TAKEN

The Vampire Syndicate

REBECCA RIVARD

Wild Hearts Press

THE VAMPIRE SYNDICATE

"A must-read series!" - Paranormal Romance Guild

THE DARK ANGEL TRILOGY

They call us the Dark Angels: Gabriel, Zaquiel and Rafael.

We're brothers. Princes. Billionaires.

The richer-than-sin heirs to one of the world's most powerful vampire Syndicates.

But we're not vampires, we're dhampirs. Half-human, half-vampire, with panty-melting good looks.

The media love us.

Vampires hate us.

And Slayers, Inc. will do anything to take us down.

Tempted (Prequel)
Pursued (Gabriel)
Craved (Rafael)
Taken (Zaquiel)

Want to be the first to hear about Rebecca Rivard's vampire romances and other steamy paranormal books?
Sign up for her newsletter:
https://rebeccarivard.com/newsletter

I

RIDLEY

Zaq Kral didn't look like a monster.

He looked like an angel in a T-shirt and jeans. A beautiful, exhausted angel.

He sprawled bonelessly on a plastic chair in Charles de Gaulle Airport, long legs stretched in front of him, in wrinkled clothes that looked like they'd been washed in a sink and hung out to dry. Sun-streaked brown hair curled over his ears, and dark stubble covered his lower face. Beneath his sunglasses, his eyes were closed.

The fatigue was genuine. He'd just spent six weeks working with refugees in North Africa, most of that underground as bombs rained down on the city. He'd been everywhere—transporting injured humans, aiding the doctors and nurses, even burying the dead. The man apparently didn't sleep.

A real live angel come down to earth, if you believed his press.

I knew better.

Zaq Kral was no angel. He was a monster in a pretty package, a rich and powerful vampire syndicate prince.

Yeah, he wasn't actually a vampire. He was a dhampir—half-human, half-vampire. But he was the son of a ruthless syndicate primus. Peel away the do-gooder veneer and Zaq Kral was just another hard-hearted, entitled blood-sucker.

I sank onto a chair two seats down, setting my backpack between us. The sunlit atrium was packed with passengers waiting for the flight to New York. French mingled with English and a handful of other languages.

I flicked a look at Zaq from beneath my own sunglasses. No visible

I

weapons, but that didn't mean he wasn't carrying a blade. A dominant dhampir like him could compel a human guard to look the other way.

The waiting area grew more crowded, but Zaq remained in his own bubble. The facial scruff and worn-out, wrinkled clothes were the perfect camouflage. The humans didn't seem to realize he was one of the famous Kral brothers, the vampire world's heartthrobs.

Still, no one but me took a seat within three yards of him. Humans have a sixth sense about these things, an instinct that warns them a predator is nearby.

The hair on my nape stirred. Somehow, I knew it was Zaq. Looking at me.

I chanced a glance. He eyed me from beneath half-open lids.

My heart jittered.

I gave him a fake-shy smile and reminded myself to breathe.

He took in my purple Baltimore Ravens hoodie and frumpy brown wig, lingering on my sunglasses.

I fought the urge to squirm. Should I take them off? But the early morning sunlight pouring through the atrium's windows hurt my eyes. Even some of the humans wore dark glasses.

And if his father's people hacked into De Gaulle's security feed, the wig and sunglasses would prevent them from getting a clear image of me.

Zaq nodded back, clearly deciding I wasn't a threat. He slumped deeper in the chair and closed his eyes again.

An incoming flight arrived and deboarded. The chatter in the lounge grew louder. Zaq's flight would begin boarding soon.

Almost showtime.

I touched the switchblade in my hoodie pocket for luck—the blade that security had been bribed to ignore—and loosened my muscles.

Jaw, neck, shoulders, fingers.

Tension distracted you. It wasted energy, added to your mental strain. When you were tense, you made mistakes.

And mistakes could get you killed.

Étan, the Tremblay Syndicate lieutenant, took a seat a couple of rows away. He'd glamoured his features, but kept his flashy blond hair and Bulgari sunglasses.

My tension ratcheted up like a screw had been turned at the base of my spine.

On a scale of one to ten, Étan had a creepoid factor of eleven. If it were up to me, he wouldn't be part of this op. Since when did Slayers, Inc. work with one vampire syndicate to take out members of another syndicate?

But it wasn't my job to understand.

I was a slayer. When I signed on for an op, I carried it out.

The end result was what mattered: One less monster in the world.

Zaq's flight was announced. Passengers started lining up at the gate. He rose and stretched, long and loose-limbed. The gray T-shirt spread across impressive pecs. He picked up his backpack and slung it over a shoulder.

I grabbed my own backpack and sank deeper into my current persona: Mary Kay Simmonds, a shy, nervy woman in her mid-thirties, a decade older than my actual age.

Zaq took his place at the back of the line.

I edged up next to him. "I hope the flight's on time." I let my voice go up on the end so it came out like a question.

"Looks like it is." His smile was reassuring. He'd taken Mary Kay's number now.

Étan got into line behind me.

"Good." I shifted from one foot to the other, sent a look over my shoulder. "I'm—" I halted, shook my head.

"What?" Zaq cocked a brow and gave me his full attention, which made his lean angel face even more attractive.

"Nothing. It's just, I need to get on that flight." I put a catch in my voice.

"Don't worry. You will."

I nibbled my lower lip. "Could you do me a favor? Pretend you know me?"

Zaq's weariness sloughed away. "Is something wrong?"

I shook my head, fast and jerky, like a terrified rabbit. "Just pretend you know me. Please?" I sent another anxious look over my shoulder.

Blaise, a Paris Syndicate soldier, stepped off the escalator and zeroed in on me. Tall and broad-shouldered, he had dark hair, a vampire's impossibly beautiful face and a boxer's fists.

Zaq's gaze followed mine. His brow creased. "Sure, okay."

"Thank you," I whispered.

Blaise cut through the crowd toward me. I gave a frightened squeak and hugged the backpack to my stomach. Everything depended on Zaq believing I was in danger. I was counting on him not being able to resist playing the hero in this little scene.

On cue, Zaq caught my hand. "Hey, it's okay." Out of the side of his mouth, he asked, "What the fuck's going on?"

Blaise pushed into the line beside me. Nobody objected. In fact, the people behind us edged back a few feet.

The big vampire crowded me with his body. "Where do you think you're going?" he asked in French. Meaty fingers clamped around my arm, digging into the soft flesh.

Prick. He knew I couldn't fight back.

I shrank from him, hugging the backpack like a pathetic shield. "Please don't make me go back. I want out. Just let me go."

"Sorry, little girl," Blaise said in English. "You don't get to decide when you leave. I do." He dragged me away from Zaq and threw my backpack to the floor.

"Let her go." Taking off his sunglasses, Zaq tucked them into his T-shirt pocket and planted himself in front of Blaise. He was two inches shorter and thirty pounds thinner than Blaise, but he radiated the calm self-possession of a man who knew how to fight.

Not that we intended to give him the chance.

Blaise flashed his fangs. "She's mine. This is not your business."

The atrium went as silent as a cemetery at midnight. The nearest humans backed away.

Zaq held up his hands, palms out. "Chill. Out." His voice was don't-mess-with-me mean. "Let her go. Find yourself another thrall."

Blaise shoved him out of the way and hustled me toward the escalator.

"Help me," I mouthed at Zaq over my shoulder.

He started after us, but Étan cut in front of him, preventing him from following too quickly. "Pardon, m'sieur," he muttered.

Blaise and I reached the escalator. I shot Zaq a panicky look, and he pushed past Étan and kept coming.

Satisfied, I faced forward. Everything was going as planned.

The escalator was too crowded for Zaq to catch up with us before we reached the ground floor. Blaise and I ducked into a side hall where the security cams had been disabled. A couple of security guards had been paid a fortune to wait five minutes before investigating.

Outside, another Paris soldier waited in an anonymous white van.

I palmed a syringe of a fast-acting tranquilizer. We'd have to move quickly. The dose would knock out a human for half a day, but a dhampir like Zaq would shake off the effects in fifteen minutes, maybe even ten. I wanted to spend as little time as possible in the van with an awake and pissed-off Zaq.

Zaq caught up with us near the exit. He grabbed Blaise's arm and jerked him away from me. "I said, 'Let her go.'"

I whipped around Blaise and jabbed the syringe into Zaq's upper arm.

"What the—?" His gaze locked with mine.

Time stopped. I'd known his eyes were green, but their intensity stunned me, rendered me immobile—a bright, leaf-green touched with gold, like a jaguar I'd once stumbled upon in a South American rainforest.

I stared into them, captured as surely as if he'd laid hands on me.

Étan appeared and time restarted. I stepped back, and he dragged Zaq's hands behind his back and secured them with zip-tie handcuffs.

Zaq lashed out with his foot, catching Blaise in the thigh. Blaise swore and slammed a big fist into Zaq's solar plexus.

Zaq's breath whooshed out. He bent over, sucking in oxygen—and spun around, still bent at the waist, and kicked out at Étan, a heel shot to the shin.

Étan hissed. "Enculé." *Motherfucker.*

Damn. Had I miscalculated the dose?

I moved forward to help, even though I kind of enjoyed seeing two vampires get their asses kicked by a man with his hands bound behind his back.

Zaq's eyes rolled up in his head. He slumped forward into my arms.

I got a noseful of his scent.

Dark, male, and somehow *right.*

I gulped and shoved him at Étan. Blaise opened the door and Étan dragged Zaq outside. The Paris soldier stood next to the van, its back door open. He tossed the keys to Blaise and went inside the terminal. He'd clean up any loose ends, including retrieving my and Zaq's backpacks, then return to Paris by train.

Étan heaved Zaq into the van. Zaq's head bounced off the metal floor. He lay where he'd fallen in an awkward heap.

I jumped into the van after him.

Étan grabbed the door handle and eyed Zaq. "You sure you can handle him?"

Typical vampire arrogance. I almost rolled my eyes. Instead, I wordlessly pulled out my knife and released the blade.

Étan grunted and shut the van door. He got into the front, and Blaise accelerated around the terminal and headed out of the airport.

I hunkered down on the metal floor near Zaq. Close, but not too close.

I was shaken, damn it. I couldn't risk smelling his dark, too-right scent again.

Zaq Kral was a monster.

And I was a monster hunter.

He could never be *right.*

2

ZAQ

I came back to consciousness with a jolt. I was sprawled face down on a dirty metal floor, arms secured painfully behind my back.

My lungs seized. For a few seconds I was back in Syria, where relief workers were always at risk of being captured.

The floor was moving. No, *we* were moving. I was in the back of a van, or maybe a closed truck.

It came back to me then. The sad-faced woman in the oversized Ravens hoodie. The syringe. The vampires.

I'd survived a bombed-out city only to be kidnapped in fucking Paris? Served me right for traveling without a bodyguard. Father had warned me I was asking for trouble, but I'd always been able to blend in with humans, even though I sucked at producing a normal, feature-changing glamour. Instead, I somehow dimmed the slight radiance that marked me as a dhampir and threw up a barrier that made the viewer's gaze slide past me.

Snick, snick. "You're awake."

I turned my head. The woman from the airport was crouched on the floor of the van, extending and retracting a switchblade. She eyed me through dark glasses like she was sizing up dinner with me as the main course.

So much for the damsel-in-distress act.

That's what you get for playing hero, Zaq.

She extended and retracted the switchblade again. *Snick, snick.*

My nape tightened. The blade was long and silver, the kind you used to stake a vampire—or a dhampir.

6

I drew my legs beneath me and sat up. The inside of the van swooped around me, an aftereffect of whatever they'd injected me with.

My stomach heaved. Bile burned my throat. I braced my feet on the floor and concentrated on not throwing up.

Snick, snick.

I gave my aching head a shake to clear it. Not a good idea. A bright bolt of pain lanced through my brain. I gritted my teeth and scooted backward until my shoulders were against the wall, my bound hands pressed into the small of my back.

The two vampires were in the front, the big dark-haired man at the wheel and the lean blond on the phone.

I gave the woman what I hoped was a death's-head glare, but was probably a helluvalot more wimpy, given that I had trouble focusing my eyes. "What the fuck's going on?"

"You'll see."

I growled. "That's not an answer."

"It's the only one you'll get."

The van rounded a curve too fast. Brakes squealed. I braced my feet against the floor so I wouldn't be thrown back onto my face.

My companion easily kept her balance, even crouched on the floor as she was. The too-big hoodie hid her upper body, but her legs were long and strong and supple. The legs of a dancer—or a black belt.

The heavy dark hair had fooled me into thinking she was older, but now I could see it was probably a wig. The color didn't fit her roses-and-cream complexion. Her real hair must be lighter—blond or even red.

And she was younger than I'd first thought—around my own age, twenty-seven.

Behind my back, I twisted my wrists, trying to work them out of the plastic cuffs. The blond asshole had cinched them good and tight.

"Who are you with? The Paris Syndicate?" It didn't make sense, because Paris was one of my father's allies, and besides, she had an American accent, but it was the only explanation my foggy brain could come up with.

A shake of her head.

I strained at the cuffs again, this time trying to break them apart. "Not the Paris Syndicate, then," I said to distract her. "The Fuentes?"

The Fuentes Syndicate had started in Chile, then crept north, first into Central America, then Mexico. Now it was trying to expand into the United States, including the Kral Syndicate territory on the East Coast.

She didn't bother to respond, just stared at me, playing with that damn switchblade.

Snick, snick.

I felt in my back pocket for my phone. My last call had been to my older brother Gabriel in New York. If I pressed *Send*, he'd guess something was wrong when he answered and heard me speaking to a strange woman.

"I have it." *Snick, snick.*

"Have what?"

"Your phone."

Damn. I closed my eyes and shifted against the wall of the van to ease the strain on my shoulders. It didn't work.

I opened my eyes again. "What's your name, anyway?" I didn't expect an answer, but once again she surprised me.

"Reaper." A feral smile. "They call me Reaper."

Ohh-kay.

"Well, Reaper, what's this about? You haven't staked me, so I'm guessing it's money."

"Yet." *Snick, snick.* "I haven't staked you *yet.*"

This time her smile was enough to shrivel my balls, but I was damned if I'd let her see it. "So it's about money?"

A shrug. "Don't ask me. I'm just the hired help."

Like hell she was. That operation had been too smooth. And tranquilizers that could knock out a dhampir weren't that easy to find.

They had to have made me as a Kral. I'd been too exhausted for my glamour to fool anyone but a human. So why kidnap me? My best guess was they planned to extort a ransom from my dad.

Hell. Father was going to be pissed off. Bad enough that I spent all my free time working for human aid organizations instead of his syndicate, but now I'd allowed myself to be kidnapped.

Reaper pulled off the wig and shoved it into the front pocket of her hoodie, then removed the sunglasses and rubbed the bridge of her nose.

I gaped at her. Her real hair was a bright, silky platinum. She had a heart-shaped face and large gray eyes fringed with dark, curly lashes.

Holy Dark Lady. I'd been abducted by a long-legged, badass sprite.

Her mouth bent down. She shoved the sunglasses back onto her face. "Take a picture, why don't you?"

"I would," I growled, "if I had my phone."

She grunted.

I kept staring. Somehow, she managed to look both delicate and edgy. And beautiful. Stunningly, jaw-droppingly beautiful.

A blur of motion. The sharp point of her switchblade pressed into my sternum. "Let me put that another way. I want you to stop staring at me. Now."

I made a scoffing sound. "We both know you're not going to use that."

She bared her teeth. "Yet."

Her scent filled my head, fresh and green, like summer grass after a rain.

My gaze went to her mouth. It was soft and full. Unpainted. Bitable.

I wanted her. Maybe because the tranq had messed with my brain, but I wanted her.

I gave her a slow smile. "Whatever you say, cher."

"Don't. Flirt. With. Me." She pressed the point in harder. The tip pierced my T-shirt but not my skin.

I raised a brow, innocent as fuck. "Was I flirting?"

"Yes."

"Mm." I forced my gaze back to her eyes, trying to see them through the dark glasses. "By the way, I'm impressed."

I heard the sound of her back teeth grinding together. "At what?"

"Your control with your blade."

Her scowl deepened. She sat back, shook her head. "I can't figure out if you're too dumb to know you're in deep shit or if you just don't care."

I moved a shoulder. "Does it matter?"

"No." She retracted the switchblade.

Snick.

I waited for the second snick, but she shoved the blade into her pocket. I decided to take that as a positive sign.

I strained against the cuffs one last time, twisting my wrists in opposite directions to break the plastic, but it was too thick. Military grade. I was definitely in deep shit. I gave up and leaned my head against the side of the van.

The burst of adrenaline that had brought me back to consciousness had worn off. I'd been dog-tired at the airport, and now I had whatever they'd injected me with to contend with as well. I slipped into a groggy, half-awake state.

A half-hour passed, maybe more. The van slowed and joined the halting Paris morning traffic—or at least, I assumed we were in Paris. Trucks rumbled, motorbikes accelerated, and pedestrians hurried past, heels tattooing the pavement. From somewhere nearby came the *nee-eu, nee-eu* of a French emergency vehicle.

The van stopped and the vampires got out of the front seat. I straightened up. My hands had gone numb. I rolled my shoulders and flexed my fingers, trying to get the circulation going again.

Reaper rose to her feet, head bent so it wouldn't hit the roof.

The back door opened. The vampires had put on hats to protect themselves from the morning sun, to go with the sunglasses and gloves they already wore.

They'd also dropped their glamours.

I strained to focus. The blond man looked familiar, but I couldn't place him until his companion said his name.

Étan. The Tremblay Syndicate lieutenant.

My stomach lurched, and not from the drug this time.

Maybe this wasn't about money after all.

❧ 3 ❧

RIDLEY

É tan and Blaise dragged Zaq out of the van and set him on his feet.
We were at the back of Philippe Moreau's mansion. The Paris
Syndicate's top enforcer, Moreau had carved out a three-level lair beneath
a gorgeous old limestone building in Saint-Germain-des-Pres, an artsy
Left Bank neighborhood.

Two wolfdogs raced up and growled lowly at Zaq. Their dhampir
handler followed. "Stay," he ordered the dogs in French.

Zaq swayed, still woozy from the drug. Étan and Blaise exchanged a
smirk and released him. He stumbled forward and would've face-planted
on the gravel drive if I hadn't leapt from the van and caught his arm.

Étan lifted a corner of his lip, showing me some fang.

Poor vampire. I'd spoiled his fun.

"Take him to his cell." He flicked his fingers at me like I was one of his
thralls.

I gave him a long look and didn't move. I didn't take orders from Étan
and we both knew it. He was only in Paris to supervise this operation for
his boss, the Tremblay Prima, and I was a Paris Syndicate employee.

At least, I was as far as Étan and Blaise knew.

When I was sure Étan and I understood each other, I hustled Zaq
toward the mansion's service entrance. The cloakroom had been
converted into a laundry with two washing machines and a dryer, but
wooden pegs still hung on the walls and the cook had stacked bins of
potatoes, garlic and onions to the side of the door.

The kitchen was state of the art: a terracotta floor, gleaming granite
counters and appliances that cost as much as I made in a month. Right

now it was empty. The vampires were on their way to their beds and the humans were just waking up.

Zaq had recovered his balance. The drug seemed to have worn off, or maybe he'd faked the stumble to keep us guessing. He zeroed in on the knife block next to the stove, but the knives were stainless steel and wouldn't do him much good even if he wasn't handcuffed. Yeah, he could do some damage with stainless steel blades, but only silver can kill a vampire.

The butler, a dhampir like me, appeared. Picture the undertaker in a horror movie, and that was Aubin: tall, long-faced and wearing a dark suit and a thin-lipped smile.

"Mademoiselle. Messieurs." Aubin took in the handcuffed Kral Syndicate prince without losing the smile. But then, he was employed by a vampire enforcer. He'd probably seen worse.

"This way, please." He indicated the salon. I didn't need an escort—I'd been on staff for three weeks now—but Aubin took his butlering seriously.

I urged Zaq forward and got another whiff of his scent. My jaw hardened. I had time to think about that scent, and I'd decided he was using his magic to amp it up. Why else would he smell so good? The man was messing with my head, trying to lure me to his side.

I sipped air through my mouth. "Move."

The salon was jewelry-box lush in a disturbing way. Hand-painted griffins and snakes in vivid greens and golds writhed across the black wallpaper. Gilded wood furniture with clawed feet hunched on a green marble floor shot with dark swirls, and old-fashioned wrought-iron chandeliers dripped with crystals.

Heavy gold curtains were drawn against the sun with blackout shades beneath. The only lighting came from the glowing amber eyes of the griffin wall sconces.

This was Moreau's public salon, the place where he conducted business with humans: politicians, CEOs, the French military. As an enforcer, his job was to bribe or intimidate humans for the Paris primus, Leo de Froulay.

It was also the setting for his famous parties. Anyone was welcome, as long as you were beautiful and had the right look.

And yes, they vetted you at the door. The parties were a pipeline, of course, bringing new thralls into the Paris Syndicate. Some of those thralls weren't really thralls, either. I was pretty sure Moreau traded in blood slaves on the side.

My mouth turned down. Enforcer Moreau was an evil S.O.B., and I hated being forced to work with him.

Aubin opened the door to what appeared to be a closet but was actually an entrance to Moreau's underground lair. Behind it was a second door, locked and reinforced with silver.

Étan and Blaise removed their hats and gloves and tossed them on a small table.

Beneath my fingers, Zaq's bicep tensed. He lurched to the side, like he'd lost his balance again, but kept going.

Ah. Of course he wouldn't go quietly. But he was bigger and heavier than me, so why fight it? I released his arm.

He hit the floor and rolled, coming up in a crouch. His fangs glinted in the low light. I felt a twinge of respect; the man had to know he couldn't escape, not with his hands bound behind his back and with three of us to his one.

Étan and Blaise moved forward. They grabbed Zaq, shoved him up against the wall and worked him over. They were pros. They went for the soft, unprotected parts—his belly, his groin. Taking their revenge for the blows he'd gotten in at Charles de Gaulle.

I stood back and let them.

Telling myself Zaq deserved it, that I couldn't stop them anyway.

But my chest was tight and my stomach clenched into a sick ball, because Zaq's grunts and heavy, broken breaths didn't sound like a monster's. They sounded like a man in pain. A defenseless, half-drugged, hands-bound-behind-his-back man in pain.

It seemed like an hour, but it was really just a few minutes before the vampires stepped back. Zaq wavered on his feet, blinking like he was having trouble seeing. He slid down the wall to the floor and sat there, legs sticking out, head lolling to the side.

Satisfaction flickered across Étan's face. He gave Zaq a last kick, then he and Blaise jerked Zaq to his feet, each taking an arm. Zaq hung between them.

The butler opened the silver-reinforced door. We followed him down three flights of stairs, Étan and Blaise dragging Zaq.

At the bottom, Aubin keyed in the five-digit code that opened a second silver-reinforced door, then headed back upstairs. I held the door open while Étan and Blaise took Zaq through.

We were deep underground in the lowest level of Moreau's lair. His private dungeon of five windowless cells carved into the bedrock and lined with concrete blocks. No one, even a vampire with their superhuman strength, could get out without the enforcer's say-so.

Four of the cells were currently empty. The fifth held an old vampire, a blood-mad woman who should've been staked. To be honest, it would've been a kindness—she'd sunk so deep into the blood craving, she was more animal than human. But apparently she was the woman who'd turned Moreau, and he had a fondness for her.

Blaise and Étan put Zaq in the middle cell and released him. The tiny lights on the walls' upper perimeter came on. Zaq's knees wobbled, but he kept upright. He faced us and tried to straighten to his full height, but couldn't. Somehow he managed to look proud, even bent at the waist like an arthritic old man.

I felt another reluctant flicker of respect. He should've crumpled by now. Maybe not all his press was a lie. The pampered prince had a tough core.

Blaise pulled out a knife and cut off Zaq's cuffs, and Étan put a hand on his chest and pushed until he was forced to back up. He hit the concrete blocks.

"Raise your hands," Étan said.

Zaq leaned his head against the wall and shook out his hands, working his fingers back and forth. Then he drew a breath and raised his head.

He bared his fangs. "You want them there, you do it."

Étan grabbed his arms and shoved them against the wall, then slammed a knee into Zaq's balls.

Zaq grunted. His face twisted. He hung in Étan's grip, panting audibly, one knee raised to shield his groin from another blow.

"Next time," said Étan, "when I tell you to do something, you do it. *Comprenez?*"

"Jesus." I pushed between the two men. "Give it a rest, already." I fitted the first cuff around Zaq's wrist.

Zaq turned his head. For the second time that day, our gazes snagged.

I *felt* him pleading with me not to do this. Felt it in my gut, a primal cry from him to me.

I set my jaw and focused on the cuff. The silver singed my fingertips but I'd tolerated pain like that—and worse—during training.

Think like a slayer. Fight like a slayer. Live like a slayer.

I touched two buttons in rapid succession and the cuff snapped into place.

The cuff burned a red line into Zaq's wrist. He stiffened, but didn't make a sound. Étan stepped back so I could get to Zaq's other arm. I snapped that cuff into place, too.

Zaq stood against the wall, arms clamped on either side of his head, a menacing expression on his angelic face. "Bastards." He glared at us, a travel-stained, T-shirted demi-god. "I'll see you all in a light-filled hell."

I swallowed uneasily. The Op Angel slayers had given each of the Kral princes a nickname. Gabriel was Prince Responsible, Rafael was Prince Charming, and Zaq was Prince Fuck-with-Me-and-I'll-Fuck-With-You.

Zaq was the quiet one. Not weak in anyway; just thoughtful, focused. And when he made a promise, he kept it.

"*Tais-toi*," Étan snapped. *Shut up.*

Zaq didn't seem to hear. His fierce green gaze fastened on me. "I'll get out of here. And when I do, I'll come after you, one by one."

Étan and Blaise snorted but alarm tripped up my vertebrae.

He meant it.

My inner thighs tightened at the picture of me and Zaq Kral locked in combat. No knives, just hand-to-hand.

And he was shirtless so I could see every move his hard, sinewy body made.

Crap. What was *wrong* with me?

I wrenched my gaze from his and left the cell.

⁂

The level above the dungeon was a labyrinth with an operations room, a gym, and bedrooms for both the members of Moreau's coven and visitors like Étan. Now he and Blaise went to their rooms to take their day sleep. I made a quick stop to change my leggings for Army green tactical pants and a fresh T-shirt, then continued to the ops room.

The room was lit by the bluish glow of a dozen video screens, the feed from various cameras around the mansion. A large digital map took up one wall, a map that currently showed the Paris streets around Moreau's lair but that could be manipulated to show any street in the world. An open-faced cabinet held an array of silver weapons—ornate daggers, solid-silver stakes, and so on.

Personally, I preferred a switchblade. Easier to conceal.

Samir, the vampire on duty, was kicked back in a chair, eyeing the feed from the security cams. "You're late," he grumbled in French.

"Things took a little longer than expected," I replied in the same language. My French wasn't great, but I could make myself understood. "Anything to report?"

"No." He rose to his feet. "It was a quiet night."

I nodded. "Moreau's asleep?"

"Yeah. He'll send for you at dusk." Samir left the room.

I sank into his chair.

We'd done it. Operation Angel was a go.

I should be excited. I *was* excited. Months of planning and preparation had gone into this day.

Op Angel was my final test. If we succeeded in eliminating Karoly Kral and his three sons, I'd be promoted to lieutenant. Instead of taking orders from above, I'd get to run my own ops and help choose our targets.

I took out my phone and sent an encrypted message to my alpha, the woman I knew only as Crow, using the code for Zaq Kral.

Reaper: *P2 has been detained.*

Her reply was immediate, telling me she'd been waiting to hear one way or the other.

Crow: *My compliments.*

From her, that was as enthusiastic as I'd get. She was happy with me.

Now if I could only drum up some enthusiasm of my own, but all I felt was tired and a little queasy.

I massaged my abdomen. I was hungry. That was the problem.

The cook should be awake by now. I put my phone back in my pocket and pushed a button to order a steak sandwich from the kitchen. "Rare," I added.

"Of course, Mam'selle."

As a dhampir—half-human, half-vampire—I could get nourishment from either blood or human food. I chose food except for a single glass of blood-wine per day.

Ridley Crawford didn't drink fresh blood. Blood was for monsters.

No one in Moreau's lair knew that. The vampires would see my aversion for fresh blood as a weakness, and my life depended on them thinking I was as strong and ruthless as they were.

Fortunately, the ruthless part wasn't a problem.

I stowed Zaq's phone in the safe of the ops room and monitored the video feed. In the kitchen, the cook was broiling my steak. In the formal garden, the wolfdogs slept in the sun. The beasts were a cheap and effective early-warning system.

Moreau didn't have a camera in his bedroom, but I watched as his favorite thrall—or maybe she was a blood slave, I wasn't sure—exited his room. Her face, throat and arms sported fresh bruises, and she had a blood addict's zombie eyes.

Bastard. I swallowed something acrid.

I turned to the cams in Zaq's cell. It was pitch-black, but I could see the darker shadow of his body against the wall, his arms bent.

I touched a control, turning up the lights in his cell so I could see his face. His chin rested on his chest. His closed eyes had dark circles under them, and he had a red welt high on his cheek.

I pressed my lips together. They could've let the man lie down.

He's a monster. What do you care how he's treated?

But something about Zaq's kidnapping didn't sit right with me. I'd been a slayer for nine years. I'd stalked syndicate vampires around the globe, and I was damn good. For me, it wasn't a job, it was a calling.

My mom and I had spent my childhood running from syndicate vampires. When they finally caught us, my mom had died, but I'd gotten away. They hadn't expected a twelve-year-old dhampir to be so fast.

Their mistake.

Six months later, I'd started training as a slayer. I staked my first vampire a week after turning nineteen. Since then, I'd notched up a dozen more kills, more than any slayer in my cohort, male or female.

And that's what felt wrong about this job.

Slayers didn't kidnap the bad guys. We staked them.

We didn't cuff them to a wall so they couldn't lie down or sleep without silver burning into their wrists and slowly poisoning them. This wasn't the clean death I'd been trained to deliver.

They were trying to break Zaq Kral. But why?

I squeezed my nape, hating that I didn't know all the facts.

The cook arrived with my sandwich, a thin-cut steak smothered with mushrooms and cradled in a crusty roll. It smelled amazing, but my appetite had fled.

I took a bite, set it down. I stared at the sandwich for a good thirty seconds, then picked it up again and made myself finish it.

You didn't waste food. You never knew when your whole life might be ripped out from beneath you like a cartoon rug and you'd sell your soul for any food you could get your hands on, even a half-eaten sandwich someone else had thrown away.

❧ 4 ❧
ZAQ

I hung against the wall, bruised and aching. Trying to keep my wrists from touching the silver in the cuffs. Attempting to make sense of what had gone down.

Anger simmered in me, anger and humiliation. I'd meant what I'd said to the three of them. Somehow, some way, I'd get out of this fucking cell.

And I *would* go after them.

If only I knew what the hell was going on.

Étan was Victorine Tremblay's second-in-command. I didn't know how Reaper and the others came into this, but I'd been kidnapped by a rival syndicate.

And not just any syndicate.

The Tremblay prima hated my family. The war between her and my father, the Kral primus, dated back two hundred years, a blood feud with numerous casualties on both sides. Something to do with territory back in Slovakia where my father had been born and spent his first few centuries as a vampire.

However, the Kral-Tremblay blood feud was finished, and had been for nearly a decade. A treaty had been signed.

Why would Victorine Tremblay risk kidnapping Karoly Kral's son? The Krals were more powerful than the Tremblays. She had to know my father would pull out all stops to rescue me—and then he'd go after her and her precious daughter.

My head throbbed. I inhaled through my teeth and waited it out.

So okay, the Tremblays had kidnapped me, and somehow the Paris Syndicate was involved too. I didn't know whose mansion this was, but it was clearly owned by a vampire in the Paris Syndicate. Probably a high-ranking member.

An hour passed, maybe two. The silver seeped into my bloodstream, beginning the slow process of poisoning me. It burned and itched, spreading out until I ached everywhere, even in places where they hadn't pounded on me.

Damn, I was uncomfortable. I shifted on my feet. Bent my knees, straightened them. Opened and closed my fingers.

The pricks could've let me sit down. Right then I would've given my last dollar for a few hours of sleep, but each time I drifted off, my body sagged and the cuffs seared into my wrists, waking me up. Sooner or later I'd pass out from exhaustion, and the gods knew what the silver would do to my wrists then.

From time to time, the cell's tiny lights brightened—a small, barely noticeable change—but after it happened a few times I realized it was so security could check on me through the video feed.

Fuck that.

I turned my head and bared my teeth at the cams until the lights dimmed again.

Night fell. I couldn't see the setting sun, of course, but I sensed the change. I'd been standing here for what—twelve, thirteen hours?

Father would come for me. I just had to hang on. By now he'd have realized I'd gone missing. He'd known I was on my way home. I'd texted him and my older brother Gabriel when I'd landed in Paris.

My aching body had stiffened. I wasn't used to healing so slowly. Usually, my dhampir blood sped the healing process, but the silver was interfering with my magic.

I bent my knees again. Straightened them. Opened and closed my fingers.

And stifled a groan, because it hurt like a mofo. I gritted my teeth and did it again. And once more after that.

Étan entered my cell. I looked past him for Reaper, but he was alone.

"You're awake." He prowled across the short distance between us, panther-quiet.

I lifted a shoulder in a shrug. "I don't need much sleep."

It was a lie. I was bone-tired and on top of that, I hadn't drunk fresh blood since leaving New York six weeks ago. The pain from the silver was a constant agony.

Étan raked his gaze down my body like I was a thrall and he was deciding whether or not to hire me. "So you're Zaquiel Kral. You don't look like a rich prince to me."

"Yeah?" I looked him up and down in return. "Well, you sure look like a hairless dick."

His muscles locked. He shoved gleaming white fangs into my face. "Someone should teach you some manners."

I knew I should shut up, but I was tired and hurting and humiliated. "Go fuck yourself."

Étan grabbed my throat. His eyes flared with the distinctive neon blue of an aroused vampire.

I kneed him in the balls. It was pure instinct, but I'd have done it even if I'd had time to think it over.

He grunted and let go of me to grab his crotch. He stumbled backward, hands clutching his groin. "*Vous—.*" He ground out something vicious in French.

I eyed him, knowing he'd come back at me hard, and I couldn't escape.

I couldn't even use my arms to defend myself.

The simmering anger boiled over. My face heated and my vision clouded. It takes a lot to make me angry, but once the lid's off, I'm not satisfied until I've kicked some ass.

I'd been drugged, beaten, and confined in a cell. I wasn't even being allowed to sleep. And my wrists burned like someone had taken a torch to them.

Anger was too tame a word for what I felt. Hell, *rage* was too tame a word.

I wanted to rip Étan's pretty blond head from his body with my bare hands.

Étan straightened up. Slammed his open hand into my throat.

The back of my head banged against the concrete. A bright light detonated behind my eyes, followed by a searing flash of pain. I barely noticed. I strained at the cuffs, trying to get at him.

Kill.

The blue circles around Étan's irises seemed to spark and flame. His fangs were fully extended. "You shouldn't have done that, dhampir."

My snarl was pure, enraged animal. I jerked my knee up, trying again to jam it into his balls.

But this time, he was ready.

He shoved my knee to one side with his thigh.

Pinned me to the wall with his body.

Smashed my face sideways against the wall, exposing the side of my neck.

And sank his fangs into my jugular vein.

🦋 5 🦋

RIDLEY

Philippe Moreau's private quarters were on the level above the ops room. Aubin met me in the hall and escorted me to the enforcer's office. As before, I knew the way, but the butler was a by-the-book kind of guy.

To get to Moreau's office, we had to go through first his salon, then his library. Like the public rooms on the ground floor, they were showpieces with silk-covered walls, gilded wood furniture and Persian carpets so old and delicate I was almost afraid to walk on them.

Moreau's office was concealed in the library behind a sliding bookcase. The door stood open. He was seated behind a large walnut desk, his trim body elegant in a three-piece suit—navy with a chalk stripe—that I'm sure had been made for him by a pricey French designer. His black hair was touched silver at the temples and a narrow mustache adorned his upper lip.

He bestowed a thin smile on me. "Good evening," he said in the precise English of an upper-class Londoner.

The accent, the clothes, the whole persona were calculated to make you think he was a stylish, classy man; but I'd played too many roles myself to be fooled. Philippe Moreau was a thug in a polished outer shell.

"'Evening." I pitched my voice just polite enough.

"May I bring you anything, m'sieur?" asked Aubin.

"Nothing, thank you." Moreau looked at me. "Unless you'd like a blood-wine?"

"No, thanks."

"*Très bien*." Aubin sketched a small bow and left, closing the door behind him.

Moreau nodded at the spindly-legged chair in front of his desk. "Sit, if you please."

I eyed the silk-covered seat askance. The chair was an antique that probably cost a fortune. I'd grown up in small-town USA, a long way from Paris. I'd never be comfortable in the opulent world of vampires.

Moreau's dark eyes took in my discomfort. The man noticed everything. But unlike Étan, he didn't try to rub it in or make me more uncomfortable; he was too clever for that.

I perched on the chair and met his gaze head on. Beneath the stylish clothes and classy manners, Moreau was still a monster.

And monsters didn't scare me. Not anymore.

He leaned back in his chair. "Report."

"The operation went off as expected. Kral is in one of your cells." As Moreau surely knew, since he had access to any security cam in the building.

"The tranquilizer worked?"

"Yes. He was out for twelve minutes and a few seconds."

Moreau stroked his mustache. "Good, good. You have his phone?"

"It's in the ops room safe."

"All right. I want you to take a photo to send to his father."

"Any message?"

"Just bring me the phone after you take the photo. I prefer to do it myself." A small smile.

The man was enjoying this. That surprised me, because I hadn't been able to uncover any bad blood between Moreau and Karoly Kral. As far as I knew, Moreau was involved only as a favor to Victorine Tremblay.

"Will do," I said. "But after that, I'm off duty."

Moreau sometimes forgot I didn't actually work for him. Typical vampire arrogance. But my paycheck came from Slayers, Inc. I'd been embedded in his coven for this job and would be leaving in a week, although only we two knew that.

He inclined his head.

"If that's everything—?" I started to my feet.

"No. Primus de Froulay has asked to see you."

I sank back onto the chair. "The Paris primus?" I asked as if I didn't know.

"Yes." Moreau scrutinized me like I'd sprouted wings and announced I could fly. I could almost hear him thinking: *What would de Froulay want with her?*

I kept my expression milk-bland.

Moreau waited a few more beats, and when I didn't say anything else, he said, "The primus is sending a car for you. Two a.m."

The location of Leo's lair was a closely guarded secret, one I wasn't supposed to know.

I nodded. "I'll be ready."

"And Reaper? Wear something more suitable. He'll expect it." Moreau eyed my Outlaw Country T-shirt and well-worn tactical pants with that special revulsion only a Parisian can summon for a fashion disaster like me. "The clothes I keep for guests. Help yourself."

Moreau was wrong. Leo de Froulay wouldn't expect it, because he knew me.

"Sure." I touched my temple in a mock salute. "I love playing dress-up." Not.

The enforcer's lips pressed into an irritated line. He disliked my irreverent attitude, but hey, a girl takes her fun where she finds it.

❦

B ack in the ops room, my mood took a drive. I retrieved the phone from the safe and headed down to the dungeon.

If I had my way, I'd stay far, far away from Zaq Kral.

I'd had that unsettled feeling all day. I'd returned to the camera feeds in Zaq's cell over and over until Moreau had called me to his office.

Now the twisted, tangly sensation was back and growing worse. The closer I got to Zaq's cell, the slower I walked until I felt like I was pushing my body through water.

For chrissake, Ridley. Chill. He's just a job. In a week, this will be over.

I pulled back my shoulders and opened the door. The stench of scorched flesh hit me. I swallowed queasily and entered the cell.

The tiny lights came on. Zaq hung in the cuffs, eyes closed. The scorched flesh was his; the silver had burned into his wrists.

My lungs constricted. Jesus, they were torturing the man.

His chin jerked up. He stared at me, wild-eyed. His T-shirt had been ripped sometime in the half-hour since I'd last looked at the security feed.

On his neck, fresh blood dripped from two bite marks. I smelled the coppery scent now.

What the hell? Anger burned my throat.

They'd fed from him. Someone in this lair had fucking *fed* from him.

The fancy chicken casserole I'd had for dinner threatened to come up. I fought to keep the shock from my face.

He's a monster. They all are. What do you care if they mess with him?

But this was just plain wrong. To vampires and dhampirs, the throat was a no-go zone. You didn't touch it without an invitation, and that went double for drinking someone's blood, especially when they were helpless to fight back.

Like my mom when the vampires had finally caught up to us.

The vampire who'd fed from Zaq hadn't even had the decency to lick the bite marks to speed his healing. His throat was bruised, the wounds raw.

Zaq showed me his fangs. "Get the hell away from me."

"Take it easy." I showed him his phone. "All I want is a photo."

"Why?" His green eyes blazed into mine. Then understanding dawned. "You're going to send it to my father, aren't you?"

"I'm just here to get a picture." I could've taken it without his permission, but sometimes simple was best. "Cooperate, and I'll bring you something to eat."

Zaq licked dry lips and considered me. Then he nodded. "A burger. Rare. And something to drink."

"Deal."

I brought up the camera. He drew himself upright, his expression defiant. Skewering me with his stare.

His goddamn scent was everywhere—his silver-burned flesh, the bloody wound, but underneath was that dark, masculine, this-is-the-one-you've-been-waiting-for smell. Filling my head, twisting me into knots when I needed to focus on the endgame.

I took two photos and shoved the phone into my pocket. "You wanna use the john?"

He blinked. "Yeah."

"I'm going to release you. Try anything and you're dead." I showed him my switchblade. "I'm fast with this. The best there is." It wasn't pride speaking; I just wanted him to have the facts. "And you don't have a weapon. Fight me, and I'll stake you."

A chuckle scraped from his throat. "I'm too fucking tired and hungry to fight off a flea. How d'you think you captured me?"

I grunted. "As long as we understand each other."

I slipped the open switchblade into a loop on my waistband and stepped to his side. The cuffs had been designed to require two hands so a prisoner couldn't somehow release himself. I kept as far from Zaq as I could, but I was too close.

I felt the heat of his body, sensed his every flinch. His breath stirred the hairs on my nape.

I released the first cuff and moved to his other side. The moment I had the second open, I grabbed my switchblade and stepped back.

"I'll be back in fifteen minutes," I said in my coldest voice.

I stepped out and locked the door. My breath came out in a whoosh. I wanted to slump against the cell door, but Samir was back on duty and would see me on the cam feed.

I went to the kitchen and ordered a couple of rare burgers. The French cook's version used chopped, not ground, beef, and added things like shallots and parsley, but it was close enough.

While she prepared the food, I took the phone to Moreau.

He pulled up the pictures and eyed them. Something dark slithered over his face. Something that made me swallow hard.

I just barely stopped myself from reaching for my switchblade.

"*Très bien*," he told me.

I grunted and escaped back to the lower levels.

My next stop was the wine cellar, where I helped myself to a bottle of blood-wine. Back in the kitchen, the cook had wrapped the burgers in paper and put them in a bag with a small baguette and some cheese. She also gave me a corkscrew to open the wine.

I stopped in the ops room to inform Samir I was on my way to feed the prisoner. "Moreau's orders," I lied.

"Okay," he said without looking away from the video screens. "But next time, secure the prisoner to the wall before you leave the cell. The boss doesn't want us to take any chances."

"Got it." I ran a hand over my hair, wanting to ask who had drunk from Zaq but knowing it was best to pretend I either hadn't noticed or didn't care. I'd have to wait until I could examine the video feed.

Blaise stopped me in the hall, eyeing the wine and bag of food. "What's that?"

"Dinner." My tone dared him to ask more.

"*Oui?*"

I moved forward like I was going to bowl him over. "Yeah."

His jaw flexed but he stepped aside at the last moment. Something about me made even vampires wary of messing with me.

Maybe they sensed that inside, I was as dead as them.

Back at the cell, Zaq was pacing the concrete floor. He'd cleaned up and washed the blood from his neck. His gaze snapped to the food in my hands. I handed over the bag.

He opened it and looked inside. His eyes closed and his nostrils flared. "Thank you." The words were ragged, raw, like I'd handed him the freaking Hope Diamond.

Uncomfortable, I glanced away. "A deal's a deal."

"Thank you anyway. And blood-wine." He zeroed in on the bottle in my hand. "That's for me too?"

"Yeah." I crouched on the floor and opened the wine.

Zaq withdrew to a corner and sat, the bag of food clasped to his chest. I set the open bottle on the concrete next to him. He drained a third of the wine in a single thirsty gulp, then unwrapped the burgers.

His hands shook. I knew it was from hunger; I'd been there myself.

The tangles in my stomach notched tighter.

I didn't want to feel empathy for Zaq Kral. I didn't want to feel *anything* for him.

I squatted on my haunches against the door. I wasn't dumb enough to turn my back on Zaq, but I needed to put some space between us.

"The main door to the cells is locked, too," I said, so he'd know attacking me wouldn't do him any good. "You can't leave without knowing the code."

"Got it," he said, his gaze on the burgers. "Loud and clear."

He tore off a chunk of bread, wrapped it around one of the burgers, and downed the whole thing in a few big bites. He let out a slow breath, then took another gulp of blood-wine and ate some cheese before starting in on the second burger. This one he ate more slowly, savoring each bite.

His jaw was strong and male. The beard scruff had thickened. It was darker than the hair on his head.

He glanced up and caught me watching. A self-deprecating smile flashed across his face. "It's been a while since I had a burger. Hell, it's been a while since I had any meat. A few weeks at least. Where I was, food is at a premium."

"In Syria."

His left brow lifted. "You did your homework."

I moved a shoulder. "Yeah."

Actually, I'd studied him for weeks—whatever I could find online and learn from others. I'd even been in northwestern Syria for a few days under an alias.

I had to admit I hadn't uncovered any evidence that he was one of the bad guys, the syndicate monsters who preyed on humans, treating them like weak, stupid cattle good only for blood and sex.

Maybe it had niggled at me, but I'd figured Zaq was just too smart to get caught.

Now those small doubts crowded into my head, clamoring to be addressed.

The biggest question was why Slayers, Inc. was involved in this at all.

The plan was to use Zaq as bait. SI wanted his father, and Karoly Kral was too powerful, too canny, to send a slayer after. And believe me, we'd tried.

So we'd taken Zaq prisoner in order to draw Karoly to Paris and away from Kral territory. When Karoly broke into Moreau's lair to rescue Zaq, Moreau and his men would quietly stake him.

But since when did SI kidnap a man's spawn to be used as bait?

My knee was jiggling. I stilled it and played with my switchblade instead, flipping it from hand to hand. The simple but challenging task soothed me, because while the handle was stainless steel, the blade was silver. Miss the handle and grab the blade instead, and I'd not only cut myself, I'd burn myself on the silver.

The alpha knows what she's doing. She's been at this for decades, a lot longer than you have.

Zaq finished his meal. He rested his head against the wall, eyelids drooping, the paper bag on his lap.

I crossed the room and shook his shoulder. "Get up." I made my voice hard to cover my doubts.

He jerked and blinked up at me, his bright green eyes clouded with tiredness.

I shook him again. "Get. Up."

He obeyed, his movements slow, like his limbs were weighted with weariness.

I pointed my switchblade at the silver cuffs. "Against the wall, arms up."

Zaq put himself against the wall. His wrists were like raw meat where the cuffs had burned into them. I set my jaw and snapped the cuffs into place anyway.

This time he didn't plead with me in any way. He didn't have to.

His eyes met mine. I felt like he stared directly into my soul, where my darkest secrets lived.

That he saw *me*.

Not Reaper, not the slayer, but *me*. Ridley Crawford.

His mouth twisted in a smile that mocked me or himself or both of us. He looked away.

That's when I realized I'd been standing there, rooted to the ground and staring into his eyes like an infatuated fool.

I blanked my face, gathered up the remains of his meal and left.

6

ZAQ

I stared after Reaper.

Who was she, really? And why would a woman who'd helped kidnap me bring me food and blood-wine?

For a few seconds there while I was eating, I'd amped up my magic, trying to sense her emotions. I got...nothing. Either she wasn't human, or she had a natural immunity to vampire magic.

And with the way she moved and fought, my bet was on dhampir.

But a dhampir who was able to suppress her vampire half, because I couldn't smell the vampire in her. And she didn't have the glow to her skin that most supernaturals had, the unearthly beauty that made us irresistible to humans when we willed it.

Not that she wasn't beautiful. She was, in a sexy-fairy way.

And she smelled amazing.

She just didn't have that inhuman look to her.

The cell's lights shut off, leaving me in the darkness. Even a dhampir needed a small amount of light to see. The utter blackness was disturbing. I wasn't used to being able to see nothing at all.

Another way the vampires in this lair were messing with my head.

At least I'd eaten. Funny what some food in your belly could do for your attitude. Things no longer seemed black as they had an hour ago when Étan had finished with me.

My jaw tightened. The bite marks on my throat throbbed. They'd stopped bleeding, but they hurt like the time I'd been bitten by the mangy dog I'd found in the woods on my family's property in Maryland and taken home to doctor.

I flexed my fingers, wanting to rub the wound, but I couldn't move my hands.

Don't think about it. Stay strong.

I had to remain calm and in control. I would *not* let these bastards break me.

Father would come for me any night now, and then, Étan was toast. Literally.

I smiled. A cold Syndicate Prince smile that would've shocked my coworkers in Syria who'd thought of me as a go-to guy, the "nice" Kral.

I deliberately turned my thoughts to Reaper. She'd seemed bothered by how I was being treated. Or was that just my imagination? She'd been all-in back at the airport when they'd first taken me.

But she didn't have to bargain with me to get those photos. We both knew she could've taken them without my cooperation.

It was like she'd wanted an excuse to feed me.

Could she be a weak link—one I could exploit?

"Yeah," I said aloud because I needed to hear a voice—any voice, even my own—in the cell's deep silence. "Keep working on her. If Father can't find you, she's your backup plan."

But he'd find me. When Karoly Kral set out to do something, it happened.

They'd have sent the photos to him in New York by now. He'd be making plans to come to Paris to rescue me, or maybe he'd send my brothers, Gabriel and Rafe.

Yeah. I pictured Gabriel and Rafe. It made me feel a little warmer, made my bruised insides ache a little less.

I hadn't seen them since the night before I'd left for Syria. The three of us had gotten together in New York at the Ruby Speakeasy and picked the three most beautiful thralls to drink from. Gabriel was the serious one, and Rafe the charmer. I was happy to lay back and be their wingman. I got plenty of ladies anyway—they all wanted a piece of the Kral Dark Angels.

I smiled; that had been a good night. Although as I recalled, Gabriel hadn't taken his thrall to a back room like Rafe and I had. Rafe said Gabriel still hadn't gotten over Camila Vittore, and maybe that was true. My older brother had fallen hard for his human girlfriend, even though he knew they could never be together in a permanent way.

Maybe when I got home, Gabriel and Rafe would laugh about my predicament. The time Zaq got duped by a slayer.

My mouth twisted. Or maybe not.

I sank back into a semi-conscious state. A little before sunrise, a big vampire arrived. He had cropped dark hair, a boxer's fists and a bronze Paris Syndicate griffin embroidered on his black uniform. A soldier, was my guess. Big Guy with the Fists released me from the cuffs and allowed me to use the bathroom.

My arms and one leg had fallen asleep. I grimaced and shook them out, trying to get the blood moving so I wouldn't fall flat on my face before stumbling into the bathroom. It was sparse, like something you'd see in a jail cell—a stainless steel toilet with no seat and a sink with one faucet.

I used the john and washed up. The water had one temperature—ice-cold. I splashed some on my face, then stuck my wrists under the tap to clean off the silver. The water stung my burned skin, but I clamped my back teeth together and kept my wrists under the stream for as long as I could stand it. The less poison that entered my system, the better.

No cup, but I stuck my head under the faucet and took a drink. But the blood craving was riding me hard now, and the water only made me more thirsty.

The burger and blood-wine had helped, but my body had burned through a lot of the energy to heal. There was nothing left to fight the silver's poison.

I needed fresh blood.

The vampire cuffed me to the wall again. I eyed his neck. If I struck fast, I could take a few mouthfuls of blood before he stopped me.

I grimaced and forced myself to look away. A few mouthfuls wouldn't be worth whatever he did to me in retaliation.

The vampire left and the cell went dark.

I passed the day in a miserable, half-starved state.

7

RIDLEY

Leo de Froulay's library was like something out of *Architectural Digest* —a parquet wood floor, cozy reading nooks and aisles upon aisles of leather-bound books.

His butler ushered me inside, announcing me to the primus, and left.

I walked the length of the library beneath a row of crystal chandeliers. Scattered among the bookcases were small tables displaying beautiful objects. A shimmering dark-glass globe, an antique Victrola, a ruby vase filled with ice-white flowers.

De Froulay waited at the back of the library behind an enormous ebony desk. "Good evening." He closed a sleek silver laptop and stood up.

Tall and broad-shouldered, he was stunning even for a vampire, with a mane of white-blond hair and the sculpted face of a Greek god. He was dressed more casually than Moreau in a midnight-blue dress shirt and black pants, but his clothes had that just-right, handmade fit, even his polished leather shoes.

In another lifetime the Paris primus had been a famous French actor. When he walked the streets of Paris, humans literally ran into lampposts trying to get a better look at him. He didn't have to lure humans to be his thralls. They lined up, begging to be taken.

"Ridley." He spoke my real name—the one my mom had given me when I was two years old—with a slight hesitation. I knew he thought it was ugly. The first time we'd met, he'd asked why I had a boy's name.

He circled his desk and held out his hands. "It's good to see you."

"*Bon soir.*" I put a smile on my lips and took his hands.

His fingers were cool. He kissed me on both cheeks with lips that were even colder. "You look *très belle, ma p'tite*. I like the dress."

I shrugged and released his hands. I'd chosen a plain, pale-blue thingy that could've doubled as a slip, the most inoffensive dress I found in Moreau's collection.

"It's not mine. A loan from Enforcer Moreau."

"Ah. Philippe has good taste." He nodded at the red leather couch in a nearby alcove. "Please. Seat yourself."

I complied, holding the slip-thingy's tiny skirt against my thighs so I wouldn't inadvertently flash him.

"Some blood-wine?" He turned to a wine cabinet.

"Yes, please." I crossed one ankle over the other.

Proving to Primus de Froulay that Ridley Crawford wasn't completely feral.

And yeah, I hated that he brought out *that* Ridley in me—the Ridley who eyed other, more girly women, wondering how they achieved those put-together looks without seeming to try.

Me, I'd had trouble walking in the high heels I'd borrowed to go with the dress. I'd never mastered those tiny, hip-swaying, pigeon-toed steps you needed to walk in three-inch heels. Besides, it took too damn long to get anywhere.

De Froulay poured two glasses of blood-wine and handed one to me, leaving the bottle on the cabinet's black granite top. He touched his glass to mine and took a seat on the couch's opposite end.

"How have you been? You are well?"

"I'm good, yeah." I sipped the wine. My cells happily soaked up the blood, my vampire-half starved for the blood fix.

It was hands-down the best blood-wine I'd ever drunk. I sneaked a peek at the label. Some vineyard I'd never heard of.

De Froulay nodded at my glass. "You like it?"

"Yeah." I heard myself and winced at my awkwardness. "I mean yes, it's very good."

"It's from my private vineyard."

"Of course it is," I said under my breath.

He heard me; he was a vampire, after all. He lifted a dark brow and let it pass.

I set the glass on the coffee table. "Why am I here, Primus de Froulay?"

He pursed his perfect lips. "Can't a father spend some time with his daughter?"

And there it was, finally out in the open. My pulse gave an agitated skitter.

Fuck, fuckity-fuck.

We'd first met three months ago. At that meeting he'd skirted around the issue, questioning me about my mom and where I'd spent the last twenty-seven years.

I had no doubt he'd had me investigated before he'd ever contacted me. He must know how things had been for my mom and me, and about that missing six months of my life before Crow had stumbled upon me.

But he couldn't know I was a slayer. My cover was too good, with layers upon layers.

To the world, Ridley Crawford had graduated from a high school in small-town Pennsylvania, then enlisted in the Army and spent the next four years in various global hot spots.

Peel away another layer, and you'd find that after leaving the Army, Ridley had become a mercenary for hire.

What you wouldn't discover was that I'd once been known by another name, one even I didn't know because I was still a toddler when my mom changed it.

That my mom had been murdered by the vampires who'd come for me a few days after my twelfth birthday.

And the biggest secret? I never attended that high school in Pennsylvania or enlisted in the Army. Instead, I'd been recruited by Slayers, Inc. and spent my teenage years working my ass off to become a vampire-slaying machine.

"So," I said. "You've decided I'm your daughter?"

And what did that mean to me?

Because being the daughter of a vampire syndicate primus was basically my worst nightmare come to life.

But I couldn't just walk out. On the way here, I'd texted Crow to tell her I'd been summoned to de Froulay's lair. She'd ordered me to play along, find out what he wanted. Of course, she didn't know he was my father. No one at SI knew that.

"I've known since January. But—" he spread his hands—"a man in my position can't be too careful. The DNA test confirmed it."

He'd had my DNA tested? He *had* been thorough. The question was why?

I pressed my lips together. "Don't worry. I don't want a damn thing from you." As far as I was concerned, he was my sperm donor, nothing more.

"No?" He leaned back against the couch arm, eyeing me.

My knee was jiggling. I forced it to still. My hand went to my pocket, seeking the reassurance of my blade. But I wasn't wearing pants, I was wearing a dress, and my blade was tucked into the pricey leather cross-body bag I'd also borrowed from Moreau. I'd had to hand over both the bag and the blade before security allowed me into his lair.

Emotions flitted across de Froulay's handsome face. Nostalgia, and a hint of tenderness. "You have the look of her. Charlotte."

A beat passed before I realized he meant my mom. By the time I was old enough to know her name, she'd been using an alias.

I dug my fingers into the soft leather cushions on either side of my thighs. "Leave my mom out of this."

I was proud of my even tone, when I wanted to carve the words into his skin with a hot knife.

His dark brows lowered. "It's a compliment. She was a beautiful woman."

I set my teeth. "I said, *leave my mom out of this.*"

"You understand that I didn't know about you. She left before she was showing. If I'd known, I would've made arrangements—settled money on the two of you. I didn't hear about you until years later, and then it was only rumors."

I shook my head. I hadn't known and I wasn't sure if I believed him.

Still, it didn't matter. What mattered was that he'd seduced my mom into becoming his thrall in the first place.

"She *loved* you. She didn't want your goddamn money."

His beautiful mouth tightened. "I didn't take advantage of her, if that's what you believe. She signed a contract like all of my thralls."

A black heat filled my head. The hell with what Crow wanted. I wasn't going to sit here and listen to this vampire—this *monster* who'd gotten my mom pregnant, then thrown her to the wolves—talk about her like she was just another thrall.

I jumped up—and wobbled on the freaking high heels. I moved my feet further apart and planted the heels on the parquet floor.

"Sit down," de Froulay said in bored tones.

"No." I balled my hands into fists. God, I wished I had my switchblade.

"Sit." His voice sliced at me.

I wavered. The prick had that much raw strength. Then I lifted my chin, spun on my heel—without, by some miracle, losing my balance—and stalked toward the exit.

"Ridley." He sighed. "Calm yourself. I have a proposition for you."

I stopped but didn't turn around. "What?"

"First, sit down. I promise not to speak of Charlotte."

I heaved a breath and reminded myself I was a pro. This connection to the Paris primus could be valuable. And Crow would be waiting for my report.

Think like a slayer. Fight like a slayer. Live like a slayer.

I returned to the couch. "Fine. What's this proposition?"

De Froulay rested a long arm along the couch back. "I'd like to hire you."

"To do what?"

"Spy on Philippe Moreau."

I blinked. Moreau was de Froulay's top enforcer. The two men went way back.

"Why?" I asked baldly.

"Something's up." De Froulay tapped a finger on the couch back. "He's...different. People are coming and going all the time in that Saint-Germain lair of his. I think his parties are a cover for something more. But I can't look too deeply into it without alarming him."

"A cover for what?"

He lifted a powerful shoulder in a shrug. "That's what I'd like you to find out. There's nothing specific, but I've known Moreau for a long time. Something's off. He's lying to me, and I want to know why—and about what."

"Why not ask one of your own people to investigate?"

"He's my oldest and most trusted enforcer, right below my lieutenant. My people are loyal to me, but all but a few report to him. That's how the hierarchy works. I can't chance him realizing I'm investigating him until I'm ready to move."

"I'm only in Paris for another week. I've been offered a better job in America," I added, in case he wondered why I was leaving Moreau's employ after such a short period.

"That will work. You can look around, report to me and leave. We both know you're good at disappearing. I'll pay you well." He named a stupid-high sum of money.

My mind worked. I was pretty sure Leo de Froulay didn't know about Zaq Kral or the Tremblay Syndicate's deal with SI. Whatever Moreau was hiding from him, that was part of it.

The money I didn't care about, except that money was security. That homeless twelve-year-old I'd once been would've given anything for even a tenth of that sum.

And I would love to take down Moreau if I could do it without compromising Op A.

I picked up my wine glass, sipped. "I'll have to think about it."

"No." His tone was you-will-do-this arrogant. "I need an answer now."

"Then the answer is no."

His mouth pulled down. He examined me from beneath lowered lids.

I returned his stare with a calm look of my own. If I agreed to work with him, it would be a transaction of equals.

Amusement glimmered in his eyes. Amusement, and a touch of respect. "Then when?"

"Friday night. Moreau's having a party. You'll be there?"

"Yes. I always stop by for a few minutes."

I nodded and rose to my feet. "I'll give you my answer then. If I accept your commission, it would be best if I don't come here again."

He stood up and I stuck out my hand. "Until Friday, then."

He looked from my hand to my face. The amusement increased. He was laughing at me, but I didn't care.

He took my hand, gave it a firm squeeze.

A chill went up my arm. I hoped I didn't regret this.

"Until Friday. The butler will see you out."

He returned to his desk but I felt his gaze on me until I'd left the library.

⚜

Outside, the night was warm and heavy with humidity. I rubbed my forehead. Sick of vampires. Sick of myself.

Moreau's car was waiting for me, but I told him I'd decided to walk back instead. The human driver nodded and left.

De Froulay's lair was just off the Seine in a quiet, exclusive neighborhood. I headed for the river and lost myself in the crowd strolling along the Right Bank.

How had he found out I was his daughter anyway? I'd thought no one but my mother and the vampires who'd murdered her knew who I really was.

And Mom was dead and I'd buried Ridley Crawford along with her. Or at least I thought I had.

I pulled out my phone and texted Crow.

Reaper: *The meeting went as expected. I may be able to use him.*

Crow: *Keep stringing him along.*

I responded with a thumbs-up and kept walking.

The moon was full. Music spilled into the air from nearby cafés, and the city's lights sparkled in the dark, moving water. I heaved a breath, willing the tension to drain from me.

The crowd thinned until it seemed that all that was left were couples, their heads together, talking in that way lovers do, like they're the only two people in the city. I eyed the couple in front of me, their arms around each other and so close they were basically one body with two heads.

A curious ache pressed against my breastbone. I massaged it with the heel of my hand and sped up until I was past them.

I'd never had a lover. Sex, yes, to see what the hype was about—but never a lover.

I wasn't even sure what that meant—to make love. Sex was sex, right?

When Crow had first brought me to SI's North American training camp, I'd been too broken to focus on anything but becoming a killing machine. Monsters were real, and they'd stolen my mother from me. The only way to stay sane was to learn how to fight back.

I'd lived for revenge.

Ate only to make myself stronger.

Worked my body until I collapsed into bed, then got up the next day and did it again, longer and harder.

Dedicated my every breath to eliminating the monsters who'd murdered my mom.

Think like a slayer. Fight like a slayer. Live like a slayer.

After I'd completed the training, I'd gone back to Pennsylvania to visit my mother's grave. That day I'd made her a promise—to stake the vampires who'd assaulted and killed her.

Unfortunately, I didn't know their names or what they looked like; I'd been too terrified to see anything but sharp fangs and blue-rimmed eyes. All I recalled was three men in black, and that they'd spoken to each other in fluent French.

But I'd bet good money Leo de Froulay could identify them.

In fact, there'd been a time when I'd wondered if he'd sent them, even though my mom had insisted he wouldn't have.

My step hitched and I almost stumbled in the high heels.

What if instead of taking de Froulay's money, I proposed a trade—the three vampires' names in return for spying on Moreau?

A corner of my mouth lifted in a smile that made a passing human blink and recoil from me.

I blanked my face but inside my smile grew. I liked this idea. A lot.

Not only would I finally learn the names of the monsters who'd murdered my mother, I could cause Moreau a world of hurt.

The only downside was Crow. If she learned I'd made a side deal with de Froulay, she'd be pissed off.

And a smart person didn't piss Crow off...unless they had a death-wish.

8

ZAQ

My heart punched in my chest.

Vampires. All around me.

I groaned, lost in a dark fog. The vampires closed in on me. I strained to fight, to push them away, but my hands wouldn't move. I couldn't even feel my fingers.

My breath felt thick in my lungs. I couldn't get enough oxygen.

Run.

I turned my head from side to side, seeking an escape through the nightmarish fog, but it was too late. I was surrounded.

My nostrils flared at their scent. Earthy and good smelling like all vampires. They could even amp up their scent to entice and befuddle humans.

But I wasn't a human, and the scent made my hair stand on end.

"So young..." A vampire swam out of the darkness, eyes glowing blue. His teeth elongated. He latched onto my throat.

No.

Pain shocked me awake. My eyes shot open.

It wasn't a dream. The vampire had his mouth on my neck, his teeth in my vein. His body pressed mine to the wall.

Not Étan, my panicked brain registered. I couldn't see the man's face, but his dark hair was silvered at the temples, and he was slimmer and a few inches shorter.

I drew a lungful of his earthy scent and almost vomited.

I cursed and bucked against the concrete, trying to throw him off. But there's not much that can dislodge a feeding vampire.

"Calm yourself," he said in French against my throat. He stroked my nape.

"Fuck. You." I thrashed against the wall like a wild man. Trying to bring my knee up. To smash my head into his. To hurt the S.O.B. any way I could.

He sucked harder.

I scrabbled against the air and tried to pull my wrists from the cuffs. Right then, if I could've chewed my hands off like a trapped animal, I would've. Anything to escape. To fight.

A wave of dizziness hit me. He'd taken too much blood from my already depleted body. Shadows crept over my vision, and I blacked out.

When I came to, he was still drinking. I went stiff with horror.

Don't pass out. Don't. Don't. Don't.

Conscious, I had a measure of control. At least, in my head, I did.

Unconscious, I was nothing but the slab of meat they were treating me as.

Another wave of dizziness swamped me. My stomach churned. My eyes closed.

Stay awake, damn it.

I tried to open my eyes, but I'd lost control of my eyelids. I was still fighting to open them when I fell backward into an endless tunnel and the darkness took me under.

9

RIDLEY

I couldn't stop thinking about Zaq. How was he? Had they released him from the wall?

I told myself it wasn't my problem, that they could fuck with him as much as they liked as long as they didn't actually kill him before it was time.

But that was a cop-out, and I knew it.

The morning after my visit to de Froulay's lair found me back on duty in the ops room. The moment I was alone, I turned up the lights in his cell. Zaq had either fallen asleep or passed out. His eyes were closed and he hung like a rag doll from the silver handcuffs.

I zoomed the video cam in on his right wrist. The silver had burned deeply into his skin. If he didn't wake up and take the pressure off, the cuffs would fuse to his wrists.

My stomach did an uncomfortable, twisty contraction. I dragged a hand down my face.

Not your problem, Ridley.

Maybe if I told myself that enough times, I'd even believe it.

I looked at another screen but kept coming back to Zaq.

Most of Moreau's lair was asleep. No one would know if I gave him a break from the cuffs. I put the cameras in Zaq's cell on a continuous loop and was out the door before I could talk myself out of it.

The cell was secured by an old-fashioned silver-reinforced deadbolt. I moved the bolt aside and opened the door, locking it behind me.

The cell's tiny lights glowed on. The air was acrid with the stench of burned flesh.

My stomach heaved. Bile burned in my throat, and I almost lost my breakfast.

Zaq snarled and jerked his head up. He glared, wild-eyed, at me.

Like I was the monster.

I took short, shallow breaths through my mouth. Frozen by what I saw on his face.

The wild-eyed expression faded. "Reaper." With a groan, he straightened his legs and moved his arms, easing the pull of the cuffs.

We both looked at his wrists. The skin was an angry, swollen red.

His gaze came back to mine. "What d'you want?" His voice was as raw as his wrists.

"I'm going to release you from the cuffs."

"Yeah?" He eyed me, clearly wondering what the catch was.

"But try any tricks, and I'll hurt you. Is that clear?" I showed him my switchblade. "I'll give you two hours to sleep, then wake you up and cuff you again."

"Understood."

I tucked my blade into a loop of my pants and crossed to him. I faltered.

Zaq's throat bore a pair of fresh bite marks.

I swallowed hard and fumbled with his first cuff.

Étan had left for Montreal, which meant another vampire—a vampire here in the lair—had drunk from him. At least this vampire had sealed the wounds.

I moved my gaze to Zaq's face. He stared back, a corner of his mouth lifted in a sideways grin like it didn't matter.

But my body was just inches from his. I felt him tense, heard his harsh swallow. It mattered, all right.

I turned back to the cuff and pressed the buttons, then released him from the second one as well. I stepped back and pulled my blade from the loop.

He brought his arms down. Winced.

He set his jaw and doggedly shook them out, but when he tried to move forward, his knees crumpled.

I swore under my breath and leapt to his aid, sliding an arm around his waist. "Easy there."

He leaned into me, lungs working overtime. "Thanks," he said in that raspy voice.

My grip tightened on him. His spicy scent filled my nostrils. My head swam with his nearness.

And I wanted to get even closer.

My throat cinched with a confused mixture of arousal and fear. I waited for him to regain his footing, then released him like he was a hot grenade.

I made my tone hard, a knee-jerk response to the confusion he stirred in me. "Don't make me regret it."

He grunted and stumbled toward the partition that concealed the toilet and sink. "I need to take a leak."

I nodded and hunkered down next to the door so he wouldn't get any ideas about opening it and escaping in the shadow dimension.

When he reemerged, he'd cleaned the blood from his throat and wrists. He sat down against the opposite wall. He bent his knees and set his arms on his thighs so his wrists didn't touch anything.

I waited for him to lie down, but he didn't.

I understood. If I were Zaq Kral, I wouldn't want to do anything as vulnerable as lie down around me, either.

He leaned his head against the wall. His lids shut and his breathing slowed.

To distract myself from his nearness and these confusing feelings I was having for him, I flipped my switchblade from hand to hand, sending it spinning into the air and catching it again. Normally, I enjoyed the challenge of trying to catch it by the handle without cutting my hand on the silver blade. But today, I couldn't concentrate. I stopped before I hurt myself.

I thought Zaq had fallen asleep when his eyes opened. They gleamed green in the dim light.

"You're a slayer, aren't you?"

I stiffened. "Go to sleep."

He ignored me. "I'm right, aren't I? You're different from the others in the lair. You do your own thing, and I can tell you're not part of their hierarchy. Hell, you're not even French. And you're wicked good with those switchblades."

I moved a shoulder.

"I don't hear a no." His smile was grim. "So you are a slayer."

"Go to sleep," I repeated.

"What I want to know is why the fuck you're a part of this? You slayers are supposed to take out the bad vampires, the insane ones or the ones who are just plain evil. Why mess with me? I'm not even a major player in my father's syndicate."

Doubt flickered through me. I rubbed a thumb over my blade's worn steel handle.

There it was, the question that had been niggling at me ever since I'd seen how bad they were treating Zaq.

Why *were* we messing with Zaq Kral? Yeah, he was bait, which was bad enough. But the plan was to take out not just his father, but Zaq and his two brothers as well.

It was like SI had been coopted by Victorine Tremblay as a sneaky way to break the treaty she'd signed with the Krals.

"Answer me." Zaq's voice was low but insistent. The voice of a man used to being obeyed. "This isn't a job for Slayers, Inc. That blond vampire—Étan? He's the Tremblay Syndicate lieutenant. This is revenge, pure and simple. His prima wants my family dead."

He was right. Victorine Tremblay hated Karoly Kral, and she probably did want his sons dead.

The flicker of doubt burned brighter. I ruthlessly smothered it. "I don't have to explain myself to you."

He didn't let up. "You don't know what this is about, do you? They give you an order, and you carry it out."

I clamped my fingers around the switchblade handle. If he thought I was ashamed of what I did, he could think again.

"That's right. Because as far as I'm concerned, take you out, and there's one less monster in the world."

"Monster?" His chin jerked back like I'd struck him. "That's what you think I am?"

"You tell me. You drink blood. You're a member of a syndicate that preys on humans. What does that make you?"

"A dhampir." He placed his palms on his knees and leaned forward. "It makes me a dhampir. Same as you."

❧ 10 ❧
ZAQ

"Take it back." Reaper flowed, lethal as a ninja, across the cell.

Her tone was cold, but her breath was agitated. She crouched and touched the switchblade to my throat.

What the fuck was wrong with her? I eyed her from beneath my lids, too damned exhausted and hungry to fight.

Let her cut my damn throat.

She pushed the point deeper. "Take. It. Back."

Blood trickled down my neck. We both smelled its coppery scent. Her nostrils flared. Her breathing sped up.

I cocked my head to the side, trying to ease the pressure. "Take what back? That you're a dhampir? You are, aren't you? Same as me."

Reaper's gaze locked on my bleeding neck. Blue rimmed her striking gray eyes. She ran the tip of her tongue over her lower lip. Fangs gleamed whitely.

Yeah, she was definitely a dhampir. Blood excited her, brought her vampire to the surface.

And that excited me. Incredibly, my cock hardened.

I swallowed, itching to sink my fangs into her plump lower lip and draw a little blood myself.

Her gaze lifted. We stared at each other, arrested. For a few seconds, I forgot where I was or who she was. I even forgot the blade pressed to my throat.

All I knew was that I wanted—no, *needed*—to drag off her pants, pull her onto my lap and sink my dick into her sweet little body.

My stomach growled, the sound loud in the small cell.

44

We took a ragged breath in unison.

Hatred flashed across Reaper's face. It was more effective than a slap. My excitement withered.

She pressed the blade deeper. "I'm *nothing* like you syndicate vampires. I don't drink from thralls. I don't use my wealth and power to prey on humans and make them into slaves and blood addicts. I *protect* humans from people like you Krals."

"Okay, okay." I leaned my head back against the wall. "You're nothing like me."

Reaper's gaze darted to the knife she was holding to my neck. "Fuck." Her eyes widened. She jerked back and closed the blade. "Fuck, fuck, fuck."

She scrambled backward and stood up, getting as far from me as she could and still be in the cell. She turned her back and put a hand on the concrete, head bowed.

"Hey." I struggled to my feet and fought to clear my head. Something told me this was important, a key to the mystery that was Reaper. "I understand. It's not easy for any of us. And for the record, I've never kept a slave in my life or turned a woman into a blood addict. My mom raised me better than that."

"Don't." Her voice was a harsh scrape. "You don't understand. You can't."

"Yeah?" The anger I'd held in for two long nights spilled over. "Why not? Because I'm a syndicate prince? I'm still a dhampir. The vampire spawn beat the shit out of me and my brothers whenever they could, and my father did nothing to stop them because he wanted to toughen us up. And he had to strong-arm the other vampires in our syndicate to accept us as his heirs—not that I even wanted to be his damn heir. But you don't leave the Kral Syndicate."

I heard the bitterness in my tone, and I didn't care. Maybe to an outsider like Reaper, I looked like a rich, spoiled brat, but she didn't know how confined my life had been. I'd been born with a silver spoon in my mouth when all I wanted was plain old sturdy, practical stainless steel.

I couldn't even choose my own career. I'd wanted to go to medical school, but my father had said, "Syndicate princes don't work as doctors."

Mom had been more diplomatic. She'd taken me aside and pointed out that humans wouldn't accept a dhampir in their hospitals. So instead, I worked on the edges of the medical profession, raising funds for organizations like Doctors Without Borders and helping out whenever I could grab a few weeks away from New York and my father's demands.

Reaper kept her back toward me. I took a step toward her, still angry.

"But I'm glad I'm a dhampir. Hell, what's so great about being a vampire? The purebloods can't go out in the day like we can or have more than one kid. Those spawn that beat on me and my brothers were jealous because they were only children, and we had each other. So what's so fucking good about being a vampire?"

On the wall, Reaper's fingers curled into a fist. She shook her head without looking at me. I had to strain to hear her words.

"You don't understand. I don't want to be a vampire. I want to be a human. Like my mom."

❦ 11 ❦
RIDLEY

I stood with my back to the wall of Philippe Moreau's public salon. The dimly lit room was crowded with gorgeous people sipping his expensive wine and flirting in multiple languages.

Servers in skimpy red dresses wove their way through the crowd with hors d'oeuvres for the humans and hand-made chocolates infused with blood-wine for the vampires. Across the salon, an up-and-coming band from Senegal played a sexy French dance-club song. A handful of couples swayed to the music.

So this was one of Moreau's famous parties.

At least I hadn't been forced to attend as a guest.

No, I was working security, decked out in a trim black uniform with a Paris Syndicate griffin embroidered over my left breast. My job was to steer guests—"Gently," Aubin had stressed as if he doubted my ability to figure that out on my own—away from the door to my right which opened to a servant's staircase leading down to Moreau's private apartment.

A man—a human—stopped a few feet away and lit a hand-rolled cigarette. His dark gaze traveled down my body.

"What's a woman so bella doing in a uniform? You should be in a beautiful dress. Like her." He nodded at a server.

I awarded him full points for a lame come-on. And he leaked emotions: lust, greed, anticipation.

I sighed, wishing I could disappear into the black wallpaper along with the griffins and snakes. Instead, I summoned my best death-stare. "I don't serve."

He dragged on the cigarette and stared at my breasts. "When's your break?"

"I don't get one." My tone dared him to keep pushing. In my current edgy state, kicking his pretty ass out of the mansion would be a pleasure.

He ran a finger down my arm. "I think you are lying."

Okay, now he'd pissed me off. I was in uniform, clearly not one of Moreau's playthings. I let my eyes flash blue and faked a knee to his balls.

His eyes widened and his Adam's apple worked. He backed up a few steps.

"A pity," he sneered from a safe distance and disappeared into the crowd.

My shoulders had crawled up to my ears. I rolled them in a circle, cracked my neck.

Two women sauntered up in tight, throat-baring dresses. They glanced at my uniform and dismissed me as unimportant.

"I hear the real action is on the lower levels," the taller woman said in French to her companion. They exchanged sly smiles and moved toward the door.

"*Non.*" I stepped in front of them. "That's private. *Interdit.*"

The tall woman's mouth tightened. She kept walking like she was going to mow me down. I rolled my eyes and grabbed her arm, preparing to twist it behind her skinny back.

Her friend gripped her other arm. "You want to get us thrown out? This woman, she's one of them. Now, come."

The woman looked back at me. This time she *saw* me. Her eyes widened. "Pardon."

I grunted and released her arm. She backed away, and the two made a beeline through the crowd to the opposite side of the room.

I retook my stance next to the door, hands clasped behind my back.

Two days since I'd last been to Zaq's cell.

Two days since I'd nearly lost control.

Since then, I'd avoided the mansion's lowest level as if merely breathing the same air as Zaq Kral would suck me into his world, the violent, man-eat-man world of syndicate vampires.

Zaq had me twisted into knots—the tight, snarly kind that you can't untangle without cutting something—and I hated it.

At least they hadn't drunk his blood again; I'd checked the video feed. I'd also ID'ed the vampire who'd attacked him the second time—Philippe Moreau.

No surprise there. Moreau was so depraved, the only thralls he could keep were slaves or blood addicts who craved the high of a vampire's bite.

So why wasn't he my target?

Behind my back, I dug my nails dug into my palms. Damn Zaq and his lean, too-beautiful angel's face. I'd begun to wish I'd never volunteered for this op.

Yesterday I'd tried to get in touch with Crow to tell her about how Zaq was being treated. But according to her assistant Stygian, she was unreachable for the next few days.

"I can take a message," he'd said, "but I don't know when she'll receive it."

"Never mind," I'd said and ended the call.

What would I have said to Crow anyway? Zaq's poor treatment didn't change the endgame, which was to draw Karoly Kral out of New York so we could slay him.

Across the salon the crowd stirred and bubbled like someone had thrown something fizzy into the mix. Someone had arrived, a VIP. These people were too hip to openly stare, but they sent casual glances over their shoulders or angled their bodies for a better view.

I lifted onto the balls of my feet trying to see who was causing all the excitement, but the room was too crowded. I sank back down and watched Moreau wend his way in their direction.

I glanced around. Jiggled my knee.

Christ, I hated standing around watching other people get drunk and flirt. Working security at a party had to be one of the most boring jobs ever.

Moreau had reached the newcomer. The crowd parted long enough for me to see it was Leo de Froulay, his dark blue suit a perfect foil for his shining blond mane. A woman stood next to him, a thrall from the possessive hand he had on her ass.

My heart banged against my chest. This was it, the moment I'd been waiting for all evening.

The band changed songs and upped the volume. A thrall wandered by, eyes glazed, high on the rush of a vampire's bite. The scent of lust and arousal mingled with cigarette smoke and the sweet-earth smell of weed.

De Froulay was too smart to head directly to me. He took his time, pausing here and there to chat like a faerie king spreading the glitter dust of his charisma. My sperm donor had serious star quality; I'd give him that.

A server offered me a blood-wine. I waved it away; I'd already had my daily glass.

And then de Froulay was standing in front of me, all that glittering charm focused in my direction. "*Ma petite*, how nice to see you again."

My lips tugged up in an answering smile. I couldn't help it. I flattened my mouth and inclined my head. "Primus de Froulay."

I glanced around for Moreau, but de Froulay must have sent him on an errand because he was nowhere to be seen. The thrall snuggled up to his side blinked lazily at me.

I stilled. *What the fuck?*

The "thrall" was Crow, hiding behind a glamour. Her hair was a short, curly red instead of its usual straight dark brown, and her nose and chin less sharp. She'd added some serious curves including large breasts that the tight black dress could barely contain.

But she'd never been able to disguise her distinctive eyes. They were a deep blue, so deep they appeared violet in the low light.

I dragged my gaze back to de Froulay. "May I help you, Primus?"

He nodded. "I'd like to speak with you. Privately."

Crow glanced between the two of us.

I gulped, then wished I hadn't, because of course she'd noticed. She noticed everything.

I gave de Froulay a small, I'm-just-the-hired-help nod. "As you wish."

De Froulay took my arm. "We'll be right back," he told Crow-the-thrall.

He opened the door I'd been guarding and steered me through it. I felt her eyes on me until the door closed behind us.

Damn, damn, damn.

Now I'd have to come up with a reason as to why I'd gone off with the Paris primus. Telling Crow that de Froulay wanted to hire me as a body-guard wouldn't cut it. A primus wouldn't take me aside for such a minor reason; he'd outsource that to his lieutenant or an enforcer like Moreau.

"You're well?" De Froulay took in my uniform and ponytail. His hand-some face looked...concerned.

I put aside my worries about Crow to focus on him. "I'm fine."

"Good, good." He hesitated as if he wanted to say more.

I didn't give him the chance. "I'll do it," I blurted.

"Ah, *oui?*"

"Yes. But not for money. I want a favor instead."

His dark brows climbed. "A favor."

Sweat prickled my palms. This was the tricky part. I *needed* him to say yes. I hadn't been able to track down my mom's murderers, not in all these years. I'd begun to think I never would.

"Yes." I drew a calming breath. "I want you to find the vampires who killed my mom."

Whatever he'd been expecting, it wasn't that. His brows lifted, his jaw slackened. "Vampires killed Charlotte?"

His shock was palpable. Any doubts I'd had about whether he'd been behind her death were laid to rest.

I nodded. "I was there. They wanted me, but she wouldn't tell them where I was. They tortured her, and she still didn't tell." My voice cracked on the last few words.

Guilt choked me. Darkness tugged at me with bony fingers, pulling me down into a muddy swamp of shame and regret.

I should've gone back. Fought by her side, even though she'd begged me to run.

I should've died with her.

No, I should've died instead of her.

De Froulay's face sharpened. A line of ice-blue encircled his irises and his fangs lengthened into gleaming white daggers.

I stepped back—I might be a trained slayer, but some responses are bred in the bone—and came up against the wall.

"Who?" he demanded in guttural tones.

I blinked. He was really, really angry. Hell, he looked ready to rip someone's head from their body.

Had my mom mattered to him that much?

"I don't know," I said. "But they were French—they talked to each other in French, anyway. I even wondered if you sent them yourself."

"No. Not me."

I nodded. Several times, because he was still making me kind of nervous. "I believe that now."

He released a slow breath. His gaze moved over me, still pressed against the wall. He retracted his fangs. "Calm yourself, little one. I would never harm you."

I dipped my chin and forced myself to outwardly relax.

"You thought they were from the Paris Syndicate?" he asked. "But why? There are other French syndicates, and I hadn't seen your mother in years."

"Why else would they want me?"

"Yes, of course." He stared over my head. "Interesting, that they knew about you when I myself didn't."

"Mom hid me. No one knew what I really was."

"Except these vampires. Very well. I will look into it. But not because you are helping me. For the information you gather about Philippe, I will pay. But your mother's killers I will find because they took something that was mine. And then—" he showed some fang again—"I will stake the sons of bitches myself."

I rubbed my forehead. I hadn't expected him to take over, and frankly, I didn't want him to. "I just need their names."

His jaw set. "Honor requires that I send them myself to their final graves. You have some objection?"

I considered him. My gut wanted to growl, *Hell, yeah, I object*, but my brain pointed out that with Leo de Froulay involved, I might finally find my mother's killers.

"All right," I said. "But only if I'm there when they die. I want to see those bastards burn and crumble to ashes with my own eyes. I want them to know they're dead because of me."

De Froulay gave a single, slow blink. Then he smiled. "You are fierce. I like that."

"Do we have a deal?"

"If it's possible, then yes. You will be there. Give me what you have—descriptions, the date it happened, where."

I compressed my lips. "I didn't get a good look at them. They came too fast. She made me run."

I closed my eyes against the images that lived in my mind. The fear in my mom's face. How she'd begged me to hide. Her screams.

And worse, the moment when her voice had cut off mid-scream.

"Tell me what you know." De Froulay's deep voice pulled me back to the present.

I swallowed, nodded. "I was twelve, so it was—" I gave de Froulay the year and date, and the name of the small town where we'd lived.

"How many?"

"Three—all men. One blond, and two with dark hair."

"The French they spoke, it was Parisian?"

I gave a helpless shrug. "I don't know. I think so."

"All right. I'll get started on this right away. If you think of anything else that might help, let me know."

"I will. You have an email where I can contact you?"

He gave it to me and I memorized it, then gave him a private, very secure email address that I'd set up just for this. "I'll use the subject line *Wine Tasting*."

He repeated the address back, then gazed down at me through hooded eyes. "This isn't right. My daughter in a uniform? You don't have to do this. I'll settle enough money on you so you don't have to work."

"I don't want your money. And I like working security."

Our gazes clashed. I moved to the door. "If that's all—?"

He inclined his head, and I escaped into the salon.

Crow was waiting a few feet from the door. De Froulay wrapped an arm around her, and she nuzzled his neck and sent me a significant look over his shoulder. They moved off together.

Ten minutes later, my phone buzzed.

Crow: *The garden. Now.*

Reaper: *15 min. I have to find s/o to cover for me.*

Crow: *Do it.*

I found a Paris soldier to take over my post and slipped out to meet her. The garden was blissfully cool and uncrowded. The wolfdogs raced up to me, and I held out a hand for them to sniff. They wagged their tails and returned to their handler.

The white pebble paths gleamed in the moonlight. I put my hands in my pockets and chose a path at random. I didn't bother to look for Crow. She'd find me.

I circled a sweet-smelling bed of lavender and creamy roses, and there she was, seated on a cast-iron bench. She fell into step beside me.

"Report." Nothing in her tone gave away the fact that she was suspicious of me, but I knew she must wonder why de Froulay had asked to speak to me privately. And why he'd called me *"Ma petite,"* an endearment meaning "my little one."

I kept my face and tone as calm as the white marble statue of a young woman we were strolling by. "I contacted Stygian, but he said you'd gone dark."

Stygian wasn't her assistant's real name, of course. Crow assigned nicknames to all of her operatives.

"And? What does the primus want?"

"He wants me to spy on—" I tipped my head at the softly-lit mansion instead of speaking Moreau's name aloud. You never knew when someone was listening.

"I see."

I dropped my voice. "The primus suspects something's going on. If I don't investigate, he'll just find someone else. This way, I can filter what he finds out."

We exchanged a look. I could tell Crow understood.

Leo de Froulay was a smart man with the resources of a powerful syndicate behind him. If he started poking around, he might discover the truth—that Slayers, Inc. had joined with the Tremblay Syndicate to take out Karoly Kral and his sons.

De Froulay could blow Operation Angel sky-high. Karoly Kral was already pushing for changes in how SI was run.

If the syndicates found out that SI had taken sides in a vampire blood-feud, we were fucked. Karoly would have the leverage he sought to force those changes through. Changes that would give the vampires more power on SI's secretive Board of Directors.

Crow pursed her lips, then nodded. "Fine. You have my okay. But only if it doesn't interfere with your primary job."

I did a mental fist-pump. *Yes.*

To Crow, I said, "Understood."

I waited for her to ask why de Froulay had called me his little one but fortunately, a pair of Paris vampires came into view, heading toward us.

Crow slipped into her role as a thrall, giving the men a bold, sensual smile. "A lovely evening, isn't it, gentlemen?"

I brushed past the three of them and hurried back to the mansion. Behind me, one of the vampires said something to Crow, and she gave a husky chuckle.

My step hitched.

Hearing Crow chuckle was like hearing a wolf baa like a sheep. It was more than odd. It was flat-out bizarre.

⚜

When I got off duty at three a.m., the party was still going strong.

I heaved a sigh of relief and headed downstairs to my quarters. With its cushy queen-sized bed and fancy bathroom, the room I'd been assigned was actually a step up from the bare-bones way I lived between ops. Why put money into a place I only used a few months a year?

Kicking off my shoes, I grabbed my laptop and sat yoga-style on the bed. The coverlet was a deep purple sateen with a huge gold griffin like the one on my uniform embroidered in the center, its lion's tail curling over its back, its beak and talons open in threat.

I opened the laptop and went into something similar to incognito mode, but more secure. I'd decided to poke around some, see if I could turn up proof that Moreau was trafficking in blood slaves on the side.

Moreau's cameras that didn't feed into the ops room? They had to be going somewhere. And I had a program that would let me access any nearby video feed.

If Moreau was a blood slaver, I was pretty sure de Froulay didn't know. He'd agreed to ban the practice of enslaving humans along with most of the other vampire primuses.

If I could take Moreau down without jeopardizing Op A, I would.

I wanted to cause the man a world of hurt.

An hour or so later, I frowned and gave up, having found nothing conclusive. But then, Moreau would do everything he could to conceal his unlawful trade in humans. Hopefully, the intel I planned to feed de Froulay about Moreau and Zaq would be enough.

Before I closed my laptop, I navigated to the feed for Zaq's cell.

He was passed out, eyes closed. Hanging from the wall with those damn silver cuffs searing into his wrists.

My wrists heated like it was me in the cuffs. I absently rubbed the left one.

Zaq Kral had been kind to me. That morning in the airport, he'd been exhausted, hungry. But he'd stepped in to save me from a vampire he thought was trying to force me into remaining his thrall.

The edgy feeling returned full force.

I bounced my knee, itching to go to Zaq's cell and give him a few hours relief. But I couldn't, not while Moreau and the other vampires were awake. I'd have to wait for dawn.

I sank my teeth into my lower lip. I didn't realize I'd extended my fangs until I smelled my own blood.

I scrubbed it away, then stared at my bloody fingers. I'd trained myself to ignore the blood-hunger, but it was always with me, scratching at my throat, drying my mouth. When it got too strong, I ran an extra few miles or did a hundred extra pushups.

Now I couldn't stop myself. I brought my hand to my mouth like it didn't belong to me and licked the blood off. Swallowed.

I stifled a moan. It tasted so good. So fucking good.

I took my hand from my mouth and stared at the now-clean skin.

Monster.

I closed the laptop and placed it on the small mahogany desk, then stripped off my uniform and hung it in the closet. In the shower I turned the water to cold and scrubbed myself down, then stood under the icy stream until I was shivering.

In the bedroom, I folded up the coverlet and set it on a chair before getting into bed.

I wouldn't allow myself to be warm tonight.

12

ZAQ

So Reaper wanted to be human.

I moved my cramped arms the few inches available to me, trying and failing to find a more comfortable position.

Gods, she was messed up.

And I was even more messed up for wondering why I hadn't seen her for two days.

Hell, I wasn't just wondering, I was worried—about the woman who'd drugged and abducted me. That wasn't messed up. That was flat-out fucked.

Still, Reaper was the only person in this lair who'd treated me halfway decently, and I was afraid she'd gotten in trouble for it. Even if I was ninety-nine percent sure she was a slayer.

The first time she'd fed me, I'd assumed she had permission, but now I wasn't so sure. She'd come alone, for one thing—both times. And in the daytime, when the lair's vampires would be asleep.

My eyes drooped. Gods, I could use some sleep myself. I shifted against the cold concrete wall.

I'd thought I'd known what it was like to go hungry and without sleep for days on end, but I was wrong. Even in the midst of a war or the aftermath of an earthquake, I'd always been able to snatch a few hours when I needed it. You learn to tune out the chaos after working a thirty-hour shift.

My head lolled to the side. I locked my knees, closed my eyes. Hoping to catch a short nap before the pain in my wrists dragged me back to consciousness.

Where in the name of the Dark Lady was my father?

I pictured him, dark-haired and dark-eyed, with peaked black brows and that not-quite-human shine to him. Me, I could blend in with humans, but Karoly Kral didn't even try.

He had to be in Paris by now, unless he'd sent someone else. His lieutenant Tomas, maybe. If anyone could track me down in a strange city with virtually no clues, it was my father.

And when he found me, he wouldn't sneak into the lair. No, he'd stalk in like he owned the fucking place and demand my release.

I shifted against the concrete again, brain fuzzy, my mouth as dry as the dust of Aleppo, the gray powder from the rubble of bombed-out buildings that coated everything. Even your food tasted gritty.

Right now, I'd give my left nut for a plate of that gritty food.

I was so hungry, my stomach had stopped growling. Instead, I had a constant, gnawing ache in my middle, and all I could think about was blood.

Rich, salty, life-giving blood.

I drew a breath through my nostrils and tried to think of something else.

Reaper, for instance. Naked. And tied up, because hey, this was my fantasy and I might want to fuck her, but I also wanted to punish her.

Her arms were open, the wrists secured to the bedposts. The position arched her back, showing off small, firm breasts.

She squirmed, eager for me to touch her, but I made her wait, feasting on her body with my gaze.

Pale pink nipples, or maybe a soft, dusky rose.

A slim waist and hips just curvy enough.

And those lean, strong legs.

I could feel them wrapped around my waist, her head thrown back in submission as I thrust into her.

My eyes closed. I dozed, lost in a hot, very erotic scene. Then my head hit my chest and I jerked awake, my dick hard.

Someone was at the door. I straightened up and willed my fuzzy head to clear—and my dick to settle down.

The door opened. A man was silhouetted in the light from the hall.

I squinted, trying to make out his face. Even the dim light was too much for my eyes after so many hours in darkness.

As he moved forward, the lights in the cell came on. It was Big Guy with the Fists.

I shuddered; I couldn't help it.

And I could tell he'd seen. His eyes flickered and a corner of his mouth edged up.

My cheeks burned. Humiliation squeezed me, fast and hard, like a giant fist compressing my ribcage.

I clenched my jaw and stood taller. I would *not* let these bastards break me.

I ran my gaze over him, noting every detail—the long nose, the full lips, the tiny notch in his right brow. I might not know the names of the people involved in this, but if—no, *when*, I escaped—I was going to make sure I could describe every damn one of them.

Big Guy allowed me to use the john, but instead of leaving after, he snapped the cuffs on my wrists and stayed behind to talk.

"You're waiting for your father to rescue you, aren't you?" His lips twisted in a nasty, knowing line.

"Yeah." My voice was a dry rasp. It had been days since I'd used it. I swallowed and tried again. "Because he will."

"He's in Paris, did you know that?"

My heart jumped and smacked against my rib cage.

Big Guy heard, of course. His nasty smile stretched. "But he's not coming for you. You know why?"

I stared back stonily.

He didn't need a response. "He's not coming because he wants you dead. You. Your brothers."

That provoked me to answer. "Yeah, right. Get your head out of your ass. We're my father's only spawn. Why the fuck would he want us dead?"

"Then why are you still in here? Moreau laid a lure tonight, a party that he made sure everyone in Paris knew about. And your father didn't show." His lip curled. "He left you here to rot."

Moreau? My stomach bottomed out. I'd been kidnapped by the Paris Syndicate's top enforcer?

"How do you know?" I shot back. "If my dad came to the party, he'd make damn sure you didn't recognize him."

"We know." Big Guy smirked.

"Then he had a good reason. He probably figured it for a trap."

"You think he loves you—a dhampir?"

"I don't think it. I know it."

Big Guy shook his head like I had rocks for brains. "You think like a human. Vampires don't love. They manipulate."

"Some vampires do both."

I should know. My father was a cold S.O.B., but he loved me and my brothers. And he was downright soft-hearted when it came to my mom, the human-turned-dhampir he'd taken as his mate.

Big Guy eyed me. His gaze lingered on my neck.

I tensed and clenched my fists. Like I could throw a punch when they had me shackled to the wall.

"Don't worry." His mouth curled evilly. "I'm not going to drink from you. Tonight."

My throat worked. "Go fuck yourself."

He chuckled. "Now why would I do that when I have all those hot little humans at the party upstairs to fuck?"

҉

A nother day and night passed. Big Guy with the Fists—whose name I'd learned was Blaise—returned again to taunt me about my father. So did some of the other members of the lair.

They were trying to turn me against him, and I knew it.

But it was working. I'd been in here how long—four, five days? Plenty of time for Father to have located me. If he was in Paris, why hadn't he done something?

He and Leo de Froulay, the Paris primus, went way back. Why hadn't he gone straight to de Froulay and demanded he do something? Then again, if the Paris primus was part of this, maybe Father had decided I wasn't worth a break with a valuable ally.

Maybe he *had* left me to rot like Blaise had said.

Father was nothing if not coldly rational. He might have decided I was the son he could most afford to sacrifice. The only son who'd refused to be made a member of the Kral Syndicate.

Stop it. That's exactly what they want you to think.

My brain wasn't reasoning correctly. I knew it.

I was one big ache. Feverish and dehydrated and seeing people who weren't really there.

Mom touched my face and murmured that she loved me.

Gabriel told me to stay strong, that this was a test, and he knew I could survive it.

And Rafe gave that crooked grin women loved. "You always did have a soft heart, asshole. Now see what you've done?"

The only family member who didn't visit me in my fever-haze was my dad.

"Karoly wants you dead. Why do you think you're still here?"

That had been the blond vampire, the female with high cheekbones. Ines, they'd called her.

My hands formed weak fists in the cuffs.

Maybe dream-Gabriel was right and this was one of Father's fucking tests.

Because he'd let the vampire spawn beat on us. He'd *known* they were beating on us and he hadn't stopped it. He'd let it happen to make us stronger.

A rite of passage, he'd called it.

They'd taunted us for being half-human, had come at us with teeth and claws. They were pureblood vampires, faster and stronger than us.

And Father did nothing to stop it. Me and my brothers had had our asses kicked too many times to count, even after we banded together to fight back. Worse, they caught Rafe alone a couple of times and hurt him pretty bad.

The second time Rafe was beaten, my mom and dad had argued about it. I'd been high in a tree in the garden of our Maryland home when they'd walked beneath the tree and I heard my mom say something about stopping the beatings. I'd strained to listen.

"You have to trust me on this, my love," Father had told her. "It's a test, a rite of passage. If I step in, the other spawn will never respect them. They'll tell their parents, and the boys will never be accepted as my heirs."

Mom had given a frustrated growl. "Sometimes I think that's all they are to you. Your *heirs*."

"Rosemarie." His tone was chiding. But he didn't deny it.

Mom had turned on her heel and stalked back to our big stone house. Father had stared after her, his expression unreadable.

"Come out, Zaquiel."

I jolted. He knew I'd overheard. I leapt to the ground and stood, shoulders hunched, waiting for him to lay into me for eavesdropping.

But he set a hand on my back and walked me toward the house. "Your mother doesn't understand."

"She doesn't understand what?"

His eyes met mine. Usually there was some warmth in them, but right now they were hard black stones.

"That you have to stand up to the other spawn on your own. If they think you boys are weak, they'll eat you alive."

I looked away, kicked at a stone. Feeling all the weight of being a dhampir. A prince, yeah, but also less.

"Not if you order them to leave us alone."

Father shook me by the shoulder. "You can't be weak. I can't protect you forever. Kill or be killed. That's our world. Do you understand? I need you to be strong for Gabriel, so he doesn't always have to fight your battles—and for Rafe, so he can depend on you."

I faced my father, lifted my chin. "I understand."

"Good." He cuffed the back of my head and we headed into the house.

After that, I doubled down on my martial arts and other physical training. Learning to fight hard—and dirty.

And when Gabriel and I got big enough, we cornered the bastards who'd beaten Rafe and gave them an ass-kicking of our own.

13

RIDLEY

The day after the party, I finally went back to Zaq's cell. It had been three days since I'd last visited. The dimly lit, black-and-white video feed hadn't prepared me for what I'd find.

He looked like a different man. The silver was eating away at his insides. His face was pale, and the blood craving was a live animal in his eyes. His features had sharpened, the human in him having been carved away to reveal the vampire beneath.

The vampire that was the only thing keeping him alive because a human would've been dead from dehydration by now.

Zaq's head wobbled on his neck. His gaze went to my throat. He swallowed, then with an obvious effort, focused on my face.

"Hey." His voice came out as a croak.

Shame sank sharp teeth into my chest. He was a dhampir. He could withstand weeks, even months, of this torture.

But that made what we were doing to him even more horrifying.

Think like a slayer.

I shoved the shame down, cramming it into a dark corner of my soul along with other questionable things I'd done in my years with SI.

"You know the drill." I put the container of steak tartare and bloodwine I'd brought on the floor and showed him my switchblade.

"Yeah." His gaze locked on the food.

I released him from the cuffs, trying not to look at the ugly wounds on his wrists, and stepped back. He brought his arms down. His agonized groan sank those sharp teeth of shame deeper.

62

And oddly, my own arms cramped. I gave them a shake at the same time he shook out his own.

What the hell? It was like I felt his pain in my own body, which wasn't just odd, it was creep-me-out weird.

Instead of going for the food, he slid down the wall and stayed there, legs sprawled out before him, head resting on the concrete.

"You need to eat." My tone was stiff. I was still stuck in the creepiness of feeling his pain.

The corner of his mouth twitched. "No shit, cher. Maybe if you could push that over here—?"

The shame returned as I realized he was too weak to get it.

I opened the container of raw steak and put it on his lap along with a fork, then uncorked the wine. He had to use both hands to lift the bottle to his mouth, but after a few gulps, he had enough strength to dig into the meat.

I crouched on my haunches near the door, toying with my switchblade and watching him eat with a satisfaction that was way out of proportion to what I should be feeling.

And it scared me.

The man was getting to me.

Why else would I risk feeding him? If I kept it up, Moreau was bound to find out I was aiding the very man I'd helped kidnap.

The enforcer would either stake me himself or report me to Crow, and God knew what she'd do to me. I'd seen her carve pieces out of slayers who disobeyed orders. The dhampirs healed, but the humans didn't always make it.

And even a dhampir remembered that kind of pain.

Zaq ate with a slow, steady focus. Even half-starved, he didn't shovel the food in. Instead, he showed impressive control, taking time to chew the steak tartare thoroughly. He chased it down with sips of blood-wine.

At least I wasn't *feeling* him anymore.

Halfway through, he set his fork down and leaned his head back against the wall. I noted with that queer satisfaction that his cheeks had regained some color.

He reached for the bottle without moving his head and drank some more wine. "Thank you," he said as he put the bottle down.

I grunted. I didn't deserve his thanks, and I knew it. Not when I was the one who'd put him in here in the first place.

He eyed me from beneath lowered lids. "So is it true my father was in Paris but didn't try to rescue me?"

I frowned. "Someone told you that?"

"Yeah. Ines and the others. They said he left me here to rot. Is it true?" His voice was matter of fact, but I heard the vulnerability beneath the question.

I knew I should tell him yes. It was clear Moreau was trying to break Zaq, both physically and mentally.

But I didn't. Instead, I told him the truth. "I don't know. I do know that according to our intel your father came to Paris. But he's made no attempt to rescue you."

Zaq's face fell. "I see."

He reached for the steak tartare and this time, didn't stop until it was gone. He took another swig of the wine. His strong throat worked as he swallowed, and I wanted more than anything to press a kiss to it. Not a bite. A kiss.

It was my turn to swallow. I looked away. "You need to take a piss?"

"Yeah." He pushed himself to his feet, careful as an old man. He blinked, then stumbled forward and nearly face-planted.

I jumped up, crossing the cell in a few swift steps and sliding an arm around his waist. "Here. Lean on me."

"Sorry." He draped an arm over my shoulders and I helped him the few feet to the toilet.

He was too warm and too damn skinny, but he still felt good. Hard-muscled and just the right height for my cheek to press against his shoulder.

I glanced up. He was looking at me, his beautiful green-and-gold eyes just inches from mine. My breath hitched and my mouth dried.

He gave me a crooked grin that was like a sneaky arrow to the heart. "I can handle things from here."

My arm tightened on him. I didn't want to release him; I wanted to help him.

I had to force my arm to remove itself from his waist. "I'll be right outside the door."

When I returned a few minutes later, he was curled up on the floor, asleep. I crouched down and watched him. Learning his features —his strong nose, his sculpted cheeks, his stubbled jaw, his full bottom lip.

I reached out and touched his mouth before I realized what I was doing. Caressed that full lower lip. It was warm, soft.

And this time I did want to bite. To bite and kiss and suck and lick.

His eyelids fluttered. I hurriedly brought my hand back to my side and backed away. But I kept watching him. I couldn't look away.

Two hours passed. I didn't dare stay with him any longer. Reluctantly, I crossed the cell and shook his shoulder. "Wake up. I have to go."

Zaq blinked and stretched. I was pleased to see he looked better. His eyes were clear and a thin new skin had formed over the burns on his wrists. He downed the last of the blood-wine and stood up.

I nodded at the wall, but instead of raising his arms, he cocked his head to the side. "Why are you doing this?"

It was the second time he'd asked that. I set my jaw. "I told you."

"No, you don't understand. I meant, why are you feeding me? Letting me sleep?"

I shook my head. "I have to go. Get up against the wall."

"Reaper." His hollow-cheeked angel's gaze beseeched me. "You don't have to do this. This is fucked up and you know it. Help me. Please."

I hesitated, a part of me, a big part, tempted to agree.

He moved closer. "My father—he'll pay you. Anything you ask."

The hair on my nape lifted. If I were a wolf, my hackles would've raised. It was precisely the wrong thing to say. He'd reminded me who Zaq Kral was—and who *I* was. A slayer who'd dedicated her life to killing monsters like Karoly Kral.

I'd put my switchblades away, but now I drew one and released the catch. "Back. Against. The. Wall."

For a tense moment, I thought he'd disobey. I stalked toward him, blade out.

He spread his arms, mouth bent in a warped grin. Daring me to stick the knife in him. "You're not going to stake me and we both know it."

"Don't bet on it." I touched the sharp point to his sternum.

"Do it, then." Jaguar eyes seared into mine.

The air between us crackled and hissed. My whole body heated.

You're pissed off, not hot for him.

Which was a barefaced lie. In some insane way, I was enjoying this, and my female parts were practically purring.

I didn't say a word. To be honest, I didn't trust myself to speak. Who knew what would come out of my mouth?

Instead, I shoved the knife into my belt loop and smacked my open hand onto his chest. "Now, dammit."

"Oh, Reaper." His voice was tender. Like he knew I was fighting myself as much as him.

When I growled, he gave me a knowing, stomach-tilting smile, and without bringing his arms down, took a step back.

I kept up the pressure. He took another step back, and another, until his back hit the wall, his wrists hovering over the cuffs. I snapped them into place and whipped around. I snatched up the container and wine bottle and fast-walked to the door like the coward I was.

I fumbled with the lock, jerked the door open.

"You feel it too." Soft words, but they slammed into me like a hail of bullets. "You can pretend all you want, but we both know there's something there."

❧ 14 ❧
ZAQ

E ight days had passed, and I was still locked in a fucking cell. Something or somebody had messed up.

Father wasn't going to rescue me.

Either he couldn't find me, or he'd decided to test me, or he'd tried to rescue me and been captured himself.

Hell, maybe he'd never even gotten the message.

Whatever. I just knew I was on my own, trapped in a living nightmare. No one was coming to spring me—not my father, not Gabriel, and not Rafe.

Not even Reaper. She'd been a long shot, but I'd hoped...

So. It was up to me to liberate myself. I was running out of time.

The silver poison had hit me hard, maybe because I'd already been rundown when I arrived in Paris. Much more of this, and it would put me into a coma. Already, I was out more than I was awake.

This morning, I'd been startled awake by a rough, agonized cry. I'd strained against my bonds, heart racing, lungs heaving.

Someone's hurt. I have to help.

Until I realized the cry had come from me.

The silver had burned through the final layer of skin and into the muscles and tendons of my wrists, fusing to my body. The pain was so excruciating, I'd cried out in my sleep.

I'd moved my wrists up and down, ripping them free of the silver. That had been so fucking painful, I'd nearly passed out again.

I'd stayed awake the rest of the day. Anything to keep my wrists from touching the silver.

Evening came. I hadn't even seen Reaper for a couple of days. My last hope of rescue drained away.

You're on your own, Zaq. No one's coming to break you out of here.

Something inside me cracked. The combination of pain, blood-hunger and lack of sleep fractured the human part of me, and the darkness—the vampire beast—surged up. The vampire beast that's part of all dhampirs, that we learn to coexist with.

Now it took control. My fangs elongated and my senses sharpened. My vision, my hearing, my sense of smell.

I growled low in my throat, but, conscious of the video cams, retracted my fangs. The vampire beast was cunning. It knew not to let itself be seen. No one could know it had taken charge, that "nice" Zaquiel Kral had been temporarily overcome.

The next time Reaper released me from the cuffs, I'd attack. The hell with this unspoken bargain we'd struck, where she fed me red meat and blood-wine right under Moreau's nose and in return, I played tame with her.

I rolled my head from side to side, shrugged my shoulders, flexed my fingers. Brought my right knee to my chest, then my left.

Moving hurt. Hell, *breathing* hurt.

But I forced my feverish, aching body to go through the entire series a half-dozen times.

I'd only have one chance to take Reaper down. I'd have to make it good.

Except when the door opened later that night, it wasn't Reaper, it was Ines and Blaise.

I prepared to fight. The beast didn't care if it lived or died.

It just wanted freedom.

"Time to go." Blaise released me from the wall while Ines stood by with zip-tie cuffs.

I brought my arms down. I didn't even bother to stifle my pained groan. Let them think I was a wuss. Easier to surprise them.

I hunched and dropped my head to my chest to cover my lengthening fangs.

"Hands behind your back," Blaise commanded. "Enforcer Moreau wants to see you."

Yeah, I bet he did. To fuck with me, most likely.

Without lifting my head, I slid a glance at my opponents. Both carried silver daggers, but the fools had left them sheathed on their hips.

I gathered my muscles to strike.

Reaper entered the cell and somehow saw what the two vampires hadn't. She leapt forward and grabbed me by the arm.

"No, Zaquiel! Moreau wants to make a deal with you."

I swung my head in her direction. "Let. Go." My voice sounded like something dragged from the bowels of Hades. Rough. Guttural. Demonic.

"No." She gave me a shake. "You can't win. Fight, and they'll shackle you to that wall again and never let you go."

Blaise dug his fingers into my shoulder. "Arms behind your back. *Now*."

"Do it." Reaper shoved her face into mine. The human part of me knew I must look like a scary mofo, but she didn't back off. "Trust me," she mouthed.

The beast hesitated, but decided to play along for now. It retreated, letting human Zaq retake control.

I drew a deep breath and growled, "No handcuffs."

Reaper glanced at my wrists and sucked in her lower lip. "Leave it," she told the two vampires. "He's not going to get away from the three of us. The man can barely keep on his feet."

Blaise shrugged. "Fine." He took out his dagger and poked me in the back. "Walk."

Ines unsheathed her dagger as well.

I stepped forward. That's when I realized how debilitated I actually was. I'd been chained up with only short breaks for over a week. I could hardly put one foot in front of the other. Reaper kept a hold of my upper arm, helping me stay upright without making a show of it.

I made it up the first flight of stairs, Reaper at my side, the two vampires breathing down my neck. When I reached the landing, I halted, lungs jerking like a human with emphysema.

"One more flight," Reaper said, low-voiced.

I closed my eyes. Then I opened them and shuffled across the landing.

That second flight was like climbing a goddamn mountain. Thirteen slow, painful steps.

By the end, I was counting them under my breath. *Eleven. Twelve. Thirteen.*

I reached the top and kept going, afraid that if I stopped, I'd pass out right there in the hall.

"This way." Reaper indicated the first door on the right. "Enforcer Moreau is in his salon."

I gave a tight nod, saving my breath to move those last few yards. Blaise strode past me and rapped on the door.

I glanced in the other direction and froze. The door at the top of the stairs, the one to the mansion's first floor, was open.

My breath hitched. My pulse sped up. Maybe I didn't have to fight—or bargain with Moreau. Not if I could escape in the shadows.

I shuffled forward. As I walked, I called on my vampire magic and started the fade.

And—nothing happened. I had no juice.

My chest clenched. Gods, I hated feeling so helpless.

Stay calm. Stay calm. Or you're dead.

The door in front of us opened. The tall, lantern-jawed man, the one I figured was Moreau's butler, inclined his head to me like I was a goddamned guest.

"M'sieur Kral. The enforcer is expecting you."

The large room we entered was old-world French: blood-red Persian rug, antique furniture, gilt-framed oil paintings. It was beautiful, but I barely noticed, instead zeroing in on the slim vampire in a tailored suit lounging on a couch like a sleek rat. A rat with dark hair touched silver at the temples.

Blood roared in my ears. It was the man who'd attacked me the night after Étan.

My vision tunneled. I forgot everyone else in the room—Reaper, the vampires who'd escorted me, the long-faced butler.

All I saw was the S.O.B. who'd drunk from a man without permission. A man pinned like an insect to a concrete wall. A man who couldn't fight back.

My vampire half surged up again. My fangs elongated, the tips itching to tear into his throat, and my fingers curved into claws.

Kill. Feed.

"Enforcer Moreau." Reaper's voice came from the other end of the tunnel. "Where would you like the prisoner?" She stepped in front of me, smoothly blocking me from charging Moreau.

She was warm, and she smelled good. Those two things penetrated my blood lust.

I took a shaky breath. *There's four of them and one of you. Attack him, and they'll take you down.*

And I'd find myself back in that thrice-damned cell.

First, I'd hear what the sonuvabitch had to say. Then I'd get that switchblade from Reaper and shove it into his goddamn heart.

"Zaquiel." Moreau nodded at a gilded wood chair near the couch. "Sit, if you please."

The adrenaline surge carried me the last few yards across the Persian rug. I lowered myself into the chair.

Reaper took a stance behind me. I spared a puzzled thought for her actions. She'd kept me from attacking first Ines and Blaise, and then Moreau. And now she hovered over me like a mama hen—or maybe a mother wolf.

She was protecting me. So she *did* feel this thing between us.

"A glass of blood-wine?" Moreau's question brought my attention back to him.

I stared at him without speaking. Wanting to tell him to stick his blood-wine where the sun don't shine.

But my starving, poisoned body craved blood.

I jerked my chin in assent.

Moreau waved a slender white hand at Aubin. "A glass of wine for M'sieur Kral."

While the butler went to a carved wood buffet, Moreau told Blaise and Ines to wait in the hall. They obeyed, closing the door behind them.

Aubin brought me the blood-wine, then left as well, leaving me alone with Reaper and Moreau.

I took a small sip of wine. It slid over my tongue like liquid silk, but it had been days since I'd last eaten. My shrunken stomach rebelled and tried to heave it back up.

I set my jaw, aware of Moreau watching me, and waited for my stomach to settle before taking another sip. This time it went down easier, my thirsty cells soaking up the blood in the wine like rain on parched earth. Energy spread through my body, warming me from the center out.

I wanted to finish the glass, but I placed it on the small table at my elbow. I knew from my work with malnourished people that you had to reintroduce food slowly.

Moreau was still staring at me. His dark eyes glowed blue at the edges.

I lifted my lip in a silent snarl.

His gaze went to the marks he'd left on my throat, and his mouth edged up.

Bastard.

I dug my fingers into the chair's wooden armrests. It was that or ram my fist down his throat. I waited until he looked at my face again, then stretched my own lips in what was supposed to be a smile but probably looked more like a dog baring its teeth. Which come to think of it, was how I felt.

"Calm down," Reaper murmured from behind me. "Listen to him."

I grunted. "Talk, then," I said to Moreau.

The enforcer picked up a gold cigarette case from the coffee table in front of him and removed a hand-rolled cigarette. He tapped the end on the case's lid and lit the cigarette. "You think Prima Tremblay was behind your kidnapping, don't you?"

"You're her sire, aren't you? You tell me."

Things were falling into place, including why a member of the Paris Syndicate had kidnapped me. Paris might not be at war with my father's syndicate, but vampires had a special relationship with those they'd turned.

Moreau dragged on the cigarette. He pursed his lips and released the smoke in a perfect ring.

"Then you know the prima and I are close, that I take a special interest in her. In fact, I encouraged her to sign the treaty with your father. It was best for both Victorine and her daughter to end the feud."

I nodded. I already knew most of this. But hey, if it got me out of that damned cell, I'd listen to Moreau drone on about the Tremblays all night.

I picked up my blood-wine again and drained the rest of the glass before motioning for Aubin to refill my glass. He waited for his boss's nod, then did so.

Moreau rested his cigarette on an ashtray. "Let me speak frankly."

"Please." My ironic tone made the skin around his eyes tightened.

Behind me, Reaper shifted slightly. I could almost hear her telling me not to poke the bear.

Fuck that. I could care less if I pissed him off. Hell, I *wanted* him to attack me. Better to die a quick, clean death than go slowly mad from dehydration and silver poisoning.

Moreau said, "You're here because you've been targeted by Slayers, Inc. A slayer has also been sent after each of your brothers."

My heart pounded in my ears. The salon's red-and-gold walls pressed in on me.

Gabriel and Rafe were in danger? It wasn't just me, it was my brothers too?

Moreau was still talking. "But you can stop it."

I drew a jagged breath and focused on him. "How?"

"By staking your father."

I recoiled, blinked. "Stake my father?" I repeated slowly, like it would make more sense the second time I heard it. "SI is after me and my brothers, but if I stake my father, I can stop it."

"Yes. His life for yours. We've decided to give you a chance to save your brothers. We'll send you to New York. Stake your father, and Slayers, Inc. will call off the contract on you and your brothers."

Okay, he was serious. I swiped a hand over my face. "So why are you involved?"

A small smile. "I have my reasons."

"Victorine put you up to this, didn't she?" I curled my lip. "She doesn't want to be caught breaking the treaty, so she's trying to get one of us to stake him instead. Well, tell her to go fuck herself."

Reaper hissed. "Listen to him, will you?"

"No. This is bullshit and you know it."

"It's the truth," she said. "Believe it."

Moreau shook his head like I was a naïve idiot. "My people tell me that you refuse to believe Karoly's abandoned you. You're so loyal to him. I wonder why. He hasn't come to your rescue, has he? And he knew you were being held in silver cuffs—I texted him the photo myself—but here you are, still in my lair. Maybe he's decided you're not worth the trouble. A dhampir."

A muscle jumped in my jaw. I shook my head and tried not to see Blaise's taunting face.

"He wants you dead. You. Your brothers."

Moreau continued, relentless. "Karoly has done nothing to get you out. He hasn't even approached Leo de Froulay for assistance, and I made sure he discovered that you were in one of my cells. So why are you still here, hmm?"

Deep inside, the beast lifted its head again. I glowered at Moreau. "You're lying. You're trying to turn me against him, and it won't work."

"It's true," Reaper confirmed. "Karoly hasn't attempted to rescue you. He was in Paris, but he left a few days ago."

No. I shook my head. There had to be another explanation. A reason.

I flexed my fingers on the armrests. I had the urge to clap my hands over my ears like a toddler and shut out his words. But that wouldn't shut out the voice in my head.

"He left you here to rot."

"If you won't believe the truth about your father," Moreau asked, "what about your brothers? Are you willing to gamble on their safety? SI has already embedded a slayer in your brother Gabriel's staff, and a second slayer has been assigned to Rafael."

I glanced over my shoulder at Reaper. She dipped her chin. "It's true." Her tone was flat, a little apologetic.

She meant it.

"Maybe your father allowed that to happen, too," said Moreau. "Perhaps he's decided to rid himself of all three of you."

My head hurt. I couldn't seem to clear it. To figure this out.

I grabbed my blood-wine and took another gulp. Fortunately, it stayed down.

"So let me get this straight. I stake my father, and in return, SI will call off the contract on me and my brothers."

"Correct."

"What proof do I have that Slayers, Inc. has anything to do with this? And even if you give me proof, since when do you speak for them?"

Reaper stepped forward. "If I may?"

The enforcer inclined his head.

She turned toward me. "I can assure you, SI is in agreement with this. It's more efficient."

"Efficient?"

"For you to approach Karoly directly. He'll let you get close to him. He trusts you."

"I see." I tried to wrap my mind around the fact that they wanted me to stake my own father. Because it was "efficient."

"And you know this how?" I asked Reaper.

"Because I'm the slayer assigned to you. Only Enforcer Moreau knows that, by the way."

My fingers constricted on the wine glass. It was what I suspected, but somehow I'd hoped I was wrong. Because a slayer working with the Tremblays and Moreau? That was fucked up.

"I can't give you any hard evidence that I'm a slayer," she added. "We carry no ID or identifying marks because they can be used against us. But if you require proof—"

She stepped forward, drew back an arm. The switchblade was somehow in her hand, its long silver blade extended. Moreau straightened from his languid slouch because the switchblade was aimed at him.

Reaper lunged at him, blade out. Moreau coolly raised his arms to defend himself, but she did a Matrix-like flip over his head and landed behind the couch facing us.

I stared at her. Shocked, and yet not.

Right from the start she'd seemed different from the other members of the lair, more professional and less invested in making me hurt.

I'd figured it was because she was a dhampir, and dhampirs stuck together. And because she liked me.

My mouth twisted. Gods, I'd had it wrong.

To Reaper, I was a job, and apparently it hadn't been in her interest to torture me.

I was a damn fool for thinking she'd help me escape. She was the slayer assigned to stake me. The enemy. She'd told me herself I was one of the monsters.

"Convinced?" She retracted the switchblade and came out from behind the couch.

I set the wine glass down before I broke it. "Yeah," I said, like she hadn't done the equivalent of smacking me over the head with a two-by-four.

I turned back to Moreau. "And you're bargaining with me because Slayers, Inc. wants it." My tone said, *Yeah, right.* I'd noticed he hadn't denied Victorine Tremblay was involved in this somehow.

"Are we bargaining? It seems to me I hold all the cards. But I agreed to it because Karoly hasn't acted as planned. Either he suspects something— or you're not as important to him as we believed. Maybe he even wants you dead."

I flinched; I couldn't help it. Just a little, but the bastard was watching me with avid eyes, like I was a fly and he was one of those boys who get their kicks ripping the wings off defenseless creatures.

"Karoly was in Paris," Moreau emphasized. Ripping off my other wing. "But he left without trying to rescue you. You're on your own, Zaquiel."

I dug my fingers into the armrests. "I see."

"*Bien.*" He reached for his cigarette again. "So, do we have an agreement?" He blew another smoke ring.

I waited until the smoke spread out and disappeared before replying. Saving face by pretending to think it over. We both knew I didn't have any choice but to accept. "Yes."

Moreau gave a small smile. "Reaper will go with you, of course. To make sure you reach New York without any...difficulties."

"That won't be necessary."

"Nevertheless, you may need help."

Like hell. Moreau wanted to send her to spy on me.

"No. If I show up with a slayer, my father won't let me get within a mile of him."

"This isn't a negotiation. You'll do as I say."

I opened my mouth to tell him *no fucking way.*

Reaper stirred. "This is non-negotiable, Zaquiel. Don't worry, no one will know I'm with SI." She bent over and murmured in my ear, "You need my help, you ass. In the shape you're in, how far do you think you'll get?"

She was right. I gave in, for now, anyway. "Fine. She can come with me."

"We'll leave ASAP." Reaper drew me to my feet and urged me to the door.

After that, things became a blur. Blaise and Ines escorted us back to my cell and left, closing the door behind them. The adrenaline that had carried me through the interview with Moreau evaporated. I leaned my back against the wall and slid to the floor like a marionette whose strings had been cut, my legs too weak to support my weight any longer.

Reaper stared down at me, her brows a ferocious inverted vee. "Wait here. I'll be right back."

I rested my head against the concrete. "Don't worry, *slayer*. I'm not goin' anywhere."

I don't know how long she was gone, because as soon as the door shut behind her, I curled up on the floor, dozing. When she reappeared, she'd changed into a gray T-shirt and green tactical pants and covered her short blond hair with the ugly brown wig from the airport. She had a backpack slung over one shoulder and an open bottle of blood-wine and two sandwiches.

I sat up and reached for the food, but she shook her head, setting it on the floor.

"Let's clean your wrists first." She showed me a bottle, telling me it was filled with a salt-water solution. "The salt will wash away the silver and neutralize it."

I nodded, because I knew that. I also knew it was probably too late—the silver was all through my body now.

She helped me to the sink and uncapped the bottle. "Ready?"

"Do it." I stuck my hands out.

The salt water hurt like a sonuvabitch, but I gritted my teeth and bore it. Fuck if I'd let her see how much pain I was in.

But she knew—and she rolled her lips in like it upset her.

She finished and waited until I sank back to the floor. "Here." She handed me the wine and one of the sandwiches. "But make it fast. I don't trust Moreau not to change his mind."

I unwrapped the sandwich. My mouth watered. She'd brought a big, juicy burger—rare. My stomach growled, and my damn hands started shaking. I was so weak and hungry. The blood-wine I'd drunk hadn't been nearly enough.

I wanted to shovel the whole burger into my mouth at once, but I hadn't forgotten how I'd almost thrown up the wine. So instead, I took a small bite. The flavor exploded in my mouth. The juices ran down my throat.

I swallowed a groan of pure animal pleasure and took another cautious bite.

On the third bite, my shriveled stomach protested. Nausea washed over me. I stopped eating and concentrated on breathing.

Reaper had crouched on her haunches across from me. She hummed with tension, jiggling her leg, glancing at the door.

But she didn't tell me again to hurry. Instead, she slanted me a compassionate look, like she knew what it was to be starving. "Try a little blood-wine."

I wanted to tell her where she could shove her compassion, but I didn't have the energy.

I brought the bottle to my mouth and sipped. My stomach clenched but I managed to keep it down. I shook my head and rewrapped the burger.

"That's enough for now."

"I'll put it in the backpack." She stood up and reached for the burger.

"That's okay." My fingers tightened the half-eaten sandwich. "I've got it."

Silver-gray eyes scrutinized me. I could tell she guessed why I wanted to keep the burger. It represented food—life—and even though I couldn't finish it, I needed to know it was there when I was ready to eat more.

"All right." She produced a cotton mesh shopping bag from her backpack and held it out. "Put it in here."

While I put the burger in the mesh bag, she recorked the wine bottle and stowed it in her backpack. "Here." She tossed me a black T-shirt. "I figured you could use this."

"Thanks." I caught it to my chest and met her eyes, as grateful for the clean shirt as for the food.

Then I looked away, angry at myself. Because she was a slayer, and I was her fucking target.

If she cleaned my wounds and fed me, it was to keep me alive long enough to get to my father. And if she brought me clean clothes, it was so I wouldn't draw attention when we left Moreau's lair.

I stripped off my torn, bloody T-shirt and pulled on the black one.

"Ready?" She shrugged into her backpack and offered me her hand.

I ignored the hand and heaved myself to my feet without help, even though it cost me. A man has his pride.

"Ready."

❧ 15 ❧

RIDLEY

We caught a taxi on Saint-Germain Boulevard and took it across the river, where I told the driver to stop next to an alley. I paid him in cash and pulled Zaq into the alley.

I risked a quick look down the street. Ines had been following on foot. My suspicions had been right; Moreau was up to something. He knew this was my op. That he'd sent someone after us told me he didn't trust me.

Ines sauntered in our direction.

I set my mouth to Zaq's ear. "Go into the shadows." I pushed him further into the alley.

"I can't." He slumped against the wall, face pale and drawn under the scruffy beard.

"Yes, you can, damn it. Now is *not* the time to turn into a fragile flower. Fade. *Now.*"

His eyelids lifted. The look he gave me was pure toothy-jaguar nasty, but he managed to complete the fade. Then his outline wavered as he started to return to the physical world. I had to reverse my fade, wrap my arms around him and pull him the rest of the way into the shadows.

Ines peered into the alley a second later. She took a few steps in and stopped inches away from me. She sniffed, testing for our scents.

I held my breath. She was close enough to hear the air that fought to push itself out of my lungs.

She spoke into her earpiece. French, of course, but simple enough that I understood. "*Oui*, I'm here." A pause. "Don't worry yourself, I'll stay with them." She headed down the street in the direction the taxi had gone.

My breath came out in a whoosh. I waited until I was sure we'd lost her, then dropped out of the shadows along with Zaq and released him. He bent over, hands on his thighs, dragging in oxygen.

I waited until he lifted his head again, then grabbed his hand and pulled him down the alley and around a corner to the Metro. It wouldn't take Ines long to figure out we'd changed taxis, but I was betting she'd assume we switched to another taxi. Syndicate vampires rarely took public transportation.

I didn't relax until the Metro pulled out of the station, heading for northeast Paris.

It had taken me two days to come up with the plan to extricate Zaq from Philippe's lair, and another two to implement it.

But in those four days, Zaq's condition had deteriorated still further. Now he could barely make it down the Metro steps, let alone to the United States.

I'd decided to hide him for a few days in the bolt-hole I kept in Père Lachaise Cemetery. The 100-acre graveyard was one of Paris's most popular parks, with tombs and headstones crammed together beneath the leafy trees, and a steady stream of tourists who came to view the graves of the celebrities buried there.

But at night, Père Lachaise belonged to the vampires, the outcasts who didn't belong to a syndicate or even a coven. A hangout for outcast vampires was the last place you'd expect to find a slayer, which was why I'd chosen it for my bolt-hole. A bolt-hole no one, even Crow, knew existed.

Zaq fell asleep as the subway left the station, his head against my shoulder. He didn't open his eyes even when the train lurched into the next station and he slipped off the seat.

I managed to grab him before he hit the floor. This time, I guided his head onto my lap. He remained there for the thirty-minute ride to northeast Paris, my hand on his shoulder.

From time to time, I stroked my hand down the back of his skull. His hair had streaks of every shade from brown to gold: walnut, pecan, wheat, corn. It felt like rough silk under my fingers.

It's all right, I wanted to tell him. *You're safe now.*

But that would be a lie. All I'd bought him was a reprieve.

We arrived at Gambetta station. I shook Zaq's shoulder. "Wake up."

When he didn't move, I pulled him upright myself. Yeah, he was exhausted and half-starved, but if I coddled him we'd never get to Lachaise, and I was growing increasingly anxious to get off the streets before a Paris vampire saw us.

I didn't trust Moreau. He'd agreed to Zaq's release a little too easily. I'd thought he was involved in Op A only as a favor to Victorine, but I was starting to wonder if he was playing some deep game of his own.

Hell, maybe he'd let Zaq go so he could take him out and blame it on someone else, even de Froulay.

Zaq stumbled to his feet and looked around, wild-eyed, until his gaze settled on me.

"We're here. Get going." I steered him off the subway car.

"Where are we going?"

I put my arm around his waist and urged him up the stairs. "Somewhere safe where you can rest up until you feel better."

At the top of the stairs, he shook off my arm and looked around, eyes narrowed. "This isn't the way to the airport. Where are you taking me?"

"You're in no shape to do anything right now. You have to take a few days to heal. Then we'll go to New York."

"Fuck healing. What about my brothers?"

"They're okay for now. I'll let my alpha know you need a couple of days."

Sweat had broken out on his forehead. He placed a hand on the wall, head bent and visibly queasy.

"All right." He drew a breath. "But only because I feel like shit warmed over. And not a few days. One day. I want to leave for New York tomorrow."

"If you're up to it, sure." I moved to put my arm around his waist again, but he held up a hand, stopping me.

"I've got it."

I shrugged and backed off.

He made it the two blocks to Lachaise on his own, but when we reached the edge, he halted and slumped against the cemetery's tall stone wall.

"Need...a minute." His eyelids drooped.

I squeezed my nape. If the cemetery's vampires saw him like this, they'd be on him like a school of piranha, latching onto him and draining his blood.

"Pull yourself together." I made my tone get-your-ass-in-gear gruff. "Or your brothers will die."

Zaq's eyelids flickered. "Fuck you," he said and pushed himself upright again.

I'd been coming to Lachaise Cemetery for so long that the vampires ignored me. They knew I wasn't human, and I'd never shown myself as

Reaper. Instead, I was a down-on-her-luck dhampir with short dark hair and the nasty attitude of a pit bull with a toothache.

What they didn't know was that I had a secret way into the cemetery. I didn't use it often, because if the other inhabitants of the cemetery never saw me coming and going, they might get suspicious.

Now I looked at Zaq's sagging body and made an executive decision. "We'll go through the wall."

"The wall?" He eyed the stones. The top was well above our heads. "What's wrong with the gate?"

"Too many eyes." I grabbed his hand and tugged him around the corner and down the sidewalk until I reached a break in the wall that I'd repaired myself without cementing the stones.

A quick glance around assured me we were alone. Fortunately, the vampires congregated near the entrances, waiting for human prey.

I crouched and shoved at a stone about two feet up from the ground, a smallish stone that held the others in place. It fell through to the other side. I pushed and pulled more stones out of the way until I had a space large enough to crawl through, then jerked my chin at Zaq.

"You first."

He cursed and lowered himself to his hands and knees. He was bigger than me and his shoulders got stuck for a few seconds, but he raised his arms above his head and wriggled through like a snake, swearing the whole time. I dropped down and crawled after him.

Zaq curled up on the ground. He was silent now, no longer cursing.

I put the stones back and helped him to his feet. For once I was grateful I was a dhampir, with a dhampir's strength. The man might've lost weight, but what was left was all hard muscles and solid bones.

I draped his arm over my shoulders. "It's just up this hill."

He grunted but shuffled forward with me taking as much of his weight as I could. The walkways started out wide but got narrower with each turn. The asphalt changed first to cobblestones, then to a dirt path barely wide enough to avoid the weathered granite tombs, obelisks and gravestones on either side.

For the last twenty-five yards, we left the path altogether. My bolt-hole was in a section of aboveground tombs that curved side by side up a hill like shrunken six-foot-high rowhomes, their worked-metal doors corroding from the elements.

By then the sky had lightened. The vampires would be seeking their day sleep, but I kept a wary eye out anyway as I half-dragged, half-pulled Zaq up the steep hill to my tomb. Actually, it was the Guilbert family's tomb, but they'd either died out or moved away. No one had visited in the two years since I'd hollowed out a small underground room beneath it.

Zaq was moving like a sleepwalker, eyes half-closed, and I was cursing myself for choosing this out-of-the-way hideout. But it was far from the cemetery's walking paths and unclaimed by any of the local vampires.

Two overgrown cypresses shaded the tomb from the rising sun. The metal door opened soundlessly because I oiled the hinges whenever I was in Paris. I pulled Zaq inside and shut the door behind us.

We were in a four-by-eight-foot space. Zaq's head almost touched the ceiling. At the far side was a bench covered by a stone slab. I propped him against the wall and heaved the slab aside.

"Almost there." I urged him toward the opening I'd uncovered.

He swayed and tripped over his feet. I swung around and caught him before he fell. We ended up facing each other, my hands gripping his torso.

"Hey." I shook him. "Stay with me."

He scrunched his face like a sleepy kid, then focused on me.

"Reaper." His tone was bedroom-husky. The gold flecks in his eyes seemed to glow.

His hands were on my shoulders to help him keep his balance.

I *knew* that was the only reason he touched me, but we were so close, gazing into each other's eyes like we were about to kiss.

His new T-shirt was damp with sweat. He should've smelled bad after all those days in the cell, but he didn't. He smelled good. Not as good as that morning at the airport—and his scent had a metallic undertone from the silver poison—but still good. Dark and spicy, like the cypress.

My spine melted, along with other parts of me lower down. I stiffened my vertebrae and ordered those other, lower parts to settle down. This was *not* an embrace, even if I was breathing in the man like a drug I couldn't get enough of.

"You—" My voice had developed a bullfrog croak. I cleared my throat and tried again. "You have to go down a ladder." I nodded at the opening. "There's a sleeping bag down there, and food and blood-wine."

He straightened up, visibly pulling himself together. "Ready."

"Okay. Me first." I helped him to the bench. When he was seated on the edge, I swung myself into the hole and braced my feet on the ladder's second rung.

Zaq followed. He had trouble getting his leg over the bench's short concrete wall, but he managed it. I guided his foot to the ladder's top rung.

"That's it. Now the other leg."

He swung his second leg over and slipped down two rungs, ending between me and the ladder. I pressed my body against his to keep him steady.

Out of nowhere, a chuckle bubbled up. A chuckle that was a shade hysterical, but it relieved my tension. "That's one way to do it."

Zaq gave a rusty laugh.

My face was up against his back. Unable to resist, I drew a lungful of Zaq-spice.

"Keep going. Four more rungs and you're there."

"Aweshome," he said in a sleepy slur.

Somehow we made it down the last few rungs without falling, me supporting most of Zaq's weight. His feet touched the dirt floor.

He turned and smiled into my eyes. "Did it."

Then his knees gave out and he crumpled to the floor in slow motion. I caught him and eased him the rest of the way, making sure he didn't hit his head on the hard dirt. He sighed, turned onto his side and went limp.

I shrugged out of my backpack and left him there to shimmy up the ladder. I moved the lid back over the opening, then dropped to the floor beside him. The underground room had fresh air from a PVC pipe I'd inserted in the ceiling, but almost no light; the cypress trees blocked the rising sun. My dhampir vision meant I could see, but everything was shadowed.

The only "furniture" was the sleeping bag and a narrow table against the wall that held dried food and two bottles of blood-wine. Above the table was a battery-powered camping lantern on a shelf I'd chiseled out of rock. I flicked on the lantern and put the bread and cheese I'd brought on the table along with Zaq's sandwich and the open bottle of wine.

I stowed the backpack under the table. It held a change of clothes, underwear, and extra switchblades. In a hidden inner pocket were two tranquilizer-filled syringes in case things with Zaq went south.

Pulling off the dark wig, I tossed it on top of the backpack and turned back to Zaq.

Jesus, Ridley. I stared down at his curled-up body. *Have you lost your mind?*

I'd gone so far off-script, I'd landed in a whole different play with a setting and characters I didn't recognize. Starting with myself.

Especially myself.

I'd pushed for Zaq's release from the cell. Karoly Kral hadn't tried to rescue him, and it looked like he didn't intend to. According to Moreau, the primus had slipped into Paris under cover of a glamour. If he had, he'd evaded the traps set for him. Either way, he'd dropped off the radar. Even our informants in the Kral Syndicate didn't know his current location.

So I'd suggested we enlist Zaq's help.

"Karoly will let him get close," I'd told Moreau. "If we explain to Zaq how Karoly has left him to twist in the wind—and possibly his two brothers as well—he'll stake Karoly for us."

Moreau and Co. had already primed the pump. Zaq had gone from waiting for his father to rescue him to doubting Karoly. It wouldn't take much to nudge him further along the spectrum to resentment and anger, and from there it was a short hop to kill-or-be-killed. Especially if Zaq believed it was the only way to save his brothers.

Initially, Moreau had appeared skeptical, but he'd liked the irony of sending the man's own son to slay him. He'd taken my idea to Prima Victorine, and when she'd approved the change in tactics, I contacted Crow and presented the new plan as their idea, not mine.

She'd immediately seen the possibilities. "I'll have to get the Board's approval, but I think they'll agree. You'll go with him, keep him on task. And if he fails, you know what to do. Eliminate them both if possible, but the father is more important."

"Acknowledged."

At my feet, Zaq hadn't moved. I unrolled the sleeping bag and unzipped it to make it wide enough for two, then rolled him onto it. He turned onto his back, one arm bent up by his head, the other by his side.

I knelt next to him. Beneath the dark facial hair, he looked...harmless. Relaxed, his expression open.

Something moved in my chest. I wanted to protect him, keep him safe.

"If he fails, you know what to do."

I swallowed hard.

You won't have to, I told myself. *This will work.*

It *had* to work.

I smoothed a wavy lock of hair away from Zaq's brow. Then it struck me what I was doing. I was hunched over the man, stroking his hair and figuring out ways to keep him alive.

I sat back on my heels.

I was falling under a Dark Angel's spell. Me, Ridley Crawford.

Just like all those other women.

The man's a Kral. He's anything but harmless. He's been raised since birth to take what he wants, when he wants. Yeah, he does some good deeds, but he's a fucking syndicate prince. If he sees you're weakening toward him, you can bet he'll use it against you.

But I couldn't shake off the protective feeling. So I surrendered to it.

For now, I'd take care of Zaq.

He'd scraped his wrists when he'd fallen down the ladder. The festering wounds wept blood. Not much, but the scent teased at me.

I picked up one of his hands and examined the wrist. Like vampires, a dhampir usually heals without scarring, but the silver cuffs had burned such a deep line, he'd probably always have scars.

If I licked the marks, though, they'd heal faster. Something in our saliva does that.

And I'd get to taste Zaq's blood.

My fangs elongated. Eager—no, aching—to bite. I stared at the bloody scrapes on his wrist and beat back my vampire self.

Not to feed. To heal.

In fact, it would be best to spit out his blood so I didn't risk taking the silver into my own body.

Okay, then. I cradled his wrist in my hand and licked it. Even with the bitter taint of the silver, the taste nearly overwhelmed my good intentions.

My vampire-half was starved for fresh blood, and like Zaq's scent, his blood was so rich, so *right*.

I clenched my teeth together and pictured myself with fangs and blue-rimmed eyes, a trick I used to keep the vampire under control.

I finished one wrist and spit the blood on the dirt, then licked the other wrist. Zaq murmured as I set his arm down, and I froze, heart beating like I'd been caught stealing, and almost swallowed the blood in my mouth.

He curled onto his side again, and I leaned over and spit it out. I scratched at the dirt to cover the blood, then got the open bottle of blood-wine and took a long drink, rinsing his taste away.

I tried to give Zaq a little blood-wine too, but couldn't wake him up. I crouched on my haunches and finished off the wine, then made a lunch of bread, cheese and a strip of beef jerky. Dessert was a handful of dried apricots.

I glanced at the unconscious Zaq and decided I might as well get some sleep.

First, I texted Crow, updating her on the situation—that Zaq was too sick to travel and we'd be in Paris for another few days before leaving for New York.

I'd have to text de Froulay at some point too, and tell him what I knew about Philippe Moreau. But that could wait.

I switched off the lantern and curled up on the sleeping bag next to Zaq.

⚜

The sun was high in the sky when Zaq bumped against me, bringing me awake with a jolt. He croaked out a string of unintelligible words, head thrashing from side to side.

I sat up and peered at him. The dim light from the air shaft fell on his face, pale except for the twin red spots on his cheekbones. He mumbled something else, then stilled.

I laid the back of my hand against his cheek. He was burning up with fever.

I muttered a curse and jumped up for a bottle of blood-wine. I opened it and kneeled on the sleeping bag. "Drink." I slid my hand under the back of his head and touched the open bottle to his mouth.

His head lolled to the side.

"Hey." I gave him a light shake. "Stay with me."

He didn't move.

Panic sleeted through me. "Drink, damn you."

I tipped his head back until his mouth opened and dribbled some wine into it. To my relief, he swallowed.

"That's it." I tipped a little more into his mouth.

He swallowed that, too. His eyes opened. "More."

I put my arm under his shoulder and lifted him partway up. He drank another few mouthfuls, then turned his head away. "Enough."

"You sure?"

"Just...need sleep."

I nodded and laid him back on the sleeping bag and examined his wrists. They looked better, although not much. At least the scrapes had scabbed over.

"I have to go out," I told him. "There's no toilet in here."

He didn't answer.

I put the wig on and left. Outside, tourists were strolling the cemetery, visiting the graves of famous people like Jim Morrison, Oscar Wilde and Edith Piaf. I made my way out of my private corner of Lachaise, then hurried down the wide, paved stone walkway until I reached the bottom and the building with the bathrooms. I used the john and washed my face,

86

then jogged to a bakery to pick up a baguette and chocolate croissants. I bought cheese at the fromagerie next door, then hurried back to Zaq.

He was still sleeping. I touched his cheek. He was still hot.

I swallowed a sliver of panic. Shouldn't he be healing by now? I'd never dealt with someone with this degree of silver poisoning.

He's a dhampir. He'll heal. He just needs rest and blood-wine.

I hunkered down against the wall and ate a couple of chocolate croissants. This time, I was able to wake up Zaq and get him to drink a few mouthfuls of blood-wine.

I passed the next few hours doing tricks with my switchblade—spinning it by the point on my finger, twirling it through my fingers. At lunchtime, I had some bread and cheese and another strip of beef jerky.

Zaq groaned and muttered in his sleep. I got a little more blood-wine into him and considered my next step.

It was time to change things up on Moreau. He'd expect us to fly out of Paris, but I didn't trust him not to be watching for us. I hadn't forgotten that he'd sent Ines after us.

So we'd take a train south to Provence and fly out of Nice. The small airport there had a direct flight to Newark. From there it was a short taxi ride to Manhattan.

Another hour inched by. Zaq woke up enough to say he had to piss. I helped him pee into a bottle, then urged him to drink some more wine. Heat radiated off him. He peered at me like he didn't know who I was.

He lay back down and went so still, I touched my fingers to his neck to make sure he was still with me. His pulse was fast and thready.

The sliver of panic expanded, filling my throat and landing with a sick thud in my belly.

He can't die. He's a dhampir. We don't die from dehydration.

But we *could* die from silver poisoning, especially festering wounds like those on his wrists.

Especially if the dhampir was already weak from blood loss and dehydration.

It was a slow, agonizing way to die.

The blood-wine wasn't enough. He needed fresh blood.

I looked at the switchblade, then at my wrist.

No. Hell, no.

I jumped up and paced across the tiny dirt floor.

I'd done what I could. Whether Zaq lived or died was on him.

I was a slayer, for chrissake. And he was my target.

I wasn't supposed to keep him *alive*.

I'd already stuck my neck out to win him this reprieve. I would *not* allow him to drink my blood.

He groaned. I swung around and stared at him.

His eyes popped open. He stared up at me, his pupils dilated. "Mom?"

That's all he said. A single, fearful word.

One goddamn word, but my chest felt like it had caved in.

I swore and slashed open my wrist.

❧ 16 ❧
ZAQ

I burned. Everywhere.

My arteries were on fire. It felt like I was being consumed from the inside, cell by smoldering cell.

And I ached like a mofo: my head, my stomach, my joints. Even my fingers and toes hurt. Merely moving my head made me want to throw up.

So I didn't move.

I lay where I was, even when my muscles cramped. I was so damn hot, my mouth dry as a crypt, but drinking—swallowing—would take energy I didn't have.

I was dying, and I didn't care. It seemed...interesting, that's all. At least on the other side, I wouldn't hurt anymore.

Something moved.

No, someone. A woman.

I peered up at her, but something had happened to my eyes. I opened them wide, but everything was ghostly gray shadows.

"Mom?"

She didn't answer me. Agitation squeezed my lungs. Why didn't she answer me?

Sadness and yearning twisted in my chest. If I hadn't been lying down, I'd have doubled over. It had been weeks since I'd seen my mom. If I could just hug her one more time, tell her how much she meant to me.

"Love you," I said. But I was pretty sure my lips didn't move.

Still, I'd realized something; I *did* care if I lived or died. There was something I had to do first. I couldn't die, not yet. Gabriel and Rafe were in danger. If I died, they'd be next—and my mom's heart would be broken.

I had to stay alive. Had to fight this poison. Had to get well.

I started clawing my way back toward consciousness, but I never made it. Blackness dropped like a boulder onto my brain, slamming me into an endless cavern of midnight.

I was out for a minute. Or maybe a day.

Time had no meaning in the midnight cavern.

The taste of blood dragged me back to consciousness. The salty, life-giving liquid touched my tongue. I instinctively swallowed.

It hurt, to swallow. But the vampire beast said, *More.*

The craving rose up in me. This is what I wanted, no, *needed.*

Fresh blood.

I sucked hard. This time, swallowing didn't hurt so much, and my shrunken stomach didn't reject the blood like it had the burger and wine. It soaked it up.

The terrible burning eased. Not much, but enough that light entered the darkness.

When I'd drunk my fill, I pried open my eyelids. Reaper's face swam into view, mouth pressed into a grim line.

I was so relieved I could see again, I didn't wonder who'd fed me, although I knew it couldn't be her.

I moistened dry lips. "What happened?" The two words were weak. They rustled in my ears like dead leaves.

I'd promised to do something. Something important. Something having to do with Rafe and Gabriel—but what?

"Never mind." She smoothed her hand over my eyes, closing them. "Sleep."

I obeyed.

Another day passed, maybe two. Twice more, I woke to drink from the vein pressed to my mouth, then fell back asleep. My fever spiked and receded, then spiked again. I shivered so hard my teeth chattered.

Then finally, the fever broke. I woke up to find I'd sweated through my T-shirt, and mercifully, my head was clear.

My eyes were gummy with sleep. I blinked and wiped them.

Reaper knelt to my left, staring down at me like an avenging warrior, eyes gleaming, platinum hair bright in the perpetual dusk of our underground hiding place. No, not a warrior. And definitely not a fairy-like creature.

She was a warrior goddess, a woman who'd stride into battle, sword blazing. A slayer. How had I not seen that before?

Silver glinted. Her switchblade was out, the sharp edge bloody.

I almost felt my chest for a hole.

But the blood wasn't mine, it was hers. My gaze went to the line she'd cut on her wrist. She hadn't staked me, she'd fed me. With her own blood.

I stared at her, open-mouthed. "You saved my life," I said in a scratchy voice.

Her lips pulled sideways. "Don't thank me. I didn't do it for you—I did it for me. I need you."

I nodded because it hurt to speak. Frankly, I didn't give a flying fuck why she'd fed me. She had, and that's what counted.

The blood craving dug sharp talons into my belly. Healing from silver poisoning takes tremendous energy.

I turned my gaze to her bloody wrist. "More." I grabbed her arm and brought it to my mouth without asking.

She went taut. Tension shrieked through her like an off-key violin string.

I sucked harder, afraid she'd shake me off. But she let me drink.

I took another few mouthfuls, then licked her wrist, sealing the punctures my fangs had made. Her skin tasted salty from the blood, and delicately feminine.

She shuddered, and I looked up at her.

Our eyes met and something arced between us. Something hot, sexual. Dark.

It shouldn't have been possible—not in my battered, dehydrated state —but my dick stirred.

Holding her gaze, I touched my tongue to one of the marks I'd made and licked a line across the tendons of her wrist to the other mark.

Her pupils darkened and expanded until the gray was a bright, thin band around a pool of blackness. Her throat worked, her swallow audible in the small space.

I inhaled, taking her fresh-grass scent into my lungs.

Her lips parted. In the dusky light, they were a soft rose.

I curved my hand around her nape and drew her down to me.

Slowly, so she could escape if she chose.

So she couldn't tell herself she didn't want this as much as I did.

When her mouth was an inch from mine, I paused.

Our gazes were still locked. Our breath mingled. Hers was short and choppy, aroused.

I brought her the last inch to me. So fucking hot for her, but knowing I wouldn't be able to take anything but this kiss.

I licked the seam of her lips. "Kiss me."

She made a low, needy sound and put her hands on either side of my head. Her mouth opened and she sucked my tongue inside.

I brought my other hand up and ran it down her side, taking in the shape of her body. The indented waist, the slope of her hip.

And then we were kissing. Deep, hungry kisses; a string of them that went on and on. She tasted like blood-wine and woman. I wanted her with everything I had.

We broke the kiss at the same time, but neither of us lifted our head. I kissed her cheek, nuzzled her behind the ear. Inwardly cursing that we couldn't finish this now.

But we would.

"Tell me your name," I said against her neck. "Not Reaper. Your real name."

She pulled back and blinked at me like Sleeping Beauty waking from a spell.

"Tell me." It was a demand now.

Her eyes widened. "Fuck." She jerked out of my grip and jumped up.

I rolled onto my side so I could see her. The room spun around me. My stomach churned. I tightened my jaw and focused on breathing.

When the dizzy spell had passed, I propped my head on a hand and studied her. She had an open bottle of blood-wine in her hand. Her chest jerked with agitated breaths.

Up until now, the woman had been mostly stone-faced in our interactions. Cold, professional. But kiss her and she got all kinds of upset.

Interesting.

I must've moved my lips because her mouth bent down. "What? What's so fucking interesting?"

I moved my free shoulder. "Nothing."

Pale eyes bored into me, but she let it drop. She took a long drink of wine and wiped her mouth with the back of her hand.

"I'm going out. I have to take care of a few things. I want you to rest. You're safe here."

"Where's here?" I didn't remember much after the Metro except walking through tombstones, which didn't make much sense. All I knew was that she'd brought me to some kind of underground bunker.

Now I took in the bunker's rough stone walls and packed dirt floor. The only light came from a small shaft in the ceiling, although a niche in the wall held an unlit camping lantern. Beneath the lantern was a narrow wood table with Reaper's wig and some basic supplies. The only other furniture—if you could call it that—was the sleeping bag.

"Père Lachaise Cemetery," Reaper said. "Under the tomb of the Guilbert family."

A corner of my mouth twitched. I shouldn't have had the energy to be amused, but I was. "Your lair is in a cemetery?"

"Yeah." Her glare dared me to say more.

So I did.

"Do you sleep with your arms folded over your chest, too? And where's the coffin?" I made a show of looking around.

Her mouth thinned. Then it lifted at the corners, and her eyes crinkled at the edges. "Okay, I guess it is kind of stereotypical."

Damn. The woman's grin was lethal.

I pushed up on both my forearms and stared at her. It was like all the light in the room had been drawn to her face, making it glow. But not a supernatural glow. A happy, sunshiny glow that was like a punch to the heart.

"But hey, it works," she added. "No one knows about my bolt-hole. And whoever the Guilbert family was, the last of the line died over sixty years ago. The graves are on the other side of the wall." She tapped the stones with her palm. "I did my best not to disturb them."

"Works."

"Yep." She held out the bottle. "Want some wine?"

"No, thanks. I'm good."

Propping myself on my forearms hadn't made me dizzy, so I decided to sit up. It wasn't easy, but I managed it. I took an experimental look around and was pleased when my head didn't spin. But I felt weak as a kitten. A newborn, eyes-barely-open kitten.

"Okay." Reaper put the bottle back on the table and smoothed down her T-shirt. It was gray with a picture of a brooding Johnny Cash and the words *Outlaw Country* beneath. "If you feel up to eating, help yourself to anything you want."

She shoved her phone and wallet into her pants pockets and tucked a mesh shopping bag into the right front pocket along with the switchblade-size bulge. She grabbed the backpack and headed for the ladder.

My hands shook. I gripped my thighs to hide the trembling. "Wait. When will you be back?"

I hated that my voice had a wobble in it, but right now Reaper was my lifeline. I felt better, yes, but I wasn't going anywhere for a while. Hell, I probably couldn't leave even if I wanted to. Not without her help.

"A couple of hours. Maybe more." She started up the ladder, lithe as a panther.

"Where are you going?" This time it came out as a demand. I was weak and sick and angry at myself for being vulnerable.

"For supplies." She set her hands on the stone slab above the ladder. It had to be heavy, even for a dhampir, but she lifted and slid it aside with impressive ease. She swung her legs out and turned to look down at me. "Go to sleep, Zaquiel. You need to heal. We've already lost too much time."

"Why? What day is it?"

"July 26. Friday afternoon." The slab dropped back in place and I was alone in the bolt-hole.

July *what*—? My mouth went slack. Panicky fingers scrabbled at my spine.

I'd been here three nights?

That's when things came back to me with a rush. Gabriel and Rafael were in danger from someone—Moreau and Victorine, Slayers, Inc., maybe even my father. Moreau had let me go, but only to stake my father.

I had to get to New York, had to save them.

I tried to stand but couldn't. My whole body shook, and my legs felt like wet noodles. I couldn't walk, so I crawled. When I reached the ladder, I dragged myself up the rungs, one by one.

I was halfway up when I lost my grip and slid down a rung. I shoved my arm through the space between two rungs and hung on, breathing hard. The room swooped around me, and my heartbeat boomed in my ears like I'd climbed a fucking cliff instead of the first four rungs of a ladder.

I gritted my teeth and started up again. First the rung I'd slipped on, then the next and the next. I think I knew it was hopeless—I'd never be able to lift the heavy slab—but I had to try.

I reached the top. I braced my feet on the ladder's rungs and used both my hands to push against the slab. It barely budged. I strained against the rough stone, heart pounding, sweat running down my face.

But I was too weak.

I lost it then, beating on the slab with my fists.

I no longer saw the slab, I saw the faces of the S.O.B.s who'd attacked and tortured me.

I was punching Étan's face. The faces of the guards who'd fastened me to a wall with no food or blood or sleep. And most of all, Philippe Moreau's sly rat-face.

The one face I didn't want to pound to a bloody pulp was Reaper's. Maybe that was because I had a bad case of Stockholm syndrome, but I didn't think so. It was because in her own stony-faced way, she was the only straight shooter in the group. Yeah, she might still stake me, but she wouldn't torture me first. She'd clearly been appalled at how Moreau and his lair had treated me.

The metallic scent of my own blood brought me to my senses. I stopped battering at the slab. I stared at my bloody knuckles, then slumped over the ladder's top rung, chest jerking.

"Don't get mad. Get even." That was my brother Gabriel talking.

"Fuck off," I told the empty room.

But just like that, I was eleven again at a gathering of local covens with my family. A couple of vampire spawn had pretended to be my friends, but as soon as they had me alone, they'd turned on me and laid into me with their fists. One of them broke my nose.

My big brother had appeared and dragged them off me. He'd pushed my broken nose back into place and stopped me from running to my father.

"He won't help. He'll just tell you to toughen up."

"Yeah. Bastard." I spat out the word, then shot a guilty look around in case an adult had heard.

"He only wants what's best for us." At thirteen, Gabriel had already been a leader; calm, controlled and fucking logical. Sometimes Rafe and I played tricks on him just to see if we could get him to break, but we both looked up to him. I'd have done anything to win Gabriel's approval.

I fisted my hands. "He thinks I'm too soft, and you know it."

"I also know he's wrong."

Nine-year-old Rafe ran up. "Ew, Zaq. What happened to your nose?"

Gabriel tugged at Rafe's curly brown hair. Rafe was the pretty one; it was his curse, whereas mine was a soft heart—at least, it was a curse according to my father and his lieutenant Tomas.

"None of your business," said Gabriel.

Rafe set his mouth and folded thin arms over his chest. "Mom's going to be pissed off at you for fighting."

I growled. "Let her be mad." I started after the spawn.

Gabriel grabbed my arm, pulling me to a halt.

My brain went dark. It was too much after the beating those bastards had given me. I bared my fangs at Gabriel. "Let. Me. Go."

His good-looking face was serious, his eyes cold beneath his peaked black brows. "Cool down, you ass."

"Fuck you." I tried to jerk my arm away, but he held on.

"You want revenge?"

My breath scraped in. I gave a short nod.

"Then don't get mad. Get even."

We stared at each other. I looked after the spawn, then back at my brother. His face wore that look, the one that meant he had a plan.

My chest heaved. But I bit. "How?"

"I'll help!" Rafe bounced on his heels like an eager puppy.

Gabriel considered him, then nodded. "All right. You can be the lookout."

And we'd gotten even—in a devious, very-Gabriel way. Those spawn had woken the next evening with mice crawling on them. Actually, more than crawling. The mice had been nibbling on them because we'd sprinkled sugar on the two boys while they were sleeping. Trust my brother to know mice have a sweet tooth.

The spawn's shrieking had woken everyone. They darted out of the room they were sharing, tearing off their clothes, slapping at their bodies, shaking mice out of their pants.

Gabriel, Rafe, and I had come out of our own rooms and laughed with the other kids.

Gabriel grinned at me out of the side of his mouth. "Guess they forgot dhampirs don't have to sleep all day."

Now I shook my head, blew out a breath and climbed down the ladder.

I crawled back to the sleeping bag and collapsed on top of it. I let myself lie there for fifteen minutes or so, then made myself get up again, knowing that I needed to eat if I wanted to get better. I vaguely recalled a burger, but Reaper must have finished it herself or tossed it. Probably a good thing, if three days had passed.

I stood up and shuffled to the table, because I was damned if I'd crawl again. I ripped off a small chunk of bread, cut myself a piece of cheese and made my way back to the sleeping bag. I took a cautious bite, washing it down with the wine that Reaper had left near the bag. When that stayed down, I tried another bite. That stayed down, too, and I kept going until I'd finished the small meal.

I lay down on the sleeping bag. Above me the cemetery was quiet except for the rustle of wind in the trees and a pigeon's mournful coo. Reaper had found an out-of-the-way corner, because I'd been to Lachaise once with my family. It might be a graveyard, but it was also a popular tourist attraction, with thousands of visitors each day.

I rubbed my forehead. The light from the hole in the ceiling had darkened. Thunder rumbled in the distance, and the air had that heavy feel it gets when a storm is on the way.

Friday afternoon.

And Moreau had released me on Tuesday.

I'd wasted too much time already, but Reaper had been right to bring me here. I'd been too sick to travel.

I stared down at my hands. They still shook.

I felt frail. Helpless. Ashamed at my loss of control. But it had served its purpose.

I was furious at Moreau and Étan and Slayers, Inc. and whoever else was behind this, and that was good. I could ride that anger, use its strength. But I couldn't let it control me. That would be suicide, and it wouldn't help my brothers, either.

So for now, I'd focus on getting well enough to travel. Do whatever it took to unravel this mess and save Gabriel and Rafe.

And then I'd get even. Because the people behind this were going down. Starting with Philippe Moreau.

Everyone except for Reaper. Her, I was going to keep.

❧ 17 ❧

RIDLEY

I was so fucked.

I left Zaq and started down the hill to the main entrance. Pretty soon I was walking fast, and then running like I was being chased by a dozen vampires. But there were no vampires, just my own horrified heart, and that came with me.

I was falling for Zaq Kral. A dhampir.

You have to stop this.

Right. Now.

He's a job, that's all.

I entered the women's room. Fortunately it was empty. I splashed cold water on my face. Too bad I couldn't take a cold shower, because right now I could've used one.

He'd looked so sexy when he first woke up, hair mussed, eyes heavy with sleep. And then he'd licked my wrist...

I stared at my wet face in the mirror. My eyes were wide, my lips red and swollen from his kisses.

You're not falling for him. You like him, that's all.

But that was fucked, too. He was my target. I couldn't *like* him.

To complete this op, I had to keep my emotions cold and my brain even colder.

After he'd licked my wrist, I'd wanted to pull his mouth to my throat and ask him to lick me there. My skin tingled like he'd actually done it.

I groaned and stuck my head under the running faucet. The cold water didn't bring clarity, but it did put a brake on my racing thoughts. When I came up for air, I removed my backpack, pulled off my T-shirt and washed more thoroughly. I'd left so quickly, I'd forgotten to put on the wig, so I did my hair in two pigtails.

By the time I left the bathroom, I was calmer.

What was I going to do? One thing was clear—Crow couldn't know. She'd order me to turn Zaq over to another slayer.

The thought made me a little nauseous. I massaged my breastbone with the heel of my hand.

Another slayer wouldn't see Zaq Kral as I did. The Zaq who seemed like a decent guy, a man who stood up to a vampire to save a woman he didn't know, and who genuinely cared about his brothers. The Zaq who wanted his mom when he was sick. Who smelled right even when he was feverish and hadn't showered for God knows how long.

And that right there was why I should remove myself from Op A.

But I also knew I wouldn't. I *couldn't*.

Okay then. I'd see this through.

And I'd make sure that what had happened back there in my bolt-hole didn't happen again.

My phone buzzed. I grabbed it, eager for a distraction.

It was Crow.

Meet me at 3 PM. She named a café near the Louvre.

My stomach did a forward roll and landed somewhere in the vicinity of my feet. I'd wanted a distraction, but not this. She was last person I wanted to see right now.

My thumbs hovered over the keyboard. I blew out a breath and texted back.

Will B there.

I hopped on the Metro and made it with five minutes to spare. Before exiting the subway, I ducked behind a partition and glamoured my appearance. When I re-emerged, I was an American teenager: curly black pigtails, light brown skin, dark eyes. I kept the tactical pants but added a silver unicorn to the center of my T-shirt.

The café was tiny, with a half-dozen tables shoehorned into the interior and another half-dozen outside under a striped awning. Despite the heat, four of the outside tables were occupied: a German family, a pair of French businessmen, three young American tourists, and a lone woman.

I took the bistro chair across from the lone woman. Today Crow was a Parisian aristocrat—short brown hair, a chic blue blazer, and a black-and-white striped Oxford shirt over dark-wash jeans. Cat-eye sunglasses hid her deep blue eyes.

She'd already ordered me a noisette, an espresso with a few drops of steamed milk. A small white cup waited on a saucer with two sugar cubes and a diminutive spoon.

I stowed my backpack under my chair. A waiter arrived to ask if I wanted anything with the noisette and I shook my head. I unwrapped a sugar cube, stirred it into my coffee.

Crow still hadn't spoken.

I set down the spoon. "What's up?"

She sipped her espresso. She took her coffee black. No milk or sugar.

"Isn't that what I should be asking you? Where have you been? You took the target and dropped off the radar."

"Some place safe. Like I told you, he's in no condition to travel."

"Mm." She eyed me through her sunglasses.

Sweat pricked my palms. I took a sip of coffee, pretending a calm I didn't feel. What if she demanded to know where I'd taken Zaq?

I'd have to lie, and I was already lying too much to her—lies of omission, yes, but still lies—about my relationship with Leo de Froulay, about how I felt about Zaq and how I'd engineered his release.

But I needed that bolt-hole, needed a safe place that no one else knew about. Mom had taught me that. After I turned ten, she wouldn't even allow me to tell her where my hideout was. The night they came for her, it had saved me. I'd managed to escape through a window.

I had a dhampir's keen hearing. Even fifty yards away, crouched in a child-sized bunker with only a narrow pipe for air, I heard them smacking her around, demanding to know where I was. She'd been able to answer truthfully that she didn't know.

"All right." To my relief, Crow didn't push to know where I'd been hiding Zaq. "So now what?"

"We go to New York tomorrow night. Or Sunday at the latest. They worked him over pretty good, and the silver poisoning slowed his healing."

"He's better?"

"Yeah." I toyed with the tiny spoon. "They drank from him while he was shackled to the cell wall. Moreau and Étan. Did you know?"

Her response was immediate, and firm. "No, I didn't know. But does it matter? He's a Kral, isn't he?"

My stomach knotted. SI was a paramilitary organization. A soldier-slayer like me followed orders and didn't question my superiors. But I came close to it right then.

Yes. Yes, it does matter. They fucking tortured the man.

And I would've said it straight to her face, except it was too revealing. I couldn't risk her yanking me off Operation Angel.

So I said, "No. It doesn't matter." The words tasted bitter, like I betrayed Zaq by speaking them.

"Mm-hum." Crow stowed the information away in her computer-like brain. Of course she wanted to know; she might be able to use the information to blackmail Philippe Moreau in the future. "You'll take a flight from Paris?"

I shook my head. "Another airport. The Paris Syndicate watches Charles de Gaulle. His father might be watching it too."

"Makes sense. You say the target has agreed to help you?"

"Yes. We told him it was the only way to save his brothers."

"And that worked?"

"Yeah." The bitter Judas-like taste in my mouth was back. My research had told me the best way to get Zaq to cooperate was to use his brothers as leverage.

Zaq's life depended on me being right. If he didn't cooperate, my orders were to stake him—and his brothers would be staked, too.

My compromise had gotten Zaq out of Moreau's clutches and given him the opportunity to save both his brothers and himself. So why did I feel like a manipulating piece of shit?

Crow's phone buzzed. She glanced at it, typed a reply.

"I have to go," she said to me, "but there's something you should know. Torch is—" She drew a finger across her throat in the universal signal for *dead*.

I swallowed sickly. Torch was the slayer assigned to Gabriel Kral. For the past year she'd been undercover as Jessa, a red-headed gym rat who worked as the cook-slash-housekeeper of Gabriel's Manhattan penthouse. She'd been the source of most of our recent intel on the Kral brothers.

"What happened?"

"P1 staked her." Crow used the code for Gabriel; as the oldest brother, he was P1, or Prince One, just as Zaq was Prince Two. "She attacked while he was occupied with a human female. I assume she thought he was distracted. She was wrong."

I stared at my alpha. She seemed more bothered that Torch had failed than that she'd died. How had I not noticed how cold Crow was?

"So they know she was one of us?" I asked.

"Yes."

"That's bad."

Her mouth twisted. "No shit."

I wrapped my fingers around my coffee cup. I was in shock; I needed something to ground me. Shock at Torch's death. Shock at the realization that if I'd been assigned to slay Gabriel, it would've been me who died.

"Wait." I frowned. "When did this happen?"

"Wednesday night, New York time."

My frown deepened. We'd left Moreau's lair early Tuesday morning, Paris time. There'd been plenty of time for Torch to have been told to stand down between then and Wednesday night.

"But...why did she attack at all? The agreement with P2 was that if he worked with me, his brothers would be safe."

Crow waved a hand like it didn't matter. "A communication misfire. Torch didn't get the message in time."

I gripped my cup. Hard.

"P2 was half-dead when we left M's lair. I *told* you we needed a few days."

"Are you questioning me?" Behind the sunglasses Crow's eyes were the chilly blue of a northern sea.

Yes, I am. "Communication misfire" my ass.

I stared back. This was the woman I'd modeled myself after. Like me, she had a vampire primus father. Like me, she'd lost her mother at a young age to the monsters. And like me, she'd dedicated her life to Slayers, Inc.

Up until the last few days, I'd followed her blindly, wholeheartedly.

I looked away first. "No. I'm sorry."

"Mm." I felt her gaze. Assessing me and my commitment. Trying to unnerve me.

I smothered a flare of resentment and shifted the conversation back to Torch's death. "Could someone have tipped P1 off?"

Crow angled her head like the wicked-smart bird from which she'd taken her slayer name. "Why do you ask?"

I moved a shoulder in a small shrug. "This informant you have in the Kral organization. Maybe he told P1 to watch his back."

"There's more than one informant, and no, P1 wasn't tipped off. None of the informants knew about Torch. But you can tell P2 what happened. Make sure he knows that just because Torch is dead, doesn't mean his brother is safe."

"You embedded another slayer?"

"We always have a backup plan. You know that." Which was a nonanswer, but I knew it was all I'd get.

A frightening thought occurred to me. The Krals now knew SI had inserted a slayer into Gabriel's household.

My mouth dried.

Damn, damn, damn.

Karoly Kral wasn't supposed to know about SI's role in his sons' deaths. The whole point in working with Victorine Tremblay was so she'd take the blame, not us. It was no secret how much she hated Karoly and all the Krals.

Now, Karoly would be doubly on guard. Worse, it gave him ammunition in his fight against SI.

Crow seemed to read my mind. "You're not getting cold feet, are you?"

I drew myself up. "Of course not. I knew the risks when I signed on for this op."

"Good." She finished her espresso. "By the way, Stygian asked me to tell you that the passport you requested for P2 is ready. You can pick it up in an hour at the current drop." Crow dabbed her mouth with a napkin and got up. "I'll contact you in a few days for an update. Don't bother contacting me—you can't reach me."

"Understood."

She put her hands on the table and leaned forward. "It's up to you and Twilight now. Don't fail me." Twilight was Lainey Q, the slayer assigned to Rafael Kral.

I raised my chin, uneasy at how she kept implying I wasn't capable of doing my job. "I won't."

"Good." She turned and left the café, chin up and shoulders back, the picture of a rich woman whose only worry was whether to wear Chanel or Valentino to the party that night. Except I knew for a fact that Crow had grown up in a small town in Oklahoma.

I fiddled with my cup, chest heavy, stomach a sick tangle.

I had the bad feeling that if I kept going with my part of Operation Angel, I'd spend the rest of my life regretting it.

But that was crazy talk.

I was a slayer. Killing monsters was what I did. I'd sworn a vow of loyalty to Slayers, Inc. That meant I followed orders, even those I disagreed with.

My switchblade was in my hand. I glanced down, blinked. I didn't even remember taking it out of my pocket. At least I hadn't released the blade.

I returned it to my pocket, then texted Twilight myself. Just to make sure there weren't any more "communication misfires."

Reaper: *You know we're in a holding pattern for now?*

Twilight: *Roger that.*

Reaper: *Keep close to the target, but don't take any further action until you hear from me or C.*

Twilight: *Everything OK?*

I hesitated. Twilight was the closest thing I had to a friend in SI. If only I could talk the situation over with her, ask if she knew why the Krals were being targeted. But that wasn't the kind of question you could ask in a text message.

I replied with a thumbs up and turned off my phone.

Thunder sounded in the distance. I put a handful of euros on the table to pay for our coffee and left the café. I had some time to kill before picking up Zaq's passport, so I picked up sandwiches for dinner, then stopped at a touristy-type store to buy him a T-shirt and a two-pack of boxer-briefs. I didn't have to guess at his size. I knew it, like I knew he liked hamburgers and the color blue, and that unlike his brothers he didn't have a Kral black wolf tattoo because he'd never officially been "made" in his father's syndicate.

So Torch was dead. We hadn't been friends; neither of us was the sort to get cozy with other slayers. But we'd been members of the same squad along with Twilight and a couple of others.

Torch had been a lot like me, actually. Efficient, focused, emotionless.

So why did her death make me feel like I'd been sucker-punched?

I shoved my hands in my pockets, wondering if Twilight knew. But informing her wasn't my job, and I'd pushed Crow enough for one day.

I came up behind a woman with a teenager girl, their arms linked. They had the same curly dark hair, the same greyhound-lean bodies, and the way they inclined toward each other like matched bookends made me certain they were a mother and daughter.

The woman nodded at the teenager as I hurried past them. "*Tu as absolument raison.*" You're absolutely right.

Longing hit me. Longing, and envy.

The woman was so clearly in her daughter's corner. Right then I'd have done almost anything to have even a few minutes with my own mom.

I needed a mom to talk to about these feelings I had for Zaq. Needed someone to hug me and tell me I was doing the right thing. Needed someone to help me figure out what the right thing *was*.

The thunder grumbled again, closer now. The breeze picked up, tugging at my pigtails.

I jogged the last few yards to the Metro entrance.

18
ZAQ

Reaper returned like moonrise on a dark night. Soundless and coolly beautiful.

The slab shifted and she dropped to the dirt floor, the mesh shopping bag in her hand. A burst of fresh air came with her through the opening, followed by a roll of thunder like giant bones knocking together.

I sat up.

Shrugging off the backpack, she took a wrapped sandwich from the mesh bag and tossed it to me. "Hope you like ham and cheese."

"I'm not picky."

I unwrapped the white paper. Nestled between crusty slices of bread was a juicy slab of ham topped with creamy Gruyere cheese. I ate slowly, savoring each bite.

Meanwhile, Reaper climbed up the ladder to put the slab back in place, then crouched nearby with her own sandwich. Her hair was in pigtails, which on most women would've looked cute but on her just looked efficient.

She ate like she did everything—with a silent, intense focus. Like being secretive and avoiding attention was a way of life.

Did she even taste the food, or was it simply fuel to her?

I couldn't finish my sandwich. I rewrapped the remainder and set it on the table.

Reaper glanced from the sandwich to me, a line between her brows. "That's all you're going to eat?"

"For now. Other than a burger in the airport and the food you brought me, it's been four, maybe five weeks since I'd had meat. I can't seem to eat more than a few bites at a time."

Disbelief flickered over her face. "You didn't eat meat in Syria?"

I clamped my back teeth together. I was tired of her assuming the worst about me. "I was in a fucking war zone. The meat went to the kids and pregnant ladies."

"I suppose you didn't feed either." Her tone was heavy with doubt.

I regarded her through slit lids. "No."

"I was there in Syria. Not the whole time, but a few days."

"You've been following me for that long?"

Silence.

"Of course you have." I answered my own question. "You've been planning this for a while, haven't you? Think about it. If I'd been feeding from those poor bastards, don't you think you'd have heard? Humans talk, you know."

She lifted a shoulder, let it drop. "You're a Kral."

"Which doesn't make me an asshole."

She grunted.

Thunder crashed, followed by a bright flash of lightning. The rain began to fall so hard, drops spattered us through the narrow air vent.

"Looks like it's going to be a big storm," I said. "You made it back just in time."

When I glanced back at her, her forehead furrowed like she was trying to figure me out. She gave herself a shake. "I brought you something." She got a T-shirt and a pack of boxer-briefs from her backpack and dropped them onto my lap.

"Thanks," I said with a rueful smile. "I must smell pretty rank. Hell, I can smell myself—that's always a bad sign."

Her mouth twitched.

The T-shirt was light blue with a graphic of the Eiffel Tower and *Paris, Je t'aime* in big red letters. The boxers were white with red hearts.

I lifted a brow at the T-shirt. "The Eiffel Tower?" I asked her. The heart-decorated boxers I wasn't even going to mention.

The left corner of her mouth hitched higher. "Best I could do."

I couldn't sense her emotions, but I was pretty sure she was lying— which meant she was messing with me.

My grin widened. "Good thinking. I'll look like a tourist."

She blinked several times. I could tell she'd expected me to insist on dressing like whatever she thought the son of a vampire primus should insist on dressing like. Then she gave a short nod, as if disguising me as a tourist had been the plan all along. "We don't want to attract attention."

I rose to my feet and reached for the hem of my T-shirt. Her eyes rounded. She spun to face the wall, giving me privacy.

I shucked my clothes and pulled on the clean T-shirt and boxers. She turned back as I zipped up my jeans.

Her expression didn't change, but her gaze went to my crotch. She moistened her lips.

I finger-combed my matted hair and watched her watching me.

She wanted me. I could smell her arousal, sharp and spicy.

Those revenge-sex fantasies I'd had? They flooded my mind, sending whatever spare blood I had south. My cock twitched and hardened, tenting my jeans.

Her mouth pulled to the side. A half-smile, but not of amusement—and not at my expense. It was twisted and a little bitter, like she was laughing at herself and her weakness.

She lifted her gaze from my crotch and met my eyes. "Nothing can hide that angel face of yours. And I know you're crap at generating a glamour. I'm surprised no one recognized you at the airport."

Angel face?

I was still processing that when she handed me a plastic bag and told me to put the dirty clothes in it. "The cemetery closes at six p.m. When the humans leave, I'll wash them out in one of the bathrooms."

"There are bathrooms? You've been holding out on me, woman."

She eyed me, brow lowered, mouth pursed, like she wasn't sure how to respond to my teasing. "Three, actually—it's a large cemetery. You wanna go with me?"

"Are you kidding? I'd like to clean up and use a toilet instead of a plastic bottle."

"Can you make it up the ladder?"

"I already did."

She glanced up—and saw the bloodstains on the slab. "I was planning on coming back, you know."

"I know. You need me, right?"

We gazed at each other for a long moment. The animation faded from her face, and I felt like a dick. But it was the truth, and we both knew it.

I might joke with her. I might even be starting to like her.

But I couldn't forget that to her, I was a monster and this was just a job, a way to get to my father.

She busied herself straightening the table, placing the half of sandwich at the back next to the beef jerky. "We'll go around seven-thirty. That'll give the cleaning crew time to finish, and still give us a few hours before the vampires wake up. There's a dozen or so with lairs in the cemetery, and even more come to feed."

I curled up on the sleeping bag. "Wake me up when you're ready."

⊙⋉⊙

I woke on my own a little before seven and rolled over, searching the dim space for her. She sat in a corner, head against the wall, eyes closed. She appeared to be asleep, but as soon as I moved, she straightened and opened her eyes.

I smiled. "Evening."

"Evening." She looked me over. "How are you feeling?"

I sat up and stretched my arms over my head. Testing how I felt. I was still weak and edgy, and my blood felt weirdly hot, like the silver was heating it. It would take a while to work its way out of my system.

But all I said to Reaper was, "Better."

She nodded and handed me the rest of my sandwich and a bottle of blood-wine. I ate a good meal—the sandwich and most of the wine.

When I was done, she grabbed the backpack and the bag of dirty clothes. She led the way up the ladder, moving the slab aside, while I followed at a slower pace.

At the top, she jumped out and offered me a hand, but I shook my head and heaved myself out of the opening. Proving to us both that I could do it on my own.

The thunderstorm had passed through, leaving the grass wet and giving the air a cool, fresh-washed scent. The setting sun sent golden light shafting through the trees.

As we walked down the hill to the bathroom, I eyed her backpack. She didn't seem to go anywhere without it. I'd love to have a look inside.

For one thing, I knew it held her wallet. That alone would be worth something to me, because I had nothing but the clothes on my back and the T-shirt and boxers. Even if I escaped, I wouldn't get far without a credit card and an ID, but even some cash would be welcome. With enough cash I could buy a cheap phone and enough minutes to call one or both of my brothers.

When we reached the bathrooms, I took the bag with my dirty clothes from Reaper, saying, "I can handle them myself."

I used the toilet, then removed the clean T-shirt to wash up. I barely recognized myself in the mirror. My dark stubble had morphed into a short beard and mustache, and my dirty, matted hair curled over my collar.

But that was good. Incognito was good. I was too drained to produce my "human," viewer-deflecting glamour.

I squirted some hand soap onto my palms and cleaned my body. Next were my hair and beard. When I was as clean as I was going to get, I washed the dirty T-shirt and boxers and returned them to the plastic bag.

Reaper appeared in the bathroom door. "Ready?"

She'd washed her hair and left it to hang in wet strands around her face. She looked younger, her eyes big, her skin dewy.

Something clenched in my chest.

She's a slayer, Zaq. She might look sweet, but don't fool yourself. She's out for blood. Your blood.

I reached for the clean T-shirt. "Almost."

In the mirror, I caught her eyeing me again. She glanced away and tucked a lock of hair behind her ear.

The pit of my stomach tingled.

I was nothing special to look at right now. I'd lost so much weight, my shoulder blades probably looked like the wings of a chicken. An underfed, scrawny chicken.

But she seemed to see something she wanted, and I took a dark satisfaction in how she couldn't seem to stop staring at me. The Kral in me couldn't help wondering how I could use her want against her.

Like the humans said, all's fair in love and war. And this was both.

I put on the T-shirt and picked up the plastic bag. "Ready."

Back at the tomb, we hung the wet clothes over some tree branches to dry.

"Take a seat," Reaper said. "We need to talk."

I nodded. I had plenty of questions. "Your neighbors aren't a problem?"

I eyed the shadows. We appeared to be alone, but that didn't mean a vampire wasn't watching us from the parallel twilight world.

"The blood-suckers?" She shook her head. "They don't bother me, and I don't bother them. If they see you, they'll think you're my lover."

Her lover? I looked her up and down. I hadn't fucked anyone in a while, but it was more than that. It was her. Reaper. I wanted to grab her jaw and take her mouth. I wanted to make her beg for me. Yeah, she wanted to wipe out me and my family. My dick didn't care.

I adjusted my jeans. "D'you have one? A lover?" The sun had dropped behind the trees now. My question came out husky.

Reaper's swallow was audible. When she spoke, her voice was rough at the edges. "I don't have time for that crap."

She took out two plastic bags, and we spread them on the wet grass and sat on them. I leaned back against a tree and stretched out my legs.

"It's been a while for me, too," I said.

"You're saying you were celibate in Syria?"

"Actually, I was. Not that it's any of your damn business."

"Oh-kay." It was just one word, but she managed to insert a lot of doubt.

A muscle ticked in my jaw. "You think you know all about me, don't you?"

A shrug.

I ground my back teeth together. "I was in a fucking war zone, remember? If you think I had time to do more than eat and sleep, then you've never been in a war zone. I barely had time to take a shit."

"All right. I'll give you that." In the twilight, her eyes shone like silver coins. "But as soon as you hit New York, you would've been out at one of your father's bars. Picking up thralls."

"So? What's wrong with hanging with my brothers, catching up with what they've been doing while I was out of the country? And yeah, I would've picked up a thrall. I was damn thirsty, because I refuse to feed from some poor shell-shocked human who's been through hell, and that includes the medics. So if I grab a thrall—who by the way is well paid by my father's syndicate—then where's the harm in that?"

Her mouth turned down as soon as I brought up being thirsty and drinking from a thrall.

The hell with this.

I let my head drop back against the tree trunk. "But that's right. You don't drink from thralls. You don't use your wealth and power to prey on humans. You protect them from monsters like me. Except you had no problem tricking me back at the airport. You didn't even take me in a fair fight. It was three against one, and on top of that, you shot a goddamn tranq into me."

She made a low, provoked sound. "Drop it, all right?"

I dragged a hand down my face. Why did I give a fuck what Reaper thought of me?

The answer was I didn't. Or at least, I shouldn't.

I glowered at her. She was the one with the problem, not me. "We're dhampirs, cher. Get used to it."

Suddenly, her switchblade was out, the click of the catch loud in the silence. I tensed, readying myself for an attack. But she merely twirled it between the fingers of her right hand in a display of dexterity she seemed unaware of.

It was a full minute before she spoke, and when she did, she spoke to the flashing blade, not me. "I'm not like you. I don't drink fresh blood."

"Where d'you think the blood in your wine comes from?"

Her lips folded in. "I only drink what I have to. A cup a day. That and red meat is good enough."

I exhaled. "Somebody really messed with your brain, didn't they? We all have a part in this thing called the universe—dhampirs, vampires, humans." I swept my arm out to encompass the tombs, the trees, the starlit Paris sky. "Just like sharks and wolves and rattlesnakes have a place."

She closed her fingers on the switchblade handle, pressed the button. *Snick, snick.*

"I made a promise," she blurted.

"To who?"

"My mom."

"What kind of mom makes you promise that?"

Her face tightened. "Forget it. I don't want to talk about it."

"No, I want to know."

"Drop it, Kral."

I frowned. Clearly her mom was a sore point. But I shrugged and let it go for now.

She slanted me a look. Sighed. "There's something I have to tell you."

Something about her tone—matter-of-fact but cautious—made me straighten my spine. "What?"

"Your brother Gabriel was attacked. In his penthouse."

My stomach lurched. "What?"

"He was attacked. By a slayer."

"He's okay?"

"Yeah. From what I heard, he didn't get hurt. Or if he did, it wasn't enough to take him down."

"One of your people?"

"Yeah. She's dead." Her tone remained matter-of-fact, but the *snick-snicks* sped up.

"When?"

"Last night."

"Last night." A red-hot fury stole my voice. I sucked an inhale through my teeth. "What the fuck, Reaper? We had a deal. My brothers aren't to be touched."

"I know."

"Then why did a slayer attack Gabriel?"

Snicksnicksnicksnick. "It was a mistake."

"A *mistake?*" I threw a look at the switchblade, tempted to rip it out of her hand. "You lied to me. You fucking lied to me."

Her eyes narrowed like an angry cat's. "No, I didn't."

Her tone was fierce—and convincing. But I was too pissed off to back down. "Then Moreau did, and you went along with it."

"No. That's not how it happened. I was told the same thing as you— that if you did your part, then you and your brothers would be left alone."

"Then what happened?"

Snick, snick. "I was told she didn't get the message to stand down."

"You were told," I repeated. "So you think they didn't tell her? Or do you think they sent a message and she didn't get it?"

"Yes. No."

"Make up your mind, damn it."

She firmed her mouth. "I mean, I think she didn't get the message. Unless—" She shook her head.

"Unless what?"

"Nothing."

"Unless they lied to you, too. Is that what happened?"

"Shut up, already. I handled it, okay?"

I glared at her—and she glared right back. I opened my mouth to demand she tell me exactly what had gone wrong, then shut it again. Demands, orders—they wouldn't get me anywhere with Reaper. We two were equals in this.

Hell, who was I kidding? We weren't equals—she had all the power, and it chafed. Big time.

And damn this beautiful assassin for forcing me to face up to how privileged I was. I might talk a good game about not wanting the perks of a syndicate prince, but people generally fell over themselves to accommodate me, and I let them.

"And my brother Rafe?" I softened my tone a notch, but I knew I still sounded angry. "What guarantee do I have that you people won't 'forget' to call off the slayer assigned to him too?"

The skin around her eyes tightened in a small flinch. "I said I handled it."

"How?"

"After I heard about Gabriel, I texted the slayer assigned to him myself. Rafael won't be hurt if you follow orders. Neither of your brothers will. You have my word."

"Fine." I wasn't happy, but I couldn't afford to alienate her. Besides, Reaper was a soldier, not the one giving the orders.

I heaved a breath. "This slayer. Was she a friend?"

"No. A colleague. You know her—Jessa."

My eyebrows climbed into my hairline. "Red-haired Jessa? The so-efficient-she's-scary housekeeper Jessa?"

"Yeah."

I shook my head. It fit, actually—the woman had always been working out. She probably could've bench-pressed me. But— "Gabriel would've had her checked out six ways to Sunday. The woman lived on site, had full access to his penthouse."

"He did have her vetted." Reaper eyed me. The sun had dropped lower, leaving her elfin face in shadows.

Silence fell. A *waiting* kind of silence.

She'd even stopped playing with her switchblade.

"So either SI is that good," I said, thinking aloud, "or someone vouched for Jessa. Someone Gabriel trusted."

"Like your father."

"Yeah. Like my father." My stomach muscles knotted. "Although that doesn't mean it was him—he delegates that kind of shit."

"But he'd approve it. If it involved one of his sons, especially the crown prince."

True. But I didn't say it aloud—that would be admitting something I wasn't ready to admit.

"Karoly wants you dead. Why do you think you're still here?"

My mind churned and my stomach felt like it was filled with acid.

Maybe it wasn't a test. Maybe Father had decided I was too weak, that I was better off dead.

Snick, snick went the switchblade.

I blew out a breath. "Do me a favor, would you? Put the goddamn knife away."

She looked at the switchblade like she'd forgotten it was in her hand. "Sorry. Habit." She put it in her pocket.

"Gabriel and Rafe will be all right as long as you do your part," she said.

"And if I don't?"

"They'll die," was the flat response.

Alarm sent a jarring spike into my chest. Prickles went up my arms, across the backs of my shoulders. Not the good kind of prickles. They were I-have-to-fucking-do-something-NOW prickles.

"I've got to let Gabriel know. I've got to let them both know." I went for my phone, then remembered I didn't have one. I stuck out a hand. "Give me your phone."

"No. You can't warn him. That's not part of the deal. What if they tell your father?"

"Fuck the deal. Give me the damn phone, or I'll buy one myself."

"With what?"

I set my jaw. Because of course I had no money. I switched gears.

"The deal was that if I helped you, you people wouldn't hurt Gabriel and Rafe. Now I find SI has already broken their part of the bargain. So why the hell should I honor my part?"

She came onto her knees. "Listen, you ass. This is your only chance. You think they wanted to let you go? I had to talk them into it."

I came onto my knees too and leaned forward, matching her determination with mine. "Then you tell them to lay off my fucking brothers. Or the deal's off."

Her eyes flickered. "I can't. My boss doesn't know that you know about Gabriel. Trust me, it's better that way."

"Fuck." I sank back to the ground, dragged a hand down my face. "Okay, here's the deal. You're going to keep tabs on Gabriel and Rafe, tell me how they're doing. And Reaper?" I subconsciously imitated my dad's voice at his most dangerous, soft and cold. "If I find out you're lying to me, I'll rip your goddamn head off."

"Fuck you."

The air crackled with anger and distrust. We glared at each other like two fighters in the ring.

She exhaled and sat back. "This isn't getting us anywhere. If you honor your part of the bargain, your brothers will be okay. That's a promise."

My mouth pulled into a nasty smile. "Then we don't have a problem."

She gave a curt nod of acknowledgment. "Okay, here's the plan. I'll get us tickets. Passports have already been handled. We'll both be traveling under assumed names."

"What if my father's not in New York?"

"Then you find him. But you don't have much time. Drag this out too long and the people above me will get impatient."

I stared at her. "This is my *father*. Let them get impatient. I'm not going to do anything until I'm sure he's the one behind this."

She matched me stare for stare. "Then your brothers will die."

"My brothers will die." I repeated her statement through clenched teeth. "Because of some trumped-up reason that your bosses came up with. And you say we're monsters?"

Suddenly, I couldn't bear to be near her any longer. I rose to my feet.

"I'm going for a walk," I told her without looking at her. "And don't worry, I won't try to escape. Like you said, I have no money, and I'm in a strange city with an enforcer who wants to make me his personal blood slave. Where the fuck would I go?"

❦ 19 ❧

RIDLEY

I trailed Zaq through the cemetery, though not because I thought he'd try to escape.

We both knew he wouldn't get far without money or credit cards. But more importantly, his brothers' lives depended on him sticking to the bargain he'd made with Moreau. I'd known Zaq and his brothers were close, but I was beginning to think he'd chew off his own hand if it would save Gabriel and Rafael.

So I didn't trail him because I was afraid he'd escape. I trailed him because night was falling fast and he was in no shape to fight off a vampire attack.

"And you say we're the monsters."

Suddenly, the night felt airless. A band wrapped itself around my lungs. Everything that bothered me about this mission was encapsulated in that short statement.

Being a slayer was all I knew. It wasn't just a job, it was my calling. I'd seen firsthand what vampires could do to a human.

Monster was too tame a word for the creatures who'd murdered my mom. I'd been too young and untrained to save her, but I'd dedicated my life to protecting others like her.

Still, I was starting to think we'd fucked up with Operation Angel.

Crow had told me that Karoly Kral was working behind the scenes to take down Slayers, Inc. He'd spread lies about SI and demanded the organization be dismantled.

The Kral primus was an apex predator. The power he'd already amassed wasn't enough for him. He wanted more.

If he got his wish, the blood-suckers would be running things at SI, and the balance between them and the humans I'd sworn to protect would be upended.

And on top of that, he'd left Zaq in Moreau's lair rather than risking his own neck to get his son out.

Karoly Kral needed to die.

But not Zaq and his brothers.

I pressed the heels of my hands to my eyes.

Think like a slayer. Fight like a slayer. Live like a slayer.

My mouth moved, repeating the words like a mantra. The simple phrases were my touchstone. They calmed me, reminded me why I'd joined SI in the first place.

We were the good guys. The heroes who stood between humans and a cold-blooded species who, if left unchecked, wouldn't stop until they'd enslaved every last man, woman and child on the planet.

I had to believe that what we did was right. Otherwise, I was as much a monster as the vampires and their syndicates.

Zaq's breathing grew labored. He slowed down but stubbornly kept walking.

"I know you're there," he said without turning around. "I'm a dhampir, don't forget. I have excellent hearing, and I can see in the dark as well as you."

So much for trying to give him space. I caught up to him.

He favored me with a green-eyed glare. "I told you I wouldn't escape."

"I didn't follow you because of that. I trust you."

"Do you? Because if you think the agreement I made with Moreau will stop me from doing whatever I can for my brothers—"

"That's why I trust you. Not because of Moreau, because of your brothers. You'll go along this as long as you think it's helping them. I'm counting on that, actually."

"Are you?" He made a sound of disgust. "Gods, you're cold."

That hurt. Maybe I shouldn't have answered so truthfully, but I thought he'd appreciate honesty.

"We should go back."

"I need air." He moved off again.

I heaved a breath and followed. As we crested a hill, a movement out the corner of my eye made me whip around.

A scrawny, ponytailed vampire crouched on top of a tomb.

Crap. The sun had set without my realizing it. And I was out here without my brown wig and dhampir-with-a-bad-attitude disguise.

The vampire eyed Zaq like he was an ice cream cone on a hot summer day. He licked his dark red lips. His fangs extended.

I drew a glamour over myself, including a hairstyle that approximated the wig, and stalked forward, switchblade out. "He's mine, asshat."

The vampire's blue-rimmed eyes moved up and down my body. Sizing me up.

My own fangs extended without my willing it. Thanks to de Froulay, my vampire magic was powerful, although I didn't call on it unless absolutely necessary. And this man was low in the cemetery's pecking order

I glanced over my shoulder. Zaq had halted. He looked from me to the vampire.

"*Go*," I hissed. "Back to the bolt-hole."

Of course, he didn't obey. No, he grunted and started in my direction.

I faced the hungry vampire, let my power surge. My senses sharpened. The blue expanded in my eyes, bringing the scrawny male into intense focus. I could see the individual black bristles on his unshaven jaw, the yellow striations in his brown eyes, the knife-like points of his fangs. His scent was musty from whatever broken-down tomb he called home, and his heartbeat was slow, weak.

The vampire's eyelids fluttered. He took a shocked breath. He hadn't expected me to be so strong.

"*Allez.*" I motioned with my blade. "*Maintenant!*" Go. Now!

He backed up without taking his gaze from me. When he couldn't go any further, he leapt off the tomb and scuttled away like a frightened rat.

I turned back to Zaq. "I had things handled."

He folded his arms over his chest. "I know—you're a badass. But even a badass can use backup. Thanks, by the way."

I shifted from one foot to the other, not sure what to make of either his badass comment or his thanks. I settled for a gruff, "You're welcome."

He held out a hand. "Walk with me."

I looked at his hand, then back to his face. What was the catch? "You want to hold hands?"

He made an impatient sound. "We're supposed to be lovers, right? Now take it already so you won't have to keep chasing off asshole vampires."

My cheeks heated. He was right; I should've thought of it myself.

I put my hand in his. His fingers were long and strong. The hand of a musician, or maybe a healer. They wrapped firmly around mine.

A zing went up my arm and he slanted me a knowing smile, even though I didn't flinch or pull away. Neither of us said anything.

We ended up at Jim Morrison's grave. Zaq opened a gate in the low metal fence that surrounded that section of graves and we went inside. I hadn't known much about Morrison before I'd started visiting Lachaise—just that he was a sixties rock star who'd died young, but his grave was one of the cemetery's most visited sites. His fans kept it decorated with fresh flowers and photos of the singer.

It was completely dark now, the sky above us a dusky blue. Someone had lit a candle and placed it on the stone above Morrison's grave. A noise behind us made me whip around. A cat's eyes glowed in the branches of a nearby tree.

"We should go back," I said. "It's not safe out here. You're still healing. If that vampire gets some friends and comes back, I might not be able to fight them off."

He blew out a breath and pulled his hand from mine. "You're fucked up, you know that? You're so worried about keeping me alive. But if I mess this up, you think I don't know you'll stake me?"

My throat worked. His gaze flicked to the small, telling movement, then back to my face.

"What if I swear that I won't?" The words pushed themselves passed the thickness in my throat, surprising us both.

He stepped closer. Searching my face. I hadn't dropped the glamour but I had a feeling he still could see me. The real me.

"Why should I trust you?"

"I'm the best chance you've got."

He gave a muted bark of laughter. "You're honest anyway."

"Yes. And when I make a promise, I keep it." I stuck out my hand. "I swear on my mother's grave that you're safe with me."

He took my hand but didn't shake it. "Tell me your name. You want me to trust you? Give me that much, at least."

I moistened my lips. "I can't."

He raised my hand. I tensed, expecting him to kiss it, but he turned it over instead and examined the faint marks he'd left behind when he'd fed from me.

His gaze came back to mine. Dark, insistent. "Yes, you can."

Longing twisted through me, a sharp, sudden craving. I couldn't recall the last time anyone had called me by my real name. Suddenly, I needed to hear it spoken—and not by just anyone.

By him. Zaquiel.

My mouth opened again. "Ridley." I kept my voice low, but it felt like I'd shouted it.

He relaxed a little. "Ridley," he repeated. His voice had a hint of gravel. My plain, boyish name sounded sexy, like we were in bed together, not standing in a graveyard. "No last name?"

I wordlessly shook my head.

"Someday." The word held a promise, like there would be a future for us, a future where I would tell him not just my full name, but all my secrets.

At that moment, I almost believed it.

"Ridley. I like it." Zaq touched his lips to the marks on my wrist. His lips were soft and warm.

Shocks and tingles went up my arm like Fourth-of-July sparklers. My head swam with his scent. My heart knocked against my ribcage. He kissed a line up my forearm, touching his lips to the sensitive skin of my inner elbow.

"Zaquiel..."

He raised his head from my arm, smiling—an intimate, just-for-me smile that set off more shocks and tingles, this time in my lower belly.

"Call me Zaq. No one calls me Zaquiel except my father—or my mom when she's really pissed off."

He's playing you, Ridley. Trying to get you on his side.

But I found myself nodding. Hell, I'd already been calling him Zaq in my head.

"Zaq," I agreed.

He released my hand and ran the backs of his fingers over my cheek. He'd moved closer, or maybe I had. We were nearly touching now. I felt his heat up and down the front of my body. My nipples prickled and hardened.

He cupped my chin, ran his thumb over my lower lip. "I wish..." He halted and shook his head.

It was maddening. I *needed* him to finish that sentence. I'd forgotten we were in the cemetery. I'd forgotten he was supposed to be my prisoner. I'd forgotten that he was probably playing me.

We were in a Zaq-and-Ridley bubble, warm and beautiful and ripe with possibilities.

I let my glamour fade. We were alone, and I could always call on it again if I had to.

"What?" I caught his wrist. "What do you wish?"

His mouth tugged to the side like he was laughing at us both. "That I'd met you some other way. So we could get to know each other like two people do. People who like each other. Because I think I could like you, Ridley No-Name."

And I could like you, Zaq Kral. A lot.

I stilled, drenched in the ice water of common sense. Nearby, an owl hooted.

I dropped his wrist. Stepped back. "We should go."

A crushing sadness gripped my chest.

Because we hadn't met in a normal, get-to-know-each-other way. And we couldn't like each other or have any kind of a future together.

I was a slayer. And he was a syndicate prince.

Zaq's smile dimmed. "Yeah. Right."

⁂

Back at the tomb, Zaq brushed me aside when I went to move the slab aside. "I'll do it."

"Be my guest." I watched as he heaved it out of the way. Clearly, he was recovering.

I looked into the bolt-hole and felt a frisson of panic. Right now, I couldn't deal with being confined in a small space with Zaq Kral.

"You go on down," I told him. "I have to do...something."

"Suit yourself." He ignored the ladder and dropped lightly to the dirt floor. "I'm going to bed."

I nodded and left, wandering aimlessly among the nearby tombs. Away from Zaq, I let my shoulders sag.

If only he wasn't a Kral.

If only I'd met him some other time, some other place.

Right then I wanted my mom so bad I could taste it. I literally ached to see her one more time. She wouldn't even have to speak, just put her arms around me and tell me everything was going to okay, that I'd work it out.

Hot tears stung my eyes. I swiped at them with the heels of my hands and realized I'd come almost to the cemetery entrance. I turned back.

The shadows next to the gate wavered like a ripple passing through dark water. Someone was there. Watching me.

My heart jerked. My knees locked. I grabbed my blade, released the catch. I'd dropped my glamour but it was too late to pull it over myself again.

I cursed under my breath. I knew better than this. Emotion wasn't something I could afford to indulge in.

Leo de Froulay emerged from the ripple, blond mane pulled back into a ponytail and wearing a suit the same midnight blue as the sky above us. He looked me up and down like he'd caught me with my hand in the cookie jar.

"What are you up to, *ma p'tite?*"

My palms were sweaty. I adjusted my grip on the blade's steel handle. How had he found me here in Lachaise? And had he seen me Zaq?

"Nothing." I schooled my voice to be flat. Thank God he couldn't read my emotions like he could a human's. "If this is about that intel you asked for, I've been meaning to contact you."

I held my breath, waiting for de Froulay to brush that aside to ask about Zaq.

But he replied, "You found something?"

I relaxed. Luck was with me. He must have just arrived.

"Yes," I said. "You were right. Something's up."

"Ah, yes?"

I couldn't tell de Froulay the truth about Zaq's kidnapping. Not yet.

But I could make Philippe Moreau's life difficult. "He's plotting something with the Tremblays. Something big."

De Froulay's face tightened. "You have proof?"

"Enough. I heard things—little things, here and there. But I don't have details. Moreau didn't trust me that far I think he's trafficking humans, too. The thralls in his lair are afraid of him, and I'm pretty sure he beats them."

De Froulay swore. "I need more."

"You'll have to find your own proof. I'm not working for him anymore. In fact, I'm leaving Paris."

Twin lines formed between his dark brows. "Why?"

"I had a better offer." It wasn't exactly the truth, but it was the best I could come up with on such short notice.

A pained look crossed his face. "If you'd let me help you..."

I shook my head. "I'll contact you if I hear anything else."

"All right." He hesitated, then stepped closer. His gaze probed my blank expression like he could see the fear and worry beneath. "If you're in trouble, I'd like to help."

No. Hell, no.

"Everything's fine. I just have another job, is all."

"Here's my personal number." He scribbled a number on a business card and held it out. "If you need anything—anything at all—call or text me. No one but me has access to it."

I stared at the card without taking it.

A muscle jumped in his jaw. He took my hand, placed the card into my palm and closed my fingers around it.

"Thanks," I muttered.

He heaved a breath. "If I could go back in time and do things over, I would. Charlotte didn't like my life—she made no secret of that. She never wanted to be with a syndicate vampire, especially a primus."

"You think I care?"

He shrugged his big shoulders. "Frankly, I think you do."

I took a step back. "I have to go."

"I'm surprised she stayed as long as she did. I should never have taken her as a thrall—that's my one regret. I knew she was different." His mouth pulled to the side in a poignant little smile. "She really did love me. You don't know how seductive that can be to a man like me."

I stared at him, hearing again my mom's screams. The screams that changed to whimpers before they were abruptly cut off.

"She died because of you." My voice shook with anger. "Do you regret that, too?"

"Of course. And I'm sorry, my dear, so very sorry. Those are just words, I know. But I truly mean them."

I fisted my hands. De Froulay's card crumpled in my fingers but I barely noticed.

"Your words mean *nothing*. Not when I lost my—my—" I stopped, unable to speak past the lump clogging my throat. "They *hurt* her. I heard her screaming. And I couldn't help. God knows what they did to her, but she refused to give me up."

"I'm sorry," he said again.

With an effort, I brought myself under control. I even managed a tight nod.

His mouth formed a hard line. "If I could go back in time and change things, I would. But I promise you this. I *will* find the men who murdered Charlotte, and they will pay. This I swear on the blood of my own mother."

"And you'll remember your promise? I want to be there."

"You have my word. And my dear? Don't wait to leave Paris. Go tomorrow, while it's daylight. In fact, leave France. You *are* in trouble, and it's not just whatever's led you to hide out in this cemetery. There's a rumor circulating among my men that you're a slayer."

I went as still as the tombs surrounding us. "That's a lie."

Shrewd light eyes considered me. "Hmm."

I opened my mouth to say something, but he raised a hand, halting me.

"I prefer not to know. Just get out of my city before I have to do something about you. You have money?"

"I—yes, I'm good."

"Good. I'll deposit the sum I promised you to a Swiss account. The details will be sent to you. Memorize that number I gave you, then destroy it."

And with that, the Primus of Paris faded back into the shadows.

20

ZAQ

On Sunday we took a train to Nice, then boarded a plane to Newark, New Jersey. As the jet took off, I let out a slow exhale. Beside me, Ridley relaxed, too.

She'd been jumpy and keyed-up ever since Friday night, and my neck had itched the entire time we were waiting for our flight. Frankly, I didn't trust that bastard Moreau to let me leave France this easily.

We landed at Newark on Monday around noon and made our way out of the jet along with the other passengers.

Ridley had ditched the ugly brown wig in favor of a dark knit hat pulled down over her own hair. She wore a ribbed black tank, Army-green tactical pants and a pair of low, flexible combat boots. Add a little makeup and a change in how she carried herself—shoulders back, chin up, like a woman who knew her worth—and she was 180 degrees from the worn-down thrall who'd approached me in Charles de Gaulle.

I'd kept the scruffy beard and donned a blue Paris soccer cap that we'd picked up at a flea market. As we exited the plane, I amped up the glamour Ridley didn't think I had, the one that instead of changing my appearance encouraged people to ignore me.

Ridley did a double take when she saw me with my head down and slightly forward, spine curved so my chest caved in. Her fine dark brows formed a disturbed V, but she waited until we were waiting in line for a taxi to say something.

"You look so *human*."

Her tone implied my dialed-down appearance was some kind of a trick, but hell, I was *supposed* to be incognito.

I set my jaw. Ridley and I had arrived at an unspoken truce. I'd accepted that I needed her help to get to New York and figure out what the fuck was going on so I could save my brothers. And she'd accepted I was going to do this my way or not at all.

Yet she continued to examine everything I did for some dark, hidden purpose.

I gave her a hard stare. "Looking human is good, right? Unless you want my father to know I'm back in New York."

"You're right." She sighed. "I'm sorry. I'm on edge and I'm not used to working with someone else. I have no social skills."

Her frankness and woeful expression disarmed me. I found my lips quirking up. "Social skills are overrated."

"Says the man who can talk to anyone."

"I work with a lot of different people. You learn how to get along. Frankly, I'd rather you tell me what you're really thinking."

"It goes both ways, you know. I won't lie to you if you don't lie to me."

Our turn for a taxi came. A yellow cab stopped at the curb. I opened the door and nodded at her to go first.

She didn't get in. "Well? Are you lying to me? And after you." She waited until I climbed inside, then followed.

She closed the door. I stretched my arm along the seat back and gave her a that-would-be-telling smile.

"Only about the important things."

⁂

The cab dropped us off in midtown Manhattan. We were a block from Times Square, and the streets were crowded with tourists, street performers and peddlers hawking New York souvenirs. On the skyscrapers, video walls streamed ads for everything from Broadway musicals to smartphones. Horns blared, and a clown on stilts walked past.

I inhaled a lungful of exhaust fumes and hot asphalt. Welcome to New York.

My mood lightened. New York wasn't home, exactly—I'd grown up in a big country house in Maryland—but the Kral Syndicate's headquarters were in lower Manhattan, and me and my brothers all had apartments in the city.

And right now, New York felt like home. We were in my territory now.

I hefted my new backpack which we'd purchased at the same flea market as my cap, along with another T-shirt (this one a plain black), three pairs of socks and a change of pants—and thought longingly of the loft I owned a few blocks away in the Meatpacking District. Actually, I owned the whole building for security purposes, the top floor for me and the middle floor for my security team. The bottom floor I rented for a dollar a month to a local nonprofit.

Right now, I'd give a dozen cases of my favorite blood-wine to take a hot shower in my own bathroom and then get dressed in my own clothes. Not to mention grabbing some cash.

I was a rich man, even if I gave most of my money to charity, keeping only ten percent of the interest from my trust fund for my own needs. But ten percent of the interest on a billion dollars is still a shitload of money. I wasn't used to someone else paying for everything, even my goddamn underwear.

"This way." Ridley moved through the crowd with an easy, ground-covering stride. "I know a squat where we can stay."

I spared a last thought for that hot shower and fell in beside her. I trusted Xavier, my chief of security, like I did my brothers. But my dad would've asked Xavier to keep an eye out for me and I didn't want to put him in the position of being forced to choose between us.

"A squat. Right. So where is it? And does it have bedbugs?" I added to make her laugh.

I didn't get a laugh but her cheek creased. "The Bronx. And don't worry, bedbugs don't bite dhampirs. Much."

I grinned down at her, happy to have drawn even a small smile from her.

She'd pulled back into her emotionless-badass shell after that night in Père Lachaise when she'd told me her real name and I'd responded that I thought I could like her, and her face had twisted with yearning.

And I hated it; I missed the Ridley behind the badass, the Ridley I had barely glimpsed but wanted to know better.

So I'd chipped away at her, encouraging her to tease me as a way to break through that flat, businesslike wall she'd erected between us.

I told myself I did it because I needed her on my side, but hell, really it was because I liked seeing her smile.

We headed into the underground maze of the Times Square-42nd Street Station. I didn't expect to see any of my dad's people—not in the middle of the day—but I tugged my cap lower and amped up my glamour.

Ridley bought two MetroCards at a kiosk. We joined the crowd fast-walking through the white-tiled tunnels and caught an uptown train to the Bronx. We came out in a neighborhood I'd never been in, a mix of low-rise apartment buildings, and brownstones, mostly well-kept although old. The signs were in both Spanish and English, and bodegas were side-by-side with Italian bakeries and hipster coffee shops.

"The squat's down this street." Reaper turned down a side street that gentrification hadn't reached yet. She stopped in front of a three-story brownstone that was in serious need of some TLC. The doors and windows were covered with plywood, and the roof was missing shingles and bowed in the middle.

We circled around to the backyard. Ridley glanced at me. "Can you keep that human look?"

"Yep. Don't worry, they won't recognize me."

She pursed her lips. "The beard helps, at least. I don't know how it fools anyone, but it seems to."

The back door had a cinderblock as its only step. Reaper stepped on the block and knocked: Two short raps, followed by a pause, then another rap and a pause, then another two short.

Footsteps sounded on the other side. "Who's there?" asked a gravelly voice.

"Tina," said Ridley.

I eyed her. How many aliases did the woman have?

The door opened. The gravelly voice belonged to a skinny man with wiry black hair. His skin was smooth but his eyes were old. He could've been any age from forty to sixty.

He jerked his chin at me. "Who's that?"

"Kevin."

"You two together now?"

She didn't hesitate. "Yeah."

He narrowed his eyes at me in a look that lasted a full three beats, then stepped back. The door swung shut. Ridley caught it mid-swing and we went inside.

The man had disappeared.

Ridley locked the door. The boarded-up windows blocked most of the sunlight, but enough leaked in around the edges for me to make out a ratty maroon rug, navy-blue couch and two mismatched chairs. In the kitchen, someone was cooking—tacos or maybe chili.

Ridley saw me glance in the kitchen's direction. "You hungry?"

"Yeah."

We'd eaten dinner on the jet from Paris, but airplane food was airplane food. Besides, my body was still healing; it craved energy. Basically, I'd reverted to a teenage boy, shoveling anything I could into my mouth, and then two hours later I was starving again.

Ridley glanced at her phone. Dismay flashed across her face, dismay and a touch of fear.

I frowned. "What is it?"

She shook her head and went to put the phone back in her pocket. I snatched it from her hand.

It was a text from someone called Crow. Cryptic as hell, of course.

PK knows. Be on guard.

"Who's PK? And what do they know?"

Ridley grabbed the phone from me and texted something back. Then she deleted the text and shoved the phone back into her pants pocket. "You wanna eat or not?"

I narrowed my eyes but allowed her to divert me. For now. "Sure."

She nodded at the kitchen. "Dex is a chef. If I give him a twenty, he'll cook us dinner."

Dex was a broad-shouldered man with a torso like a tree trunk and dreadlocks halfway down his back. He wrapped his big arms around 'Tina.'

I waited for Ridley to pull a blade on him, or at the very least, shove him away. To my surprise, she hugged him back with equal enthusiasm. "It's good to see you."

Dex released her. "Where the hell have you been? And who's this?" He looked me up and down.

"A friend. Kevin."

"Your friend, huh?" He relaxed—and grinned.

Ridley crossed her arms and jutted her pointed chin. "Yeah."

I stuck out my hand. "Good to meet you, Dex."

We shook hands, then he had me take a seat at the scarred plank table. "You hungry?"

"Oh, yeah."

He was cooking something called Chimi burgers, ground beef which had been sliced and grilled, then served on a pita-bread-like sandwich with cabbage and what he said was his abuela's secret sauce. We washed it all down with Cokes.

My sandwich was fucking amazing, and I told him so.

He gave a regal nod, an artist accepting his due. "I got the recipe from my abuela. Every family has its own recipe, but my abuela's is the best, of course." He grinned.

"Dex is from the Dominican Republic," Ridley said.

"Yeah?" I said around a mouthful of Chimi burger. "I may have to visit just for the food."

"My abuela will cook for you. Say the word and I'll let her know."

"Thanks. I'll do that." I stuck out my hand again and we shook on it.
Ridley looked from me to Dex, a tiny line between her eyes.

"What?" I said. "I mean it. This food is good, and I love the islands."

"You've been?" Dex asked.

"Not to the Dominican Republic." I was about to tell him about my
family's private island off the coast of Florida when I recalled I wasn't
supposed to be a rich man. "But a few other islands—St. John's, Puerto
Rico, Haiti. On business."

He gave a knowing nod. I was pretty sure he thought "business" meant
"illegal drugs," when actually I'd been coordinating medical crews in the
aftermath of hurricanes, but he stopped asking questions.

Ridley's room was on the second floor. To get there we had to climb a
ladder. Upstairs were three bedrooms and a bathroom. Ridley's was the
room on the end.

It was hot and cramped and airless, with barely enough for a queen-
sized mattress and a chair. The only lighting came from a bulb screwed
into a ceiling fixture. The two windows were closed and covered with
cheap brown blinds.

Ridley sent me an apologetic look. "I know, it's like an oven up here.
And smelly." She wrinkled her nose. "I haven't been here for a while."

She set her backpack on the chair and turned the window air conditioning unit on high.

"Dex liked you." She examined me like that was something suspicious.

"Yeah? Good. I liked him too."

She grunted. "Humans like you. You're good with them."

"Doesn't mean I take advantage of them."

She pursed her lips. "No, I don't think you do. But before I met you, I
thought you did."

Well, hallelujah. The wall of her suspicion had developed a crack.

"I figured you used your volunteer work to cover up work you did for
your father's syndicate," she added, "or to troll for thralls. Or both."

I expelled a breath. "You must think I'm a first-class asshole."

"Not anymore. But all you syndicate men are entitled pricks."

"Well, fuck you too."

She lifted a shoulder. "Hey, I call them like I see it."

Something about her expression—dark, but because she was remem-
bering something—made me move closer.

"What happened?" I softened my tone. "This isn't just about you
being a slayer, is it? Something happened to make you hate the
syndicates."

She looked down and to the side as if trying to decide how much to tell me. Then she raised her head and gave me a clear-eyed gray look that almost made me take a step back.

"My mom was murdered by syndicate vampires."

A sharp shard of compassion lodged in my chest. "I'm sorry."

She gave a little shake of her head, like she didn't want my concern. "It was a long time ago."

"When?"

"Fifteen years ago. I was twelve. They wanted me, too—they asked her where I was—but she didn't tell them. I got away by fading into the shadows, but she was a human. She couldn't hide like me. She told me to run and then faced them down by herself." Flat, matter-of-fact statements that made my heart constrict.

"Twelve years old." I squeezed my nape. "Shit."

She shrugged and looked away.

"So that's why you're a slayer?" I asked

She dipped her chin. "SI saved my life—in more ways than one. I was on my own for six months until another slayer found me and took me in. I was in pretty bad shape by then—physically, emotionally. Jumpy. Stealing food, eating out of garbage cans. Terrified they'd come back for me. And so full of hate..." She passed a hand over her face. "The slayers gave me a chance to do something about all the hate—gave me a target for it. I was one step away from going feral. I like to think I would've killed myself first, but I don't know." The last few words were a whisper.

I sank onto the mattress. My belly was full for the first time in weeks, and I'd been feeling a confidence I probably shouldn't have. I was safely in New York and Ridley had warmed up to me—a little, anyway.

Now a sick sensation settled in the pit of my stomach. What if it had been Kral Syndicate vampires who'd killed Ridley's mother? My father didn't make a habit of killing human females, but if the woman had been a spy or betrayed him in some other way...

Ridley sat against the water-stained wall, legs out, the switchblade in her hand. She'd taken it out at some point during her story, although she hadn't released the blade.

I didn't want to ask, but I had to know. "Do you know what syndicate they were from?"

She understood immediately. "Not yours. They had French accents."

"We have a few French vampires. Cajun-French, from New Orleans, and even a couple from France."

"They were from the Paris Syndicate. Three men."

The sick sensation eased. "You know who they were?"

"Not their names, no. And I didn't get a good look at their faces. But they were from Paris, trust me. That, I'm sure of. It wasn't the first time they'd attacked us." She glanced at her switchblade and firmed her jaw. "And I *will* find them. I have a lead now, someone who might be able to identify them."

"Good. And when you do, I hope you send them to a bright, sunny hell."

Her smile was all teeth. "I intend to."

We fell silent. It had been a long day. I'd been doing okay, but now a wave of tiredness rolled over me. I yawned and knuckled my eyeballs like a kid.

"Go to sleep." Ridley nodded at the bed. "You need it. We're safe here."

"I think I will."

I made a trip to the john. It was basically a mildewed closet with a toilet, a shower and a sink with a faucet that only spouted cold water. At least we didn't have to use a hole in the backyard.

Ridley followed me but stayed on the other side of the door. Back in the room, I stripped to my T-shirt and boxers and curled up on the mattress.

Ridley took off her combat boots and socks and resumed her position against the wall. The switchblade rested on the floor beside her.

I moved closer to the wall. "There's room for both of us."

She closed her eyes. "I'm good."

I sighed and went to sleep. But when I woke up a couple of hours later, she was curled up next to me, still in her tank and tactical pants, her breath slow and even.

I came up on an elbow. Her dark lashes curved against soft, pink-touched cheeks, and her cap of shiny hair was sleep-mussed. She'd taken a shower. She smelled of clean soap and fresh-cut grass.

My chest hollowed out.

Holy crap, she was young. She should be in college or working a first job, not risking her life on a daily basis.

Those vampires who'd murdered her mom deserved to be chained to a post and left to burn in the summer sun. They hadn't just taken her mom's life, they'd stolen the life Ridley should've been living, pushed her into a high-risk profession.

And she didn't risk only her life when she went out on a mission, she risked her freedom as well. Not every vampire staked the slayers they captured. Some kept them as blood slaves.

I brushed a hand over her hair. "I should hate you," I said lowly.

"You're the enemy. I don't care what you say. You think I don't know that you'll have to kill me if I fuck this up?"

She didn't respond. She was passed out, too exhausted to be wary. I knew the feeling; I'd been there myself a few times.

I drew in her fresh, clean scent. I wanted to cuddle her, to whisper promises I probably couldn't keep, like that if I got out of this alive, I'd help her find and slay the vampires who'd killed her mom.

She drew a soft breath. Her breasts rose and fell. They were small, but I'd seen enough of her to guess they were perfectly formed.

I enjoyed the view for a few moments, then moved my gaze from her chest—and to the backpack on the floor next to her head.

I tensed. Shot another look at Ridley.

She lay like a vampire in the day sleep—unmoving and almost impossible to wake.

I eased off the mattress, picked up the backpack and moved to the other side of the room. I slid the buckle out of the catch. Slowly, slowly. Keeping an eye on her the whole time.

Because even though her story had gutted me, we weren't on the same side.

And this wasn't just about me. My brothers' lives were in danger, too.

The backpack held clothes and her wallet but no phone. Concealed in an inner pocket were a syringe and two vials of a clear liquid—probably the tranquilizer she'd used on me in Paris.

Insurance, I supposed. Well, fuck that. I set the vials aside.

A second pocket held three switchblades and my wallet. To my joy, the wallet hadn't been touched—it contained my ID, credit cards, thirty-five euros and a hundred dollars. The cards could be traced, but the cash I could use.

Score.

Ridley's wallet held about a thousand dollars, the MetroCards and a credit card in yet another alias. I kept a MetroCard, two hundred dollars and one of the switchblades and returned everything else to her pack. Then I scooped up my wallet, leather boots and the vials, and slipped out the door.

21
RIDLEY

Zaq had left the squat. I jolted awake, heart in my throat.

I turned over to make sure. His side of the bed was empty, the sheets cool, like he'd left a while ago.

Stupid, stupid, stupid to let myself fall asleep. To count on the fact that I was a light sleeper.

I *knew* I couldn't trust him.

He was my prisoner, even if sometimes things between us felt...different. Like we were friends, or at least colleagues. Two people working together.

But I'd been getting by on three or four hours of sleep ever since we'd left Moreau's lair, and it had finally caught up with me. On top of that, I'd eaten a big meal. The combination had taken me under like I'd been drugged.

I flipped to my other side. My backpack was still where I'd left it. Maybe I was wrong? Maybe he was still in the squat?

I sprinted down the hall to the bathroom and banged on the closed door. In my panic, I almost called Zaq's real name but remembered in time.

"Kevin? You in there?"

"It's me." A woman I didn't know responded. "Gigi."

"Oh. Sorry."

Damn damn damn.

I darted back to my room, where I pulled on socks and shoved my feet into my boots, then grabbed my backpack and scrambled down the ladder.

Cursing myself for not tying Zaq's ankle to mine. Hell, I should've chained his goddamned arms and legs together.

The front door was nailed shut. I pulled open the back door and leapt over the cinderblock to the ground.

In the yard next door, a middle-aged man in a Yankees shirt was barbecuing ribs. I waved an arm. "Hey!"

He regarded me from under lowered brows. "You talkin' to me?"

"Sorry, sir." I dredged up an apologetic smile. "Can I ask you something?"

He shrugged a beefy shoulder. "You can ask. Don't mean I'll answer."

"Have you seen a man wearing a blue cap? He's about this tall"—I held my hand above my head at approximately six feet—"and he has a dark beard."

"Yeah, I seen him. He went that way." He pointed toward the street.

"Thanks."

"About thirty minutes ago," my informant added. "Maybe more. No way you'll catch him now."

Thirty minutes? He could be in Manhattan by now. Or on his way to Maryland.

Damn damn damn.

He could be anywhere.

I jogged around to the front of the brownstone. The light from the setting sun slanted down across the street, warming the buildings' weathered chocolate-colored stones. People sat on stoops, staring at their phones or talking with friends. A group of kids kicked a soccer ball around, their happy cries filling the air.

It seemed like everyone in the neighborhood was outside taking in the cooler evening air. Everyone, that is, but Zaq.

My blood pounded in my ears. I'd fucked up—bad. I wiped my sweaty palms on my pants.

I returned to the house and questioned Dex, who confirmed that Zaq had left about a half an hour ago.

"He didn't say when he'd be back?" Who was I kidding? He wasn't coming back.

"No." My friend's broad face creased with concern. "Why? Is there a problem?"

"No."

I passed a shaky hand over my eyes. He was gone. He could be anywhere by now. He knew this city as well or better than I did.

Damn damn damn. I'd have to contact Crow, let her know.

Despite the heat, the thought of my alpha's anger sent a chill down my spine.

I returned to my room and rummaged through my backpack. He'd taken one of my blades but left the other two. I undid the hidden inner pocket. The syringe was still there but the vials were gone.

I grabbed my wallet and looked inside.

Great. He not only had a weapon, he had cash and a MetroCard.

A heavy stone of disappointment lodged in my chest. I sank into a crouch, my arms wrapped around my knees.

I'd *trusted* Zaq. Maybe I shouldn't have, but I had. We'd made a deal and I'd expected him to keep his side of it.

He's a syndicate prince. What did you expect?

Hell, he'd warned me himself not to trust him, said he only lied *"about the important things."*

I knuckled my eyes.

Think. Where would he go?

Not to his father. Moreau had planted enough doubt that I was reasonably certain Zaq wouldn't contact Karoly. Not yet.

But he might try to get in touch with his brothers. Last I'd heard, Rafe was in Montreal, but Gabriel was in New York.

So what was the worst that could happen if Zaq got in touch with Gabriel? Gabriel knew his attacker had been from SI. Zaq couldn't add much to that except to tell his brother about me.

Okay. I drew a centering breath through my nostrils.

I knew I should contact Crow, explain what had happened and ask how to proceed. If I stayed at the squat, Zaq might return with reinforcements, but I didn't think he would.

He was smart enough to know that if he returned with reinforcements, he might make things worse. Taking me out wouldn't save his brothers. They'd still be in danger.

Plus, the man was a lone wolf. He went his own way, did his own thing —like taking a commercial flight instead of a private jet, and traveling without a staff to smooth his way.

So if Zaq had left, it was to do his lone-wolf thing, something he wanted to investigate on his own.

So. I'd leave the squat but remain in the area in case he returned.

And I wouldn't contact Crow. Not yet, anyway.

I waited for hours. Forcing myself to remain within sight of the squat even though every muscle and bone and nerve in my body screamed to go after Zaq.

Finally, around one a.m., my patience was rewarded.

I'd moved every half-hour so as not to attract attention. Currently I was hunkered down on the curb outside a bodega, nursing a cream soda. The street had emptied until it was just me and a couple a half-block away who were simulating sex without removing their clothes—or at least, that's what it looked like.

A packed car drove by blasting Pitbull's "Don't Stop the Party." Somewhere nearby a siren wailed.

I took another drink of soda. At one point, I'd gone back inside to use the bathroom and change into a clean tank top and jeans shorts. I'd also tucked my hair up into a knit hat—even though it was too damn hot for a knit hat and my head was sweating—and dimmed my dhampir-glow.

It had worked; nobody except for a couple of douchebag men had paid me any attention. And they'd backed off when I'd taken out my switchblade and started tossing it from hand to hand.

The hair on my nape lifted. Someone was watching me. I palmed the switchblade and rose to my feet, scanning the area.

In the alley next to the bodega, the shadows seemed thicker, darker. I took a fighting stance, legs apart, knees bent, and moved my thumb to the blade's catch but didn't press it.

"Who's there?"

The shadows stirred, and Zaq stepped out of them and walked toward me. He stopped a foot away, gazing down at me with hooded eyes. "Hey."

Relief flooded me. Relief and anger.

I shoved the blade back into my pocket. "Where the fuck have you been?"

"I had some things to do."

"Yeah?" I gripped the front of his T-shirt and got in his face. "Next time," I said between my teeth, "take me."

He grabbed my wrist and dug his thumb into a pressure point, forcing me to release him. "You knew I'd come back."

"No, I didn't know. Not for sure, anyway." I rubbed my wrist, barely noticing the pain. "You snuck out while I was sleeping. Why would I think you were coming back?"

Zaq grabbed my upper arms and jerked me closer, brow lowered. "Because my brothers' lives are on the line, that's why."

We glared at each other. Beneath the beard-scruff, a muscle jumped in his cheek.

The bodega door opened, and a woman pushed past us, juggling a toddler and a bag of groceries.

Zaq cursed and pulled me into the alley. "You want to have this out? Fine."

I blew out a breath. "Not out here. Let's go back to the squat."

I waited for him to start walking and followed on his heels like a sheepdog with one sheep. Zaq tolerated that for about three seconds before dropping back and putting an arm around my shoulders. I gave his arm—and his shaggy-haired and somehow-still-sexy self—the side-eye.

"We're supposed to be 'friends,' remember?" he said out of the corner of his mouth. "Act like you like me."

"Right." I leaned into him, pretending to play up to him. But it wasn't all pretense, because honestly? I leaned into Zaq because it felt good. I turned my head and took a surreptitious sniff of his spicy scent.

I was still pissed that he'd snuck out like that. But he'd come back. I'd been right to trust him.

My whole body went loose with relief. I wouldn't have to inform Crow he'd gone AWOL.

Zaq didn't know—or maybe he didn't care—what a tightrope we were walking here. One misstep, and he was dead. And maybe me along with him.

Back in the room, I dragged off my hat and scraped my fingers through my sweaty hair. "All right. Talk. Where did you go?"

He fingered his stubbled chin like he was deciding what to tell me. Or whether to tell me anything.

"Look," I said, "this isn't going to work if we can't trust each other."

"But I can't trust you," he said almost gently. "Can I?"

That hurt. "I gave you my promise that I wouldn't stake you."

"Actually, you didn't. Not in so many words."

I thought back and he was right. I opened my mouth, but he crossed to me and laid his hand over my lips.

"Don't say anything. That way you won't have to break your word if it comes down to it."

"Bu..."

"No. Don't." He pressed harder. "I mean it. Okay?"

I heaved a frustrated breath. "Okay."

He took his hand away.

"But I wouldn't break my word."

"Quiet." He set a finger back on my mouth.

Our eyes met. I felt a jolt, and suddenly, the anger and distrust between us morphed to sexual tension. The air almost crackled.

Zaq took his finger from my mouth. But instead of moving away, he combed his fingers through my hair, tucking a strand behind my ear, playing with the ends.

He curved his fingers around my nape. "Your hair is so pretty. Like sunlight in Greece. Or the Caribbean."

His husky tones rumbled through me like a purr. I wanted to rub my head against his palm like a cat.

But the discipline instilled in me from a young age made me push at his arm.

His eyes sparked with something I couldn't interpret—aggression? possessiveness?—and his fingers tightened on my nape. Then he exhaled and released me.

I stepped back, trying to put some distance between us, but came up short against the wall. Zaq moved with me like we were partners in a slow, sensual dance.

Too close. He was too close.

Too. Close.

My skin prickled with awareness. His body warmed mine from my breasts to my thighs, and his hot male scent filled my nostrils.

I closed my eyes, but that made it worse. Now he was all around me. Zaq—everywhere.

And I wanted more.

More heat.

More scent.

More touching. Because paradoxically, he was both too close and not close enough.

Zaq set his hand on the wall beside my head. I opened my eyes—and got lost in his green-and-gold irises. He had a dark, almost black line around the outside.

What were we talking about?

Trust. Right.

I brought my focus from his eyes to his nose. Filled my lungs with air and expelled it again.

And with regret, turned back into a slayer.

I slipped under his arm and put some space between us. "Fine. You don't have to trust me, but you do have to work with me."

He faced me. "I came back, didn't I?"

"Yes, but..." I tightened my jaw and decided to save my breath. Arguing with him would get me nowhere; he clearly intended to do whatever he thought best. I'd just have to make sure he didn't give me the slip again.

"I took some cash and a switchblade," he said. "I bought a burner phone and some minutes, but I haven't used it yet. And no, you can't have the phone—and no, it's not on me. I hid it before I showed myself to you."

Okay, that was honest. "Fair enough."

"And I found the tranquilizer."

"Standard procedure. I had to be sure." I sounded defensive, even to myself. Still, it was the truth.

Zaq's nostrils flared. He took a step closer.

"Fuck your procedure. I'm willing to work with you because I need you and because I don't want to be glancing over my shoulder everywhere I go, wondering if and when you'll catch up to me. But you tranq me again and I will make you hurt, understand?"

All the spit left my mouth. Goosebumps popped up on my arms, and I had to fight the urge to back up.

Even after nine years and thousands of hours of training, an angry vampire still made me uneasy, and right then my brain didn't see much difference between Zaq and a vampire.

My fingers flexed at my sides. I wanted the comfort of my blades, but I suspected that would only piss him off more.

And I wasn't afraid of him. Not really.

The fear was a primitive reflex, a throwback to the twelve-year-old who hadn't been able to fight back.

I dipped my chin in a terse nod. "Understood."

He stared at me for a long moment. Then he shut his eyes, shook his head. Angry at both himself and me.

And don't ask how I knew—I just did.

"I went to the library," he said.

I blinked. "The library?"

Not what I'd expected him to say. Not that I knew what I *had* expected, but definitely not that.

"Yeah. The humans follow my family—you know that. Social media, the tabloids. I wanted to see what they were saying about me and my brothers."

"And?"

"There was a picture of Gabriel and Rafe the night after I was captured. And after that, nothing for two weeks. Until today when some paparazzi put up a picture of Gabriel with a woman named Camila Vittore. You know who she is?"

"Just that she and Gabriel were together for a couple years and then when things seemed to be getting serious, she took off."

He nodded. "Well, she's back. They were photographed near Gabriel's building on the Upper East Side."

"Is that a problem?"

"Hell if I know." He dragged a hand down his face. "Gabriel must have heard I'm missing. Father would've told him, and besides, he knew I was on my way back to New York. So why bother with Camila now unless she came to him? And if that's true, the timing is pretty damn suspicious. Maybe she's working with someone—Jessa, for example."

"Not Jessa." I shook my head. "Vittore's not with SI, and we wouldn't send anyone but a trained slayer into a situation like that. But I suppose she could be working for the Tremblays."

Zaq pounced on that. "So the Tremblays *are* part of this. Victorine's lieutenant was there in the airport, and later at Moreau's lair. SI's working with them."

I hesitated, not sure how much to admit to him. But I needed him to trust me. "Not by my choice. The decision to work with Prima Victorine was made by someone higher up. I can tell you that she came to us first."

His lip curled. "That's fucked up. Since when does SI take sides in a syndicate feud?"

"They don't. Not usually. In fact, this is the first time I've ever heard of it."

"That you know of."

I shrugged and glanced away, flashing on the video of Étan with his teeth in Zaq's throat. Guilt slunk, weasel-like, through my chest and settled in the pit of my stomach.

Stepping closer, I touched Zaq's arm. "I had no clue they'd drink your blood. That was never part of the plan. I'm sorry I couldn't stop them. I had to pretend I didn't care or Moreau would've kicked me out of his lair."

His muscles hardened under my fingers. Darkness smoldered way back in his eyes. "They'll pay. Étan—and Moreau, too."

It was the first time Zaq had let me see behind his mask—and he *had* been wearing a mask, more than I'd realized. A cool, controlled, let's-get-this-done mask. I felt weirdly honored that he'd allowed me to see the anger he must feel at how he'd been treated.

Zaq glanced at my hand on his arm, but not like it bothered him. No, it was a thoughtful look, like he was considering what it meant—and recalling that night in Père Lachaise.

His gaze returned to my face. The darkness remained, but now it had a sexy, speculative edge.

Heat stabbed from my breasts to my womb. I released him and stepped back. "What else did you find out?"

"Who said I found out something else?"

I shrugged. "I don't know." I couldn't explain it myself, but I was sure he was keeping something from me. "You seem upset. More upset than you'd be if this was just about Camila Vittore."

"Well, you're right. I am upset. I'm afraid we may have a traitor, someone high up in the hierarchy."

"A traitor? You found that out at the library?"

"Not at the library. I also went to a couple of vampire dives in Manhattan. And don't worry, they didn't know it was me. I can pretty much make myself invisible to vampires—it's a quirk of my glamour—and they bought it. I was trying to pin down my father's location, but no one's heard anything since he left for Paris." He shook his head. "Anyway, I heard a rumor that the Krals have a traitor. Too many things are being leaked. People are on edge."

I didn't say anything, but his gaze sharpened. "You know something."

I moved a shoulder. I wasn't ready to tell him that someone had been feeding us high quality intel—and I didn't mean Jessa. These were things that only someone high in the Kral hierarchy could know.

"Tell me, Ridley."

I shook my head.

His green eyes tracked over my face, reminding me I was dealing with a smart man, one who'd been raised by an equally smart—and ruthless—centuries-old vampire.

"You don't have to say anything. I can guess. We *do* have a traitor." He cursed. "They've been feeding you intel about me and my brothers. That's how you knew I'd be in the airport that day."

"I can tell you one thing. You didn't find any media mention of Rafe because he's undercover in Montreal. Your father sent him there to work on Zoe Tremblay. He told Rafe he believed the Tremblays were behind your kidnapping."

"So you're saying Father was suspicious of the Tremblays from the start?"

"Or he pretended to be."

"What's that supposed to mean?"

I angled my upper body forward, willing him to believe me. He seemed to view his father through rose-colored glasses, which was insane.

In the cold-blooded world of syndicate sharks, Karoly Kral was a big-ass, razor-toothed Great White.

"Think about it. If your father was trying to kill you and your brothers and wanted to throw suspicion on someone else, Victorine Tremblay would be the perfect choice."

"True. But you can turn that argument around and say that if anyone wants us dead, it's Victorine. She only signed that truce because she was forced to." He shook his head. "No. The vampires in Moreau's lair tried to tell me the same thing, and I'll tell you what I told them. We're my father's heirs, his only spawn. He forced the vampire world to accept us. Why the fuck would he be trying to kill us now?"

"I don't know. Maybe he's well aware that Victorine's behind this and he's decided to take advantage of it. Maybe he's tired of fighting your battles."

"What the fuck's that supposed to mean?"

"I know he had to fight to get you accepted by the Kral vampires. And I know some of them still aren't happy about it. Maybe they've convinced him that dhampir heirs aren't worthy of him."

Zaq's mouth tightened. "Maybe you'd be right if it was just me. But not Gabriel—he's the crown prince. And Rafe's the face of the syndicate, the man Father uses to charm the humans. He's not going to toss them aside, not heirs of his own blood."

"Are you willing to risk it?"

He stiffened. "How do you know so damn much about me and my family, anyway? The fact that Father had to fight for us to be accepted isn't general knowledge."

"Does it matter how I know?" Actually, I'd heard it from Twilight, and I wasn't sure where she'd learned it.

"Yes, damn you. I don't like knowing you were picking through my life without my knowing it."

"Don't tell me your father doesn't keep files on his enemies."

He ignored that. "What else did you discover?"

I compressed my lips.

He huffed an unpleasant laugh. "That bad, huh?"

I cleared my throat. "If by bad you mean, did I find out anything a good detective couldn't find out, then no."

He hooded his eyes. "You don't know me, Ridley. You might think you do, but you don't."

His words hung in the air like a threat.

I licked my lips and his gaze went to my mouth. That sexy edge was still there, and God help me, I liked him a little dangerous.

He took me by the shoulder, gave me a little shake. "You're wrong about my father. He loves us. Maybe not like a human loves, but in his own way he loves us. And even if he didn't, he has no other heirs of his blood."

I remained silent. Frankly, I believed Karoly Kral was perfectly capable of eliminating his own sons if he had a compelling reason.

Or maybe it was just Zaq. Maybe Karoly had seen a chance to rid himself of the son who caused him the most trouble, and he'd taken it.

Zaq released me and sank onto the mattress. He tugged his fingers through his hair. "He *loves* us," he repeated like he was trying to convince himself.

I crouched down and placed my hands on his knees. I had to make him face facts.

"Look, you're right; the Kral Syndicate does have a traitor. Somebody's feeding us intel. But if you tell anyone I told you, I'll call you a liar."

His whole body went rigid. "Someone's been feeding intel to SI?"

I nodded. "It's how we knew exactly when and where you were landing."

"Who?" he bit out.

"I don't know."

His fingers flexed like he wanted to grab my throat and shake it out of me. "Tell me, damn you." He shoved his face into mine. "Who. Is. It?"

I reared back and pulled out my switchblade, releasing the blade. "Back off, Kral."

"For fuck's sake." He scraped a derisive look over me. "I'm not going to attack you. I just want some answers."

"I don't know who it is. I swear I don't." I retracted the switchblade and touched the handle to my heart. "I only know it's someone high up. Someone who knows things only Karoly or one of his top people would know."

His jaw set. "Doesn't mean it was my dad."

"They told us what plane you were taking to New York."

"Any hacker could've found that out."

"But would a hacker have told us that Rafael was in love with Zoe Tremblay? Or that Gabriel never got over Camila Vittore?"

Zaq blinked. Rubbed a hand over his face. "Not too many people know both those things," he admitted. "Rafe didn't even tell Gabriel the whole truth about Zoe. Just me."

Putting the switchblade on the floor, I set my hands on his thighs again and leaned forward. Hating myself a little for pushing him like this, but it was in both our interests for Zaq to realize Karoly Kral was a callous prick.

"Your father could've found out. Rafe's bodyguards would've known, for example."

"Hell, I suppose you're right. And ultimately, they report to Father. He's our primus. But I still can't believe..." He shook his head.

"What if your father did more than see an opportunity to get rid of you and take it? What if he somehow manipulated things in the first place so Victorine thought Karoly was after her daughter? You know she's a little crazy when it comes to Zoe. And that summer he was in Montreal, Rafe did go after Zoe like a heat-seeking missile."

I sat back on my heels, allowing that to sink in. I had to open Zaq's mind to the possibility his father might be behind this whole thing.

Because I was starting to wonder about it myself.

"It could be his lieutenant," Zaq said. "My dad tells him everything."

"Tomas Mraz?"

He heard my doubt because he grimaced. "You're right. That doesn't make sense. Mraz is more than just my dad's right-hand man. Hell, he's his only real friend. And he's like an uncle to me and my brothers."

I turned over my palm in a you-see-what-I-mean gesture. "He could be working with your father. But I don't see him working on his own. He's not the type."

"So I can't trust my father. I can't trust anyone." His mouth twisted. "Even you."

I rose to my feet, my mind a cloud of conflicting emotions. I'd been honest with him, telling him nearly everything I knew about this situation, but here we were, back to trust again.

"We'll be fine as long as you're straight with me."

He stood up too. "Yeah? What about those vials of tranq?"

My gaze slid from his. "I told you, that's standard procedure."

"Well, to hell with your 'procedure.' I smashed the vials and tossed them in a garbage can."

He closed the space between us. His eyes weren't dark anymore. They were a bright jungle-green. They dared me to get angry about the smashed vials, but in a way, I was relieved.

It was one thing to drug and kidnap a man I believed to be a monster. But I knew Zaq Kral better now, and he was no monster.

"So, Ridley No-Last-Name." His gaze challenged me. "Can I trust you?"

I stared up at him. I wanted to argue that yes, he could trust me, but when it came right down to it, could he?

Yes, I was doing everything I could to help him, to keep him alive. But if Crow gave me a direct order to stake him, would I disobey?

It felt like my heart was being ripped in two. When you stripped all else away, who was left?

The slayer? Or the woman?

Then Zaq cupped my face and I forgot everything but him. "Say it." A low murmur that vibrated down my spine. "Tell me I can trust you. Even if it's a lie."

I closed my eyes, unable to take the intensity of that jungle-green gaze.

He made a pained sound low in his throat, touched his lips to my temple. "Lie to me, Ridley."

My heart lurched like it was trying to jump from my chest to his. I took a shuddering breath, and then the words tore themselves out of my lungs like a small explosion. "It wouldn't be a lie."

Because, somehow, someway, I was going to find a way to keep Zaq Kral alive.

I grabbed his shoulders, raised onto my toes and smashed my mouth to his in a desperate, you-can-believe-me kiss.

22
ZAQ

Ridley's kiss felt like the truth.

Her heartbeat sped up and she pressed her body against mine with a raw urgency that seemed real.

But maybe I was lying to myself.

She could be playing you.

I'd heard the stories. Slayers would do almost anything to get to their target. Maybe she thought that if she had sex with me, I'd be easier to control.

That didn't stop my arms from wrapping themselves around her and pulling her up against me. And it didn't stop my mouth from kissing her back.

She tasted warm and wet, her mouth moving seductively beneath mine.

Who cared if she was playing me? I'd just play her right back.

I palmed one of her ass cheeks, working my fingers under the frayed threads of her jeans shorts.

Gods, the woman did something for frayed shorts. She should wear them all day. Every day. Even in the winter.

Watching her from the shadows, I'd itched to take hold of the threads and jerk, ripping the shorts off her trim little ass. And then I'd drag her panties off and bend her over...

Ridley took a breath, changed the angle of her mouth and dove back in.

But I'd had time to catch my breath as well, and I wanted to slow things down. Otherwise things were going to end too fast.

Hot and heavy could be good, but I wanted to savor her. Do a couple of the things I'd fantasized about.

I threaded my fingers through her corn silk hair and broke the kiss. Her eyes were closed. She made a needy sound and tried to bring her mouth back to mine, but I tightened my grip on her hair, halting her.

Her eyelids fluttered, then opened. "Is something wrong?" Her gaze darted between my eyes.

"No. I'm just—" I started to say I was slowing things down, but she didn't let me finish. Instead, she pushed at my chest, straining to get away.

I resisted for a few seconds, then let her go.

She took a stumbling step backward until her back hit the wall. A loud exhale escaped her lips. "You're right. This is a bad idea."

A harsh laugh tore from my throat. "No. It's not. It's a very good idea."

She set her feet a little apart. A warrior's stance, hands fisted at her sides. A pulse beat at the base of her soft, pretty throat.

A throat I literally ached to drink from—and if that made me a monster, then I was guilty as charged.

Her head tilted. She studied me. "You want this—me?"

"You have to ask?" I gestured to where my erection strained against the fly of my jeans.

She glanced down. "Oh." The corner of her mouth edged up in a sassy little smile that was like an erotic lick up my spine.

I dragged off my shirt, because it was damn hot in here even this late at night, and eased my zipper open because my dick needed the space.

Her gaze tracked my movements. Her swallow was audible. Her mouth opened. Closed.

Triumph surged through me. She wanted me. And by the Dark Lady, I wanted her.

The beast was alive, but this was no longer about revenge or punishment or bending her to my will. Well, maybe it *was* about bending her to my will, at least in part.

Whatever. All I knew was that I wanted Ridley No-Last-Name with a blood-pounding, can't-run-from-it craving.

"Like what you see?" I closed the space between us.

A faint flush tinged her cheeks. She nodded, swallowed again, the movement working the muscles of her throat. A movement that drew my gaze to her long, creamy neck.

Without my willing it, my hand reached out.

Her eyes widened but she held her ground. I touched her throat. Her heartbeat leapt in response, and she shuddered.

I stroked a fingertip over her throbbing pulse, then continued down her silky flesh. Tracing her collarbones, one at a time, then moving lower to the upper curve of her breast beneath the plain gray athletic bra.

That plain, utilitarian undergarment was so Ridley, I almost smiled, but I knew she'd misunderstand. The bra—so different from the sexy underthings most of my women went for—sent tenderness curling through me.

No. Not tenderness.

This is fucking. Nothing else.

I removed my hand from her breast. "Take off your bra."

It was a demand, not a request. I was determined to keep this about sex. Not tenderness.

Her eyes flashed. I waited for her to tell me to go to hell or pull one of those damned switchblades on me.

But she didn't. Her gaze flicked to my mouth. She licked her lips and I stifled a groan.

I stepped back and folded my arms over my chest. "Do it."

Her eyes came back to mine. Her pupils had expanded. They were huge and black, edged by a thin rim of gray that was almost silver.

I'm not sure what I'd have done if she'd said no. The beast was riding me hard.

I wanted her submission. I wanted her real and raw and begging me for anything I chose to give her.

But she didn't say no.

She crossed her arms over her torso and pulled her bra over her head, holding my gaze the whole time. The bra dropped to the floor.

I looked at her breasts. Hell, I devoured them with my eyes. They were as I'd pictured them, only better. Perfect apple-sized globes. Glowing, fine-grained skin topped with soft pink nipples.

My dick jerked and thrust against my boxers.

I crossed the step between us so I could caress her breasts. The skin was even softer than it looked. I brushed my thumbs over the points of her nipples. They hardened and I gave them a pinch. She moaned low in her throat.

I crowded closer, trapping her between my body and the wall.

Her eyelids lowered to half-mast. She put her hands over mine, helping me touch her.

Fuck that.

I wanted her to suffer—just a little.

I wanted her to beg—more than a little.

I caught her wrists and set them against the wall by her head. Growled, "Keep them there."

She blinked at me, then glanced from one arm to the other.

I think we both realized at the same time that I'd put her in the position I'd been forced to hold in the cell.

She grimaced. She opened her mouth and started to apologize—and I didn't want to hear it. Not again.

I believed she was sorry about how I'd been treated. What I didn't know was if I could forgive her. But at this moment, it didn't matter.

I covered her mouth with my left hand and touched my lips to her throat. She tensed, and I could tell she was afraid I was going to drink from her. She apparently had issues around blood-drinking.

Right then I'd have given up the rest of my trust fund to sink my teeth into her throat. She was beautiful, we were alone. She'd kissed me first. Taken her own bra off.

And the dark bastard in me growled that she *owed* me.

But I'd never taken blood from an unwilling woman in my life, and something wouldn't let me do it now.

A vampire would probably shake their head, say I was a weak dhampir. Hell, Étan had said it straight to my face. But Étan was an asshole.

So instead I murmured, "You're sorry? Then make it up to me," and scraped my teeth over her skin.

She shuddered and grabbed my shoulders. "Zaq, I—"

I licked the scrape I'd made. "Shh. I know."

More and more, I seemed to *know* what she wanted. Right now she wanted kisses and maybe a little teeth, but she didn't want me to feed from her.

I nipped her under her jaw. "I'm not going to drink from you. Not today. But someday you're going to beg me to drink from you and, Ridley, it's going to lead to the best fucking you've ever had. But for now, I want you to put your hands against the wall like I told you."

"Is this payback?"

I hesitated. "Maybe. A little. But it's not just payback. It's me showing you how good things can be when you let me take charge."

Her breath hitched. "Oh."

"But," I added, "move those hands from the wall again and I *will* stop."

She immediately set her hands on either side of her head.

I stepped back a few inches so I could take her in. "Higher. Stretch them over your head."

She obeyed, moving her hands up the wall. The position raised her breasts. She looked so beautiful, so ready for anything I wanted to give her.

"Good girl." I caught a rosy nipple between my fingers and twisted it a little. "I've had fantasies about you."

"Me, too. About you." She grimaced. "That's so messed up, isn't it?"

"Maybe." I tugged at her other nipple, harder. She sucked in a breath and squeezed her thighs together. Her legs were long and supple. I could've watched the muscles flex in her thighs all night. "But who cares?"

She licked her pretty lips. Her breasts heaved like she couldn't take in enough air.

I set a hand on her stomach. "Stay where you are."

Her chin dipped in a jerky nod. "Okay."

I bent my head and tongued her areola, sliding my hand beneath her waistband and into her boyshort panties. I worked my hand lower and used my middle finger to toy with her clit.

Her body twisted against the wall. "Zaq…"

I went to my knees, sending her a stern look. "Remember what happens if you move your hands?"

She licked her lips. "Yes."

"Good." I undid her shorts and jerked them and her panties down her thighs.

She moaned and I glanced up. Her fingers opened and closed, but she kept her hands above her head.

I moved my hands down her waist and over her hips. The darkness—the beast, my vampire-half—loved having her confined by her clothes and her hands against the wall.

Hell, I'll be honest; it wasn't just the vampire that loved it. *I* loved it—Zaquiel Kral. It was fucking erotic to have this strong, tough woman at my mercy.

And she was loving it. If she didn't, she wouldn't be moaning my name and keeping her hands where I'd told her.

I dug my fingers into her ass and kissed her clit. Then I tongued it. Her moans turned into whimpers

I kept licking and kissing her. Tasting her. Lapping up her sexy, salty woman-spice.

She tried to widen her legs to give me greater access but her shorts only allowed her to open them an inch further. She brought her hands down and tried to push them lower herself.

"Uh-uh," I said against her sex. I grabbed her hands and held them to the wall by her hips. "Do I have to stop?"

Her breath hitched. "No. Don't stop."

"Then be good." I licked a circle around her clit. Making her wait.

She cursed me, and then she pleaded. "Don't stop, don't stop, don't-stop, pleasepleaseplease."

Oh, yeah, I liked hearing Ridley beg.

I sucked her clit into my mouth.

Her body bowed and her thighs flexed around my face. "I want—"

I sucked and tongued her for a minute, then stopped and looked up at her. "What do you want?"

She looked down at me, dazed, her lower lip reddened from where she must have bitten it. "You."

"Say it." I nipped her taut little stomach. "Where do you want me?"

"I want you. Inside me."

My answer was more growl than speech. I stood up and dragged off my jeans and boxers.

Ridley stared at me, dazed, still against the wall.

I stalked back to her, put my hands on either side of her head, caging her in, and gave her a long, wet kiss. "Get undressed." I stepped back.

She lurched into motion, tugging her clothes the rest of the way down her legs and kicking them off in a couple of lithe moves.

I took her by the waist and swung her around. Walked her backward until her calves hit the mattress.

She sat down and I knelt between her legs. My hands were on her thighs. Her gaze went to my wrists. The wounds had finally healed over, but the silver had left a thick band of scar tissue.

Her teeth dug into her lower lip. "I'm sorry about that, too. I wish things were dif—"

I was tired of her apologizing. I pushed her legs further apart.

"You don't have to keep saying you're sorry. And don't make this more than it is. This is just fucking, and we both know it."

I said the words, even though I wasn't sure I believed them. Maybe I was saying them for myself, not her.

Something flashed in Ridley's eyes. Sadness, but I pretended I hadn't seen.

She put her hands on the mattress. I waited for her nod, then took my hand from her mouth and trailed my fingers up her inner thighs. Touched the deep pink flower at the center. She was flushed and slick with arousal.

I played with her clit. It was swollen, and I could tell from how she sucked in a breath when I caressed her with my thumb that it was sensitive.

"I want to taste you here." I ran my finger down her slit. "Would you like that?"

Her inner thighs constricted. She moistened her lips, nodded.

"Say it. Say you want me to taste your pussy."

She obediently repeated the words in a low, needy voice. "I want you to taste my pussy."

I didn't move.

"Zaq," I prompted. "Say you want me—Zaq—to taste your pussy."

She said it again, adding "Zaq" in husky tones that made my balls clench.

The mattress was on the floor, too low to make it easy to kneel between her legs and kiss her the way I wanted. I gave her a little spank on the side of her hip. "Scoot back."

She shimmied backward. Propping herself on her forearms, she watched as I bent forward and hooked my hands under her thighs. I captured her gaze, and, bending forward, brought my mouth to her clit again. It pulsed beneath my tongue.

Her eyes closed. She tensed and dug her heels into the mattress.

I kept licking and kissing her. Still somehow knowing what she wanted, exactly what worked for her and what didn't.

So I gave it to her. I kissed her, sucked her soft, pulsating flesh.

Her hips rocked up and I lightly closed my teeth over her clit. That made her groan and start saying please again.

I slid two fingers into her passage and swirled my tongue over and around her sex. It took only a few more licks until she went off, her inner muscles convulsing around my fingers, a raw sound on her lips. I eased off, lightening the pressure until she relaxed onto the mattress.

I grabbed a condom—I'd picked up a box while I was out because I'd decided we were definitely going to fuck, if not tonight, then soon—tore it open and crawled back over her.

She opened her legs for me. I knelt between them without entering her, took her head between my heads and gave her a hard, hungry kiss. She squirmed beneath me, rubbing her belly against my dick.

"Now," she said when I broke the kiss. "I want you inside me."

I reached down and fitted myself to her entrance. She tilted her hips up, and I slid inside.

It was my turn to groan. Holy fuck, she was hot and tight, and I was primed from all the foreplay. I gritted my teeth and slowed. Determined to make it last.

I thrust in again, a sweet, slow slide. Her fingers dug into my ass, urging me to take her harder—and I complied. Firm, leisurely strokes. Angling myself so I was rubbing against her clit.

"Yes," she said. "That. Please."

I nipped her ear. Loving how she jolted.

"Faster," she said.

"No, I think we'll take it slow." I raised my head so I could see her face. "Do you know why?"

She wordlessly shook her head, her eyes huge in her heart-shaped face.

"Because when we're in bed, I make the rules. I say whether we go fast or slow."

Her breath caught and her pussy clenched around me. Oh yeah, she liked me dominating her.

I pulled almost all the way out and halted, putting my mouth to her ear.

"And right now," I growled, "I want to fuck you nice...and...slow." I punctuated each word with a hard stroke.

She whimpered.

I thrust in again, hard. Rubbed myself against her clit. Repeating the sequence over and over until she was pleading with me to finish it.

"I'm so close, so close."

I increased the speed of my strokes and she rasped my name and climaxed, arms and legs wrapped tight around me. The sensation of her sex milking my cock sent me over the edge.

Lightning zinged up my spine. Sparks exploded far back in my brain. I gave a guttural growl and thrust again and again, emptying myself inside her.

After, I brought my forehead to hers. My breath shuddered out.

Ridley traced a lazy path up and down my back with her fingers. "Mm," she murmured.

It was a very satisfied "mm," which made me move my head enough to give her a soft kiss. "You're beautiful," I said against her lips.

I was more than satisfied myself, and a helluva lot more relaxed than I'd been in months. I didn't want to move. I could happily have fallen asleep inside her. But I eased myself out of her and rolled to the side.

We lay on our backs, staring at the ceiling. I wanted to pull her into my arms, wanted to feel her head nestled into my shoulder, but I didn't. Cuddling her would make this into something it wasn't.

It's just fucking.

Still, I moved my hand and covered hers. I felt her look at me. I turned my head and smiled at her, and she smiled back.

I turned my gaze back to the ceiling. The smile slid off my face and the after-glow faded, leaving a hollow space in my chest.

Sex with Ridley didn't change anything except make me feel like maybe I could trust her, and that would be thinking with my balls, not my brain.

The hell with it. I was too exhausted to keep worry at the problem of Ridley No-Last-Name. I got up to dispose of the condom, then took my place on the mattress next to the wall. Closing my eyes, I dropped like a stone into sleep.

❦

Two hours later, Ridley's cell phone vibrated, waking us both. She got up and dug it out of the pocket of her shorts.

"It's a text from my alpha." She sat down on the mattress and frowned at the screen. "She says you're going to get a call and I should let you take it."

"A call?" I rubbed a hand over my face, still half-asleep. "Did she say who?"

She shook her head. "No."

The call came within minutes. Ridley handed the phone to me.

I didn't recognize the number. I rolled onto my side, propping myself on a forearm, and brought the phone to my ear. "Yeah?"

"Zaquiel Kral?" A woman's voice, tinged with a French accent.

I exchanged a baffled glance with Ridley, who lifted a shoulder in a shrug.

"That's me," I said.

"This is Zoe Tremblay."

That made me sit bolt upright. What the hell could Victorine's daughter want with me?

"You heard that?" I mouthed at Ridley.

She nodded, a perplexed line between her eyes.

"Yeah?" I said into the phone.

Zoe expelled a breath. "I'm calling about your brother. Rafael." Her tone was so empty, so devoid of emotion it chilled me even through the phone.

I gripped the case, white-knuckled. "Go on."

"He's been captured."

"Who?" I went taut, my muscles and sinews snapping to attention. "Who has him?"

"I can't tell you that. But I've been instructed to tell you that you have one week to complete your mission. If anything goes wrong, Rafael will be sold to a brothel as a blood slave."

I didn't say anything. I couldn't speak over the anger and fear.

"Did you hear me?" Her robotic tone fractured into something frantic. Like Zoe Tremblay gave a fuck about my brother. Two years ago, she'd stood by while Victorine's goons had beaten Rafe into a pulp. "Do you understand?"

"Why are you telling me this?"

"I—" She gulped, then spoke in a rush like at any moment the phone would be taken away from her. "Because they're forcing me to. But I can tell you that they mean it. If I could help, I would."

Yeah, right. "Then get him away from them."

"I can't," she said in a voice I had to strain to hear.

"I see." A hot fury clamped like a band around my chest. It was an effort to speak. "Tell them I'm already in New York," I said and ended the call.

Ridley took the phone from me and set it on her backpack.

I met her eyes. Whatever she saw in my gaze made her flinch.

Smart woman.

It took a lot to make me really, truly angry, but I was there. Scorch-the earth, take-no-prisoners enraged.

"You heard what she said?" My voice sounded harsh in my ears. I didn't wait for her nod. "She said they captured Rafe. My *brother*, Ridley. If I don't kill my father, they'll make my brother a fucking blood slave."

"God *damn* it." She spun and smashed the side of her fist against the wall.

I glared at her, my anger wanting an outlet. But unless she was a world-class actress, she was as upset as me.

"This whole thing is so messed up," she bit out. "I don't know who's running the show, us or Victorine and Moreau. But I swear I didn't know anything about this. I didn't even know Rafe had been captured."

Her chest heaved. Her gaze willed me to believe her.

"Okay." I dragged my hands down my face. "Okay. The motherfuckers have my brother. Do you know where he is?"

She shook her head. "I don't know. Montreal, maybe. But I think I can find out." She grabbed her phone and sent a text.

The reply came back almost immediately.

Ridley's lips pressed into a thin line. "He's not in Montreal. He's in Paris."

"In Paris? Why?"

"Probably to rescue you."

I cursed and closed my eyes. Getting up, I pulled on a pair of boxer-briefs and paced across the room. "Tell me Moreau doesn't have him."

Ridley pulled on a tank and a pair of boyshorts. "I don't know."

Her phone buzzed again. We were both on our feet now. She snatched it off the mattress and let out a vicious curse.

"What?" I grabbed the phone and stared at the message.

Twilight: *With M.*

"'With M'?" I showed her the text. "Is that Moreau?"

"Yeah." She swallowed audibly. "I'm sorry, but it looks like Moreau has him. Twilight is a slayer; she'd know."

Blood pounded in my ears. My brain felt like it was going to explode.

Not Rafe. Please, not Rafe.

Not my kid brother. This wasn't supposed to happen.

My fangs extended. The scars on my wrists burned and itched.

"That sonuvabitch." I tossed the phone onto the bed. "That mother-fucking, lying sonuvabitch."

Ridley's mouth was white around the edges. "This is so effed up."

I took a deep breath, willing myself to calm down. "He's dead. I'll stake the bastard myself."

Another text arrived. We both went for the phone. I got there first and read the message aloud. It was from Twilight again.

Someone informed on him. They knew he was here.

I felt sick. I shoved the phone at Ridley. "Ask who informed on him."

"Okay." She typed the question and hit *Send.*

We waited, both of us staring at the phone. The short delay seemed endless but was actually only a couple of minutes. The screen lit with the reply.

Don't know. But P3 took out Étan.

"P3 is Rafe?" When she nodded, I said, "Rafe sent that bastard Étan to his final grave?"

"Guess so." Ridley didn't seem concerned. Apparently she hadn't liked the Tremblay lieutenant any more than me.

"Good." My lips peeled in a smile.

Étan had been sent to his final grave—and by my own brother? Another so-called "weak dhampir"? Talk about poetic justice. The only thing better would've been if I'd skewered the prick myself.

I focused on the first part of the text. "So either Twilight doesn't know who's the informer—or they're not saying. Fuck, Ridley. We have to know. Tell them that."

She shook her head. "Won't do any good. Twilight won't know. Intel is on a need-to-know basis only. That way if we're captured, they can't torture it out of us."

Gods. Ridley sounded so matter of fact about the possibility she could be captured and tortured.

It made my stomach clench and my heart burn. I shouldn't care about her. But I did.

I brought my brain back to Rafe. "We have to do something."

Ridley texted back a *TY* and returned the phone to her backpack. "At least Rafael took out that prick Étan before he was captured."

"I thought you two were working together."

"I told you, that wasn't my choice." She hesitated. "Slayers, Inc., has changed in the last few years. I'm not sure whose side we're on sometimes."

I felt a stirring of hope. "What do you mean?"

"Just...I don't know why SI took the contract on you and your brothers. Your father's another story. But I don't care how much Victorine is paying us to take you three out, too, that's not how we work." She grimaced. "Especially the contract on you. Now that I know you, it makes even less sense. Before I met you, I figured you must be doing something undercover for your father's syndicate—maybe recruiting blood slaves while pretending to help those poor displaced people. But that's not true, is it? You really do all those things—those good things—that they say you do. You're for real."

"I don't know how 'for real' I am, but yeah, I was in Aleppo because I was trying to help. And the Kral Syndicate doesn't keep blood slaves, not these days. My father banned the practice years ago. And if we did, we could find displaced humans right here in New York or Baltimore or Atlanta or New Orleans." I named the cities where the syndicate had a large presence, adding, "I'm not even a made man in the syndicate. Yeah, I work for my father from time to time, but I wouldn't recruit blood slaves for anyone."

"I see that now." Her lips pressed together and to the side in an ashamed expression. "I wanted to think the worst of you, so I did. I can be too single-minded. It's a fault, and I know it."

Her immediate, obviously sincere apology defused my anger somewhat. I jerked my chin in acknowledgment.

Ridley pulled at her lip, thinking. "Whoever informed on Rafe is someone high up. Your father wouldn't have told many people that he was sending him to Montreal. And apparently, they knew he'd gone to Paris with Princess Zoe."

I sank onto the mattress. "So again, we're down to my father, his lieutenant, and maybe a few other people. Gabriel probably knew, for instance. And he could've told Camila, although I doubt it."

I was still tired and my joints ached. Even my fucking eyes burned. The side effects from the silver poisoning seemed to ebb and flow, and right now I was pretty sure I was spiking a fever again.

But what did that matter compared to what Rafe was going through?

I pressed the heels of my palms to my burning eyes.

Desperate to do something. Right. Now.

But that could play into their hands. Whoever the hell "they" were.

While I was in Manhattan, I'd heard something I was still trying to make sense of. Andre Redbone, a Kral kapitán, had been slain by one of our own men. His elimination, along with my disappearance, had sent shock waves through the Kral Syndicate.

"Zaq?" Reaper's concerned voice made me lower my hands.

"Yeah." My mind was spinning five different directions like a juggler rotating a plate on his right index finger, his left index finger, a foot, his knee and his nose. "We need a plan."

"They can't know I'm helping you." Her brows were lowered, her mouth pulled into a distressed, sideways oval.

I focused on her. She was Rafe's best chance to get out of this alive. "We had a deal, and I kept my part of it. You'd better fucking make sure my brother stays safe or I'm walking."

"No, you won't."

"Try me."

She rubbed her forehead. "Look, I kept my part of the deal. I'll help anyway I can. Tell me what I can do."

I eyed her. In her own way, she was as trapped as me. If I didn't complete the mission, she'd have to stake me. Yeah, she'd sworn she wouldn't. But when it came down to it, would a slayer really choose me over her mission?

"You want the truth?"

"Of course."

"I don't know where the fuck my dad is. Those vampire dives I went to were full of rumors. He's been in and out of the city. No one knows what's going on. Apparently he's gone dark. Right now, Tomas and Gabriel are running things."

"So we find him. You must have some idea, some place you haven't looked yet."

I considered her for a beat and made up my mind. "Yeah. I do."

❧ 23 ❧

RIDLEY

"This way." Zaq put a hand on my lower back and steered me toward a dumpster on West 42nd Street.

I tugged at my short red skirt and slanted him a glance. He'd been on edge ever since Zoe Tremblay's call last night. His face was grim, his body taut with tension.

"Relax." Zaq unbent enough to caress my bottom. "Let those hips sway."

It was late Wednesday evening, and we were on our way to meet with Zaq's contact in the New York underworld. Apparently, if I wore my usual clothes, I'd stick out like a sore thumb—or to be exact, a slayer—which would open us to attack and mean we learned zilch.

That's what Zaq had said anyway. I had serious doubts, though. The man was a closet sadist. At least he'd let me wear my combat boots instead of the kitten heels he'd wanted me to buy.

I shot him a you-will-die look. "Easy for you to say. And take your hand off my ass."

His lips twitched, which made me glad I'd taken a chance and teased him a little.

"Those legs of yours are the best camouflage," he said. "Everyone will be looking at them instead of your face. And my hand is staying right where it is, babe." He squeezed my butt cheek. "I'm your master, remember?"

I snorted. "Don't push your luck, *babe*."

And then I gave him a wide smile, because I was supposed to be a thrall.

Zaq's thrall.

But not the pampered, well-paid toy of a rich syndicate prince. No, I was the blood-addicted thrall of a sleazy underworld vampire.

The sleazy underworld vampire would be Zaq. A barber had trimmed his beard back to a sexy dark stubble and given him an 80s-style haircut with sideburns and bangs that dipped over the center of his forehead. For tonight's outing, Zaq had slicked down his hair and donned a bronze sharkskin suit that we'd picked up at the same thrift store where we'd bought my skirt.

We'd both put on pale makeup, and I'd painted dark circles under my eyes and bite marks on my throat. Zaq had bought braided leather bands to hide the scars on his wrists.

Zaq slipped around the back of the dumpster and ran his hands up the brick wall behind it. He pressed a brick and a door slid open, revealing a flight of rusty metal stairs.

We started down, him going first.

"Careful," he told me. "They're steep and a little shaky."

I nodded. "Don't worry. I have good balance."

"I noticed. There's not much you're not good at, is there?"

I stopped and stared down at his back, mouth ajar. He'd said it so matter-of-factly, like it was a given: Ridley is good at pretty much everything.

I only wished it were true, because this thing between me and Zaq confused the hell out of me. I wasn't good at relationships. I was a relationship-virgin, in fact.

I'd never really had a boyfriend. I hadn't even dated. I'd had hook-ups, of course, but that was it.

Zaq liked me. I could feel that. And the sex had felt like more than fucking, despite what he'd said.

But I wanted more. I wanted his trust, even though I probably didn't deserve it.

I heaved a sigh. Gods, I was messed up.

And he was already ten steps below me. I jogged down the steps after him.

We descended several flights before arriving in an abandoned subway tunnel. The white tiles were cracked and grimy. Water dripped from the ceiling and puddled on the concrete floor between rusty metal tracks. The only light came from a long way to our right where subways rumbled by out of sight; without my enhanced night vision, I'd have been walking blind.

Zaq took my hand and we picked our way along the wet concrete floor. "When it rains," he said, "the tunnel floods to your waist. Even the homeless stay away. The only things that live here are vampires and rats."

On cue, a pair of eyes glowed red a few yards away at ankle height. A frisson of fear went up my spine. A rat, and it was a good sixteen inches long. I swallowed—hard—and hoped it had eaten recently, because it appeared to be sizing up my ankles for its next meal.

"Damn, Kral. You sure know how to show a girl a good time."

"They don't attack. They're too smart to attack anything down here that walks on two legs."

His barely concealed amusement made me want to stick something sharp in him, but we weren't carrying weapons. Zaq had said they'd only confiscate them. "Down there, it's their world. We have to play by their rules." We'd left my phone at the squat for the same reason.

I kept a wary eye on the rat until it scampered off.

We drew even with a tunnel leading off the main tunnel and Zaq stopped. Several other pairs of eyes glowed at intervals down the side tunnel. These eyes weren't at ankle height, and they shone blue at the edges.

"Here we go," Zaq said out of the side of his mouth.

I nodded.

Every big city in the world had vampire outcasts like those in Père Lachaise, the vampires who'd never joined a syndicate or had been thrown out. In New York, they lived in the abandoned subway tunnels beneath Manhattan. I knew about them, of course, but I'd never been down here before. Slayers who entered the underworld without an invitation tended to disappear.

Zaq released my hand and stepped in front of me. "It's Batman. I'm here to see Spider."

Batman and Spider? I swallowed a sudden, inappropriate urge to laugh.

The closest pair of eyes came nearer, and I saw they were attached to a lanky vampire with a face like the hot billionaire in *Crazy Rich Asians* and a shock of purple layered over his black hair.

"George." Zaq nodded hello.

George didn't return his nod. "Who's the woman?"

"Mine."

George leaned to the left so he could see around Zaq. His eyes tracked up and down my body like I was for sale and he was in the mood to buy.

My shoulders tightened with a mix of anger and uneasiness. Inside, I cursed myself for agreeing to Zaq's "no blades" edict.

Zaq reached back and pulled me up next to him. He tucked me under his arm, making it clear I was under his protection. I leaned into Zaq and fluttered my eyelashes at him, playing the dazed, love-struck addict for all I was worth.

"I said, *she's mine*," Zaq told George in menacing tones.

My inner thighs constricted. God, I liked hearing me claim me, even if it was only for George's benefit.

The vampire brought his gaze back to Zaq. "Spider know you're coming?"

"He'll see me."

"Arms out."

Zaq obeyed and nodded at me to do the same. Two vampires stepped out of the darkness and patted us down for weapons.

"They're clean," they told George, and he waved a hand for us to precede him down the track. I felt him staring at my ass the whole time, but like Zaq had predicted, at least he wasn't paying attention to my face.

We came to a Y in the track. "Take the right turn," George said.

We did and kept walking. The darkness grew thicker until I could only see a few feet in front of me.

Abruptly, a torch on the wall burst into flames. The sudden light seared my eyeballs. I screwed them shut and threw up a hand in front of my face.

When I opened my eyes again, two new vampires—a male and a female—waited a few yards away in a large, surprisingly homey cavern lit by kerosene torches.

"Spider." Zaq strode forward and shook the male's hand. "It's good to see you."

The underworld lord was thin and darkly gorgeous with an Afro the size of a basketball and long, spiderlike fingers that I surmised were the reason behind his nickname.

The female stood at attention a few feet behind him, her thick black braid falling forward over one shoulder. She had the face of a South Asian goddess, a Barbie doll body and a pair of silver daggers strapped over her short red skirt.

Spider clapped Zaq on the shoulder and eyed his sharkskin suit. "Upped your style game, I see."

Zaq barked a laugh. "The flashier you are, the less they see."

"Truth. So what brings you here?"

"That's for your ears only."

Spider jerked his head at George. "Wait at the end of the tunnel. And keep everyone else out."

George nodded and headed back the way he'd come.

Spider eyed me. "Who's this?"

Zaq shrugged. "No one important."

"Hmm." Spider's appraisal was 180 degrees from George's. His eyes were hard and all-knowing, and he focused on my face like he was trying to memorize my features—or figure out where he'd seen me before.

Beside me, Zaq tensed. I dulled my dhampir-shine even further—we'd agreed it was better if the underworld vampires believed I was human—and gazed at Spider's shoulder.

A full thirty seconds ticked past before Spider indicated a couch at the rear of the cavern. "Wait there, beautiful."

I'd passed inspection. I released a soundless breath of relief and minced past Spider and the Barbie doll.

The cavern was basically an underground apartment, and we were in the kitchen/living room. I sat on the couch and ran a hand over the soft red fabric. The couch had been dressed up with orange-and-bronze throw pillows, as had the armchairs set at angles on either side of the couch. The walls were draped with red curtains bordered in orange, and on the slate floor was a colorful braided rug.

The cavern also held a large barbecue grill and a long wooden table with a dozen chairs. To my right was a walk-in pantry stocked with food, blood-wine and other staples, and in a smaller cave to the left I glimpsed a big bed.

Compared to the Lachaise vampires, Spider and his people lived in a palace.

Zaq and Spider moved to the side of the room and conducted a heated discussion in subvocal tones. The Barbie doll remained where she was, her eyes trained on the two men, clearly straining to hear what was said.

I slouched against the couch's arm like the blood addict I was supposed to be and strained my own ears, but all I caught were a few words here and there.

"Father..."

"My brothers..."

"Redbone is..." Spider drew an index finger across his throat.

What? I fiddled with a cushion, keeping my expression carefully blank. The only Redbone I knew of was Andre Redbone, the kapitán of the Kral Syndicate's Louisiana Coven.

Zaq nodded like he already knew about Redbone. Something he hadn't told me, apparently.

Spider said something else.

Zaq's head snapped back in shock. "A coup?" Then he lowered his voice, and maddeningly, I didn't catch anything else.

The whole discussion took less than ten minutes. Then Spider pressed a buzzer and a young, hard-bodied human appeared from the end of the tunnel along with George.

"Refreshments for our guests," Spider told the man.

"Yes, sir."

Spider invited us to sit down. Zaq took a seat on the couch next to me, and Spider took the armchair near me. George and Barbie remained standing.

Spider's man servant poured Zaq and the vampires each a glass of blood-wine and brought it around. Me, he gave a glass of regular wine.

Zaq nudged me with his thigh, but I didn't need the nudge. If a vampire invited you to have a drink with him, then you did.

Zaq raised a glass to Spider. "May you always drink from young throats."

"And may you have your choice of blood and beautiful women."

He touched his glass to first Zaq's, then mine, honoring me as Zaq's guest even though he believed I was human and a thrall at that. He obviously held Zaq in high regard.

I murmured, "To your health," and sipped my wine as if I wasn't dying to know what Zaq had found out.

Thirty minutes dragged by while we made small talk. At last Zaq rose to his feet, pulling me up with him. He thanked Spider for his hospitality and steered me toward the exit.

Spider unfolded his long legs and stood as well. His long fingers closed on my arm. "Go on," he told Zaq.

I concealed my alarm. What could he want with me? I was supposed to be unimportant. A blood-addicted thrall.

Zaq bared his fangs. "She stays with me."

Spider growled and showed his own fangs. Suddenly, the air was thick with testosterone.

My adrenaline was pumping. I allowed my heart to speed up like a nervous human's would, but not too much, so Spider wouldn't think I was hiding something.

I gave Spider a smile and a helpless shrug, playing up to him as the alpha of this little vampire cell. To Zaq, I said, "It's okay."

He flicked me a glance. "No. It's not. Let her go," he told the vampire lord in a cold, syndicate-prince voice, and took my other arm.

The Barbie doll moved forward, a dagger in each hand, and she obviously knew how to use them.

Ok-kay. Not a Barbie doll after all. Unless she was Slayer Barbie.

Spider heaved a breath. "Chill, man. I don't have designs on your woman. I just have some business with her. Alone."

Zaq's mouth thinned.

"It's okay," I said again.

"Fine," he said after another tension-filled few seconds. "I'll wait over there." He moved a few feet into the tunnel and turned to face us, arms folded over his chest.

Spider jerked his head for Slayer Barbie to move back. "Keep an eye on Batman."

She nodded and walked over to Zaq. He gave her a crooked smile and raised his hands in an I'm-harmless gesture. Her back was to me, but something in the way she tilted her head made me sure she'd smiled back.

Jesus, the man could charm the skin off a snake.

Spider lowered his head. "A warning," he murmured. "The Crow flies crooked."

"Excuse me?"

His eyes slit. "Let's not play games, okay? I know who you are and why you're in the city."

I stilled. "Oh?"

"Don't worry. The others bought the lie that you're Batman's thrall. But information is my business. Knowing things no one else knows pays for this cozy crib." He indicated the cavern, his mouth bent in a self-mocking smile.

I hesitated. But Spider had put himself out to deliver the cryptic warning—and I wanted to know more.

"What do you mean, 'the Crow flies crooked'?"

He dipped his head so his mouth hovered next to my ear, so close I felt his breath, cool and dry. "Your boss is out of control. She'd sacrifice anyone or anything for the cause. Even the famous Reaper."

A chill tripped down my spine. My stomach churned uneasily.

He's lying.

Crow was like a mother to me. A hard-ass, tough-love mother, yeah—but she'd been there for me when no one else had.

"And you're telling me this because—?"

He shrugged. "I make more money when things are stable with the syndicates. Your bosses are fucking that up for me. So, this time, the info's on me. Next time, you pay."

"Understood." Suddenly, the cavern's dank air was oppressive.

Zaq had been staring at us, brow lowered, his stubbled jaw tight. Now he returned to the cavern and took my arm.

"We're done here," he told Spider. "I'll transfer the money to your account ASAP."

The underworld lord stuck out a long-fingered hand. "A pleasure doing business with you."

Zaq shook it and hustled me back into the cavern.

We took the subway back uptown. When we arrived in the Bronx, the sun had risen. Zaq pulled me to the side before we entered the squat.

"You go ahead. I need to go back to Manhattan."

"To do what?"

"I can't tell you."

"Can't—or won't?"

His face was drawn, his shoulders slumped in tiredness. He massaged the bridge of his nose. "Won't, then. And don't give me that crap about trusting you—unless you intend to tell me what Spider told you."

I pressed my lips together. I felt as tired as he looked, and hollow inside.

"No. It's a lie, anyway. It makes no fucking sense."

"All right." He turned to leave but I caught his arm.

"Where are you going? To your father?"

"No. Spider didn't know where he was. He hasn't been seen for over a week. Spider thought he was out of the country, actually."

"Then don't go. You're tired. You need sleep. You've been up—what, twenty hours now? And I know you only slept a few hours on the plane."

"I have to." His expression was stark. "Rafe... Spider told me something, something that worries me."

"What?"

"Andre Redbone. He was staked sometime last week. You know who he is?"

I released his arm. "A Kral kapitán."

"Yeah. I actually heard a rumor about Redbone last night, that someone in the Kral inner circle staked him—Tomas or Gabriel—which is bad enough. But Spider doesn't believe it. He thinks it must have been my father, and I don't know why Father would've staked Redbone. Hell, I don't know why Tomas or Gabriel would've staked him unless he was the traitor."

I scrunched my mouth to the side, thinking. "You say he was staked last week? Do you know what day?"

"No. Spider heard Thursday night—that's all he could tell me."

"It's possible Redbone was a traitor, but we've had intel since then."

"Fuck." Zaq lowered his eyes in a slow blink. "I have to..." His whole body seemed to droop. "Actually I don't know what to do."

"Then sleep on it. You have a week. You said yourself your father may not even be in the country. Keep pushing yourself like this and you're going to collapse again and then you won't be any good to anyone, especially Rafe."

"Do you care? Really?" His voice was harsh. "About me or Rafe?"

I flinched and tried to cover it by rubbing my nose.

But he noticed because he looked away. "Fine. I'll lie down for a few hours." He released a breath. "I *am* tired. So damn tired."

Back in my room, we got ready for bed. I had my daily glass of blood-wine, and Zaq downed a couple of glasses in rapid succession.

We stripped to our underwear and lay side by side on the mattress.

I wondered what I'd do if he made a move. Then I wondered what he'd do if I made a move.

But neither of us made a move.

Instead we stared at the ceiling unmoving. Zaq's right pinkie was a scant inch from my left, but it felt like he was on the other side of the planet.

❧ 24 ❧
ZAQ

I woke up around noon the next day, tired and a little achy. I still hadn't shaken off the aftereffects of the silver poisoning.

But I couldn't lie around, waiting to get better. I had to keep pushing. Already, two of the seven days they'd given me had passed.

Spider had told me the Kral Syndicate was like a ticking bomb. One more spark could blow everything sky-high.

Andre Redbone's passing had sent a shock wave through the syndicate, and then Tomas had disappeared too. With my father away, rumors were flying fast and thick.

Some said Redbone was a traitor who'd been staked when he attacked Gabriel.

Others insisted the kapitán had been loyal, that it was Gabriel who was the traitor. They said Redbone was only the beginning, that Gabriel—or maybe me or Rafe—had staked Tomas, too. That we three brothers were coming after all the kapitáns, one by one. With my father's inner circle eliminated, it would be easy to take him out next. It didn't help that neither Rafe nor I had been seen in over a week.

Then there were the people who blamed it all on my father, said he'd gone blood mad and was staking all his top people.

My father, blood mad? That was like saying Macbeth had been insane when he'd murdered his king.

Cold, ruthless and complicated as fuck? Yes.

But not insane.

And yet I *knew* Gabriel wasn't planning a coup with me and Rafe. So either Andre Redbone had attacked Gabriel and been staked by my brother in self-defense—or my father was somehow involved in this.

I was drenched in sweat. Ridley's window air conditioning unit was no match for the heat and humidity of a New York City summer.

I got out of bed and dragged my hands down my damp face. Unsure what to do or who to believe. Just knowing I had to do something.

Ridley sat up and swung her legs to the floor. "You're still here."

"Yeah. I'm going to take a shower and head back into the city."

"I'm coming with you."

"No."

She let out a put-upon sigh. "I'm not asking for your permission, Kral. Either take me with you, or I'll follow in the shadows."

I sent her a hard look. "Maybe I shouldn't have smashed those vials of tranq."

"Yeah?" Her pretty mouth formed a stubborn line. "Something you should know—I don't respond well to threats."

That did it. Bending down, I planted my hands on either side of her thighs.

Her bare thighs, since all she'd worn to bed was a tank and a pair of boyshorts—and damn the woman for making me notice when I should be thinking of Rafe, and only of Rafe.

"Maybe I'll tie you up and leave you here."

Her eyes flickered. "You have to catch me first."

My smile was slow and nasty. "Try me."

Her inner thighs clenched. The spicy scent of her arousal filled my nostrils.

So the idea of being restrained turned her on. My dick twitched, liking the idea a little too much.

She chewed on her full lower lip. I tracked the movement, itching to sink my own teeth into her soft pink flesh.

And that itch gave my next sentences a rough edge. "Fine. Come to Manhattan then. But you can't come with me into headquarters."

Her eyes narrowed. "You're going inside Kral headquarters? Why?"

"To get some answers. I have an idea, a way to get information that might help me figure out what, exactly, is going on. But I'm damned if I'll take a slayer into our headquarters."

"You can get in and out without anyone knowing?"

"Yeah. Which is why you can't come with me—it'd be like handing you the keys to the front door."

Her chest rose and fell. My gaze flicked to her breasts, the nipples hard points beneath the soft black tank.

Her throat worked, and beneath my boxers, my half-hard dick went to full mast.

I pulled back a few inches and focused on her face, trying not to think about how easy it would be to drag off her boyshorts, press her to the mattress and sink into her wet, pretty pussy.

I needed to keep my head clear, and that meant no sex with Ridley No-Last-Name.

"Look," I told her. "I'm not going to do anything stupid. Not when my brother's life is on the line. No one will know I'm there. I'll get in and get out as fast as I can."

She growled. "Fine." A lithe twist of her body and she stood a few feet away, looking down at where I was still crouched over the mattress. The woman was a freaking eel. "You take me with you, and I promise to wait outside the building. But I want a shower too. And food."

I rose to my feet. "We can get something to eat in the city."

⚜

By the time we got to lower Manhattan and ate lunch, it was after three p.m. I left Ridley at Washington Square Park and slipped into the shadows to walk the last few blocks.

The Kral headquarters were tucked beneath a brownstone in Greenwich Village. I approached the building from the small, well-kept garden at the side.

Headquarters was never empty. There'd be a couple of dhampir or human soldiers on security detail, and the cleaning crew and maintenance men would be doing their thing. But if you wanted to sneak inside—and your father had built a secret underground entrance known only to five people—him, his lieutenant, and his three sons—then mid-afternoon was hands-down the best time. Even the PAs and other administrative staff didn't arrive until five.

I'd already rejected going directly to Father's office. It was located three floors below the surface and behind multiple layers of security. Instead I shadowed the cleaning crew—a man and a woman—until they were on the floor above his office where Gabriel and Tomas's offices were located.

No one else but me and Rafe knew this, but Father, Tomas and Gabriel all had a way to put their security cams on a continuous, repetitive loop so to security, it appeared their offices were empty.

The man went into Gabriel's office and the woman into Tomas's. I followed the woman.

Tomas's office was like an upscale version of a 1940s private eye's office. Plain mahogany furniture and no computer because he didn't trust modern tech other than cell phones. He kept his notes in old-fashioned manila folders and stored them in metal filing cabinets.

Father shook his head over it, but Tomas was the Kral Syndicate's muscle, not the brains. Not that he wasn't smart, but he was smart like a grizzly bear, preferring brute force over diplomacy. He and my father made a perfect team, their strengths complementing each other.

If anyone knew what had really happened between Gabriel and Andre Redbone, it would be Tomas.

I pressed myself against a wall and waited until the cleaning lady finished and left, locking the door behind her. Then I dropped out of the shadows and hit the button under Tomas's desk to activate the security cam loop. It was set to erase the last ten seconds so my presence wouldn't be detected.

At first I couldn't find any reference to me or my brothers until I realized he referred to us each by code. The code was simple enough. He'd named us *One*, *Two* and *Three* in the order of our birth. The tricky part was he used the Slovak words, not English. Fortunately, I'd picked up enough Slovak from him and my father to figure that out.

After that, locating our three files was easy—and yes, Tomas kept files on all three of us.

No surprise there.

I wasn't even that surprised at the undercurrent of disdain in his notes on us. Most vampires looked down on half-human dhampirs like me and my brothers.

Unfortunately, most of his notes were written in Slovak except for the occasional memo or clipping in English, and my knowledge of Slovak didn't extend that far.

I focused on his recent notes about Gabriel. I sorted through them, reading what I could.

I found references to Camila Vittore, including photos of her from the years after she'd left Gabriel. So Tomas had been keeping an eye on her. I wondered if my brother knew that.

I found copies of memos that Gabriel had sent Father, reporting on work he'd done for the syndicate, and suggestions for future business. At times Gabriel's impatience bled through. He wanted more responsibility, and my father was reluctant to give it to him, even though as crown prince, Gabriel was next in line to take over the syndicate.

I kept looking. Yeah, it was interesting that Tomas had copies of Gabriel's private correspondence with Father, but I needed more.

I pulled out a handwritten note about Andre Redbone. It was in Slovak, but I could make out a few words, enough to tell me it was a record of Redbone's passing, and that yes, it had been Gabriel who'd sent him to his final grave.

I turned it over and stared at the scribbled English words on the other side. They were in pencil, like Tomas had been working out what he wanted to say in English before writing a more formal note.

He hadn't bothered with his code. Instead, he used our initials—G, Z & R.

G, Z & R plotting against you? Feeding intel to SI. All or just G?

My fingers tightened on the piece of paper. I wanted to shred the damn thing, but I forced myself to release it before I crumpled it.

Did Tomas actually believe we were plotting against our own father, or was he simply noting something he'd heard?

And had he passed it on to my father?

I snorted. Of course he had. No way Tomas would've kept quiet about something like that.

So the real question was, did Father believe it?

I pressed the heels of my hands to my eyes, mind racing and circling like a hamster in a wheel.

What had made Tomas write that note? A stray rumor? Or something more, something I wouldn't have heard because I'd been out of touch in Syria?

I took my hands from my face. I'd allowed myself an hour in Tomas's office. Time to finish and get out.

I flipped the rest of the way through Gabriel's folder and set it aside. I still had a few minutes of the allotted hour left, so I paged through Rafe's. There were multiple references to Princess Zoe. Rafe thought no one knew about his short affair with Zoe two summers ago, but apparently, Tomas had known all along.

I set Rafe's folder down and opened mine. It was thinner than my brothers' folders, mainly a record of my travels—where I went and why. He'd even noted that I'd never boarded the flight to New York.

I closed the files and returned them to his cabinet. After unlocking his door, I went back to his desk, hit the button that restarted the cam and shot out the door, starting to fade into the shadows as I did so. I pulled the door shut behind me just before I lost contact with the physical world.

The hidden exit was concealed in the wine cellar. There was a cam in the hallway, but I knew my dad didn't have a cam on the wine. If you were a syndicate vampire with access to headquarters, then you were welcome to help yourself.

I left the shadows, grabbed two bottles and escaped through the hidden door behind a large shelf of bottles. I returned to the shadows until I was out of sight of headquarters, then ducked into an alley and dropped back out.

Reaper was waiting beneath a tree near the Washington Square Arch. She'd glamoured her hair so it was purple, pulled it into two stubby pigtails and changed her features so she looked about sixteen. A sleeveless gray tee showed off her lean, sculpted arms.

"Hey." She searched my face. "Find anything?"

"Yeah. I'll tell you, but not here. And I got us some wine." I showed her the bottles.

"Good. We can use it, that's for sure. Here, give them to me." She shrugged out of the backpack and took out her Ravens hoodie. She wrapped it around the bottles and stowed them at the bottom of the pack.

I reached for the pack. "I've got it."

Ridley shook her head and settled the pack on her shoulders. "You think I don't know you're still fighting silver poisoning? I'm not a human, remember? Stop treating me like one."

"And I'm not as weak as you think."

She sighed and started walking. I fell in beside her.

"I know you're better," she said. "But I can carry a couple of bottles, okay?"

She was right. I was treating her like I would a human woman, when she was a supernatural like me.

"Fine, carry the damn bottles then. But the same goes for you. I'm not that guy you had to practically carry into the cemetery—I'm much better."

"Agreed." She gave me a sidelong glance from beneath her sunglasses. "So, what did you find out?"

I waited for a trio of twenty-something women in baggy shorts and cropped tops to pass us before answering. "We're not far from the High Line. We can talk freely there—it's sunny and open."

"Sounds good."

The High Line was an old elevated train line that had been repurposed as an urban park. Jogging up the stairs, we joined the stream of people walking the trail.

The Hudson River flowed by on our left, a broad silver ribbon under the late-afternoon sun. A cool breeze blew off the water, a welcome break from the summer heat. A sailboat darted like a dragonfly among the tugboats and barges, and an ocean liner glided downriver like a queen among her subjects.

We walked until we found a park bench set back from the path under some shade trees where we could sit and talk in relative privacy. From thirty feet below came the muted sounds of the city: the hum of traffic, a barking dog, children at a playground.

Ridley put her backpack on the bench between us. I got out a bottle of blood-wine, unscrewed the cap, and offered it to Ridley.

With a nod of thanks, she took a drink and handed the bottle back to me. I took a drink myself, then capped the bottle and put it on the ground at my feet.

"Okay, here's what I found out." I laid it out for her—that it had been Gabriel who staked Andre Redbone, the rumors about a possible coup against my father, Tomas's note. The only rumor I didn't share was the one about my father being blood mad. I refused to give SI any more ammunition against him.

"A coup." Ridley's mouth made a silent *Wow*. "That's one serious motivation for wanting you and your brothers dead. Especially if he thinks you're feeding intel to SI, too."

"Yeah, but—" I looked unseeingly at the people passing on the trail fifteen feet away. "Father can't believe we're trying to kill him. Hell, I've been in Syria. I barely had time to text my family, let alone plot a fucking coup."

"This goes back longer than a couple of months. The planning for this operation began a year ago."

"Gods." I grabbed the bottle; I needed another drink. "I have to tell Gabriel. Warn him about these rumors of a coup."

"*No.*" She grabbed my arm. "You can't."

I shook her off. "Not your decision."

"You're forgetting they have Rafael."

"Like hell I am. He's all I think about. I go to sleep thinking about him, and I wake up in a cold sweat, picturing what they're doing to him."

"Sorry." She heaved a breath. "I didn't mean it that way. I meant you have to play by their rules if you don't want them to sell him to a brothel. And they don't want you contacting anyone in your family. Besides, what if Gabriel warns Karoly? That would make him impossible to get to."

She was right, and I kind of hated her for it.

I curled my lip. "But that's what you would say, isn't it, *slayer?*"

Her chin jerked up like I'd smacked her. "Okay, I'll give you that. But this operation—it's been fucked up from the start. I'm not in control. I thought I was. I was in on the planning, but so many things don't make sense."

I frowned. She appeared genuinely upset, her brow furrowed, her small white teeth worrying her lower lip.

"And meanwhile, they've got my brother. How the fuck did that happen anyway? You said he was in Montreal."

"I don't know." She shook her head. "I just don't know."

"So what now?"

She stared out at the river. "Twilight might know more. I'll give her a call. But not here. Let's go back to the Bronx."

❧ 25 ❧

RIDLEY

The subway uptown was packed with commuters. Zaq and I had to stand. We held onto the same pole, his front to my back, where he'd put himself.

The man was still protecting me, this time from being jostled by the crowd. He couldn't help himself. He was an alpha male to the core, in the best way: strong, caring, comfortable in his own skin.

And I liked it.

Yeah, I could protect myself, but it made me believe he cared, at least a little. That I belonged to him.

It had been so long since I'd belonged to anyone, or had someone who belonged to me. Not since my mom had died, in fact.

His free arm came around my waist, and I leaned back against him. Soaking him in—his hard body, his special Zaq-scent, his breath against my hair.

We rode like that through Upper Manhattan. We couldn't talk, of course—not about anything important—but I didn't want to talk anyway.

I didn't want to think, either, but I couldn't help it. My chest was a tight mass of apprehension. Something was very wrong at Slayers, Inc.

The Crow flies crooked.

Zaq angled his head and looked at my face. "You okay?"

I blanked my expression. "Yeah. Just thinking."

"Hmm." He squeezed my shoulder and fell silent again.

My doubts about Operation Angel just wouldn't go away. They drummed relentlessly at my brain.

Maybe Karoly Kral needed to be eliminated. Maybe those changes he was pushing for were the first step in taking away SI's autonomy, and he wouldn't stop until the syndicates ruled the show.

But why had the contract included his sons, too?

I was starting to wonder if Crow had a personal vendetta against the Krals. Yeah, the Board of Directors had approved Op A, but Crow had been the driving force behind the order to take out the entire family. It was what Victorine Tremblay had demanded, of course, but the Board could've refused.

I desperately needed to talk this over with someone.

It's not like I could go to the BOD and ask. Like all of us, they used code names and switched identities regularly, and I didn't know anyone on the Board anyway.

Directly below the BOD were the alphas, and Crow was the alpha of the North American Division, the division my squad of five slayers was assigned to. Crow was obviously out, and so was my squad lieutenant. I didn't trust him not to report my doubts to her.

And Torch was dead, which left Twilight.

Back at the squat, I gave Dex another twenty bucks to cook supper for us again. He told us it wouldn't be ready for at least an hour, so we went upstairs to wait in my room.

Zaq took off his boots and lay on the mattress, fingers interlaced behind his head, staring at the ceiling.

I texted Twilight. *Can we talk?*

Five minutes passed during which I second-guessed myself. My phone buzzed and I snatched it up.

Twilight: *15 min? I'll call U*

I replied in the affirmative and stood up. "I'm going for a walk," I told Zaq.

He turned his head to look at me. "To talk to Twilight?"

"Yeah."

He didn't ask to come with me, just nodded. "The syndicate's on edge. I know we haven't seen anyone up here, but sooner or later they're going to figure out where we are. Be careful, okay?" He meant it. His brow was wrinkled, his mouth tight and pulled toward the side.

His concern was like a shiv to my heart. How could the man worry about me after what I'd done to him? After what I might still do to him?

I scraped my fingers through my hair. "Zaq. Don't."

"Don't what?"

"Don't worry about me. Don't *care* about me."

"Ridley." He imitated my tone. "I'll worry about you if I want. I'll *care* about you if I want. That's on me, okay? And how you respond is on you."

No, it's not okay. Because you're making me care right back.

"You're too nice," I blurted.

"It's a weapon," he said—and smiled. A *nice* smile, but a knowing one, too.

A flare of panic went over my skin.

I stared at him. Wanting. Wishing.

He spoke the truth. His niceness, his innate decency, *was* a weapon. A powerful, damn-his-sexy-ass weapon.

I fumbled for the doorknob. "I have to go."

"Ridley?"

I huffed a breath and glanced over my shoulder. "What?"

He crossed the room and I turned around, my back to the door.

He captured my chin in his hand. His gaze snagged mine, and I flashed back to that morning at Charles de Gaulle. The intense green of his irises and how they'd reminded me of a jaguar's.

A beautiful cat, yes, but one you'd be wise not to underestimate.

I licked my lips and his gaze dropped to my mouth. His eyes darkened and he leaned in like he couldn't help himself, like he was drawn to me as much as I was drawn to him, and nipped my lip. He soothed the small bite with his tongue, and then he was kissing me, a slow, thorough kiss that scrambled my brain and turned my knees into mush.

He lifted his head and released my chin. "I'm nice, not weak. Don't confuse the two."

My fingers were digging into his shoulders. I inhaled, made myself let go. "Got it."

I fumbled behind my back for the doorknob and slipped into the hall.

Outside, I turned south toward the Bronx's less populated, industrial section.

Twilight called right on time. "It's me. What's up?"

I touched my lips. I was still back in the room with Zaq, my body humming from his kiss.

I took a centering breath and concentrated on my reasons for contacting her. "You alone? It's safe to talk?"

Our smartphones were encrypted in three different ways, and we changed them out every few weeks so that even if someone managed to infect them with spyware, they didn't get much info. However, we still used a verbal code because no matter how good your tech, someone's always raising the bar.

"Um...yeah." Her caution came through loud and clear.

I understood. Twilight was my closest friend—we'd looked out for each other, back when we were teenagers at the same SI training facility —but even she didn't know me that well. No one did.

I chewed my lower lip. How could I put this without giving too much away?

"Something's off." I stopped short of saying something was wrong at SI. I wanted to feel her out first. "The brothers—do you know why they're involved?"

Why are Zaq, Gabriel and Rafe targets?

"You're asking me? You've been on this op longer than me."

"Yeah, but everything's on a need-to-know basis. I thought if we pooled information..."

She expelled a breath. "What's this about? Really?"

I glanced around. I was in a concrete wasteland of warehouses and auto repair shops that smelled of motor oil and the garbage cooking in a nearby dumpster. The only living things within sight were the spindly locust trees poking through grates in the sidewalk and the man spray-painting a car across the street at Juan's Body Shop.

And I had to trust someone or I was never going to get to the bottom of this.

"Okay. Here's the way it went down." I dropped the code except to refer to the Krals by their numbers. "We took P2 as planned, but after that, it turned into a shitshow. P2 was chained to a wall with silver hand-cuffs day and night. The blood-suckers drank from him—twice—while he was restrained. The man couldn't even defend himself. Much longer in there, and they'd have drained him dry."

"Jesus."

"Yeah. And the Bird approved it." Twilight would know the Bird was Crow.

Twilight drew a shocked breath. "All of it?"

"I don't think she knew they'd drink his blood. But the silver cuffs burned into his wrists. And he wasn't allowed to sit or lie down, so he couldn't sleep. It was torture, and she didn't care. The only reason they released him was because I worked out a deal for him. If he stakes his father, they'll let him and his brothers live."

"Jesus," she said again. "And they have P3 now."

"Yeah. The bastards are using him to up the pressure on P2. He was told that if he doesn't stake his father by Tuesday, they'll sell P3 into blood slavery."

"Fuck. That's seriously messed up."

"Yeah," I said grimly.

"You sure about this? You have proof?"

"I was with P2 when they called. I heard every word. They said he has seven days to finish this. If anything goes wrong, they'll sell P3 to a brothel."

She exhaled, a worried, drawn-out sound, and fell silent.

"What is it?" I asked.

"It's just—I saw something the other day. Something strange. The Bird was going into Philippe Moreau's mansion."

"I think she's been working undercover as PF's thrall." PF was Leo de Froulay.

"She wasn't with PF, and she wasn't pretending to be a thrall. She was in her fancy-French-bitch disguise. I wouldn't have recognized her—I wasn't close enough to see her eyes—but I know that glamour."

"Yeah. Me, too." My head started to throb. "Did she see you?"

"No. I was in the shadows. She wasn't alone—she was with PT."

Prima Tremblay.

I massaged my forehead. "They were together?"

"Oh, yeah. They seemed real cozy, if you know what I mean."

"Maybe it was something to do with the contract." The contract between Prima Tremblay and Slayers, Inc. that the Board planned to use to pin this on Victorine Tremblay and the blood feud. "Maybe the Bird needed more intel from PT."

"What intel?" asked Twilight. "Op A has been launched. We don't need anything from PT."

"I don't know. Maybe..." I trailed off. I was grasping at straws and I knew it.

The Crow flies crooked.

My chest ached.

No, not my chest—my heart. Crow was my mentor, the slayer I most admired. I'd *modeled* myself after her.

I switched the phone to my left hand, and with my right, removed my switchblade.

I extended and retracted the blade. Trying to calm myself.

Snick-snick. Snick-snick.

"P2 has contacts in the New York underworld," I said at last. "One of them pulled me aside and warned me that the Bird is 'crooked.' I figured the guy had his head up his ass, but now I'm not so sure."

"That's all the guy said?"

"Yeah. He was cryptic as fuck, to be honest. But why would he lie? He has no skin in this game. He's some kind of underworld lord with no connection to PK's syndicate."

A pause. I waited it out, giving Twilight time to think. Her current cover might be Lainey Q, an airheaded, hashtag-spouting "Stylist to the Stars," but beneath those trendy, carefully curated outfits was a brilliant strategist.

"If you're saying what I think you are..."

I let out a puff of air. "I'm not sure what I'm saying. Except that this op has felt wrong from the day we kidnapped P2. After nine years, I *know* when a vampire is bad—and P2's not. He feels like you or me, know what I mean?"

"Yeah. After a while you just know. Same goes for P3—he's not all sweetness and light, but he's not *bad*. He was only in Moreau's lair to get P2 out. They wouldn't have caught him if someone in his own syndicate hadn't ratted him out."

"So why are they targets? Other than because of their father, that is?"

"Damn if I know. But I don't think Crow's a traitor. I think she's obsessed. You know how she gets."

"Yeah. If she had her way, she'd wipe out the syndicates completely."

"She probably saw this chance to take out PK and his sons in one blow, and took it. Losing that many people at the top will throw their syndicate into disarray for years."

I grunted in agreement. "There'd be challenges, infighting... Fuck. You might be right about Crow."

Twilight made a low, confused sound. "The hell with it. I'm going to get P3 out. You know how they caught him? He was protecting the Ice Queen's daughter from her own mom and that creepy blond lieutenant. They were slapping her around in front of a roomful of people."

"Huh. Didn't think Prince Charming had the balls to go up against a roomful of vampires."

"Man's tougher than he looks."

"So's his brother."

She grunted. "You like him, don't you? P2."

A dirty white semi-truck rumbled by on the way to one of the Hunters Point food distribution centers. I gripped my switchblade. My lips still tingled from that last kiss, and I could feel his fingers firm on my chin.

"Yeah," I admitted.

"Just...be careful, all right? These guys are smart. They'd never have lasted as dhampirs in a vampire syndicate if they weren't. P2 could be playing you."

"Noted." But I'd gone way past careful already. And if Zaq was playing me, could I blame him? "So you can do that? Spring P3?"

"Yeah."

"Then I vote you go for it. This whole op stinks like a pile of three-day-old shit."

"Agreed." She took a deep breath. "Okay, I'm on it. But we never talked, okay? Nobody can know it was me."

"Not even P2?"

Because damn, Zaq could use some good news. The pressure was getting to him, and he'd never completely recovered from what those pricks had done to him. He was still too thin, and he seemed hungry all the time.

"Especially not him," was her reply. "He can't know until everyone else does—you don't know who he might tell or how it would change how he acts. This can't point back to me. If it does, I'm dead. You know that."

I rubbed a hand down my face, wanting to argue but knowing Twilight was right. She was risking a lot as it was.

"Got it. We never talked."

"And lose this number," she added. "I won't be answering it anyway. If I succeed, this cover will be blown."

"Will do." I ended the call, put away my knife and headed back to the squat. I'd only gone a half-block when my phone buzzed again. Somehow I knew it was Crow even though I didn't recognize the caller ID.

I stared at the screen, my thumb hovering over *Accept*.

Ignore it. You can make some excuse, tell her you were tied up.

Except then I'd still have to contact her later.

And what was *wrong* with me? Did I honestly believe that my alpha—the woman who'd saved me from the streets and given me a reason to live—would go after innocent men?

Yeah, said a small voice. *She would. If they were part of a vampire syndicate.*

I accepted the call and kept walking. "It's me."

"You clear?"

"Yeah." I turned at the corner and headed down another industrial block toward the East River.

"Good. Where are you?"

My hand was sweaty. Damn heat. It even radiated off the pavement.

I switched my phone to the other hand, wiped my damp fingers on my pants—and lied to my alpha. Again.

"In Brooklyn. A rented room."

"P2 is still with you?"

"Of course."

"I wondered. You haven't made contact with PK, so..."

My brow puckered. Crow was right, but why did she sound so certain? Unless her informant in the Kral Syndicate had told her.

"No. He's stayed on the move. We haven't been able to pin down his location. He seems to have gone dark."

An exasperated breath. "You've been here in the city for three days. That's all you've got for me? Can P2 get to him or not?"

I paused by a small park, a tiny emerald oasis in the industrial desert. The centerpiece was an abandoned cemetery, its moldy gravestones knee-deep in weeds. Above the East River, a jet sliced a trail through the blue sky.

I had to give Crow something. I couldn't tell her Zaq was digging for the truth, trying to figure out whether if his father had been framed or if he really was manipulating things behind the scenes.

And that I was helping Zaq because I wanted to know the truth myself.

"Zaq's sources tell him there's a coup in the making against PK."

"That's it?" she asked coldly. "You know how many coup attempts PK has fought off? At least five, maybe even more. The man has nine lives."

Yeah, but was his own son behind any of those attempts?

I didn't say it. I had no proof Gabriel was behind this, and I wasn't sure how Crow would use the information.

"Time's up," she said. "Tell P2 to come up with a plan for taking PK out—stat—or the deal we made with him is off."

"Understood. He—*we*—need a couple more days, is all."

"Who's in charge, you or him?"

"Me. But without his cooperation, I wouldn't get within fifty yards of PK." As Crow damn well knew.

"Hmm."

I winced. The woman could infuse more doubt in a simple *hmm* than most people could in an entire paragraph.

She expelled a breath. "Not tonight, though. I just received intel that PK took a helicopter out of the city with his mate, his son and some human woman. My source says he won't be back until tomorrow night, or Saturday at the latest."

Yes. I mentally pumped a fist. "I'll pass that on to P2."

"Pass this on to him, too—maybe it will get him off his ass. His own people are saying his father's blood mad."

I blinked, frowned. "You sure?"

Usually you heard whispers when a vampire had started to lose it, and I'd heard nothing about Karoly Kral being blood mad.

"Positive," Crow said.

"I see." A cold fear skated up my spine. A blood-mad vampire was scary as shit, cunning in the way a serial killer is. They craved blood—lots of blood—and would do anything, break any rules, to get it.

"He'd be in the early stages, then," I said, thinking aloud.

Then my breath hitched as a traitorous thought occurred to me. Was Crow telling the truth about Karoly?

I shook my head, telling myself she wouldn't lie about something this big.

"He's been purging the syndicate of his own men," Crow added. "A kapitán named Andre Redbone. Apparently all the kapitáns are hunkered down, wondering who to trust."

"I see." I didn't tell her I already knew about Redbone. But the fact that she mentioned it made me inclined to trust the rest of her intel, because Redbone had definitely been staked, although according to Zaq, it had been Gabriel doing the staking, not his father.

"There's more," she said. "PK is working the phones, pushing for a seat on the Board. Telling people we made a deal with Victorine Tremblay. The BOD has denied it, of course."

"Hell." I briefly closed my eyes.

"We can't let him get a seat on the Board. There's no telling what a blood-mad vampire would do with access to the kind of intel the Board has. And we can't slay him ourselves. He's too prominent. The other primuses trust him, and now with him telling this story about Zaquiel, all hell will break loose if we go after him directly. That's why it has to be one of his sons."

"Understood." I raised my chin, even though she couldn't see it. "Don't worry, I have this under control."

There was a long silence. A disbelieving silence.

My mouth flattened. "Have I ever let you down?"

The question hung there for several beats. "Not yet," she said and ended the call.

I stared at the phone. *Not yet?*

Fuck. The last thing I needed was her deciding I couldn't handle this and interfering. I grimaced and started back to the squat.

I was a block away when I stopped dead.

"Hey!" A woman nearly ploughed into me.

"Sorry," I muttered and moved to the side. She hurried past with an exasperated look in my direction.

Crow had said *here*, as in, "You've been *here* in the city for three days." Not "You've been *there* for three days."

She was in New York. But why hadn't she told me? Unless she was working her own angle—or having doubts about me.

And she hadn't mentioned Rafe Kral either. She must know he'd been captured by Philippe Moreau. Twilight would've informed her. So why hadn't Crow told me?

I should never have let her see how much Moreau's treatment of Zaq bothered me. She was keeping information from me now.

Added to the fact that she'd followed me and Zaq to New York, and a horrible certainty welled up in me.

Crow was here to stake Zaq if he failed to kill his father. Because she didn't trust me to do it—and she was right.

I swallowed sickly.

Damn, damn, damn.

A fine perspiration prickled my forehead. I swiped it away with the back of my hand. Thank God I hadn't told her our real location, and she couldn't track me through my phone.

You still have time. She won't do anything with Karoly out of the city.

She was clearly waiting to see if Zaq could get to his father.

So I'd just have to see that he did.

<hr>

B ack at the squat, I found Zaq in the kitchen, learning how to make another of Dex's abuela's special dishes. Dex had Zaq slicing tomatoes, the two of them chatting like old friends. Zaq's sun-streaked hair was tucked behind his ears, his T-shirt loose around his too-thin body.

Longing welled up in me. I wanted to go to him, wrap my arms around his waist and rest my head against his back the way I'd seen other women do with their men. Beg him to leave New York before it was too late, to save himself.

Think like a slayer.

For once, the mantra didn't energize me, and it brought me zero comfort. I couldn't even bring myself to finish it.

Because I wasn't just a slayer. I was a woman, too. A woman who wanted the same things most women did.

A life partner, an existence outside my rigid world of training and undercover operations.

Maybe even a child.

Joy.

Something deep in my chest constricted. I wasn't happy and hadn't been for a long time. The idea of happiness hadn't even been on my radar.

Zaq frowned at me. "What's up?"

I gave a small shake of my head. "After we eat."

He gave me another searching look, then glanced at Dex and went back to the tomato he was slicing.

To my surprise, I enjoyed dinner. We were joined by two other people from the squat and several of Dex's friends, all human. We talked about their world—the economy, politics, music, the best place for fried chicken. We laughed, me and Zaq sharing *did-you-get-that?* looks across the plank table.

After helping clean up, Zaq and I went for a walk, ending up in a park by the East River. Dusk was falling and the park had started to empty. We found a path along the river and took it.

Zaq caught my right hand and interlaced his fingers through mine. "You're worried. Why?"

I was no longer surprised at his ability to pick up my emotions. It went both ways. Something between us—something I refused to examine too closely—made it possible.

Guilt tightened my throat. Dex's excellent meal turned to lead in my stomach.

I pulled my hand from his. "It's about your father. I know you're having a hard time believing he's behind this. But what if he's blood mad? He wouldn't be thinking clearly."

He recoiled and narrowed his eyes at me.

"What?" I asked.

He shook his head. "Just...there's a rumor going around the syndicate to that effect."

I pounced. "What if it's the truth?"

"It's not. You don't know my dad. He is *not* blood mad."

"You might not know."

"I'd know. And even if he hid it from me and my brothers, you think he could hide it from my mom? They're mates. Sometimes you'd swear they have one brain."

I folded my arms over my chest. "Have you ever met a mad vampire? Because I have. They're smart, insanely so. Some have hidden it from everyone for years, especially in the early stages."

"How many of them had mates?"

"None," I admitted. "But this came straight from my alpha. A blood-mad vampire is irrational—your father might honestly believe you three are plotting a coup. He may even believe you've figured out that he's going insane and he wants to take you out before you report him to SI."

He started to argue and I lifted a hand. "Just consider it, okay? She says it's not just you and your brothers, that he's purging the syndicate of his top people. Andre Redbone was just the first."

His mouth turned down. "But then, there are the rumors that it's me, Gabriel and Rafe who are going after the syndicate's kapitáns." He fingered his chin. "I wish I knew where these rumors are coming from. Your alpha, did she say anything about Rafe?"

"No," I said, too quickly. It was the truth, though. Crow hadn't said anything new about Rafe, Twilight had.

His gaze sharpened.

The promise I'd made to Twilight grated at me. But it was her call, not mine.

"Your turn," I said before he could push me on it. "Any other intel you want to share?"

"That's it—that rumor, and the ones I already told you about. What about you?"

I heaved a breath. "My alpha's in the city."

"I take it that's not good."

"No, it's not. She didn't tell me straight out, either. I figured it out from something she said. So that's...odd, that she's hiding it from me. We have to be careful. *You* have to be careful. There could be other slayers in the city, too—I don't know. She did pass along a useful piece of intel—your father's not in the city tonight and he may not be back for a couple of days."

I deliberately chose not to tell him his father was with Gabriel. There was nothing Zaq could do about it anyway, and I honestly didn't care if Gabriel lived or died.

Zaq was my priority.

"Hell." He rubbed his forehead. "So we lose another night. Your alpha didn't tell you where my dad was going?"

"No. I don't think she knew."

"All right." He glanced at the sky. "It's getting dark. We should get back."

"She's a dhampir," I blurted. "My alpha, that is. Most of us are."

"I know; dhampirs make the best slayers. And yeah, I get it—we have to stay alert no matter what. We go out at night, we have to worry about my father's people. And during the day, it's the dhampirs. We'll just have to be careful."

We headed out of the park.

"I need to feed," Zaq said. "I'm still feeling the aftereffects of the silver poisoning. I'm going to—" He named a block in Hunters Point known for its prostitutes. They were primarily sex workers, but for the right price, some would let you drink their blood. "Wanna come?"

"I told you, I don't drink it fresh."

He moved a shoulder. "Suit yourself."

"You have enough cash?"

"Yeah."

"Take this anyway." I slipped him a handful of twenties.

"Thanks." He slanted me a curious look and tucked the bills into the pocket of his jeans.

I answered his unspoken question. "You shouldn't have to ask every time you need money."

"Well, again—thanks. And don't worry. I'm good for it."

"Hey, it's not my money."

"So SI is picking up my tab?" His mouth twisted in a sardonic grin. "Well, isn't that ironic?"

❧ 26 ❧
ZAQ

Ridley trailed me to Hunters Point. She didn't even try to hide it.
I wasn't sure if she was protecting me or making sure I didn't
take off again, but I was pretty sure it was the first, which made me
mentally roll my eyes.

At least she hung back while I negotiated a fee with the woman I
selected in exchange for her blood.

The woman told me to call her Bella and took me to a room above an
auto repair shop that smelled of gasoline and sex. The only furniture was
a nightstand, a three-legged stool and a daybed covered with a crumpled
pink sheet. Tucked behind a rattan partition at one end of the room were
a toilet and a rust-stained sink.

Bella sat on the bed and brushed her long dark hair over one shoulder
so I could access her throat. "Your fifteen minutes start now," she said
with a nod at the small clock next to the lamp.

Putting five twenties on the table, I sat down and gave her an easy
smile to hide my distaste—not for Bella, for the situation. I'd met enough
sex workers in the course of my volunteer work to know she'd probably
been pushed into this life by a pimp or to feed her family, or both.

I took the minimum amount of blood, finishing before my fifteen
minutes was up.

And yeah, I got a hard-on. For vampires and dhampirs, sex and the
blood craving are wired along the same primitive pathways.

I wiped the blood from my mouth on the back of my hand and started
to get up.

Bella stopped me with a hand on my crotch. "For another seventy-five, I can take care of that for ya, too."

"I'm good." I removed her hand. I was horny as hell, but Bella wasn't the woman I wanted.

"You sure?"

"I gave you all my cash." I lied because it was the quickest way to end this.

Bella's plucked black brows jumped in surprise. Her painted mouth turned down. "Like hell. If you don't wanna, all you hafta say is *no*. Everyone knows how rich you vampires are."

I ignored that to wash up. "Thanks," I said as I opened the door. "You have a good night, now."

"Yeah, sure." Her lips twisted in a way that was too old for a twenty-something woman. She eyed my cheap Paris T-shirt and faded jeans. "Funny. You look like one of them Dark Angels. Anyone ever tell you that?"

"Yeah," I said with a shrug. "I get that a lot."

Outside the night was hot and humid. Overhead, thick clouds had piled up, wiping out the stars with a heavy hand. Ridley waited on the corner near a woman wearing leather shorts and thigh-high boots.

The woman in shorts made a beeline in my direction. "Hey, handsome."

Ridley cut her off. "He's mine."

"Hey." The woman started to argue until she took a second look at Ridley's face. She closed her mouth with a snap. "Yeah, sure."

Ridley fell in beside me. Her mouth was pinched, her shoulders tight. And not because I'd fed.

She was jealous.

I smothered a smile. "I only took blood, you know."

Her pinched lips smoothed out. She moved a shoulder. "You don't owe me an explanation. You needed to feed. You look a lot better, to be honest."

"I feel a lot better." I grabbed her hand and pulled her to face me. "And I think I do."

She blinked up at me like a suspicious owl. "What?"

"I do owe you an explanation."

"No. I—we're not—"

I took her face between my palms and stopped her sputtered protest with my mouth. Her breath hitched and her body melted against mine.

A haze filled my head. I was still horny, still craving sex.

But not just any sex. Sex with Ridley.

The hell with the fact that I wasn't sure how far to trust her. I wanted this woman more than I wanted my next breath.

"Actually," I said against her lips, "we are. At least for these few days. I want to fuck, but not her. You."

A sigh escaped her. She rubbed up against me like a cat, and I went from half-hard to hell-yeah-we're-doing-this, my dick trying to push out of my jeans.

With a groan, I wrapped my arms around her. Her body fitted itself to mine like she was my other half, her abdomen taut against my erection, her small, perfect breasts pressed to my chest. The nipples were hard points that I was wild to taste again.

Ridley ran her lips along the stubble on my jaw. "I shouldn't say this."

I nibbled her full lower lip. "Say what?"

"I want to fuck you, too. So much."

My breath snagged in my chest. The raw, needy words ricocheted from my brain to my balls like she'd tasered me.

I gripped her nape and thrust my tongue into her mouth. She sucked it deeper, and the kiss got hot and heavy in a hurry. She twined a leg around mine and rubbed her crotch over mine.

The pressure of my zipper against my cock hurt, but in a good way. I rocked my hips against her and maneuvered us so her back was against the wall of a nearby store.

Keeping my grip on her nape, I eased her T-shirt up with my free hand and ran the thumb over the stretchy black material of her bra, playing with her aroused nipple.

A passing car honked, reminding me we were on a busy street. I broke the kiss and lifted my head, chest jerking like I'd run a 100-meter dash. For a few seconds, neither of us spoke. I don't know about Ridley, but my mind was too revved to form a coherent sentence.

She drew a jagged inhale. Her gaze tracked from my mouth to my eyes and back again.

I eased her shirt down over her stomach. "Let's go back to the squat."

She swallowed. Nodded. "Okay."

Back in our room, we dragged off our clothes and boots. Ridley finished first, me right behind. I tossed my T-shirt, boxers and jeans on a chair and crossed to where she stood by the bed.

She put her hands on my chest and ran her fingers through the hair on my chest. "You are so hot." She played with my nipples. "My beautiful Dark Angel."

I blew out a breath.

"What?" Luminous gray eyes met mine.

"I hate that nickname. It's not...me. It's someone the media made up."

"Really? Then I won't use it again. But I have to say, I have a thing for angels." She traced a finger down my unshaven cheek. "Especially the dark ones. They're pretty sexy."

"Yeah?" My mouth curved in a slow smile. I took her hand and sucked her wandering digit into my mouth. "Then you can call me Angel anytime you want."

Her lips formed an 'O.' "It feels like you're touching me. Down there."

"Here?" I said around her finger and slid my other hand between her legs, cupping her.

She was hot and slick. I dipped my middle finger into her juices, then toyed with her clit.

"Yeah. There." She removed her finger from my mouth and clutched my shoulders.

Without stopping what I was doing between her legs, I nibbled on her ear. "Remember what I said about not being that nice?"

A jerky nod.

"Right now, I'm not feeling nice at all. I want to do bad things to you."

Her breath hitched. A gush of liquid heat wet my fingers. "Yes."

Oh, yeah, that's what I wanted to hear.

"So here's what's going to happen." I traced the rim of her ear with my tongue. "First, I'm going to make you come, and then I'm going to take you against the wall. Hard. Is that what you want?"

She moaned.

"Talk to me, Ridley."

She gulped. "Yes. God, yes."

I growled low in her ear. "You're such a bad girl," I told her, and proceeded to do exactly what I'd promised.

I took my time. Making her beg me a little, because we both liked it. And then I gave her what she was pleading for.

She came twice. Once with my mouth and fingers on her, and once when I was pounding into her against the wall, her inner muscles squeezing rhythmically around me.

The sight and sound and feel of her coming apart dragged me over the edge after her. I thrust a few more times and with a shudder, emptied myself into her.

After, I let go of her legs and she slid them down my thighs to the floor.

She rested her forehead on my chest with an exhale. "I saw stars."

I chuckled. A wave of tenderness washed over me. I tamped it down, reminded myself not to let her get under my guard. Sex—even incredible sex—didn't make her any less my enemy.

I set her from me. "Be right back."

Wrapping a towel around my waist, I went to the john to clean up and dispose of the condom. When I returned, Ridley was curled up on the mattress.

"Move over," I said.

She did, and I got into bed next to her. For the first time, she was the one by the wall and I the one nearer to the door.

It was a sign of trust on her part. A simple gesture, but somehow, it made my defenses collapse.

The hell with it. I hooked an arm around her waist and drew her into me so I spooned her, my front to her back.

"G'night," she said sleepily.

I nuzzled the silky skin of her temple. "Good night."

৩২৩

F riday night we went back to Manhattan again. Traveling to the heart of Kral territory after dark was iffy, but I donned my human camouflage and Ridley had an actor's ability at disguising herself.

We spent the night trying to track down my father without tipping him off. It didn't work, of course. Even when things were normal, he was a secretive bastard, and it wasn't like we could walk up to people and ask where he was. I worked what contacts I had, but if anyone knew his location, they weren't telling.

Maybe he hadn't even returned to the city yet.

By the time we returned to the Bronx Saturday morning, I was fighting down panic. The week I'd been given was more than half over, and I had no idea where Father was.

And meanwhile, Rafe was at the mercy of those sick bastards in Paris.

When I awoke around six that evening, I felt dark, irritable, twitchy. The vampire beast wanted out. I'd managed to keep it leashed since Paris, but now it wanted to kick some ass—or fuck.

Ridley was curled on her side, facing away from me. Naked.

When we'd returned that morning, we'd been too tired to do anything but strip off our clothes and fall onto the mattress.

The black sheet covered her legs. Her upper body emerged from it like some fairy creature glowing palely against a shadowy forest floor. I eyed her hungrily: the delicate wings of her shoulders, the beads of her vertebrae, the curve of her hips.

The dark part of me wanted to close my fingers around her nape, hold her face down and take her from behind.

I turned onto my back and fought for control.

I wasn't angry at Ridley. Not really. She was part of this, but she wasn't the prime mover. In her way, she was as trapped as me.

She rolled over and touched my chest. "Morning."

Her fingers slid down and wrapped around my erection. I bit back a groan.

The roughness with which I'd taken her up until now was nothing compared to how dominant I felt like being right now. I wanted to hold her down and sink my fangs into that pretty throat of hers while I pounded into her until she was screaming with pleasure.

But fuck if I'd let her see the monster in me. I wasn't ashamed of my vampire; it was part of me. But she didn't feel the same way.

I put my hand on her wrist. "Go back to sleep. You don't want me right now."

But I didn't remove her fingers.

"Shut up, Kral." She squeezed me. Hard and so good.

My mind blanked. I shut up.

Rising up over me, Ridley kissed her way down my body. My throat, my chest, my cock. She licked the cap, then stroked me with her tongue.

"Suck me," I growled.

She took me into her mouth. I speared my fingers into her hair and guided her, showing what I liked. She was a fast learner, licking and sucking and making sexy little moans. It wasn't long before my balls were drawn up tight and I was close to coming in her mouth.

I tugged at her hair. "Come here. I want to be inside you."

She released me with a last suck and crawled her way back up me. Grabbing a condom, she rolled it onto my dick, then straddled my thighs and lowered herself onto me a slow slide that seared me from my toes to the top of my head.

I wrapped my fingers around her nape and pulled her down for a rough kiss.

We didn't speak after that. She moved on me slowly at first, then faster. I met her downward movements with hard upward thrusts. I pinched her nipples and she gasped and bit my ear.

The sex was crude and hungry and just what I needed. We were both close to climaxing when I stopped and lifted her off me.

Her dark brows formed a confused 'V.' "Something wrong?"

"Let me..." I laid her on her stomach.

"Oh. Sure." She lifted her hips. I shoved a pillow under them and crawled over her.

Her cheek was on the mattress, her hair a spill of moonlight on the dark sheet. I nuzzled the turn of her shoulder, and my fangs extended without my volition.

I scraped the tips over her soft skin. Craving her taste and so damn tempted to sink them into her neck and drink deep. She didn't know what she was missing. I could make this so much better for both of us.

She stiffened and pushed at the mattress. "No."

I stilled, fangs against the side of her throat, then lifted my head, inhaling deeply. It took all my self-control, but I managed to retract my fangs and focus on sex.

I braced myself on my forearms and slid my dick over her ass. She lifted her hips, encouraging me to enter her. I took myself in hand and teased her entrance with the tip.

She whimpered. "Please."

"You like it this way? Tell me." I pushed in a little.

Her fingers dug into the sheet. "Yes."

"Me too." I liked it a lot. The badass, take-no-crap Reaper underneath me, moaning and begging and desperate for my cock.

"I'm in the mood for slow." I pulled out, thrust in a bit deeper. "And hard." I rocked my hips forward in a firm thrust.

She groaned. "Yes. Oh, God, yes."

"Touch yourself." I stroked in and out again. "Like this." I reached a hand between her and the pillow and rubbed her plump little clit.

She obediently slid her hand between her thighs.

"Good girl. Don't stop until you come."

Her inner muscles tightened on me, telling me she liked me taking charge, telling her what to do, praising her.

I pushed in, smacked the side of her ass. "Say it," I told her. "Say you won't stop until you come."

"I...won't stop. Until I come." Her muscles clenched around me again like the sensations were so good she couldn't help herself. "Zaq..." She drew out my name, turned it into a low, primal sound of want and need.

I slapped her ass a couple of more times, enjoying how she moaned and wriggled beneath me, then gripped her hips and started fucking her in earnest.

We climaxed one after the other. She came first, a series of small contractions that sent waves of pleasure up my spine.

And then my balls exploded, and my cock jerked in a shock of bliss that made my brain go first bright, then blank.

I heaved myself to the side and collapsed on the mattress beside her.

Inside, the beast gave a toothy grin and settled back, satisfied. For now.

Ridley remained on her stomach. I opened my eyes to find her staring at me. There was something unguarded in her expression, something that made my throat catch. Before I could analyze it, her face blanked and her coffee-colored lashes swept down.

I nuzzled her neck and got up to take a shower.

When I returned, she was seated naked on the mattress, legs folded yoga-style, waiting her turn at the bathroom.

I took a single, greedy look—I had a feeling I'd never get tired of her lean ninja body—then grabbed my clothes and got dressed.

"I think it's time I call my father. I'm never going to get to him this way."

She pursed her lips, then nodded. "But not here."

"No. I was thinking Times Square subway station. Even if he was able to pinpoint our location, we'd be gone before anyone got to us."

We set out a half hour later, me in my human camouflage and Ridley wearing her purple-haired, cute-sixteen-year-old glamour.

We hadn't even reached the subway station when Ridley nudged me. "Look. On the newsstand."

I followed her gaze to a tabloid with a large photo of Rafe and Princess Zoe on the first page.

Rafe had escaped from Moreau?

I tossed the newsstand operator a five and snatched up a copy, holding it so we could both see the headline: *Angel Thaws Ice Princess's Heart*. A smaller subhead read, "New York's own Prince Charming Finds Eternal Love."

According to the short article beneath the picture, Rafe and Zoe had been photographed in Paris, their arms around each other, locked in a clinch. The reporter speculated that this would end the Kral-Tremblay blood-feud once and for all.

"He's free." Ridley bumped my shoulder and grinned at me.

I studied the photo. "What if this was taken before Moreau got ahold of him?"

"No, he escaped." She moved a shoulder in an apologetic shrug. "I'm sorry I couldn't tell you earlier, but I had reasons. Anyway, he's free. Believe it."

She sounded satisfied, like we were on the same side, which made no damn sense.

I frowned down at her. "You're happy Rafe got away from Moreau? I thought he was a target."

"Fuck that." She gripped my arm, her brow furrowed in an earnest, believe-me expression. "This isn't what I signed up for. We don't torture our targets. We take them out cleanly."

I studied her. So the slayer had a code of ethics.

"The important thing," she added, "is this buys you some time. He's free, Zaq."

That's when it hit me. Rafe was free. He'd escaped from that thrice-damned dungeon.

Relief shuddered through me. Ridley was right, it bought me some time, or at least eased the pressure.

"Okay. Okay." I blinked, rubbed a hand over my face. "What now?"

"There's still your father. SI isn't going to release you from your promise. As long as he's alive, you and your brothers are still targets."

"Yeah." And there was the reminder—if I'd needed it—that Ridley No-Name and I weren't on the same side. "Let's go, then."

We got on the subway and took it to Times Square, where we found a quiet corner. Earlier, while she was in the shower, I'd retrieved the burner phone I'd purchased earlier in the week from its hiding place. Now I punched in Father's most recent number, hoping it still worked.

I was still looking for a way forward and had decided to ask for a meeting. Somehow I'd ditch Ridley and talk to him, face to face.

And if I had to, I'd stake him.

What I didn't expect was for Tomas Mraz to answer.

"Who's this?" he asked suspiciously.

I opened my mouth, then shut it. My thumb hovered over the *End Call* icon.

Hadn't Spider said Tomas had gone missing? But Tomas wasn't just my father's lieutenant, he was a family friend. Almost like an uncle.

"It's me," I said. "Where's Father?"

"He's not available." He didn't ask how I'd escaped Moreau or if I was okay. But then, he wouldn't. The big blond lieutenant was old-school. If I'd survived, that meant I was okay.

"Why not?"

"He's gone dark."

Frustration gripped me at Tomas's short, uninformative sentences. "This is urgent, damn it. Can you at least get a message to him for me?"

"No," Tomas said. No explanation. Just *no*. "Where are you?"

I pinched the bridge of my nose and glanced at Ridley. A word to

Tomas, and my father's people would descend on us. She'd be taken into custody and I'd never see her again.

And the way the vampires in Moreau's lair had fucked with me? She'd be lucky if they treated her that well.

She might be my enemy, but I just couldn't do that do her.

I looked away. "Somewhere safe."

"Where? New York?"

I shifted my feet, aware that Tomas would be trying to trace me. If I talked much longer, he'd be able to triangulate my location using nearby cell phone towers.

"Look, I have to go. If Father contacts you, tell him I want to meet with him."

"Tell me where you are."

His insistence sent a cold prickle over my skin. Something was wrong. I thought uneasily of his note about the coup.

G, Z & R plotting against you? Feeding intel to SI. All or just G?

The cold prickle changed to alarm. "Goodbye."

"Wait," he barked, but I pretended not to hear and ended the call.

Ridley eyed me. "Who was that?"

"Mraz."

She stilled. "Is that usual—for him to answer your father's calls?"

"Not usual, no. But yeah, he's done it before."

"So you trust him."

I rubbed my unshaven jaw. "Not enough to give him our location."

Her mouth opened like she wanted to say more, but she closed it again. "Agreed. The less people who know where we are, the better."

Ridley's phone vibrated. She pulled it out of her pocket and read the message aloud.

"PK is in New Orleans. Due back Sunday."

"PK is my dad?"

"Yeah." She texted an acknowledgment and returned the phone to her pocket.

"Fuck." It meant we'd have to delay another day. I shoved my hand through my hair. "We might as well go back to the squat."

Sunday evening I woke up feverish and shaking. Another fucking relapse from the silver poisoning.

I would've crawled into Manhattan anyway but Ridley told me not to be ridiculous. "You're in no shape to face your father."

I passed out in the midst of arguing with her.

Ridley spent the night by my side, sponging me down. And at some point, she crawled into bed with me and let me drink her blood again.

I closed my eyes sometime after midnight and didn't open them again until Monday afternoon. I rolled over, weak, but clearheaded. The fever was gone.

Ridley sat on a chair, watching me, her light eyes unreadable. An unopened switchblade hung loose in her hand. "You're better?"

"Yeah." I rubbed a hand over my unshaven face. "Thanks for the blood. Again."

She lifted a shoulder, let it drop. "I need you to be at your best."

My gratitude evaporated. "My bad. I forgot I'm just a tool."

"I would've done it anyway, okay?" Her face had that naked, unguarded look to it again. "For the record, I'm sorry. About all of this."

Beneath the leather wristbands, my wrists itched and burned. I slid my right thumb beneath the left band and rubbed the raised scar left behind by the silver cuffs.

I huffed a laugh. "For what? Blindly following orders? Believing me and my brothers are monsters without any evidence? Helping another fucking syndicate kidnap me?"

"Yeah." Her throat worked. "All of that."

I shook my head and got out of bed. "I'm going to take a shower."

When I returned, Ridley was downstairs.

I took out my phone and hurriedly dialed Gabriel. The cold shower had helped clear my mind. I'd decided that for now I'd keep stringing Ridley, and thus SI, along.

But I had to get my father to back off. I knew he had people hunting me. If I could get him to back off, maybe I could come up with a plan to salvage this without staking him.

I had to go through a couple of layers to get to Gabriel, but when he finally came on the line he sounded so goddamn normal, I started to shake.

"Zaq? Where are you? Are you okay?" Despite the questions, he sounded distracted. And he was apparently outside, because I heard wind crackling over the microphone.

"I'm fine."

"Then where the hell are you? Father's been look—"

I blew out a breath. "Shut up and listen. I don't have much time—they could trace this call any second. We've been on the run for the past week." That last wasn't exactly the truth, but it was close enough.

"Who's we?"

I made a frustrated sound. I didn't have time for this. It had taken me good ten minutes just to get through to him. Ridley could come back at any second.

"Listen, damn it. The short version is I was kidnapped by the slayers."

"We know. But who's we? And where are you now?"

"I can't tell you. Not over the phone." The soft scrape of the ladder against the floor warned me Ridley had returned. "Fuck. I have to go." I dropped my voice. "Tell Father to call off the hunt. I'll be in touch. And bro?"

"What?"

"You and Rafe be careful. They're gunning for all three of us. Whoever's behind this wants to bring Father to his knees."

Gabriel started to say something, but I cut the connection and returned the phone to my pocket.

Ridley opened the door and frowned at me. "Who were you talking to?"

"My brother Gabriel."

She grimaced. "You shouldn't have done that."

I folded my arms over my chest. "Wrong. I should've called him sooner. If SI has targeted us, he deserves to know. Besides, I wanted to check in. He must've been going out of his mind wondering where the fuck I am."

She sucked her lower lip in. "I'm just afraid it will come back to bite us. My alpha—" She shook her head.

"Don't worry, I didn't tell him where we are."

She nodded, sighed. "I don't have any brothers or sisters. It's hard for me to understand"—she waved a hand—"families."

"I'm sorry," I said. And I meant it.

Her eyes flickered. "You don't miss what you've never had."

I wasn't so sure about that. She must have seen the compassion on my face because she added, "SI's my family now."

And that was just sad.

"Ridley—"

Her expression blanked. "Time to eat." And she turned on her heel and went out the door.

🦊 27 🦊

RIDLEY

I crouched beside Zaq on a rooftop across from the Hotel Garnet, staring down at the courtyard.

It was Tuesday night. A few hours earlier, Zaq had received word from Spider that Karoly Kral and Victorine Tremblay were meeting here at midnight. Supposedly Rafael and Princess Zoe would be present, too.

Zaq shifted on his haunches. I glanced at him, glad to see him looking better. He'd scared the crap out of me the other night. I'd woken up to find him incoherent and shivering. I hadn't even hesitated to let him drink my blood. I'd have done pretty much anything to make him better.

I swallowed over something large and prickly in my throat. I'd become too invested in him; I knew that.

I returned my gaze to the empty courtyard. To Zaq's dismay, we hadn't been able to conceal ourselves inside the restaurant. Karoly had locked down the entire hotel earlier that day.

Suddenly the scene exploded into action. Expensive cars zoomed up to the hotel—sleek, supercharged machines that looked more like rockets than street vehicles. Within seconds, the courtyard swarmed with black-suited vampires and uniformed soldiers from the Kral Syndicate.

Two enforcers appeared from inside the hotel to update the newcomers. "Mraz staked the prima," said one.

"Victorine?" asked one of the black-suited vampires.

The enforcers exchanged grim looks. "Yeah."

What the—? I strained to hear the details.

But I'd heard correctly. Karoly Kral's lieutenant had staked the Tremblay prima, and in retaliation, Karoly had sent Mraz to his final grave.

I glanced at Zaq. He gazed down at the courtyard, a muscle jumping in his jaw. He palmed a dagger that he'd scared up from somewhere to go with the switchblade he'd taken from me.

So Karoly had staked his own lieutenant. Crow's intel had been correct. The primus was indeed purging his top people.

Karoly himself emerged from the restaurant. He strode into the court-yard, rapping out orders at his people.

Zaq inhaled sharply and leaned forward.

Where was Rafe?

My stomach soured. If Rafe died, Zaq would never forgive me. It wouldn't matter that I hadn't staked Rafe myself. I was a part of this, and we both knew it.

He'd been cool to me all day. Withdrawn and polite in a nerve-grating way. I was pretty sure it wouldn't take much for him to hate me.

I sipped a breath through my teeth. I didn't want Zaq to hate me.

I don't want to lose him. That was Starry-eyed Ridley talking.

Practical Ridley snorted. *You never had him.*

That's not true. He likes me. *He can't get enough of me.*

Liking isn't love. Lust isn't love, either.

I stifled a growl at my own confused heart and nudged Zaq. "Now d'you believe me?" I asked in an undertone.

He took an audible breath.

"Zaq?"

He shook his head and didn't answer.

I pressed my point, even though I felt like a slimeball. Karoly was his father, after all. But if Zaq didn't act soon, he was dead. Crow wouldn't hold off much longer.

"If you don't do something about your father, Rafael and Gabriel are next—if he hasn't already staked them."

He threw a hot-eyed look at me. "You don't give a flying fuck about my brothers."

I flinched. He was right—but he was also wrong.

I did care about his brothers, but only because they mattered to Zaq. And he mattered to me.

Rafe Kral came out of the restaurant, Zoe Tremblay held protectively against his side.

Zaq straightened and stared down at his brother like a pointer spot-ting a bird, muscles locked so tight they trembled with the strain.

"Karoly must have a reason for not killing him yet," I murmured.

"Like what?"

I moved a shoulder and scanned the street. All these Kral vampires swarming the premises made me edgy. We needed to get the hell out of here before we got caught.

Zaq expelled a breath and rose to his feet. "I have to think."

I stood as well and put a hand on his arm. "Where're you going?"

He jerked from my grip. "Don't. Touch. Me."

I pressed my lips together. He might as well have doubled up his fists and slammed them into my gut. It would've hurt less.

He rubbed a hand over his face. "Sorry." His chest heaved. "I've seen enough," he added in even tones. "I need to think."

"You're tired. Let's go back to the squat, talk it over."

I glanced at the alley below and froze. For a few seconds, the world simply stopped. I didn't breath. Even my heart stuttered and ground to a start.

Crow stood in the alley as herself. Slim, sharp-featured, her shoulder-length brown hair scraped back into a ponytail. She must've arrived in the shadows.

She was watching the action, not me and Zaq, but she had to have seen us. If she turned her head even a few inches, we'd be in her line of sight.

My heart lurched, scrabbling like a panicked animal against my rib cage.

How had she known we were here? Because I sure hadn't told her.

And had she come alone? I didn't see anyone else, but that didn't mean they weren't somewhere around.

Zaq had seen her too. His fingers tightened on his blade.

I grabbed his arm and rose onto my toes. "The shadows—*now*," I said against his ear. "I'll meet you in Times Square. Outside the Minskoff Theatre."

He gave me a long look. Then, mercifully, he trusted me enough to begin the fade. I followed him into the shadows, praying we'd make it before Crow turned her head.

I flowed over the side of the wall and into the alley. Crow might sense me in the shadows, but she couldn't follow.

She was gazing up at the roof we'd just exited. "Reaper?" she said, low-voiced. "Show yourself."

Crap. I closed my eyes and considered pretending I hadn't heard, but the habit of obedience to my alpha was too strong. I dropped back into the physical world still clutching my switchblade.

Her gaze darted from me to the rooftop. "Where's P2?" she whispered.

"He took off after he saw his brother was okay."

She took me by the arm and hustled me around the corner and out of sight of the hotel. "You lost him?"

"No. He's on his way back to Brooklyn." I pointed east with my switchblade.

I didn't even question the lie this time. My entire being was focused on one goal: Protect Zaq from my alpha.

Her cobalt eyes glowed in the darkness like a Siamese cat's, the rims a paler, vampire-blue. "You let him leave without you?"

Something about her tone sent a chill chasing up my spine. I squared my shoulders. "Yeah. He's been straight with me. And he knows his brothers' lives are on the line—he's not going to try anything funny."

"Give me the address of the room you rented."

My mouth went dry with fear. "In Brooklyn?"

She hissed in irritation. "Yes, of course."

"Can I ask why?"

"Because as of now, you're off Operation Angel. I'll handle Zaquiel from here."

I lifted my chin and somehow managed to reply calmly. "That's not necessary. I've got this."

"No, you don't. You've been here for over a week now, and Karoly Kral is still standing. In fact, he's won a few more primuses to his side with his story about Zaq's kidnapping."

"Zaq tried to get to Karoly and couldn't." Another lie, but I didn't care. "He's gone dark, and you know yourself Karoly's been out of the city half the time."

She made an impatient sound. "I don't have time for this. Clearly, Zaquiel either can't or won't contact his father, and you're too close to him to think straight. Now give me that address."

"He trusts me—"

A flash of silver. "Zaquiel's location." She touched a switchblade to my throat. "Now. That's an order, slayer. The Krals have been a pain in SI's ass for too damn long."

I moistened my lips. "Bedford-Stuyvesant. Second floor." I gave her an address on Atlantic Avenue where I'd once stayed.

She retracted the blade and jerked her chin for me to leave. "Report to your lieutenant. He'll tell you where to go next."

"Yes, Alpha." My hands were shaking. I pressed them to my sides to hide it.

I'd lied to my alpha. Again.

And this time I wouldn't get away with it. I'd gone rogue, a death sentence for a slayer.

My mouth had made the decision before my mind caught up, but I was all in now. For Zaq.

"And Reaper?" Crow stepped back. "You're lucky I'm not writing you up for insubordination. Now get the fuck out of here."

"Yes, Alpha."

I retracted my blade, faded back into the shadows—and took off for Times Square and Zaq.

28

ZAQ

Times Square isn't actually a square, it's a bow tie, with triangles on the north and south, and the intersection of Broadway and Seventh Avenue at the center. I dropped out of the shadows at the bow tie's south end. The video walls lit the seething carnival of humanity with an eerie radiance.

I pulled on my human glamour and dodged through the crowd, keeping an eye out for Kral vampires. Times Square after midnight is prime hunting ground. And yeah, the vampire-human treaties say we're not supposed to feed on unwilling humans, but it's not hard to find a willing human when you're beautiful and filthy rich.

I didn't seen anyone I knew, though. The call must have gone out to get to the Hotel Garnet.

I arrived at the Minskoff Theatre before Ridley. The theater was dark. I pretended to study the Lion King posters in the windows.

If only I knew what, exactly, had gone down back at the Garnet.

Tomas was ashes, but Rafe was okay.

Princess Zoe had been hanging on to Rafe like he really was her mate. Still, it was hard to wrap my head around the idea that my brother had mated with a Tremblay.

And had Tomas really staked Victorine Tremblay?

On my way to the meeting, I'd told myself it was time to face facts. Ridley's doubts had infected me.

What if she was right? What my father *was* behind my kidnapping? What if he was in the first stages of blood madness?

If so, then Rafe was fucked. If he'd died in that restaurant, I would've never forgiven myself.

But now I didn't know what to think.

Rafe was still alive. That single, indisputable fact pushed the pointer on the balance back to my father's side.

With Tomas dead, Father could've staked Rafe and blamed it on Victorine, but he hadn't.

Why not? If he wanted us dead, what the fuck was he waiting for?

I squeezed my eyes shut. I was exhausted, too tired to think straight.

Time. I needed time.

A man jostled me, a beefy weight-lifting type.

The toothed beast surged up and took over my mind. I whipped around and bared my fangs at him. He whitened and swerved into the street to get away from me. Car horns blared and brakes slammed, but he didn't stop until he was on the other side.

I shook my head at myself, disgusted. *Way to fly under the radar, Zaq.*

I took a steadying breath and, with an effort, leashed the vampire.

Ridley still hadn't arrived.

You could just leave.

But I couldn't. Something linked us, the same thing that had kept me returning to the Bronx when I could've escaped multiple times.

A soft footstep behind me, accompanied by the scent of fresh-cut grass, out of place in this concrete-and-glass jungle. I was turning to meet Ridley even before she said, "Hey."

Half her face was shadowed, the other half bathed in bright light from the video walls. She'd kept her own clothes but used a glamour to change her face and paint her hair black with lime-green roots. She looked like Billie Eilish, if Billie had a twin who was an assassin.

"Let's go." I tipped my head toward the west, where the crowd was marginally less thick. "I haven't seen any Kral men, but that doesn't mean they're not around."

Ridley nodded and fell in beside me. "We have to find a new place. We can't go back to the squat."

"Because of that woman in the alley?"

She shrugged—and I *knew.*

"So it was someone from SI. Your alpha?"

Her face tightened. "Just take my word for it, all right? The squat is out for now. In fact, we probably shouldn't go back at all."

I squeezed my nape, thinking. "I have a loft on the West Side."

"The Meatpacking District. I know."

Of course, she did.

"But I'm sure my father's watching it," I added, "and I don't want to put my people in the position of having to lie about my whereabouts."

"What about the underworld?"

I nodded. "You read my mind."

"Spider will let us stay there?"

"For a fee, yeah. Hell, for enough money, he'd let us move in for a year. But I only trust the guy so far. Tomorrow we'll have to look for a more permanent solution."

"Agreed. Same entrance?"

I said yes, and she faded back into the shadows, me a few seconds after her.

When I arrived at the dumpster, Ridley was leaning against the wall behind it in a deceptively casual pose, one knee bent and her boot resting on the bricks, her eyes scanning for trouble.

I exited the shadows—and was blindsided by a wave of weakness.

I rested my forearm on the wall and sucked in air. Gods, I was sick of feeling like a fucking fragile flower. But I was burnt. Too much time in the shadow dimension on top of powering a glamour had sucked all the magic juice from my still recovering body.

Twin lines formed between Ridley's brows. "You okay?"

I straightened. "Just catching my breath."

She gave a disbelieving grunt, which I ignored. I opened the door, and we jogged down the rickety stairs to find George waiting at the bottom, fangs bared and a big-ass dagger in his hand.

He gestured with the dagger at the stairs behind us. "Go back to whatever hole you crawled out of. Spider doesn't want you here."

Adrenaline kicked in, bringing with it a surge of energy. "Then he can tell me himself." I pulled out the switchblade I'd taken from Ridley and the dagger I'd picked up in a pawn shop.

Ridley's own blades had already leapt into her hands. *Snick, snick.*

She'd kept her glamour but a wolfish grin lit her face. The woman was enjoying this.

George fell back—it was that or get mowed down. He glanced at Ridley and did a doubletake. "That's your thrall?"

She gave a goaded growl. "I am *not* his thrall."

Uneasiness pricked me. Ridley looked nothing like the mini-skirted blood addict of last week. How did George know she was the same woman?

"I wouldn't mess with her," I advised. "She's wicked good with those blades."

Out of the corner of my eye, I saw her brow lift. "Why, thank you."

I showed George my fangs. I couldn't compel him like I could a human, but I could use my dominance against him. I was stronger than George, even though he was a vampire and I was a dhampir, and that's why he disliked me—that and the fact I was a rich syndicate prince who could buy and sell him a hundred times over.

I put all the force of my vampire-half into the command. "Take me to Spider. *Now.*"

George shuddered, followed by a look of intense hatred that should've incinerated me where I stood. But he gave in.

"Your blades." He stuck out a hand, his mouth an insolent curl.

No fucking way.

"I don't think so. But as a sign of good faith—" I returned the dagger to my pocket and retracted my switchblade, and Ridley did the same.

"You first." George jerked his head at the tracks.

Ridley and I exchanged a glance. I could tell she didn't want him at our backs any more than I did, but I judged that I'd pushed him as far as I could.

I started walking, Ridley alongside me, and George following close on our heels.

My neck crawled like he was eyeing it. Probably wondering if he could get away with severing my spine. And I'd have bet serious money that a couple more vampires watched from the shadows.

I moved my thumb to the catch of my switchblade. Just in case.

Inwardly, I frowned. What was up with Spider? I'd come and gone in his section of the underworld for years.

He wouldn't have let my brothers past the outer door, but everyone knew I was the Kral family rebel, the brother who'd refused to be "made" in the syndicate. More importantly, I was the Kral who brought him gifts of cash and blood-wine. I'm sure Father knew about our friendship—he had spies everywhere—but he'd never brought it up and neither did I.

I wasn't sure why I'd first set out to win Spider's trust. Probably because I'd needed somewhere to go where I wasn't a Kral. And not just a Kral, but a Kral Dark Angel, to spread the icing on the things-I-wished-I-could-change cake.

I hadn't asked for this life. I didn't want it.

But there was no way out. Made man or not, I was still a Kral. You could be born into a vampire syndicate, or "made," or both.

But you didn't leave. Not when your father was Primus.

Ahead of us the darkness shifted and solidified, and Spider faced us, stiff-legged and expressionless, a silver dagger gleaming in his hand. "Batman."

"Spider." I gave him an easy nod. "My apologies for intruding."

His eyes glittered blue like a *Danger, Keep Out* sign. "What do you want?"

"A night's sanctuary for me and my woman."

A smile that wasn't a smile. "Yeah? What the fuck have you been smoking? You think I wanna be dragged into a goddamn syndicate war?" He pointed the dagger at the tunnel behind us. "Get your sorry asses out of here or I'll chain you and that bitch of yours to a wall and cut you up for the rats to feed on. It's been a while. They're hungry."

Ridley made a subtle, agitated shift from one foot to the other.

My jaw hardened. "Twenty thousand. Cash."

Spider rubbed a thumb over the dagger's carved ebony handle. "For one night?"

"That's right. We'll leave tomorrow. We just need to disappear for a few hours, let the trail cool."

"Nobody saw you come down here?"

"No."

"Make it fifty thou."

"You've got it." I transferred the switchblade to my left hand and stuck out my right.

He eyed my hand without taking it. "Deal's only good until tomorrow at noon."

"Understood."

"Then you've got your sanctuary for the night." He shook my hand and glanced over his shoulder. "Velma?"

His long-legged, black-haired lieutenant stepped forward. "Here."

"Show Batman and his woman to our guest room."

George sniggered at the "guest" room, but Velma tilted her head at me and Ridley. "This way." She had a deep, soothing voice like the kind you hear on late-night radio.

We followed the lieutenant through a labyrinth of dirty, badly lit tunnels until we reached a dead end, a short passage with only one room. The room's thick, silver-reinforced oak door stood open.

The toothed beast stirred uneasily. The set-up was too much like the one I'd escaped in Paris, and even if it hadn't been, it was never smart to get boxed into a place with only one exit.

Ridley blew out a breath, clearly not liking our accommodations any more than me.

"You're Spider's guests," Velma reminded me. "You know his word is good."

It was clear that if we refused Spider's "hospitality" now, he'd be insulted. And it's not like we had another option.

We followed her into the tunnel.

The guest room was a step up from Moreau's dungeon, although not by much. At least it had a bed—a mattress on a sagging metal frame covered by a threadbare quilt the color of dried blood. The rest of the small space was taken up by a table and a pair of chrome chairs upholstered in cracked yellow vinyl. A single bottle of cheap blood-wine stood on the table.

"Help yourself to the wine, and the john's there." Velma pointed to a door behind the table. She dropped her voice. "You know the way out?"

"Yeah." I'd made it a point to note each twist and turn, and I was sure Ridley had done the same.

"Make sure you leave by noon. Spider won't break his word, but he might bend it if you overstay your time by even a minute. He likes you, but—" her mouth twisted wryly—"he likes money more."

"So there's money in me?"

A clear-eyed look. "What d'you think?"

Hell.

I jerked my chin in acknowledgment. "Thanks. I appreciate the heads-up."

Velma turned to leave.

"Wait," I said. "I have a question."

She turned around, black brows lifted. "Go ahead."

"What did Spider mean about a syndicate war?"

"You didn't hear what went down at the Garnet Restaurant?"

"I heard something. I just wondered what you'd heard."

"Your father and brother butchered Tomas Mraz and Victorine Tremblay. What makes it dicey was that Karoly had granted the prima a safe-conduct pass for twenty-four hours."

"I see." So my father had broken his word—or at least, it appeared like that to the vampire world. My heart sank. Things were looking worse and worse. "What about Princess Zoe?"

"She stood by and allowed it. Apparently Rafe has his hooks deep into her. They're saying she was in New York to defect to your syndicate."

"Huh." I glanced at Ridley. She had a crease between her brows.

"I have to go." Velma went to the door, hesitated. "If I were you," she said in a voice barely above a whisper, "I'd leave as soon as it's daylight. But you didn't hear that from me."

"Understood. And thanks, I owe you one."

"Just leave Spider out of this."

"Will do."

Velma left. I shut the door and threw the deadbolt. The bolt was steel and wouldn't stop a determined vampire, but at least they couldn't sneak into the room in the shadows.

Ridley sat on one of the vinyl chairs. I sank onto the bed, my stomach hard with tension.

Could Ridley's alpha have been correct after all? Could Father be in the first stages of blood madness? Because why else would he have staked Tomas?

He didn't stake Rafe, pointed out a small, insistent voice.

But was that proof he didn't intend to? Maybe he hadn't wanted witnesses. Zoe had been there, for instance, and probably a couple of bodyguards.

Ridley shifted under my gaze but didn't speak. She'd withdrawn into her detached, I'm-an-emotionless-badass shell, and it was my fault. I'd been cool to her all day, and at the Garnet I'd been a downright prick.

Still, I didn't apologize. Maybe a little distance was a good thing. We'd gotten too cozy, and it was affecting my ability to think clearly where she was concerned.

"I have to contact Gabriel and Rafe," I said. "Tell them about Father..."

"Tell them what? That your father is trying to kill you all? That he's in the first stage of blood madness?" She shook her head. "They'll think you're the crazy one. Or that Moreau brainwashed you into believing it."

"Maybe." I massaged the bridge of my nose. I was so damn tired, and not just physically. My brain was exhausted, my ability to reason pretty much nil. "But I have to do something. At least if I warn them, they'll be on their guard."

"Can you trust them not to go straight to Karoly?"

I scowled. "Of course."

"Are you sure? Even if they honestly believe you've been brainwashed?"

I swallowed. Hating her a little for making me doubt my own brothers. I looked down at my hands on my thighs. Spread the fingers apart and relaxed them again.

"I don't know," I admitted.

"If they go to your father with this story, he'll be forced to act. He's been holding back for some reason. Maybe he's trying to get to you first, I don't know. But he knows where your brothers are. Are you willing to risk that?"

"So what am I supposed to do? Say nothing and let them die?"

She zeroed in on that. "So you do believe he's a danger to you and your brothers."

"Yes. No." I was on my feet again. "I don't know, all right? *I don't fucking know.*"

"Zaq." She leaned forward, her expression intent. At least she was showing some emotion, even if only to argue with me. "You have to face facts."

"What facts? I've been running around New York for over a week and I don't know jack shit."

"I think you *do* know. You just don't want to believe your own father wants you dead."

"And you don't want to believe that maybe someone else set things up so that it looks like he wants us dead. You don't know my father—you know the Kral Primus. He's a cold S.O.B. but he does have a heart. Like with me—I used to take in hurt animals, you know?"

"No. I didn't know."

"It's true. Birds with broken wings. Three-legged cats. I even had a blind dog that adopted Father as its alpha—and he let it." I huffed a laugh. "He let that damn dog live out its life on the rug in front of the fireplace in his library in Maryland, and he built a big shed on our property for me to care for the other animals. And I know he wondered if I was too weak. Tomas did—he told me so straight to my face. But Father told Tomas to let me be, that what I wanted to do in my free time was my own business. And later, Father wanted me to become a made man like my brothers—and yeah, he pressured me pretty hard. But when he saw I really meant it, he backed off."

"Okay." Ridley raised her hands in surrender. Humoring me, and we both knew it. "So your father doesn't want you dead. Someone in your syndicate does, though. Whoever's been feeding intel to SI."

I picked up the wine, unscrewed the lid and offered it to Ridley. She drank and handed the bottle back to me. I took a long slug and put the bottle back on the table.

"If only I knew what really went down in that restaurant," I said. "Why the fuck did Father stake Tomas? Unless—"

"What?"

"What if Tomas was the traitor?" I sat on the mattress again and rubbed my forehead. It fit. "He knows—he *knew* everything my father did. He would know the plane I took to Paris. He knew all our movements—me, Gabriel, Rafe. My dad trusted him like a brother."

She pursed her lips. "It's a possibility," she conceded. "I suppose he could've been the one feeding us intel."

"Fuck." I squeezed the bridge of my nose. "I'd have said he'd cut off his own hand before betraying my father."

But the suspicion was turning into certainty. If it wasn't me or my brothers—and I *knew* it wasn't—Tomas was the logical suspect.

"Sleep on it," Ridley said. "We can't do anything more tonight."

I nodded. "I'll take the first watch."

"No, I will. You need rest."

I opened my mouth to argue, then shut it again. She was right, I did need to rest. Not only was I wrung out, my blood craving was so strong I'd found myself eyeing a rat in the tunnel. Ordinarily, I'd ask Spider to lend me a thrall, but in his current mood he might send an assassin instead.

I slugged down some more blood-wine and used the john. When I came back, I told Ridley to wake me in three hours and settled on top of the quilt. She used the john too, then retook her seat.

I turned my head to look at her. She had a switchblade in her hand and was eying it.

"I wonder how George knew I was the woman who pretended to be your thrall last week."

"Yeah," I said. "I'd love to know that too. Another leak. It's like someone knows every fucking move we make, almost before we make it."

Her face closed up. Both switchblades were in her hands now. She released the catches and the knives sprang free.

I narrowed my eyes. "You know something."

"Maybe. But I have to think, okay?" The long silver blades danced through the air too fast to follow, even for a man with my supernatural vision.

I set my back teeth. "Damn it, Ridley. I can't figure this out if I don't have all the information. This is my family we're talking about."

She shook her head. "It's not something I know. Just a...suspicion."

"Tell me."

She exhaled. "Let me think it over, will you?"

"Fine," I growled. I thumped the hard, flat pillow and laid my head on it again, staring at the ceiling.

It took me a long time to fall asleep. The mattress was lumpy and the quilt smelled like somebody's armpit, but I'd slept on worse.

No, I was awake because I was becoming increasingly uneasy. Velma's advice to leave at daylight replayed in my head. Had coming to Spider been a mistake?

Ridley was on edge, too, maybe more so than me.

I rolled onto my side and watched her from beneath my lashes.

She'd stopped playing with her knives. She stared at the door, a blade in each hand, her wiry body tense.

Then she started pressing the catch on the blade in her right hand.

Snick, snick. Snick, snick.

I shifted onto my back and put an arm over my face.

"Sorry," she muttered, and stopped.

She didn't retract the switchblades, though. She kept both of them in her hands and ready, and when it was my turn to keep watch, I did the same.

As the hours passed, my uneasiness increased. The moment I sensed the sky outside lightening, I crossed to Ridley. "Time to go." I touched her shoulder.

She was on her feet in one smooth move. We eased open the door and hurried back through the tunnels, blades out and ready.

We'd only gone partway when my shoulders tightened and crawled higher. Someone was watching us. I glanced behind me.

The passage was empty.

"The shadows," Ridley mouthed at me.

"Yeah." I tightened my grip on my knives. We turned sideways and crab-walked down the tunnel, backs to the wall, keeping an eye out both behind and in front of us.

Two rats erupted, squeaking, out of a side passage. We both jumped. Ridley swore under her breath. The rats scurried down the tunnel toward whoever was following us.

Ridley's eyes met mine. I knew she was thinking the same thing as me.

Run.

We took off, sprinting through the twists and turns until we were on the homestretch. Sometimes you can hear a person in the shadows, and now I did. They weren't breathing hard—the sprint hadn't been that strenuous—but they were breathing a little louder than normal.

At the bottom of the staircase, I grabbed Ridley's arm and tried to push her up the stairs ahead of me. "You first. I'll hold them off."

She flicked me a flat, you've-got-to-be-kidding look and took a stance next to me, knees bent, blades ready.

George stepped out of the shadows, the big-ass dagger in his hand. He stalked forward, his dark irises encircled by blue fire.

I snarled. "What the hell? Spider gave us sanctuary. Does he know you're here?"

His smile iced my bowels. "I'll make it good with Spider. The reward for the two of you is worth ten times what you're paying him." He turned his smile on Ridley. "We know who you are, *Princess*. Or should I call you Reaper?"

Ridley winced and brought her chin up like she'd taken a fist to the belly.

I glanced between her and George, shock warring with confusion.

Princess?

And the reward was for both of us?

Ridley recovered. She snorted. "You have the wrong woman. Trust me, I'm no princess."

"No?" George smirked—and lunged at us. Ridley tried to throw herself in front of me, but I was there first. I parried George's blow with my dagger. The clang of silver against silver echoed in the tunnel and reverberated up my arm.

I came back hard, targeting the sweet spot beneath George's ribcage where I could angle the blade in and up to his heart. He evaded the thrust and slashed down with his dagger, aiming for the tendon in the crook of my elbow.

Just in time, I jerked my arm back, dancing away. Ridley had circled to his right.

My lips pulled back in a toothy grin. *Got you, mofo.*

Then three more men materialized from the darkness.

❦ 29 ❦

RIDLEY

Zaq and I stood back-to-back, forcing the four vampires to come to us. The pricks fought dirty. One aimed a kick at my kneecap that I barely avoided, and the other tried to slash my left hamstring.

I was afraid the street-fighting moves would throw Zaq, but he clearly knew a few of his own. When George tried to knee him in the balls, Zaq deflected the blow with his thigh, then grabbed George's arm and jerking him close, using his momentum against him. Zaq's blade flashed, slashing through George's eyeball and half his cheek.

George made a sound that was part groan, part shriek.

All-righty, then.

I stopped worrying about Zaq to focus on my own opponents. They moved in on either side, trying to divide my attention.

I bared my teeth. I'd trained with the best, but I was up against two full-blood vampires. They might be able to take me down, but first, I'd make them hurt.

One man came at me high, the other low. I slashed out with my switchblades, tracing a pattern in the air that caught the high man's blade and knocked it out of his hand. But the low man evaded the pattern and managed to stick me in the side.

I felt a shock of heat as the silver slid in. Then the pain got lost in the buzz of fighting.

The movement had brought Low Man within inches of me. I brought my left hand up and under his ribcage and shoved my switchblade into his heart.

He grunted and looked at me, eyes wide and mouth ajar, like he couldn't believe he'd been bested by a dhampir.

I pushed him away. He stumbled back and sank to the concrete, body smoking as fire consumed him from the inside out. The acrid stench of his burning flesh mixed with the metallic scent of my own blood.

Low Man's dagger was still in my side. I yanked it out to replace the switchblade I'd left in him.

Behind me, Zaq had staked one of his opponents, too, and was fighting with George.

I parried another thrust by High Man. He moved closer and struck again.

Fear closed my throat. He was my match in fighting skills and uninjured, whereas my side burned and my knees felt like rubber. The silver blade had gone deep into my side. Already, the poison was spreading through my bloodstream.

I managed to evade his dagger and struck out, but he sidestepped my thrust and closed in. His leg swept behind me, hooking the back of my knee and knocking me off my feet. I hit the ground hard, my breath whooshing out of my lungs.

Meanwhile Zaq had somehow gotten George's dagger away from him, leaving George weaponless. From the corner of my eye, I saw Zaq stab George in the chest. The knife bounced off bone with a sickening thunk, and with a growl, he threw Zaq off.

Blood ran down George's face. He swiped it away and backed up, a hand to his chest wound, squinting at Zaq through his good eye.

He bared his fangs. "Bastard. Why don't you go running back to your daddy? Oh, that's right. He thinks you're trying to overthrow him."

Zaq came at George a second time. George bobbed and weaved, trying to strike at Zaq with his fangs.

I didn't see what happened next, because my opponent lunged at me. I threw my body to the side and his blade whistled past my shoulder. The momentum sent him flying over my prone body. He rolled and jumped to his feet.

I pushed myself onto my knees. Bracing myself with one hand on the concrete, I grit my teeth and somehow managed to bring my switchblade up between me and High Man, hissing as the movement sent pain spiking through me. It felt like someone had inserted a hot poker into my side.

Two things happened almost simultaneously. Zaq staked George, shoving the dagger into the vampire's chest so hard, his body bounced off the wall; and High Man lunged at me with his dagger. As I thrust out an arm to block him, my blade flew out of my hand. I watched, horrified, as it landed a couple of yards away. I'd lost coordination in my fingers.

I threw myself to the side and he missed again, stumbling past me. I curled up on the dirty, blood-soaked concrete, prepared to die. My last thought was a fervent prayer that Zaq would live.

Suddenly, High Man slammed to the ground, his dagger flying out of his hand. That's when I realized he'd stumbled because Zaq had knocked him away from me. Zaq kicked High Man's dagger away and snatched up my switchblade. He stabbed it into the man's heart, pulling the blade down like he was gutting a fish.

High Man let out a low, agonized grunt. He gripped the switchblade's handle, attempting to pull it out, but he was already too weak. He took his smoking hand from his chest and looked at it like it wasn't attached to him.

He gave Zaq a baleful look. "Fucking rich S.O.B."

Zaq came to his knees, breathing hard. "Who put out the hit on us?"

High Man smiled, a fuck-you curve of his lips, and closed his eyes.

Zaq shook his shoulder. "Tell me, damn you!"

"Go...to...Hades," he said without opening his eyes, and started crumbling into ashes.

Zaq heaved a breath and turned his head toward me.

I managed a small smile. "Nice work, Kral."

He grinned. Then his nostrils flared. "You're hurt."

I grunted assent.

"What the fuck?" Emotions chased across his face. Fear, worry.

For me.

Despite the pain—or maybe because of it—wonder filled my heart.

He scrambled the few feet to where I was curled on the concrete and eased up my bloody shirt. He sucked in a breath.

"Damn you, Ridley. You're not supposed to get hurt."

"Didn't...plan...to."

"Don't talk. And don't move. You'll make the bleeding worse."

He ripped off his T-shirt, tore a large patch off the bottom, and pressed it to my side. "Hold that against the wound."

My hand fluttered. I tried but failed to move it to the T-shirt he held over my wound. My hand fell back to my side.

Zaq cursed, low and vicious. "We have to get you out of here."

Blackness edged my vision. My arms and legs had turned to wet noodles and my side burned like a motherfo. I pushed ineffectually at his thigh with the back of my hand.

"Go. I'll just slow you down."

He gave an animal-like snarl, his green eyes rimmed an Arctic blue. I blinked. I'd never seen him look so fierce.

"You really think I'd leave you for those scumbags?"

He scooped me up and jogged up the steps, while I pressed my forearm against the makeshift bandage covering the wound and concentrated on not screaming at the spiking pain.

I moistened my lips. "No," I rasped.

"What?" He gave me a distracted look.

"Didn't think...you'd...leave me." My voice seemed to be coming from a long way away, but it seemed important to make that clear.

At the top of the stairs, he turned sideways so he could reach the door handle. "Put your arm around my neck and kiss me."

I lifted my brows. *Seriously?* I thought but didn't have the energy to say.

He growled. "*Do it*. And if anyone stops us, you're drunk, got it?"

I understood then. I wriggled an arm free and somehow managed to loop it around his neck.

I touched my lips to the corner of his mouth. "But...where...go—?"

"Let me worry about that."

He kicked open the door and stepped into the dawn.

❧ 30 ❧
ZAQ

I peered around the dumpster, Ridley cradled to my chest. Forty-second Street was empty. The late-night crowd had gone to bed and the morning rush hour hadn't begun yet. The few humans left were drunk, on drugs, or smart enough to mind their own business, and the vampires would have returned to their lairs to take their day sleep.

I pulled my glamour over me, nuzzled Ridley's neck to hide her face, and strode down the sidewalk like a man with sex on his mind.

There was too much I didn't understand about what had just gone down. Still, one thing was clear—someone had put out a hit on not just me, but Ridley. And with her injured, the best thing was to go to ground while she healed. Somewhere safe with both food and blood-wine, and maybe access to a thrall for fresh blood.

I racked my mind for options, but the only place that checked all the boxes was my own loft. I decided to take the chance.

As long as we got inside without being spotted, we should be good. Xavier, my dhampir head of security, was loyal to me, not my father. Five years ago I'd rescued Xavier from a dicey situation in Mexico City, and he'd turned around and rescued me the next day. I'd offered him a job and he'd been with me ever since.

It was the getting inside without being spotted that was the tricky part.

I ducked into a doorway and worked the phone from my pocket while trying not to jar Ridley.

Xavier answered immediately.

"It's me," I said, low-voiced. "Don't act surprised. And *don't* say my name."

"Okay."

"Is anyone with you?"

"No."

"Good." I glanced around, calculated we were roughly two miles from my loft. "I'm in the city, about twenty minutes away. Is anyone watching the building?"

"Not since last night. Something big went down. I don't know if you heard."

"I heard. But okay, perfect." I released a relieved exhale. "Wait on the top floor for me. I'll come around the back and ring the bell. I'll be in the shadows, so you won't see me. Buzz me in, then open the door to my loft. But only you, understand? Don't tell the others." Besides Xavier, my security team had three other members.

"Understood. Just in case, I'll send Katie out front to create a diversion. We've been doing it off and on just to keep them busy—and to cover you when you finally came back."

And that right there was why I loved the man.

"Good thinking. See you in twenty." I ended the call and set off for the Meatpacking District.

My T-shirt was soaked with Ridley's blood. I glanced over my shoulder, hoping we weren't leaving a trail. We weren't. Not yet anyway.

At least the sun was up—still hidden behind the skyscrapers, but up—because a vampire would be able to scent that much blood a block away, and the same went for a dhampir.

I couldn't walk the entire two miles with a bleeding woman in my arms; even a New York City cop wouldn't turn a blind eye to that. I flagged down a cab and climbed inside, settling Ridley carefully on my lap.

She moaned; a low, hurting sound that hit me in the heart.

The cabbie frowned at me in the rearview mirror.

"Drive." I let the vampire-blue into my eyes. "Syndicate business."

His mouth dropped open. "Yes, sir."

"Drop us on the corner of Ninth and Fourteenth. Chelsea Market." I named a corner a block from my building so he wouldn't know our true destination. "And take it easy. She's hurt. I don't want her getting banged around."

The cabbie's swallow was audible. "Yes, sir."

I made Ridley as comfortable as I could, her head supported in the crook of my arm, her legs on the seat. Her skin was pale, her mouth tight with pain, and dark bruises had bloomed on her cheek and jaw.

I set my lips to her temple. "Hang in there, badass. We're almost there."

Her eyelids fluttered. "I'm...fine."

I huffed a laugh. "Sure you are."

Back there in the tunnels when I'd turned and seen that bastard stick Ridley with his knife, the bottom had dropped out of my world. I would've gladly taken the blade myself.

I pressed a kiss to each of her closed eyes. Without her trademark energy, the inner vibrance that made her seem so much more than she was, she felt too light, almost fragile. Too damn breakable.

My chest squeezed like she'd reached inside and grabbed my heart— and that's when I knew I was holding my mate.

God damn it to Hades.

I didn't realize I'd spoken aloud until the cabbie glanced uneasily at the mirror.

I flashed my fangs. "Keep your eyes on the road."

I waited until he obeyed, then rested my head on the back of the seat. The adrenaline from the fight had worn off. I stared tiredly at the passing buildings. My eyes drooped, my head nodding on my chest.

I straightened and blinked rapidly, willing myself to remain awake until the cabbie stopped in front of the tall brick building that housed the Chelsea Market.

"We're here, sir."

I handed him a fifty and pointedly eyed his identification. "You tell anyone you saw us, and I'll hunt you down."

The fifty disappeared. "Saw who?"

"Good man."

I got out of the taxi, Ridley in my arms. She'd passed out, probably a blessing.

The market didn't open until seven a.m. I slipped into the entryway. When I was out of sight of the sidewalk, I faded into the shadows with Ridley. The building I owned was on the next block, the middle unit in a row of three-story buildings that had once been factories.

When I reached the corner, I saw a woman pounding on the front door of my building—Katie, disguised by a glamour. At least, I assumed it was her.

I circled around the back, dropped out of the shadows and slapped my hand onto the doorbell for the third floor. Xavier immediately buzzed me in. Not for the first time, I thanked the lucky star that had led to that chance meeting in Mexico.

Pulling open the door, I stepped over the threshold and back into the shadows.

My head spun. I took a stumbling step forward. I was running on fumes, my energy all but depleted. I set my jaw and strode with Ridley up the steps.

The first floor was rented at a low rate to a local nonprofit, who had no access to my private staircase. The door to the second floor, where my security staff's quarters were located, was closed.

Xavier waited at the top, holding open the door to my loft. I walked out of the shadows and into the kitchen—and got slammed by a wave of nausea. Beads of sweat broke out on my forehead. I swallowed and kept walking.

Xavier closed the door and fell in beside me. His gaze bounced between me and Ridley, taking in our torn, bloody clothes.

"What the fuck, jefe?" He insisted on calling me *boss*, even though I'd told him to call me Zaq.

"We got jumped by four underworld SOBs. Apparently there's a reward for anyone who stakes us."

He let out a low whistle. "Where do you want to put the woman?"

"My bed."

The loft took up the entire third floor. It was built on an open plan with the kitchen and living room taking up the front half. On the street side, a wall of windows ran the length of the living room. I glanced at them, relieved to see someone had closed the custom-made blackout blinds I'd had installed inside the glass.

Xavier followed my gaze. "I closed them," he said. "The blinds in your bedroom, too. No one can see in."

I nodded my thanks and headed down the short hall to my bedroom. Xavier slipped past me to turn on a small brass lamp and pull down the covers.

I laid Ridley on the bed. Her hair was damp from perspiration, its brightness dimmed like a tattered, but still beautiful butterfly. I stroked it back from her face, and her eyelids fluttered but didn't open.

"Scrub the video of us," I told Xavier, "then put the cam on a loop so it looks like no one is up here." The longer we kept my return a secret, even from my staff, the safer Ridley and I would be.

"I'm on it, jefe."

While he was out of the room, I removed Ridley's boots and eased up the hem of her sleeveless black tee. Blood seeped out of her wound. The blades used as stakes are long and thin, which meant the hole was small in diameter—a couple of centimeters across—but deep. Still, it would've scabbed up already if the silver had prevented it from healing.

My first priority was to clean out the silver. The longer the poisonous metal remained in her body, the sicker she'd get.

Xavier returned. His deep brown eyes moved from Ridley's pale face to the bloody hole in her lower left abdomen.

"She took a knife in the side?"

"Yeah. A silver knife. She's a dhampir."

His thick black brows lifted. I could see his intelligent brain working, but all he said was, "What can I do?"

"I need to irrigate the wound."

He nodded. "I'll boil up some salt and water and sterilize a meat baster."

"That'll do." The salt water would clean and disinfect the wound, and I could use the meat baster as a syringe.

"You gonna stitch it up?" he asked.

"Nah. Better to leave it open so the silver can work its way out. If it gets infected, I might have to clean it again."

Xavier left and I heard him in the kitchen, running water and putting it on to boil. I turned to Ridley, easing off her shirt and pants.

Her bra and boyshorts I left on. They weren't in the way, and the possessive beast in me who'd just realized I'd found my mate didn't want another man looking at her naked body.

I threw away the shirt and put her pants aside to wash later, then turned back to her. Not only her face was bruised; red-and-purple marks and cuts marred her arms and torso as well.

My lungs fisted with a dark anger. I only wished I could stake George twice.

I pulled the sheet over her legs and went into the bathroom. I scrubbed up, then gathered gauze, self-adhesive first-aid tape and a pair of surgical gloves. Back in the bedroom, I set everything on the nightstand and pulled a chair up to the bed.

Ridley's head moved from side to side. "Zaq?"

"Right here." I took her hand and brought it to my lips. Her skin was clammy. Dismayed, I laid her hand back on the sheet.

Her lids fluttered again. This time she managed to get them open. Fever-bright eyes searched my face. "You—okay?"

"I'm fine. You're the one with a goddamn hole in her side."

She raised her hand and hovered it over her abdomen without touching the injury. "Hurts."

My throat constricted. "I know." My voice came out a froggy croak. I cleared my throat, tried again. "I'm going to clean the wound out for you, okay?"

"Tired."

"I know, cher. Just let me get you fixed up and then you can sleep all you want."

A tiny nod. Her gaze took in the room—the high ceiling, the king-sized bed with a leather headboard, the exposed brick walls on two sides of the room, the bronze pendant lights. Her fingers plucked at the sheet, a soft linen in a color my interior designer called fog but to me was a plain old gray.

"Where...are we?"

"In my loft."

The corners of her mouth turned down. "Not safe."

"It's okay. I snuck us in and Xavier here—" the other man had walked in with a metal basin of hot water, a plastic meat baster and a stack of white kitchen towels—"will make sure nobody talks."

"Oh."

I got the nightstand from the other side of the bed and set it next to me. Xavier laid the baster, pan and towels on it.

"No one can know we're staying here," I told him. "Not my father. Not my mom. Not even Gabriel and Rafe."

Surprised flickered over his face. "Not even your brothers?"

"No."

"Understood. You need anything else?"

"Some blood-wine for the lady."

"Be right back." Xavier returned in thirty seconds with a stemless glass of merlot.

I cupped the back of Ridley's head. Her gray eyes were clouded with pain.

My mouth flattened. Fuck, I hated seeing her hurting like this. She was such a badass, and I loved that about her—but she shouldn't have to be a badass. She should be able to live a normal life with a job that didn't mean risking her life on a daily basis.

"Drink." I brought the glass to her lips. She took a small sip. I kept the glass against her mouth. "More."

She took another tiny drink, then turned her head. "Done."

"One more sip." I used my sickroom voice, soft but firm.

She wrinkled her nose at me but obeyed.

"Good girl." I finished the wine and put it on the nightstand.

To Xavier, I said, "I'm going to roll her onto her side and clean as much of the silver out as I can. You catch the overflow with the towels."

"Got it." He picked up the towels and moved to my other side so he could reach her more easily.

I turned back to Ridley. "Okay. Let's do this."

She tried to turn onto her right side herself. I guided her the rest of the way over, packed some of the towels around her and pulled on the surgical gloves.

"This is going to hurt," I warned as I filled the meat baster/syringe with the warm salt-water solution.

She nodded. Her fretfulness had vanished, replaced by a grim determination.

I pulled the wound a little apart with my gloved fingers. She tensed but didn't make a sound.

I winced along with her. "Relax, sweetheart." I kept my tone low and easy. "Breathe in. Breathe out."

She nodded and I felt her muscles loosen.

I made a small, approving sound. "Perfect. Just like that."

I squirted the saltwater solution into the wound multiple times while Xavier sopped up the blood and pus that ran out of it. Ridley remained outwardly relaxed, her breath loud but even, for the entire procedure.

Hell, I was more tense than her. I knew it had to hurt like a mofo.

At last I finished. The blood ran clear, and the wound had started to close up.

I sat back and released a long exhale like a tire leaking air—which was pretty much how I felt.

Xavier patted Ridley's side dry. "Nice work," he told me. "I think you got all the silver."

"I hope so." I ripped open a gauze packet and bandaged the wound, then stripped off my gloves and dropped them on top of the dirty towels.

"Almost done," I told Ridley. "Now I'm just going to clean you up."

Xavier handed me a damp washcloth, and I cleaned the blood and sweat from her face and body. "There you go. All done." I tucked a lock of white-gold hair behind her ear.

"Thank you," she whispered. She closed her eyes and a few seconds later was asleep.

Xavier gathered up the towels, basin and supplies.

"Bring me a glass of the merlot," I told him. "No, bring the whole bottle. And some cheeseburgers—rare. I'm hungry as fuck."

He nodded. "What about a thrall? You look like hell."

A thrall? My fangs pricked at my gums and my mouth watered. I needed fresh blood, bad.

I reluctantly shook my head. "Better not risk it."

"Leave it to me. I'll get Sierra—offer her triple her usual rate and put her up here for a few days. But I'll have to tell the team you're here."

I hesitated, but I needed to feed. "All right, but don't tell them about Tina." I indicated Ridley, using her current alias. I trusted Xavier like a brother, but the less people who knew her identity, the better. "And if anyone leaks that I'm here, I will personally send them to their final grave."

"Don't worry. They'll keep quiet."

I sat back on the chair, legs stuck out in front of me, and considered the sleeping woman. So Ridley No-Last-Name was a princess—and someone wanted her dead.

I pursed my lips. "You've been keeping secrets, badass."

If she really were a princess—and why would George have lied?—that meant her father was a primus. And my bet was on Leo de Froulay.

I considered her pale hair and delicate features. Why hadn't de Froulay claimed her? The man didn't have a mate who might object to Ridley. He didn't even have an heir of his bloodline.

I massaged the bridge of my nose. "But that's not the biggest problem here, is it?"

First we had to figure out who had put out the hit on us. My father? Slayers, Inc.? Or someone else altogether? Because how the hell would my father or SI know Ridley was a princess?

Xavier arrived to inform me the food was ready. I nodded and with a last glance at the sleeping Ridley, followed him down the hall to the main part of the loft.

The kitchen table was a one-of-a-kind piece I'd bought from a Maryland woodworker who'd cut up two old oak doors into rectangles of different sizes and fit them back together into one large rectangle. I pulled out the steel chair in front of a platter of cheeseburgers and sat down. Xavier took the seat opposite and sipped a blood-wine while I started on the first burger.

"So I take it you know what went down at the Garnet last night," I said between bites.

He nodded. "Victorine Tremblay was staked when she attacked your father. Mraz got caught in the cross-fire."

I stopped eating to stare at him. "That's the official story?"

"Yeah. You know different?"

I shook my head and took a gulp of blood-wine. "I was there, but not in the restaurant. I was watching from a roof across the street. I got word that Father and Rafe were meeting with Victorine and her daughter, and I—"

I stopped short of saying I'd been there to stake my father before he could kill Rafe. Some things Xavier was better off not knowing.

"I was there to help if I could," I said instead. "I don't trust Victorine."

"Well, she's not a problem anymore, is she?" He flashed a white, sharp-toothed grin.

"No." I stared at him. "She's not, is she?"

In all the excitement, I'd almost forgotten. The prima had always been out there, the woman who wanted me and my brothers dead.

At least something good had come of last night.

"So where the hell have you been?" he asked. "And why couldn't anyone get in touch with you?"

"First I was in a fucking cell in Paris and then I was holed up recovering from what the bastards did to me. Since then I've basically been dark."

"A cell?"

I nodded. "An enforcer from the Paris Syndicate had me kidnapped and kept me in a cell, cuffed to the wall. Silver cuffs."

Xavier's gaze went to the braided leather bands on my wrists. He pursed his lips. "The enforcer's still alive?"

"Moreau? For now." We exchanged grim smiles. "But enough about me. Tell me what's been happening with my brothers."

"Here's what I know." He sat back, wine glass in hand, and brought me up to date while I helped myself to a second cheeseburger.

Gabriel was fine despite having been almost staked—twice. In fact, he'd impressed some of our most vocal detractors in the syndicate with how he'd kept things together while my father had been out of touch.

And the thing between Gabriel and Camila Vittore was legit. She'd accepted his blood bond at the Ruby Speakeasy in front of a roomful of Kral Syndicate vampires.

"You didn't hear this from me," Xavier added with a sly smile—he prided himself on being the first to know anything—"but Gabriel took the Vittore chica as his mate."

"No kidding." So Gabriel's Mila really had come back. I smiled. "That's good news."

"They haven't been seen since last Thursday, though. Somebody told me he took her to his house out on Long Island, and she's undergoing the transition to dhampir for him."

"Wow. That's some heavy shit." As a human, Mila only had a 50 percent chance of surviving the transition. No wonder Gabriel had seemed distracted when we spoke on Monday.

"Yeah," said Xavier.

"And Rafe?" I asked.

My younger brother was fine too, and had apparently mated with Zoe —in fact, the princess had intended to defect to the Kral Syndicate, which was why they'd been meeting with Victorine Tremblay.

"You can guess what the prima thought about that," Xavier added dryly.

As a dhampir, he'd been treated like scum by the Mexico City primus. The only vampire he truly liked and respected was my father.

"So Victorine attacked first?"

"That's what Feehan says, and he was inside the restaurant."

I straightened. "He was? Tell me exactly what he said."

"Exactly?"

"Yeah. This is important."

Xavier stared into his glass for a few seconds. "Okay, here's what he told me. Your father accused Prima Victorine of breaking the truce. He had proof, said Princess Zoe had shown him the evidence herself. He mentioned Philippe Moreau, said he'd been stripped of his rank as enforcer for detaining you and Rafe."

His gaze flicked again to the leather wristbands.

"Excellent." I showed my teeth in a smile that would've surprised those vampires in Moreau's lair who'd believed I was soft. "It will make it easier when I stake the sonuvabitch. Go on."

"There was more talk about the feud. Your father pushed Victorine to put the feud behind them for good. Rafe and Zoe had bonded, he'd said, and if Victorine staked Rafe, Victorine's bloodline would end with Zoe."

"So they really mated."

Xavier nodded. "The prima gave in. You know how vampires are about their bloodlines. She took an oath that the three of you were safe from her, that she'd never try to harm you. That's when things blew up."

I leaned forward, literally on the edge of my seat. "What happened?"

"Only two guards were allowed in the room—Feehan and another man. But the other soldier was really Lieutenant Mraz using a glamour. He staked the man who was supposed to be there and took his place."

"But my father must've known—"

A decisive shake of his head. "No. Your father had been looking for the lieutenant. Mraz wanted you dead. That much everyone agrees on. There's talk he was working with SI."

I considered that. It fit, and yet... "But what if it wasn't Tomas who was working with SI? What if it was my dad?"

"The primus?" Surprise splashed across Xavier's broad face. "Why would he want you dead?"

"I don't know, damn it. It doesn't make sense to me, either. But I was told by both Moreau and Tina that he knew I was in that damn cell, and he did nothing to get me out."

His sturdy shoulders lifted in a shrug. "I suppose it could be true. It fits the facts, and everyone knows Tomas was an extension of Karoly. But why would your father want to take out his heirs?"

"That's what doesn't make sense to me, either. Unless he believes we're planning a coup."

"You heard about that?"

"So it's true? People are saying the three of us are planning a coup?"

"Yeah. Your father disappeared around the same time as you, and suddenly Gabriel was in charge. It looked bad, *sí*? And Mraz seemed edgy. He supported Gabriel in public, but behind his back, he was trying to find out where your father had gone. Mraz even flew to Paris, which didn't make sense at the time, but if that's where you were—"

"Yeah."

"But Monday night, your father marched into the Ruby Speakeasy and put a stop to the rumors. Said he'd put Gabriel in charge himself, and if anyone said different, he was lying. Sounds like somebody was trying to make trouble." Xavier fingered his chin. "Maybe Mraz?"

I grunted. The gods knew, I wanted to believe my father was innocent. But he and Tomas had been so close. Either one—or both—could have been working with SI. Whatever you said about one man applied equally to the other.

And there was that note I'd seen in Tomas's office, the one that had implied the rumors of the coup came from someone else...

"So how did Tomas and Victorine die?" I asked.

"Tomas attacked Rafe out of nowhere and all hell broke loose. Feehan said it happened like that—" Xavier snapped his fingers. "Victorine took advantage of the confusion to grab Zoe's dagger and went for your father. Then a funny thing happened. When Mraz saw Victorine attack Karoly, he went for her himself."

"So it was Tomas who staked Victorine?"

"That's right. And your father staked Mraz."

"That's what I heard last night." I stared unseeingly over Xavier's shoulder, recalling the scene in the Hotel Garnet courtyard. "What I don't understand is why Father would stake Tomas when he'd defended him against Victorine? Unless he's going blood mad…"

"Your father?" Xavier looked at me like I'd sprouted a second head. "No way. He might be old, but my master in Mexico was going blood mad, and I can tell you your father is not. He's not giving off that odor, is he?"

"Not when I last saw him. But that was a couple of months ago. Suppose he's in the early stages?"

Xavier spread his hands. "Anything is possible. What makes you think this, anyway?"

My gaze jumped toward the bedroom.

"Ah," he said. "The woman. But how would she know?"

I shrugged, not ready to answer that.

Xavier tugged at his lower lip, something he only did when he was worried or upset.

"What?" I asked.

"The last thing Tomas said is, 'Zaquiel is ours. You will not find him until it is too late.' Everyone is looking for you, jefe. There's a rumor going around that you secretly joined SI. They say that's where you go when you disappear, that your so-called humanitarian missions are a cover."

My jaw dropped, along with my stomach. "Holy fuck. Leave for a few weeks and the world goes crazy. So I'm the bad guy? Tomas really said that?"

Xavier nodded. "You have to admit, it looks funny. First you disappear like you got sucked into a fucking black hole. Then when you reappear, you don't go straight to your father, you hide instead. You can't blame people for getting suspicious. Most of the vampires in the syndicate go way back with Mraz, and you're the Kral brother who never officially joined the organization." He spread his hands. "If you were them, what would you think?"

"Damn." I exhaled through my teeth. "It actually makes a weird kind of sense."

And to be honest, I *had* been up to something. I'd come to New York with a fucking slayer to stake my own father.

Hell, if I were a Kral vampire, I'd be suspicious of me, too.

Xavier glanced toward my bedroom. "So how does the woman come into this?"

"It's complicated." I blew out a breath.

Something was bothering me. Something Tomas had said. *"Zaquiel is ours."*

And that's when I knew. My view of the past few weeks' events shifted and realigned.

I sat up straighter.

Tomas was the traitor. He had to be. It was the proof I'd been searching for. Why else would he have said I was "theirs"—whoever the hell "they" was?

And if he was in his final grave, then Gabriel and Rafe were safe.

The back of my throat stung and my eyes prickled. It had been such a long few weeks.

I swallowed and brushed a hand over my eyes. Xavier reached across the table and refilled my wine glass. Not saying anything, just making it clear he was on my side, no matter what.

I took a gulp of wine. By the time I set it down, I had myself under control.

"It was Tomas. It has to be. He's been feeding intel to Slayers, Inc.— and they were the ones who kidnapped me. They were working with Moreau and Victorine Tremblay. I have proof. Tina will back me up."

But would my dad believe me? Or would he believe Tomas's last, vicious accusation?"

A sliver of apprehension worked its way into my happiness.

This wasn't over. Not for me, anyway.

Especially with Ridley—a slayer—here in my loft. Even I had to admit that looked damn shaky.

"So," said Xavier. "This woman. She's a slayer, isn't she?"

I gave a tight nod. "But no one else can know that. Swear it, Xavier."

His mouth flattened. "*Dios mio*. What in the name of the Dark Lady have you gotten yourself into?"

"First, swear you'll keep her secret."

He snorted, clearly insulted I had to ask. "You know I will."

"Thank you. And I'm sorry. You know I trust you with my life. If I didn't, I wouldn't be here."

"Damn right you can," he muttered in Spanish, then added, "And why didn't you come straight to me? How long have you been in the city anyway?"

"Nine nights," I admitted.

"So you don't trust me to keep my mouth closed?"

"It's not that. I didn't want to put you into the position of lying to my father. I may still end up with a stake in my heart."

His head lowered like a bull ready to charge. "You think I'm afraid?" He smacked a fist to his chest. "Me?"

"Hell, no. I've seen you in action, remember?"

He nodded, somewhat mollified. "And what about Tina?"

"What about her?"

"Are you loco, bringing her here? I don't care if she's hurt. You could've left her on the street for them to find."

"She's also the one who arranged that deal for me in Paris. Otherwise I might still be in that fucking cell. And they didn't just have me cuffed to the wall in silver without allowing me to eat or sleep—they were feeding from me."

Xavier's brows lowered. "Thrice-damned blood-suckers." His primus had planned something similar for him before I got him out of Mexico.

"Anyway," I continued, "this morning, when those underworld pricks attacked us, I told Tina to get the hell out of there, but she wouldn't go. She stayed and helped me fight them off—and ended up getting knifed. So don't worry about her. She's with me now. You can trust her."

"Whatever you say," he said, clearly not convinced. "Okay. I'll tell you what. Tonight I'll go to the Ruby Speakeasy, see what people are saying. See if they've bought this story that you're working with SI to overthrow your father."

"Fuck the syndicate. The only thing I care about is what my dad believes."

"You still need to know what they're saying."

"I know. It just pisses me off, that's all. I was kidnapped, for fuck's sake. How did I become the bad guy?"

He slanted me a look. "Why did you come to New York with a slayer, anyway?"

"To stake my father."

He reared back. "This is the truth?"

"Yeah. They said it was the only way to save my brothers from SI. And once they got hold of Rafe, they turned up the pressure. Threatened to sell him as a blood slave if I didn't do exactly as they said."

"Does Karoly know any of this?"

"Not as far as I know. But who knows what Mraz told him?"

He dragged his fingers through his straight black hair. "Holy Mother of Darkness. This isn't good. This isn't good at all."

"Yeah. I know."

By the time Xavier and I wrapped up our little convo, I was so tired I was seeing two of him.

I stumbled into the bathroom and stood under the rain showerhead, eyes half-closed, letting the water wash away the blood and sweat and smell of the tunnels. I toweled off, then crawled naked onto the mattress beside Ridley.

I touched my fingers to her carotid. Her pulse was weaker than I liked, but steady. I set my head on the pillow next to hers, and the next thing I knew, it was late afternoon.

Ridley was still asleep. She'd pushed the sheet off and lay flat on her back, one hand touching my hip, the other curled near her head.

Her body radiated heat. Too much heat. And her lips were dry and pale, her eyes sunken. She was dehydrated, her dhampir body sucking up energy to heal itself.

I sat up and lifted a corner of the gauze, checking the wound. It had closed up already and was a healthy pink. I sniffed, but there was no sign of infection.

I got up and used the john, then hurried back to try and get some fluids into her. Xavier had left an open bottle of blood-wine on the nightstand. I poured some into a glass and brought it to her lips, but I couldn't get her to wake up enough to drink. I swore and set the glass on the nightstand.

Xavier tapped on the bedroom door. "It's me."

I opened the door, and he looked me over with a critical eye. "You look better. Too skinny, but better. What about the woman?"

"The stab wound is better, but she's burned through a lot of energy." I dug out a clean T-shirt and boxers and put them on.

Xavier eyed Ridley coolly. "She needs to feed."

"She won't. She has...issues about fresh blood."

"Figures." He curled his lip. "Typical fucked-up slayer. Anyway, I came to tell you Sierra is here."

"Good." Sierra was one of my longtime thralls. Xavier had suggested I have her stay on the middle floor for the next few days. I'd agreed, telling him to take away her devices so she couldn't communicate with anyone. In return, I'd instructed him to pay her triple her usual fee. "She agreed to the terms?"

"Yeah. She and Katie are a thing now, so she's happy to move in for as long as you need her." Katie was a member of my security team, along with two men.

"Good."

"And Katie and the men said to say they're behind you a hundred percent. They'll keep your secret."

I nodded. "But I still don't want you to tell them about Tina." I nodded at the sleeping Ridley. "Somebody wants her dead, and they're willing to pay a boatload of money to make it happen."

"Hmm." His look said the jury was still out on "Tina."

He withdrew, and I pulled on a pair of shorts and tried again to get Ridley to drink some blood-wine. This time, she woke up enough to take a small amount.

I left her to rest and went out into the living room where Sierra waited on a couch. A curvy, black-haired woman, she rose to greet me with a wide smile, and we air-kissed.

"It's good to have you back, Zaquiel."

"It's good to be back."

We sat on the couch, and I took the blood from her wrist. Energy surged into me. Somehow I knew my body had finally eliminated the last of the silver.

I felt like myself again. Focused, in control.

Back in the bedroom, Ridley was struggling to sit up. Her skin had an unhealthy flush and her eyes were blood-shot.

"Hey, take it easy." I hurried across the room and guided her to lie back down. "What can I get you?"

"Thirsty," she croaked.

I filled the wine glass and brought it to her lips, and she gulped it down.

"George." She plucked at my wrist. "Knew who I was."

"Rest." I laid her head back on the pillow. "We'll talk about it later."

"No." Her throat worked. "*Listen*."

"Okay." I took her hand. "What do you want to tell me? You really are a syndicate princess?"

A slight shake of her head.

"You're not?"

"Not...that. He knew...I was Reaper—with you."

"And you're wondering how?"

Her fingers dug into my palm. "Crow. In the city."

"Crow?" She was worried about a bird?

"My...alpha."

Understanding dawned. "Your alpha's name is Crow, and you think she's the one behind the hit?"

She dipped her chin.

"But why?" I asked. "I understand why she'd put a hit out on me, but why you?"

Ridley moistened her cracked lips. I released her hand and brought the wine to her mouth again. She took a small sip, but when I tried to get her to drink more, she pushed the glass away.

I put it down and turned back to her. I would've preferred to tell her to rest, that it could wait, but her urgency had communicated itself to me.

I touched her cheek. "I'm listening."

"Back at the Garnet. She was there."

Understanding dawned. "The woman in the alley?"

Ridley nodded. "She took me off the op. Wanted to know where you were. I gave her an address...in Brooklyn."

"I see." I frowned, working it out in my head. "So you lied to your alpha. In fact, you should have left me last night. You shouldn't even have met me in Times Square. Is that what you're saying?"

"Yes. I'm...a rogue."

"A rogue?" I sat back abruptly. "A rogue slayer?"

She squeezed her eyes shut like it hurt even to think it. "Yes."

I swore under my breath. "So they want you dead. They put out a hit on both of us. It's not my father, it's SI. They're trying to take us both out."

"I don't know. But maybe—?" She moved a shoulder. "I'm on your side now, Zaq. And my alpha wants you dead. I think she's always wanted your whole family dead—you, your brothers, your father. And when she sets her sights on something, nothing stops her."

The vampire beast awakened. I felt my eyes change, blue rimming the irises. When I spoke, my voice sounded harsh in my ears. "I'll keep you safe."

Her gaze bounced between my eyes. I knew she saw the vampire, but for the first time she didn't recoil or tense. That was progress, and it calmed me a little.

"It's not me I'm worried about," she said.

"Too bad. They touch you, and I won't stop until the whole damn organization goes up in flames."

"No." She moved her head from side to side against the pillow. "I... don't want that."

I growled. "You think I'm going to stand by and let them kill you?"

"Please." She caught my hand, her breath coming in short, agitated pants. "I'll help...as soon as...I'm better. But...wait."

"Okay, okay." I brought her hand to my lips, pressing a kiss to her soft skin. "Calm down. I'm not doing anything tonight anyway—I'm staying right here with you until I'm sure you're better. Plus, Xavier is going to a Kral speakeasy to see what he can find out."

"Okay." She closed her eyes, the spurt of energy gone like she'd sprung a leak.

My heart constricted. She appeared so small and vulnerable against the gray sheets.

Enough. Stripping off my T-shirt, I got back into bed and brought her mouth to my throat.

"Drink, baby. Please. You have to get better."

She made a small, negative sound and turned her head away.

"Damn it, Ridley." I guided her back to my throat, but she'd passed out again.

I held her to my heart. "I'll keep you safe," I murmured, silently vowing to protect her with everything I had.

My position. My money. My life.

I left her sleeping and went into the living room to try and catch Xavier, but he'd already left, so I buzzed the second floor on the intercom and asked him to come back to the loft.

"Be right there," he said.

He'd changed into a dark suit and crisp button-down shirt, required attire for the Ruby Speakeasy. No tie, though; Xavier didn't don a tie for anything but funerals and mating rituals.

I explained what Ridley had told me about why she'd been targeted.

"A rogue?" He lifted a brow. "You sure she's not playing you? A slayer will lie like a snake if they think—"

I cut him off with a slash of my hand. "She's telling the truth."

"How do you know?"

"I just do. Trust me."

His expression changed. "She got to you. You've been fucking the bitch."

My hand wrapped around his throat. We might be friends, but he'd just crossed a bright, hard line. "Don't. Call. Her. That."

A muscle in his jaw worked. "Sorry."

I gave him a shake. "You *will* respect her, got it? She's my woman."

He dipped his chin.

I released him, blew out a breath. "We're linked. That's how I know she's telling the truth. I can feel her emotions, and she meant it."

His brows crawled up his forehead. "You mated a slayer?"

"Not yet. It's still new—I just realized myself. I'm not sure if she knows it herself."

Xavier smoothed down his jacket, straightened his shirt collar. "I'm sorry; I didn't know." This apology sounded sincere, unlike the first.

"Apology accepted," I said with a curt nod. "I need you to get out there, see what you can find out. Who put up the money for the hit? Somebody has to know something. Start at the Ruby, but if SI is involved, you may have to work your underworld contacts. But be careful. From what George said, Spider didn't know about the reward—and if he doesn't know George attacked us first, he'll be gunning for me."

"Understood."

"You have cash for bribes?"

"Fifty thou."

"Good. If you need more, get it. I want answers, ASAP. But don't go into the underworld itself—Spider knows you're my chief of security. Oh, and transfer 50K to his account. I want to act as if nothing happened until I can work this out with him."

"Got it."

I waited until he left the loft, then headed for my office and my stash of burner phones. I'd decided to chance a call to Gabriel.

I hadn't forgotten what Xavier had said about Mila undergoing the transition to dhampir. Gabriel must be standing guard over her gravesite, waiting and worrying until she'd made it safely through the transition. But I hoped he could give me a few minutes. He was smart and pragmatic, and closer to the top people in the syndicate than I was.

More importantly, he had Father's ear. If anyone knew what Karoly Kral was thinking, it was my older brother.

Plus, the thing about George knowing Ridley was a princess niggled at me. There was something odd about this, some piece I still didn't understand, and I was hoping Gabriel would have some insight on it.

I put a SIM card in a phone and activated the number. I sent a text with my identification code so Gabriel knew it was me, then pressed the Call button.

What I hadn't figured on was my father answering instead of Gabriel. "Zaquiel? Is that you?"

I jolted, took the phone from my ear. Father must be out at Montauk with Gabriel, unless he was having my brother's calls routed through him.

"Zaquiel?" he repeated. "Where are you?"

He sounded so normal. Like he hadn't staked his own lieutenant last night.

He certainly didn't sound like he believed I was a traitor who might be working with SI to plan a coup.

My heart hammered in my throat. I opened my mouth, then shut it again.

Part of me wanted to talk to him, to plead my case. But I flashed to

Ridley, pale and helpless in my bed, and knew I couldn't risk it. She was sick, unable to defend herself.

It was one thing to ask Father to forgive me for doubting him. But Ridley was a slayer, the slayer who'd kidnapped me and encouraged me to go after him. What if he insisted on taking her into custody, or even staked her on the spot?

Both parts of me—the vampire and human—snarled a *hell, no*. She was my mate, and I wasn't letting my father anywhere near her until I was sure it was safe.

I hit *End Call*.

The screen immediately lit up with a return call from Gabriel's number. I hit *End Call* a second time and powered off the phone.

I was pretty sure I hadn't stayed on the call long enough for Father to track me, but I couldn't take the chance. Removing the SIM card, I dropped it into a desk drawer along with the phone, then returned to the bedroom and Ridley.

❧ 31 ❧
RIDLEY

"**D**rink, baby." Zaq's voice, a low croon in my ear, pulled me from somewhere black and nameless.

My face was pressed to his neck. His throat was covered with stubble. I could smell his dark Zaq-fragrance, and I wanted to taste him. So bad.

Hunger gnawed at my insides like a ferocious little animal. My fangs tingled with the need to sink into his neck, to reach the blood pumping in the artery beneath my lips.

I licked the hollow of his throat. My mouth watered.

His muscles moved beneath my lips. "That's it, sweetheart. Drink. You need to feed."

Yes...

Without opening my eyes, I slid my hand around the back of his neck. He was strong, masculine, his skin rougher than mine even here. His upper body was bare, as was mine except for an exercise bra. His chest hair pricked my nipples through the stretchy material.

My fangs lengthened. I dragged the tips over his carotid.

His arms tightened, drawing me closer.

A stabbing pain in my abdomen made me groan and suck in a breath. My left side burned but I couldn't remember why, and I didn't care. I just wanted to feed.

"Easy, easy." Zaq arranged me so the burning lessened, and I returned my attention to his throat, pressing kisses to the stubbled skin.

His cock pushed against my hip, hot and insistent.

"Drink, baby." He stroked the back of my head. "It's okay."

I opened my mouth to obey—and froze, flashing back to the last time

I'd drunk from anyone. It had been my mom, and I'd been five-and-a-half-years old. Up until then, she'd let me feed from her because it was clear I wouldn't thrive without it.

But that last time, I'd glimpsed her expression, mouth turned down, nose scrunched like she smelled something bad.

Distaste, aversion—I didn't know what to call it then, but I felt it in my belly. Not for me—Mom had showered me with love—but for what I was.

A monster.

Like the men Mom had to hide me from.

A sick shame gripped me. I pushed away from her. "I'm not hungry."

She rolled her lips into her mouth. "You sure?"

I jerked my chin in a nod. "Yeah."

Her sigh of relief told me everything I needed to know. She kissed the top of my head. "How about I make you a hamburger?"

I'd said yes, and the next time I needed to feed, she'd somehow located a supply of blood-wine.

Now I pressed weakly against Zaq's chest, but he wouldn't let me go. "Please, Ridley. You're hurt. You need to feed."

I retracted my fangs and raised my gaze to his face. His expression was the opposite of distaste or aversion. His brow was furrowed, his striking green eyes pleading.

The link between us was stronger than ever. His concern swamped me, like a huge wave slapping down over my head and knocking me off my feet. The air left my lungs in a whoosh.

I was still reeling when Zaq brushed my hair back from my face. A tender gesture that made my heart somersault in my chest.

"You need fresh blood," he said. "You won't heal without it. You were stabbed with a silver blade. I cleaned out the wound as soon as we got here, but some of the poison had already entered your bloodstream. You've been out for almost twenty-four hours with a high fever. You're sick, dehydrated."

I gulped and looked around. We were in a strange room, one I vaguely recalled seeing before.

"We're safe?" And I was pretty sure I'd asked that before, too.

"For now. This is my loft." Before I could object, he said, "Don't worry, it's okay. My staff knows I'm here, but no one knows about you except my head of security. But we can't hide here for very long. My father's bound to check the loft sooner or later. We need to get back out there, find out what the hell is going on, and I can't do it without you. I need my badass."

His lips lifted in a small, crooked grin. A grin I felt in my whole body.

"Damn you," I muttered. He was manipulating me—I *felt* it through that odd, powerful link—and it was working.

"So you'll drink."

I blew out a breath. "Yes. Thank you."

Now that I was fully conscious, I knew he was right. I was in bad shape—weak and feverish, my body working overtime to counter the silver's toxic effect. I'd be useless in the event of another attack.

And there *would* be another attack. Too many people wanted us dead. Karoly Kral. Crow. Maybe even Spider.

Zaq guided my mouth back to his throat. I extended my fangs and sank them into his skin.

A dark excitement surged up in me. *Yes. This. Feed.*

Zaq hissed like he was in pain.

I recoiled, horrified. *Monster.*

But not him, me.

"I'm sorry," I said. "I—"

"No, no." His fingers clamped around the base of my skull, bringing me back. "I like it. It feels good."

Unable to help myself, I licked the blood from his throat. "My mom... my promise."

He caressed my nape. "Look, I know she meant well. But she was wrong. You're not a human, you're a dhampir. And drinking blood is necessary for us. Making you promise not to feed is like forcing a tiger to be a vegetarian. You need this, cher."

Tears leaked from my eyes. I pulled away from him, swiped at them with my hand.

"It's the only thing she wanted from me." My voice wobbled.

"I know." He laid his head on the pillow and looked into my eyes. "But she loved you. If she were here in the room right now, do you honestly believe she'd hold you to that promise?"

I retracted my fangs. "She didn't actually ask me to promise I wouldn't drink blood," I admitted. "It was my idea, because I knew how she felt."

"Mm." He traced my mouth with his index finger. "It's up to you, sweetheart. But if you're worried about me, don't be. I liked it. Especially when it's you."

"Yeah?"

"Yeah—it's a major turn-on. You must've heard that before."

My gaze returned to his throat. Zaq fell silent. He'd made his point, now he was leaving the decision up to me.

I moved back into his arms. They closed around me, lean and hard.

Nuzzling his throat, I extended my fangs, scraping them lightly over his skin. My mouth watered and a shiver of anticipation went up my spine.

"Yes," he encouraged. "Go ahead." He cupped the back of my head and held me to his throat.

With a slow inhale, I sank my teeth into him, taking a tentative sip.

Energy filled me, along with...wonder. It was so much better than blood-wine. Rich, a little salty. Luscious.

I sucked harder.

Zaq's throat muscles worked. "That is so fucking hot," he said thickly.

I moaned agreement against his skin. Lord help me, it *was* hot. Heat pooled in my lower abdomen and my panties dampened.

I took a half-dozen deep, greedy sucks. With each mouthful, I felt stronger, more energetic.

A fine sweat broke out on my body, bringing a lovely coolness. The throbbing in my side eased. I retracted my fangs, not wanting to take too much, since Zaq had only just recovered himself, and licked the marks I'd left behind. They closed up within seconds, but I kept licking.

He tasted so good, so male. So right.

I twined a leg around his and pressed my mound against his thigh.

He swore, rough and growly, his throat vibrating beneath my mouth. "Damn it, Ridley. Stop it already."

"Why?" My licks turned to kisses. I was drunk on him. I couldn't get enough.

"You're sick—you have a fever."

I cupped his cock through his boxers. He was hard and ready. "I feel better."

He removed my hand. "Let me take care of you instead."

"I'm fine." I pouted—and who was this woman, pouting? Ridley Craw-ford didn't pout and tease. But with Zaq, it felt like foreplay.

His gaze went to my pushed-out lower lip. He gave a hard swallow, then shook his head. "No. You're not. You don't know how sick you were."

He gathered me into his arms and carried me into a ginormous bath-room, all pale blue glass and black-and-white subway tiles. One side was a long, walk-in shower with multiple showerheads.

He turned into a cozy alcove where a porcelain slipper tub nestled, and put me down on a thick blue rug. "How about a bath?"

I nodded and kissed the side of his jaw. "I'd love it. But first, the toilet?"

"Toilet's in there." He pointed at a sliding door tucked next to the shower. "You need any help?"

"I'm good."

"Okay." He turned me toward the sliding door and smacked me on the ass, a casually possessive slap that made my inner thighs clench. "I'll draw you a bath."

"Make it...hot," I said with a sassy over-the-shoulder grin.

He just chuckled.

When I returned, soft music played on hidden speakers, and the tub was half-full. Zaq removed the gauze dressing on my side and discarded it, then had me lift my arm so he could examine my wound.

He gave a satisfied nod. "It's healing nicely. You should be okay to go in the water."

I examined it in the large mirror that ran the length of the bathroom counter. The hole in my side had closed up, the scab a healthy-looking dark red.

"Nice. You do good work, Kral."

"Thanks." He dropped a kiss on my nose. "Let's get you undressed."

He removed his leather bracelets and set them on the counter. I lifted my arms and he eased off my bra. His gaze fixed on my breasts like he couldn't look away, which made my nipples bead.

He groaned. "Keep teasing me, and you're going to get fucked so hard."

Arousal lanced from my breasts to my core. I slanted a look at him from beneath my lashes, testing my newfound flirting powers, my mouth stretching in a pleased smile. To hear Zaq, you'd think I was a freaking femme fatale, which couldn't be further from the truth. Still, I couldn't help being happy—no, *thrilled*—that he thought so.

His eyes darkened. "What?" He ran his thumb over my lower lip.

"You're looking at me like you want to eat me up."

"Because I do."

A warm, liquid heat twisted through my belly. My breasts felt heavy, sensitive.

I put my hands on his chest, letting my nipples brush against his curly dark hair, and kissed him on the lips. "Hold that thought."

"Oh, I will." His big hands palmed my ass, squeezed. "Now get in the tub."

I stripped off my boyshorts and Zaq helped me into the slipper tub. It was long enough for me to stretch out in with a foot or two left over. Behind it, nooks set at different levels in the tiled walls displayed fat white candles and a few perfect shells.

I eased back into the steaming water with a contented sigh.

"Too hot?" he asked.

"No. It's perfect. It feels so good." I sank lower in the water.

"Good." He turned off the faucet, soaped up a cloth and started washing me—my breasts, my throat, my arms.

He brushed his fingers over a deep bruise on my right triceps. "Whoever sent George after us is going to pay for every damn bruise," he promised in a harsh, syndicate-prince voice. "I thought Spider had more control over his people."

I moved a shoulder. "I've had worse."

A muscle in his jaw ticked. "Like fuck you have. How many times have you almost died, anyway?"

"I don't know—five times, maybe six? You can't think about it. If you do, you're constantly afraid. And when you're afraid, you make mistakes. You're too cautious—or worse, too bold. The blood-suckers can't sense my emotions, but they're not stupid. They can read body language, same as a human—maybe even better because they've been around for so many lifetimes. They can tell when you're afraid."

His brows lowered. "You shouldn't have to live your life like that."

"I went into SI with my eyes wide open. I knew what I was getting into."

"You must've been a teenager when you started training."

"Well, yeah," I said, not sure where he was going with this. "We all are."

"That's too damn young to give your life to a cause."

I stared up at him. He seemed angry—but not at me, *for* me—and I wasn't sure why. "What else would I do?"

"I don't know. Move in with me. Go to college. Open a business. You decide—you've got a long life ahead of you. But not if you stay in Slayers, Inc."

My heart thumped. Move in with Zaq?

I gave a slight shake of my head. "I took a vow."

"So? You can leave, can't you? It's not like you signed your damn life over to them."

"Of course I can leave. It's not easy, but I could. But I believe in what I do. I don't want to lea—" I halted, biting my lower lip. Because suddenly, I wasn't so sure I didn't want to leave. "Of course I can leave," I repeated.

Zaq grunted and soaped up the cloth again. "Sit up. I'll wash your back."

I complied, and he moved the cloth in slow circles over my shoulders, my spine, my lower back. I made a low sound of pleasure. "That feels so good."

He dropped a kiss on the place between my shoulders. "Want me to wash your hair?"

"Yes, please."

"I like you like this." His voice held amusement. "All sweet and submissive."

I turned my head to frown at him, but I felt too relaxed and my mouth tugged to the side into a droll smile.

He chuckled and set the washcloth on the edge of the tub. "Relax and enjoy it." He guided my head down to my chest and squirted shampoo from a wall dispenser into his hand.

I bent my legs, wrapping my arms loosely around them, and rested my head on my knees. Giving into the relaxed, good feeling.

Zaq massaged the lemon-scented shampoo into my hair and scalp, then used a shower attachment to rinse it out. "Conditioner?"

When I nodded, he got a palmful of conditioner from another dispenser and worked it in. "You're not bad at this, Kral," I said against my knees.

"Thanks."

"You must do it a lot." And yeah, I was fishing, but I needed to know.

He shocked me by saying, "Not really. I've never had a woman in my loft before. Well, except for my mom or a member of my security team. But I've had a few girlfriends, if that's what you're asking."

"And you like to take care of them."

He rinsed the conditioner from my hair, then helped me lie back in the water again, my head against the tub. He rubbed his lips over mine. "I like to take care of *you*."

Moving onto my right hand, he cleaned each finger, then kissed my knuckles and picked the left hand.

Gradually, memory returned. Or to be precise, I allowed myself to think. The last I remembered, Zaq had been cold, withdrawn. "You're not pissed off at me anymore."

"I was never pissed off at you." The washcloth moved down my body to my legs. He cleaned them with the same thoroughness he had my arms and hands, ending with my toes.

"Not true." I straightened my spine. "Even in the underworld, you acted like I was the enemy."

And it had *hurt*, even though I'd told myself it didn't matter. That I was the cool, pragmatic Reaper, the badass who never needed anyone.

Zaq draped the washcloth over the faucet and took my face in his hands. "I was an asshole. And you're right, I was pissed off, but at the situation more than you. I'd decided I couldn't do it anymore, the whole enemies-sex thing with you. It was messing with my head, making me think you were on my side. When you weren't. But now—" His mouth pulled sideways and he released me.

I grabbed his wrists. "What?"

"You put your life on the line for me. D'you remember telling me? You said you lied to your alpha, that you're a rogue now."

"Yeah." My chest squeezed. Panic slithered through me. "But if I'm not a slayer, what am I?"

Nothing, that's what. My skills weren't easily transferable to the human world.

"Hey." Taking hold of my wet shoulders, he touched his forehead to mine. "We'll figure this out. No one is going to hurt you. I'm sorry I was an ass."

His expression was so tender, his tone so sincere.

Jesus, this man. He was going to wreck me if I wasn't careful.

I swallowed over the obstruction in my throat. "It's all right. I didn't blame you."

"I'm sorry anyway."

My gaze went to the scars on his wrists. Scars I'd helped to put there. Guilt twisted and pulled at my stomach, spreading to my chest.

I turned my head and kissed the scar on his left wrist. "I'm the one who should apologize. I should've never helped kidnap you. I should've told my alpha no."

He caressed my shoulders. A corner of his mouth lifted in a wry smile. "I'll admit I did want to make you hurt, there for a while. But if you hadn't taken the job, SI would've assigned it to someone else."

"Still doesn't make it right."

"Ridley." Warm lips touched my temple. "We've all done things we wish we could go back and do over. And in the end, you saved me, didn't you? You brought me food and blood-wine, and you got me out of that hellhole."

I closed my eyes. I didn't deserve his understanding, and I definitely didn't deserve his forgiveness.

"I had doubts," I admitted lowly. "Almost from the beginning. But I ignored them, told myself you were too perfect to be true, that it had to be a smokescreen. No syndicate prince could be such a do-gooder."

"And I'm glad you did. Because you know what? If you'd told them no, we might never have met—and that would've been a goddamn shame."

I opened my eyes. The lump in my throat grew three times larger, like the Grinch's heart. "I—"

"How about if we start over?" His hands moved down my arms. "I'm Zaq Kral, and I think you're the most beautiful woman I ever met."

I couldn't help huffing a laugh. "So the first time we meet, I'm naked in your bathtub?"

"Yeah." He looked down at himself, grinned. "Come to think of it, I'm overdressed."

He rose to his feet and pulled off his boxer-briefs. His cock sprang free from a nest of curly black hair. It was darkly flushed, the veins prominent.

I licked my lips and it gave a happy little jerk.

He held out a hand. "What's your name, beautiful, and how did I get so lucky to find you naked in my bathtub?"

I took his hand. "Ridley." I hesitated, and added, "Crawford."

His eyes gleamed. A slow smile curled his mouth.

"Ridley Crawford. Nice to meet you." He drew me up. The water streamed off my body into the tub. He took a long look. A look so hot I wouldn't have been surprised if steam rose from my skin. "Very, very nice."

He snagged a towel from a warming rack, wrapped me in it and lifted me out of the water, setting me on my feet on the thick, fluffy rug.

"Likewise." I twined my hands around his neck and raised on the balls of my feet to kiss him. For now, I set aside my guilt and the fact that I didn't deserve Zaq's forgiveness.

He wanted this, and so did I. So bad.

Despite everything, these days in New York with Zaq had been some of the happiest of my life. And like a greedy child, I wanted more, even if it hurt me in the end.

He opened his mouth and I slid my tongue inside, running it over his teeth, playing with his tongue. The towel slipped down between our bodies. He twitched it away and moved his hands to my breasts, rolling the nipples between his thumbs and first fingers.

Pleasure moved through me in a slow, sensuous stream. His erection was a spike of heat against my abdomen. He sucked my tongue deeper and my knees melted. I moaned and pressed against him.

We kissed and kissed and kissed. Exploring each other's mouths, caressing each other's bodies. One kiss flowed into another and another in a string of loveliness.

I'd never spent so long simply kissing. I hadn't wanted to with other men. But with Zaq, this—kissing him, feeling his body warm and hard against mine—was so perfect. Necessary, even.

I'm not sure who lifted their head first, but even then, our lips clung to each other.

We inhaled in unison, a rough, needy sound.

Zaq slipped his fingers around my nape and moved his other hand to my ass, pulling me up against him. His mouth roamed over my face, kissing my eyelids, my nose, my lips.

"You want this?" He touched his lips to the tender hollow beneath my ear. "It's not too soon?"

A broken laugh scraped from my throat. "Stop now and I might have to hurt you."

He chuckled. "My badass." He made it sound like a compliment. "My beautiful, sexy badass." He bent his knees, and then I was in his arms and he was striding with me into the bedroom.

He laid me on the bed and followed me down, crouching over me like a big cat. He started at my throat, placing a ribbon of kisses from one side to the other, then continued down, biting and sucking my left breast, tracing the nipple with his tongue.

Time stretched like warm, sweet taffy. I drifted in a hazy, dreamlike state, alone in the world except for the sexy angel who loved me with his hot mouth and strong hands.

He moved his head to my other breast. I combed my fingers through the springy hair on the back of his skull and urged him closer. He nipped the beaded tip, shooting a thrill straight to my core.

I let out an "Ah," and arched my back, trying to get closer to him. He blew on the sensitized skin, then nibbled his way down my body.

When he reached my thighs, I bent my knees. He pushed them further apart and nuzzled my wet lips. The salty scent of my own arousal filled my nostrils.

He licked and kissed me, slow and perfect...now touching my clit, now swirling his tongue around it.

Tension gathered in my lower abdomen. "Zaq." I lifted my hips, wordlessly asking for more.

He obligingly sucked my clit like it was a piece of candy. Then he lifted his head and met my eyes. "I'm going to do this slow. You may as well lie back and enjoy it."

I blinked a couple of times. "But—"

He scraped his teeth over the soft skin of my thigh. "Trust me, cher. You'll like this."

"Hmm." I had a feeling I would like it, very much. But part of the fun was pushing back at him. "Don't I get a say?"

His smile was dark and very male. "Not if you want me to fuck you." A soft, I'm-in-charge-now statement that made my mouth drop open—and my sex clench.

He didn't give me time to process that, simply dove back in, teasing me with his tongue and fingers until my legs trembled and I was producing small, needy whimpers.

"More, more, more..." I twisted beneath him, begging him to finish it, and even then he drew it out for a few more endless minutes.

And then—at last—he sucked my clit into his mouth. Light and heat shot up my spine and exploded in my head. Even my fingers and toes tingled.

Zaq slid two fingers inside me. "That's it, sweetheart. Come for me."

My back arched. My sex constricted around his fingers. The sensations went on and on—and yet ended too soon. When I came back to myself, I let out a sigh.

Zaq gave me one last lick and kissed the inside of my thigh. "Beautiful."

He took a condom from a drawer in the nightstand and came onto his knees to open it. I rolled over to watch.

Christ, he was gorgeous: all lean, compact power. Hard shoulders, tapered waist, cut muscles. Soft hair covered his chest and thighs.

While he rolled on the protection, I stroked him—his waist, his hips, around his balls. His breath hitched, and the corner of my mouth edged up.

"You're not the only one who gets to tease."

"Yeah?" He took my hands and crawled over top of me, pinning my hands on either side of my head. "Tonight, I am," he growled against my neck.

He released one of my hands and reached down to bring his tip to my entrance, then brought his hand back to mine. I interlaced my fingers in his.

He pushed into me, just an inch or so. I moaned, the pressure against my already-sensitized flesh almost too much. Pleasure and pain spiked through me, a sharp, sweet agony.

He pushed deeper, slow and unstoppable. The pleasure increased. I wrapped my legs around his hips and tightened my inner muscles around him.

His dark lashes drifted down over his cheeks. "Yeah," he said in rough tones. "Do it again."

I squeezed him again, and he began to move, gliding in and out, in and out, a little harder each time.

He rested his cheek against mine. His musky aroma filled my head.

I nuzzled his ear, breathing him in. Nothing and no one would ever smell as good as Zaq.

He released my hands and cupped my face. "Gods, I want you," he muttered against my mouth. "I can't get enough of you."

"I want you too." I stroked his back. His skin was slick with effort, the muscles rock-hard. "So bad."

He angled his thrusts so he could stroke my clit with his cock.

"Yes." I moved my hands to his muscular ass and squeezed. "Like that."

But it wasn't quite enough, and he slowed further, then pulled out all together. "Turn over."

I rolled onto my front and got onto my hands and knees.

He came back into me—and stilled. "You sure you're okay? Nothing hurts?"

"I'm fine." I wiggled my ass, enjoying how he inhaled sharply. "Really." Just a slight twinge in my side, but that was to be expected.

"Good. Because I want to fuck you hard."

I'd always had a thing for dirty talk. A hot lick of lust went over my skin. I jerked my head in assent.

He scraped his teeth over my nape. "Say it. Tell me you want it hard." A low voice in my ear.

"Yes." I swallowed, then added a "Please," because he seemed to like that.

He made a sound deep in his throat, part growl, part groan, and thrust slowly in and out. "You feel so damn good."

He stroked in a few more times, then scraped his teeth over my nape. I jolted and arched my back.

"Fuck me, Ridley."

I willingly pressed back against him, moving myself over and around his cock. He bent over me and slid his hand between my legs, stroking me and murmuring dirty, sexy things against my shoulder until I gave a small scream and broke again.

He straightened up. He gripped my hips, keeping me where he wanted me, and pumped into me, hard and fast, his groin smacking against my ass.

I whimpered into the pillow and pushed back against him. Pleasure rolled through me, wave after wave. Overwhelming. Perfect.

And when I climaxed a third time it felt like I'd exploded into a thousand flaming pieces.

Zaq gave a last firm thrust, then groaned and stilled, his dick jerking inside me.

After, he hung over my back, both of us breathing hard. Dropping a kiss on the sensitive spot between my shoulders, he rolled onto his back and reached out a long arm to pull me closer.

"Mm." I nestled my head in the hollow between his neck and shoulder. Warm and comfortable and at peace for the first time in forever.

He nuzzled my temple. "How about a burger?"

My stomach growled, and he chuckled. "I'll take that as a yes."

⚅⚅⚅

While I was flat on my back, healing, someone had washed my pants. Zaq got them for me along with my phone, wallet and a ribbed white tank, saying, "I had to throw out your shirt."

I nodded and washed my bra and boyshorts in the bathroom sink. Zaq ran them through the dryer while I dried my hair and brushed my teeth.

By then my underwear was ready, so I got dressed and put my phone in my pocket without turning it on. The wallet I left in Zaq's bedroom for now.

The last thing I did was reach for my blades, but I'd lost them in the underworld. I made a mental note to borrow some from Zaq.

As an undercover slayer, I'd seen a lot of rich vampires' lairs over the years, but Zaq's loft felt like a home in a way none of those lavish, expensively furnished lairs had. Yeah, it clearly belonged to a rich man—it had to be at least two thousand square feet with high ceilings, wood beams and exposed brick walls. The kitchen had gleaming graphite counters, pale orange cabinets and top-of-the-line appliances.

Still, the loft felt lived in. The walls that weren't brick were painted a tranquil sea green. The living room was furnished in buttery-soft, midcentury leather chairs and couches, and the coffee table held a thriller by Harlan Coben and a stack of well-thumbed travel magazines. In one corner stood a pool table with the balls racked up and ready to play, and two of the leather chairs were pulled up to the gas fireplace in the living room's center. Scattered here and there were family photos and an eclectic mix of First Nations pottery and statuettes.

Zaq stood at the kitchen stove with his back to me, his only clothing a pair of gray jogging pants cut off at the knees. He flashed a smile at me over his shoulder. "Burgers will be ready in five minutes."

"Can I help?"

"Nah, I got it. Make yourself at home."

"Thanks." I drifted around the living room, looking at things without touching them.

What would it be like to live somewhere like this? Somewhere that felt like a home, not just the place where I stowed my stuff?

A home where the man cooking in the kitchen belonged to me?

My eyes turned toward Zaq like he was a man-sized magnet. Savoring the smooth, efficient way his muscles worked as he flipped the burgers and added slices of cheese on top. The cut-offs hung low on his hips, showcasing a pair of deep dimples on his lower back, dimples I wanted to lick and fondle.

My chest hollowed out with longing.

Move in with me. Go to college.

He sent me another smile like he felt my eyes on him. "Almost done."

A sharp pang constricted my lungs. "It smells good," I managed to say.

Zaq made it sound so easy, but it wasn't. I'd taken a vow when I'd joined Slayers, Inc. A vow I'd meant to the depths of my soul. The idea of breaking that vow made me my heart jitter and thump against my ribcage.

But you've already broken the vow. You're a rogue.

Ohgod, ohgod, ohgod.

That's when I realized how completely I'd burned my bridges. They'd even put out a hit on me.

Emotions welled up in me. My throat closed.

Ohgod, ohgod, ohgod.

I took a couple of calming breaths, tamping the emotions down. I couldn't deal with this right now. Later, when Zaq was safe, I could consider how thoroughly I'd blown up my life. That is, if I'd somehow managed to evade SI's long arm.

But not now.

I took a few more deep breaths and looked around, focusing on my surroundings in order to ground myself.

I stood in front of the fireplace. Scattered along its thick wood mantelpiece were a mismatched set of framed photos. I picked up the first, my mouth twitching at Zaq and his brothers standing with their arms around each other, mugging for the camera. Zaq must've been about ten, which made Gabriel twelve and Rafe eight. The three of them were so freaking cute, like half-grown puppies.

I put it down to examine the photo of Zaq and his mom at some fancy event. He was sleek and sexy in a tux and she wore a long red dress, their dark heads inclined toward each other as they grinned at the camera. I'd seen photos of Rosemarie Kral, of course. I'd even remarked that Zaq took after her side of the family. This photo made it obvious—he was clearly the male version of Rosemarie down to the tiny smile lines at the corners of their mouth.

I flashed to Zaq calling for his mom back at Père Lachaise when he'd almost die and swallowed a spasm of guilt. Had I really become so single-minded that I'd ignored the fact that Zaq and his brothers had a mother, too? A mom they clearly adored, if Zaq was anything to go by.

The third photo made me do a double take. A younger Zaq—he couldn't have been more than twenty-one—stood with his arm curved protectively around a tiny, stooped nun with a shaved head and dark red habit, her lined face wreathed in smiles.

Zaq reached around me to pick the photo up. "She's the toughest human I know. And the kindest." His tone was admiring and full of affection.

I turned my head so I could see his face. "A Buddhist nun?" I don't know why I was surprised; by now, I should be used to this man surprising me. But I was.

"I met her on my first trip to Tibet." His mouth curved in an almost bashful smile. "She said the world needed more people like me. Told me to keep up the good work. That it didn't matter if they thought I wasn't for real, as long as I knew the truth."

I winced. I'd been one of the people who'd believed Zaq couldn't be for real.

"She was right," I said.

He put the photo back on the mantel. He was right behind me, his breath warm on my nape. A prickle of awareness slid over my neck and shoulders, followed by another pang of longing.

Move in with me.

My mouth twisted. The idea of us together was impossible. Hell, laughable.

And I knew it even if Zaq didn't.

He rubbed his hands up and down my arms. "Time to eat, cher."

32

ZAQ

There was something viscerally satisfying about feeding Ridley.

I liked taking care of her.

I liked having her in my space, and I fucking loved having her in my bed.

Having her in my loft felt right, even necessary, like there'd been a Ridley-sized hole in my life, one I hadn't even been aware of until she'd come along. Now, I couldn't envision going forward without her.

She was my mate. I was sure she felt the link between us, same as I did, and had been ever since that first morning at Charles Le Gaulle. But she was fighting it, pretending it didn't exist.

Well, tough shit. I wasn't letting her go. If I had my way—and I intended to—she was going to move in here permanently, and I'd show her what it meant to be part of a family. People who had your back no matter what. She didn't need to be a slayer to have that.

But first I had to know what, exactly, we were up against.

When we finished eating, I loaded the dishwasher while she wiped down the table. Then I poured us both another glass of wine and we went into the living room.

I sat on one of the couches. "I think it's time we talk, don't you?"

Her gaze flew to mine, and her grip tightened on her wine glass. But by the time she'd seated herself on a leather chair catty-corner to me, it was like that flash of tension had never happened.

"What d'you want to know?"

"Why don't you start by telling me why George called you Princess?"

She gave a tiny, tell-tale flinch. "Damn if I know."

My teeth clamped together. "You're lying," I said evenly. "I thought we were past that."

She puffed out her cheeks and released a breath. "You're right, and I'm sorry. I do know why he called me Princess, but he's got his head up his ass. I'm not a princess and never have been. I was raised by my human mom in small-town America."

"I figured your father was some lowlife like George, but he's a syndicate vampire, isn't he? He never claimed you as his spawn?"

"No. I knew who he was, but I never had any contact with him, even when Mom was alive. And after she died, I stayed far, far away."

"Because he's a primus. De Froulay?"

She blinked several times. "How did you know?"

"You look like him." I lifted a shoulder in a half-shrug. "It wasn't hard to guess once I knew you were a princess. He doesn't want to acknowledge you? Claim you as his heir?"

"Lord, I hope not." Her lip curled. "Until this year, he didn't even know I existed. To be honest, I don't know how he found out. I sure didn't tell him."

"But someone put out a hit on you. Someone who knows you're his daughter. Maybe it's not SI who put out the hit. Maybe it's something to do with your father."

"Sperm donor," she corrected absently. She frowned into her wine. "I suppose you could be right. Someone in his syndicate, maybe."

"Who knows he sired you?"

"No one. For a long time even he didn't know. My mom was afraid to tell anyone, even him. But someone obviously knew—or found out. We were hunted for years by Paris Syndicate vampires."

My heart squeezed for that young, defenseless girl. No wonder she thought all vampires were monsters.

"How did de Froulay find you, anyway?" I asked.

"I don't know." She turned her palm up. "He just sent for me one day. I thought he was going to hire me as a mercenary or bodyguard—that's my cover. I'm a merc for hire. Unless..."

"What?"

"The vampires who killed my mom. They wanted me. As far as I know, I'm de Froulay's only spawn. They demanded she tell them where I was that night. And when she wouldn't, they—" She rolled in her lips, shook her head.

I touched her leg. "I'm sorry."

She dipped her chin in acknowledgment and continued, "I thought I'd buried that part of me for good. I lived on the street for six months. The official story is that I died along with my mom but that my body was never found. But maybe they never stopped looking. Maybe they've been looking for me all this time, and when de Froulay sent for me in Paris, they put two and two together."

"Mm." I hesitated, but it had to be said. "I wonder how your alpha comes into this, Crow."

She heaved a breath. "I've been wondering about that too. Because George said the reward was for both of us."

"And you thought SI might have put out the hit on us. Who is your alpha, exactly?" I only knew bits and pieces about the secretive slayers' organization.

Ridley's silver eyes clouded. I could tell she didn't want to think about this—she clearly idolized her alpha—but Crow was rapidly becoming my number one suspect for the person behind George's attack.

"She's in charge of the entire North American operation."

I whistled. "So she's a biggie, a VIP."

"Yeah."

"Does she have another name?"

"Yeah, of course. But I don't know it."

"It worried you to see her at the Hotel Garnet. Why?"

She gave a you-still-don't-understand shake of her head. "Because of you."

"Me?"

"I was afraid she was there to stake you."

All the air went out of my lungs. I sat back. "You're saying you would've stopped her?"

Ridley rubbed her hands down her pants. "I couldn't let her do it."

"But I'm your target. You—"

"I told you. I'm on your side now."

"But why?"

She stared at me with her heart in her eyes. I waited for her to say she loved me, that she could never hurt me because she knew we were mates.

But her gaze slid from mine, and I tried not to be disappointed.

"Because you don't deserve to die," she told my chin. "You're a pawn in the battle between your father and SI. There's no other reason they would've kidnapped you."

"I see."

"Anyway, SI doesn't tolerate disobedience. The minute I lied to my alpha, I was a rogue. I'm—" She snapped her mouth on the words shut like merely releasing them into the room would be a betrayal.

"—fucked?" I finished for her. "So what you're saying is you would've protected me from your alpha. Me—a Kral."

Triumph flooded me. Triumph and love and all the things you feel when you've finally found your other half.

Her shoulders lifted in a shrug like the fact she'd chosen me over her mission didn't matter. "I should leave. Get far, far away from you."

Like hell.

I took her wine and set both glasses on the coffee table. "Try it and see how far you get." I pulled her onto my lap. "You're mine now, and I'm not letting you go."

She started to speak and I shook my head. "Let's save that argument for later, okay? I have things to tell you, too."

She opened her mouth to disagree, and I said, "Believe me, you want to hear this."

She compressed her lips. "Go ahead."

I brought her up-to-date on what Xavier had told me about what had happened in the Hotel Garnet restaurant, including Tomas's last words, "Zaquiel is ours."

Ridley had rested her head on my shoulder to listen, but now she pulled back to look at me.

"And there's a rumor going around you're the one who's been working with SI?"

"Yeah."

She stiffened and tried to push off my lap, but I tightened my grip on her.

She shook her head. "And here you are hiding a slayer. Holy bat crap, Zaq. You have to let me leave. If your father finds out—"

"I'll handle him. I'm not letting you go. We're mates. You just haven't accepted the bond."

"No." She shoved my arms away and rocketed off my lap like I'd touched a live wire to her ass. "Hell, no. I have to consent to it. Don't I?"

I stared at her, hurt and a little angry. Would I be that bad of a mate?

I took a deep breath. Ridley's objection came out of a place of fear; I would've guessed that even if I hadn't felt the panic radiating off her.

"Well, yeah. But you're not going to find it easy to leave me. There's a link between us, a connection. You think I don't know you *feel* me, just like I feel you?"

And right now, her anxiety was off the charts.

"Sometimes it's like we're in each other's heads," I added. "I've seen you wince when I was hurting. And you *knew* I'd come back that night in the Bronx. You knew I couldn't stay away."

Her eyelids flickered. "I wasn't sure."

"Then why was the famous Reaper—the roughest, toughest slayer on the planet—sitting outside a bodega drinking a soda and waiting for me to return instead of tearing apart the city looking for me?"

She wrapped her arms around her body and gave me her back. "*No.*"

Her anxiety was still off the charts, but I sensed something beneath.

Longing.

Hope.

And that gave me hope.

I went to her. "Ridley."

"What?"

"Turn around and look at me."

Her shoulders heaved but she turned to face me, chin lifted, fists clenched like I was her opponent.

I took her right fist, smoothed out the fingers. "It's okay, sweetheart. Nobody's going to make you do anything you don't want to. Just think about it, okay?"

She blew out a breath. "It would never work, Zaq. This isn't some fairytale. In the real world, rich and powerful syndicate princes don't mate with slayers."

"I'm not that powerful. You're thinking of my father, not me." *And you're not a slayer anymore.*

But I didn't say it aloud. That would be cruel, even if it was the truth.

She snorted. "Yeah, right. And I suppose you're not that rich, either."

"I'm not. Yeah, I have a nice-sized trust fund, but I only keep ten percent of the interest for myself. The rest goes to charity."

"Really?"

"Really."

Her brow creased. "How did I not know this?"

I almost laughed. Finally, something she hadn't discovered about me. "Nobody knows but my brothers."

"Huh." She shook her head. "But it's not just that. I don't do this, Zaq." She pulled her hand free and waved it between us. "Relationships."

"Never? But you've had sex before." Something dark and primitive moved through me. "You don't mean you only had sex with your targets?"

"No!" She recoiled. "I never have sex with my targets. Until you, that is," she added with a shake of her head. "I told you, my cover is a merc for hire. I go in as a bodyguard or a member of their security like with Moreau. Those men I had sex with, they were mainly other slayers who didn't want a relationship any more than I did. I spent my high school years at an SI training camp. I had hook-ups, but never more than once and not very often. I don't know how to do this whole man-woman thing. With a man I know. Not that we're *together*—you and me, I mean." Her face reddened. "Crap. This is so awkward. I'm so awkward..."

Tenderness filled my chest.

Gods, this woman.

But she'd told me something important. This was real. She wanted me as much as I wanted her. She just didn't know how to deal with it.

I caught her by the waist. "You're not awkward. And we *are* together."

Her mouth formed an 'O.' "We are?"

"Yes." I brushed a kiss over her rounded lips. She smelled good from her bath, clean and lemony. "We're together, involved, exclusive—I don't care what you call it as long as you understand you're mine. So get used to it. When this is over, you're not going to just walk away. I'll do whatever it takes to keep you."

"Zaq. I can't."

I was tempted to remind her that she'd gone rogue, that as far as we knew, her own alpha had put out a hit on her. Where the fuck did she think she'd go?

But her entire world had been knocked off its foundation. Being a slayer wasn't just a job, it was who she was. She needed time to adjust to the changes.

I could be patient. For Ridley Crawford, I'd do just about anything—except let her go.

"We'll take it slow." I caressed her hips. "Get to know each other."

Her mouth quirked wryly. "If we live long enough."

I couldn't help it. I laughed. "That's what I like about you. You're such an optimist."

She chuckled. "That's me, little Miss Sunshine. It's my superpower."

I laughed harder. We leaned into each other, laughing.

When our laughter died down, I pulled her into a hug. "I love you, Ridley Crawford."

She drew a shuddering inhale. "Oh, Zaq." Her arms curved around me, hovering over my back like a dragonfly's wings.

I caught my breath.

And when her arms tightened around me, it felt like a gift.

33

RIDLEY

I'm used to waiting. A slayer learns to exercise patience, or they don't make it past their first op.

That doesn't mean I like waiting. In fact, waiting is on my Top Ten List of Least Favorite Things to Do. No, make that Top Five.

Right now, waiting was torture. I wanted to be out in the city, gathering intel. I wanted to know who, exactly, was willing to pay 500 grand to eliminate me and Zaq.

And then I wanted to kick their ass.

But we needed Xavier's intel; and to be honest, I wasn't up to kicking ass right now.

So I paced the living room while Zaq watched from one of the couches, his long arms spread along the back, seemingly relaxed, which kinda made me hate him.

I stopped and did some easy pivots at the waist, letting my arms swing loosely around my torso. Testing how much the hole in my side could take, and considering our next step, although that depended on what Xavier found out.

What I *didn't* do was think about what Zaq had said about us being mates.

Well, okay, I did. In fact, I conducted an argument with myself in my head. Telling myself all the reasons it wouldn't work, why I couldn't let myself love him.

All I did was make my brain hurt.

Around the time I started my tenth circuit around the loft, Zaq rose from the couch. "Why don't we shoot some pool?"

I considered that, then said, "What I'd really like is a switchblade. Or maybe a couple."

"Come with me." He crossed to a beautiful, honey-colored mid-century cabinet with metal legs that stuck out at angles like an old-style TV antenna and opened the doors. "Take your pick."

I stared at the array of daggers, stilettos and switchblades like other women would a case full of jewels. I literally salivated.

I swallowed, licked my lips. "I can have anything I want?"

"Yep. Take two or three, actually. Wanna spar with me?"

"Yeah." I shot him a grateful look. "I'm going crazy here."

The corner of his mouth twitched up. "I noticed."

I hefted several blades, testing their weight and feel, before deciding on a pair of identical switchblades with stainless steel handles. I released the knives and traced a pattern in the air with them. "These'll work."

Zaq selected two switchblades for himself. "I'm not as good as you with the left hand, but I'll give it a try."

He moved a couch and a couple of chairs to the side of the room, and we faced off on a large kilim rug.

"Step off the rug and you lose," he said. "Otherwise, first person with three touches wins the round."

I nodded my agreement, and we circled each other, moving slowly, testing out moves. I was stiff—everywhere—and my wound twinged every time I raised my arm too high.

I worked through the stiffness until my muscles loosened.

Zaq parried my first thrusts but kept circling without attempting to strike at me. It took me a minute to realize he was giving me time to warm up. Making sure I didn't overdo it.

Taking care of me.

Warmth bloomed in my chest like a big fat flower and spread to my mouth. I was still feeling good from laughing with him. From knowing that he wanted a chance with me.

That good feeling made me grin at Zaq. A wide, happy grin.

His brows raised. "What?"

"Nothing. Just—" I retracted my blades and leaned in for a kiss. "That."

His lips clung to mine. "If this is a sneaky plan to distract me, it's working."

I grinned and danced back as his arms closed around me. He gave a play-growl and let me go.

I extended the blades again and feinted right, then came in left. The first touch was mine.

The next one, he must have been watching for the shift in weight because he was ready for me, parrying the move. He came back at me in an underhand thrust and touched the tip of his knife to my ribbed tank between my breasts.

The next touch was again mine.

He was still holding back, but I was practical enough to accept that. It felt good to move, but if I didn't take it easy I was going to end up back in bed.

Zaq got a touch, but I slipped one under his guard a moment later and won the first round. The next round went to him by one point.

He flashed me a grin, and I saluted him with a switchblade, not caring that I'd lost, just enjoying the game.

We returned to the center of the rug. He eyed my flushed face. "One more round, badass. Then you're going to lie down."

I rolled my eyes. "Yes, doctor."

His smile was pure fallen angel. "On second thought, I believe you need a thorough examination before you undertake any more physical activity. Just to make sure you're okay."

I tilted my head and pursed my lips. "I do have a hurt that you need to kiss better."

He grabbed my hand and marched me down the hall and into his bedroom. "Take off your clothes." He used his Prince Zaquiel voice, the one that made my lower abdomen all hot and liquid.

I obeyed, taking my time about it. Enjoying how his green eyes darkened.

When I was naked, he curved a hand around my nape and pulled me up against his still-clothed body. He nipped my earlobe. "Tell me where it hurts."

Electricity spiked from my breasts to my core. "All over," I said in a husky voice.

"Poor baby. Let me take care of that for you."

He backed me up to the mattress and guided me to lie down with my feet on the floor. Kneeing apart my legs, he proceeded to kiss me *all over* with an attention to detail that left me breathless and begging for him to come inside me and finish things already.

Only then did he remove his clothes and take me, him still standing, me on the bed looking up at him. He thrust into me, slow but firm, his face hard with desire.

I tightened my thighs around his lean hips. "More."

"Ask nicely." He paused his thrusts and circled his pelvis instead, teasing my opening with the root of his dick.

I pushed the fingers of my right hand into my hair, needing an anchor. I felt taut and flushed and needy. "Damn you, Kral."

"Beg me. And call me Zaq when I'm inside you."

He stroked into me again. So slowly sweat beaded his forehead. So slowly I thought I'd die.

It was both excruciating and amazing at the same time.

"Please!" The word burst out of me. "Please give me more."

"Zaq," he said.

"Zaq," I repeated. "*Please.*"

He rumbled his approval. "That's it. Now touch yourself."

I slid my hand between us and fingered my clit. I moaned with pleasure. It felt good—so good—but I needed him, too.

"That's it." He started thrusting again. Forceful. Perfect.

I had the fleeting thought that he was completely healed now, his body strong and lithe.

Then a white-hot static filled my head and I stopped thinking of anything but Zaq and how good he was making me feel.

Zaq said my name in a rough voice and thrust a half-dozen more times before stilling and emptying himself into me.

He hung over me, breathing hard, then crawled onto the mattress and pulled me into his arms. I nestled my head the crook of his neck, limp and satiated, my arm around his waist and one leg draped over his thigh, and closed my eyes.

I awoke a few hours later to find him easing himself out from beneath me. "Wheraryougoin'?" I mumbled.

He smoothed a hand down my spine. "It's three a.m. Xavier will be back soon."

"'Kay." I rolled over, stretched.

"How're you feeling? Any pain?"

"Nope." I touched my side. "It barely even hurts."

"Good. I'm going to take a shower. You get some more rest."

"Wake me up in an hour."

He nodded and got out of bed. I rolled onto my side and watched him walk to the bathroom. Damn, the man had a fine ass, firm and muscular.

Interest stirred in my belly.

He flashed me a grin over his shoulder. "Hold that thought."

I furrowed my brow. "You can read my mind?"

He turned back. "No. Just your emotions. Especially when you're excited or angry or horny. I told you we're mates."

Suddenly, I wasn't at all sleepy. I swallowed a spurt of panic and sat up in the bed.

He turned back. "What?"

"We really are mates?" I honestly hadn't believed him the first time. Not that I thought he'd lied, he was just...confused.

He nodded, his eyes on my face. His mouth tugged sideways in a whimsical smile. "Would it be so bad?"

My heart hammered in my chest. The panic spread out from my center to my fingers and toes. Fight or flight. I recognized the symptoms, but I could do neither. So I stared at him, mind whirling.

"I figured it was all in my head."

He crouched in front of the bed and took one of my hands in his. "Talk to me, Ridley. Tell me why you're scared."

"Because."

"Because what?"

"Because you're a freaking syndicate prince! And even if you weren't, I'm a rogue slayer. If we get out of this alive, I'm going to have to disappear."

"Fuck that." He grabbed my arms. "If you think I'm going to just let you walk away when this is over..."

"You have to. I'll only bring you down."

"No way." His eyes narrowed and his lips firmed. "We'll figure it out. You're it for me. I'm not letting you go."

"Zaq. Be reasonable. Even if we could make this all go away—SI, your father—it would never work. No." I gave a firm shake of my head. "I won't accept the bond."

A muscle ticked in his jaw. I could tell I'd hurt him, and that hurt me. But he deserved my honesty.

"Then I'll just have to change your mind," he gritted.

"You can't."

"No?" He stood up, pulling me with him. His mouth came down on my mine. Hard, demanding.

I pushed at his chest, but it was like fighting myself. With a whimper, I opened to him. His tongue swept into my mouth, telling me without words I was his and he was never letting me go.

Our bodies pressed against each other, fitting together like we were made for each other. I felt myself weakening.

A part of me—my soft, vulnerable underbelly—longed to agree. To believe that love could actually happen to a woman like me. A woman who'd closed herself off to emotion. A woman who lived only to kill.

Zaq sensed me softening. Of course he did.

He eased the kiss. Gave my lips a sweet, hot lick.

His breath sighed out. He rested his forehead against mine, one hand stroking my lower back.

"I love you, Ridley Crawford. I love you because you're a badass. I love you because you're a survivor. I love you because you're not the emotionless killing-machine you think you are, and most of all, I love you because you're you—complicated as fuck, but that just makes you interesting."

The words reverberated up and down my spine like he'd twanged a string deep inside me. I was gripped by a yearning so powerful I could barely breathe.

My chin quivered. "You can't love me." They were the hardest words I'd ever said. But I knew they were also the right thing to say.

"Yes, I can."

I opened my mouth and he touched his lips to mine, stopping my words.

"Don't say anything right now. Just promise me that when this is over, you won't disappear."

"Don't." I closed my eyes so I wouldn't have to look at his earnest expression. "I can't promise you anything."

I can't love you.

But that was a lie, because I could.

And I did.

My throat worked.

I *did* love him.

Zaq Kral didn't just smell right to me, he *was* right for me—in every way. His compassion, his work ethic, his love for his family. He was a beautiful man, inside and out, and I wanted him with every particle of my being.

His tongue licked at my mouth. "I'm not asking you to promise to stay forever. Not right now. For now, I'm asking for a few days. You can give me that much, can't you?"

I opened my eyes. He was so close, his gaze intent on me. I felt surrounded by him. His heat, his scent, his hard body.

I swear I intended to say no, but instead what came out of my mouth was, "A day. That's all."

His hands moved lower to stroke and squeeze my bottom. "Seven. You can give me a damn week."

"Two."

"Make it three." He nibbled the outer edge of my ear, flicked his tongue inside.

A hot thrill scalded the base of my spine. I pushed him away. "Fine. Three."

"Promise?"

"Yeah."

"Say it. When this is over, you promise you'll give me three days."

I heaved a breath. "When this is over, I promise I'll give you three days. But I'm not going to change my mind."

His mouth curved. "We'll see."

❦

Shortly before dawn, Xavier texted Zaq to say he'd be back soon.

His next text said: *The hit on you? It has a Paris connection. I'll explain.*

A few minutes later the back door buzzer sounded. Zaq checked the surveillance camera to make sure it was Xavier, then buzzed him in.

Zaq introduced me to Xavier as Tina. We murmured polite hellos and sized each other up.

Zaq's security chief was a compact, hard-muscled man with a shiny cap of black hair and a broad face that would've appeared kind if not for the cynical twist to his lips.

"You're out of bed. You're better?" He somehow managed to sound both concerned and to make it clear I'd have to prove myself before he'd roll out the welcome mat.

That was fine with me; I liked that he was protective of Zaq. "Much better, thanks."

He'd left the back door ajar. When I moved to close it, he looked at Zaq and lifted his shoulders in an apologetic shrug.

"I'm sorry, jefe."

Zaq's brows beetled. "What—?"

The air near Xavier wavered and coalesced, and Karoly Kral stepped out of the shadows, lean and dark, his eyes rimmed a fiery blue.

My stomach lurched and dove for the floor like an out-of-control airplane. I fumbled for my borrowed blades and ranged myself beside Zaq.

The Kral primus was slim and only a little above average height, but he dominated the kitchen like he was Keanu Reeves here to kick ass. Dark suit, broad shoulders, and a narrow, sharp-cheeked face with peaked black brows. His gaze flicked to my knives, but he made no move to defend himself.

Zaq reached out a long arm and swept me behind him. He'd pulled a switchblade too, although unlike me, he kept it at his side. "Father."

The blue fire surrounding Karoly's irises winked out. "Hello, Zaquiel."

I leaned around Zaq and took a surreptitious sniff. The primus smelled like a typical vampire—a little earthy, like a forest after a rain. No rotten taint. And he was clearly in control.

Zaq had been correct. His father wasn't blood mad...unless he was in the very early stages.

Xavier was still apologizing. "He followed me out of the Ruby. Said either I brought him into the loft with me, or he'd come back with a dozen men and break down the door."

"It's all right," Zaq said without taking his gaze from his dad. "I was going to contact him anyway."

"You couldn't have stayed in hiding much longer anyway," Xavier said. "There are all kinds of rumors about you. You would've had to show yourself."

"It's all right," Zaq said again. "Go back to the second floor. I've got this."

Xavier glanced uneasily at Karoly. "You sure?"

The primus slitted his eyes at Xavier. "Go."

Xavier went.

Zaq's nostrils flared, testing the air like I had earlier.

His father looked taken aback. "You thought I was blood mad?"

I slipped back around Zaq and stood next to him again. I appreciated that he wanted to protect me, but I wasn't the cower-behind-her-man type.

"That was me," I said. "I had intel to that effect."

"Hmm." Karoly's cold dark eyes moved over me. "So you're the famous Reaper. Or should I call you Ridley?"

I lifted my chin. If I was going to die, I'd do it with my head up and my shoulders back. "Reaper's fine."

"The slayer who kidnapped my son."

It wasn't a question, but I answered it anyway. "Yes."

"She's also the woman who got me out of Moreau's dungeon," interjected Zaq.

"Is she?" He turned back to his son. "On the other hand, you wouldn't have been there if not for her."

Zaq tightened his grip on his switchblade. He'd recovered from his surprise and donned his stern syndicate-prince face. "She's mine."

There he was, claiming me again in no uncertain terms.

And like when he'd said it earlier, my chest compressed, my emotions a tangled coil of yearning and wariness.

"Mm." Karoly cut another cool look at me.

Zaq moved forward, interposing himself between me and his father again. "Why don't we sit down?"

He indicated the couch and chairs in front of the unlit fireplace, and we all moved into the living room. "I'll stand," I said.

"Ridley." Zaq looked at me and gave a slight shake of his head.

"Let her stand," said Karoly.

Zaq sat on a couch and his father took a nearby chair. I stood behind the couch a little to Zaq's right, deliberately choosing a defensive position, my blades out but at my sides. I wouldn't attack first, but if Karoly went for Zaq, all bets were off.

Karoly's small smile acknowledged my body language. "I see you've acquired your own personal wolf-dog," he said to Zaq.

Maybe he meant to be insulting, but I wasn't insulted.

"Damn straight," I said under my breath.

Zaq's mouth twitched but he kept his focus on his father. "I don't need an attack dog, do I? Unless you're here to stake me."

Karoly's brows lifted. "The way I hear it, you're here to stake me."

Oh-kay. Way to bring things out in the open, guys.

But my apprehension eased. It was a good sign that they were both laying it out there, as well as further proof that Karoly wasn't blood mad. He was too relaxed about the fact that his son might be here to stake him.

A bitter taste filled my mouth. Another thing Crow had lied about.

But no, I couldn't put this all on her. Shame filled me. It was another thing I'd been blind about, because in my head, a vampire father was no father at all.

Zaq had put his leather wristbands back on. He slid a fingertip beneath the wristband of the hand holding the switchblade, itching the scar.

His father's eyes flickered. "Moreau?"

Zaq's jaw hardened. "Silver burns from the cuffs."

"I saw the photo."

Zaq bared his fangs and leaned forward. "He's dead. And I claim the right to be the one who takes him out."

"Of course." His father smiled back.

Zaq gave a satisfied nod and sat back.

"So," said his father. "What is this I hear about a coup and you joining Slayers, Inc. and coming to New York to stake me?"

"It's a fucking lie, all of it," said Zaq. "But first—." He retracted his switchblade and laid it on the coffee table.

I tensed, my gaze darting to the primus. I bent my knees, readying myself to move quickly. If he attacked Zaq, I was going over the couch.

Karoly's face softened. "Tell me."

My eyes widened. I straightened, my gaze bouncing between the two men.

The primus loved his son. Zaq had been right about that, too.

"These stories about a coup are a lie. But I did come to New York to stake you, and for that I'm sorry." Zaq's jaw worked. "So damn sorry. But it was the only way to get out of that fucking cell."

❦ 34 ❦
ZAQ

Father's gaze assessed me, but I didn't feel judged. He simply wanted to know how damaged I was, and who was to blame.

"Tell me," he repeated.

I heaved a breath. "I will. But first, how's Mom? She in New York?"

"She was." His dark eyes warmed like they always did at the mention of my mother. "She left for Baltimore earlier tonight."

"She's okay? She's not worried about me? Or Rafe?"

"She's fine. I told her you'd decided to extend your stay in Syria for a few weeks. She was disappointed, but she understood. And we told her that Rafe was away on syndicate business."

"Good." I swallowed thickly. "That's good."

My mom was all right. My brothers were all right.

And my faith in my father had been justified.

"Okay. So..." I looked up and to the right, not sure where to begin.

"Start in Paris," he suggested. "We lost you after you reached Charles de Gaulle. I flew to Paris a few hours after I received the photo, but by then the trail had gone cold. I didn't track you down until that weekend, and I suspect that was only because Moreau wanted me to find you."

"He did," Ridley confirmed.

"Okay," I said again, and launched into the story, glossing over Ridley's role in it—no sense in stirring up trouble—except the parts where she'd snuck me food and blood-wine, and later, how she'd let me drink her own blood when I was dying of silver poisoning.

Father turned that assessing stare on her.

My vampire stirred. Hopefully, her actions after I'd been kidnapped

272

would tip the balance in her favor. If not, I'd *make* him accept her. The two of us were a package deal.

Father looked at me again. I held his gaze, making it clear that to get to her, he'd have to go through me first.

He gave a small nod, and I continued talking.

I'd reached the part where Moreau's people had told me Father had been in Paris but had left without attempting to free me. I spoke calmly, but my anger must've been evident because he pressed his lips together.

"I couldn't," he said. "I had to let it play out. I wasn't sure where Leo de Froulay stood in all this."

"So this wasn't one of your fucking tests?"

"No." He looked at me like I had my head up my ass. "I had to let them show their hand. And by the time I was ready to make a move, you'd left Moreau's lair."

Behind me, Ridley stirred. "I can tell you that de Froulay had nothing to do with Zaq's kidnapping. In fact, he hired me to spy on Moreau because he suspected something was up."

"Ah," said my dad. "That's what I believed, but I wasn't sure, especially when I almost got caught in Philippe's trap."

I looked at him, dumbfounded. "The sonuvabitch tried to trap you?"

"The second time I was in Paris, yes." He gave a small, cool smile. "The men he sent are in their final graves."

"Moreau wanted you to try and rescue Zaq," said Ridley. "You would've been accused of entering his lair without permission."

"That's what I suspected," Father said. "Philippe thinks he is so clever, but he's wrong. In fact, he's distressingly predictable." He looked back at me. "I'm sorry, Zaquiel. I took too long, and then it was too late."

I gulped. My father never apologized. Ever.

Ridley moved restively. "He almost died."

Father exhaled. "I had faulty intel that sent me back to America. I was told that you'd escaped and were on your way back to New York. I returned to Paris as soon as I realized you must still be there, but by then, you'd left Moreau's lair and the trail had gone cold. I had people watching for you at the airports, but they missed you."

"Because I didn't want them to see me," I admitted.

"I'm sorry you didn't trust me." His tone was even, but I heard an undercurrent of hurt that stunned me. My father had always seemed too cold, too remote, to be hurt by anything I did.

I looked away. I hadn't considered how Father would feel if he were innocent.

"I'm sorry, too. So fucking sorry." I met his eyes so he'd see my sincerity. "But I couldn't take the chance. Not with Gabriel and Rafe's lives on the line."

"We didn't give him a choice," said Ridley. "If he would've refused, he would've died in Moreau's dungeon—or been sold as a blood slave. And after they captured Rafael, they threatened to sell him as a blood slave if Zaq didn't slay you."

Father inclined his head. "You made the right choice," he told me. "If you'd come to me, I would've told you to protect them."

"I pushed Zaq," Ridley said. Taking all the blame on herself because that's the kind of woman she was. "He refused to believe you were trying to kill him and his brothers. I don't know where the story of the coup came from, though. That wasn't SI." She paused. "As far as I know, anyway."

"I see," Father said.

I turned on the couch so I could see her. "What she's not saying is everything she did for me. In Paris, she hid me to give me time to recover. She even fed me her own blood when I was out of my mind with silver poisoning. And here in New York, she did everything she could to save me from SI."

"Is this true?" Father asked her.

She nodded. "If Zaq didn't stake you, my orders were to stake him. But if he did, not just his life would be saved, SI would call off the attacks on Gabriel and Rafael, too."

"I see," he said.

"But when it came down to it," I added, "she couldn't stake me. She helped me get away from her alpha."

Ridley shifted on her feet, clearly uncomfortable, and changed the subject. "This faulty intel. Was it from Lieutenant Mraz?"

Father gave a heavy sigh. "You know?"

"So it's the truth?" I asked. "He was working with SI to slay us?"

Father dipped his chin. "He said as much before he went to his final grave. He apparently disagreed with my decision to make you my heirs and prepare Gabriel to rule the syndicate after me. He learned his mistake."

I shook my head. Tomas had always been there, my father's friend and advisor. Yeah, he wasn't exactly a warm and fuzzy guy, but it was hard to wrap my mind around the idea that he'd wanted me and my brothers dead.

"Hopefully," Father added, "that is the end of this nonsense. The slay-ers, of course, are another story."

Ridley's spine went ramrod straight. Dislike emanated from her. Dislike, and fear.

Father returned her scrutiny with the air of a scientist studying a particularly interesting insect.

I didn't like knowing Ridley was afraid. She could dislike my dad— Lord knows she wouldn't be the only one—but I wanted her to feel safe. And I wanted him to accept her.

Before it turned into a staring match, I rose and asked my father if he'd like a glass of wine.

He took his gaze from Ridley to accept. "I would, thank you."

"I'll be right back." I went into the kitchen, Ridley on my heels.

While I opened the bottle, she shifted her blades to one hand, and with the other got three glasses from the cabinet. The whole time she kept a wary eye on my dad, who stared into the unlit fireplace, his profile to us.

"Put those blades away, would you?" I muttered. "This is a negotiation; he wouldn't be here otherwise. He would've sent men to drag us to head-quarters."

She glanced at my dad. "Yeah?"

"Yeah," I said as I filled the glasses. "He came alone, didn't he?"

She grunted, but retracted the switchblades and returned them to her pockets.

Back in the living room, Father came to his feet and accepted the glass I held out to him. His eyes warmed.

"Welcome home, Zaquiel," he said, touching the glass to mine.

I smiled back. "Thank you, sir. It's good to be here."

Then it was Ridley's turn. He raised his glass to her, unsmiling. "And welcome to New York, Miss Crawford."

She stilled in the act of touching her glass to his. Dismay flickered across her face. "How do you know my name?" She glanced at me.

I shook my head; I hadn't told him.

"You kidnapped my son," was his reply. "Did you think I wouldn't do everything I could to find out exactly who you were?"

Ridley took a small sip of her wine and set the glass down. She lifted her chin. "So now what?"

"That depends," he said. "I'd like some answers first, starting with everything you know about this plan to kill me and my sons. But first, sit."

Ridley looked at me. I gave her a small nod, and this time, she sat next to me on the couch. I took her hand, underlining that despite having kidnapped me, she'd earned my loyalty and trust.

Her fingers were cold. I curled my hand around them, trying to warm them.

Father noticed, of course. But he didn't say anything, simply retook his seat. He leaned back in the leather chair, eyeing Ridley. A trick he used to make underlings uncomfortable.

Ridley eyed him back. Nothing betrayed that she was nervous or upset—not her heart rate nor her breath nor even her expression.

But I knew she was. Even if I hadn't been able to feel it through our link, I'd have known. The more emotionless Ridley Crawford got, the more she was feeling.

I wanted to pull her into my arms, but I settled for squeezing her hand.

Father arched a brow. "Talk, slayer."

All the fight went out of her. Her shoulders slumped. "Don't call me that. I'm not a slayer. Not anymore."

Father frowned. "So you're not the Reaper?"

"No, that much is true. I was known as Reaper. It's because I'm a rogue." Her voice was toneless, but I *felt* the pain underlying her statement.

"Because of me," I inserted. "She wouldn't give me up to her alpha. Two nights ago, her alpha took her off the operation and demanded to know where I was. But Ridley wouldn't tell her."

Father pursed his lips. "Indeed."

Ridley took a deep breath, let it out.

"It's okay," I told her. "You don't have to tell him anything you don't want to."

"I want to," she told me. She looked at my dad and seemed to come to a decision. "I don't know the whole of it," she said, "but SI has declared war on you. The plan is to take out you and your sons. It's called Operation Angel. Op A, for short. You know a slayer was sent after Gabriel."

Father nodded, and Ridley continued, explaining that the plan had been to slay Gabriel and Rafe while kidnapping me. I would've been staked eventually, but first, I was to be used as bait.

"At first all we intended was to use Zaq to draw you out of New York. The end game was always to get to you. Even in Paris, the only reason they let Zaq go was because I convinced them it was the smartest way to get to you."

"I see." Father steepled his fingers and brought them to his mouth. "I can't say I'm surprised. This is why the syndicates need an ally on SI's Board. SI has changed from the early days. The work you slayers do is necessary—the vampire world can't always be trusted to police itself—but there are some bad actors using SI for their own ends, like Prima Victorine and my own lieutenant."

"I'm afraid you may be right." Ridley rolled in her lips like it pained her to admit it. "I believe in what we do. But this vendetta against your family—it's personal. And it's wrong."

Father tapped his steepled fingers against his lips. "You will tell your story to my allies? Verify that this Operation Angel was implemented to take out me and my sons?"

Ridley's eyelids fluttered. She slid her free hand into her pocket, and I knew she was fingering a switchblade.

My father tensed and brought his hands back down. I gave a little shake of my head and he settled back.

My heart hurt for her. I released her hand so I could rub her lower back.

She might be a rogue, but she was still about to betray the organization that had given her a home, a purpose, a reason for living. SI wasn't a job to her; it was her surrogate family.

"Tell me something first," she said. "In fact, I want your word on it. The only thing you've requested is a voice on SI's Board, is that right? You're not spreading lies about us and demanding the organization be dismantled."

My father looked taken aback. "No. Absolutely not. As I said, the vampire world needs you slayers. I agreed to that back when SI was first incorporated."

"I see." Pain flashed across Ridley's face. She took her hand from her pocket. Released a noisy breath. "Then yes," she said. "I will tell your allies everything I know about Op A."

❦ 35 ❦

RIDLEY

Blood rushed to my head. My skin prickled. A feeling of unreality descended, like I observed the scene from the outside.

Had I really agreed to help Karoly Kral in his fight against Slayers, Inc.?

I swallowed and rubbed my palms over my thighs.

So many lies Crow had told me. So goddamn many lies.

I couldn't go back and change things. All I could do was make this right going forward.

Zaq was speaking. I forced myself to focus on his words.

"There's more," he told his father. "Yesterday morning we were attacked in the underworld. Four of Spider's men. Apparently someone put out a hit on me and Ridley for half a million. Ridley took a blade to the side."

Karoly nodded. "Xavier mentioned that on the way here. You took care of the men?"

"They're all four in their final graves." Zaq quirked his mouth at me. "We make a good team, me and her. Anyway, Ridley thought they might've been sent by SI, but Xavier texted me something about a Paris connection.

"He told me that as well," said Karoly. "That the bounty is being paid by the Paris Syndicate."

"What did he say, exactly?" Zaq asked.

"That whoever succeeds in killing you should apply to Philippe Moreau for payment."

Zaq and I exchanged a glance. "So Moreau's behind it?" he asked.

278

"It appears so," said his father.

"Why am I not surprised?" Zaq muttered.

"I already knew Philippe was behind Zaquiel's kidnapping," his father added. "Rafael and Zoe Tremblay verified that. I've spoken to Leo de Froulay, and Philippe was reprimanded for his part in detaining my sons, and stripped of his rank as enforcer. This hit on Zaq could be his way of striking back at me."

I shook my head, trying to make sense of this new information. "But why me? Why not just Zaq? If SI isn't behind the hit, why would the hit include me? Unless..."

I blinked rapidly. This couldn't be related to my being Leo de Froulay's spawn, could it?

"That, we'll have to determine." Karoly set his wine glass on the coffee table. "Here's what I want you to do. For now, I want you both to stay undercover. Don't go out without a glamour. Let Slayers, Inc. worry about where you are. Meanwhile, I'll put out the word that I have evidence that SI targeted my sons. We'll say you fought them off. It's close to the truth, and I'd prefer not to give anyone an excuse to think you're vulnerable. In the meantime, I'll consider the best way to use Ridley and her information."

I nodded, still numb but agreeing with his logic. "I have one stipulation. I won't give you any intel that can be used against another slayer. We're not the problem. The BOD is." My mouth twisted. "And maybe my alpha."

"Her alias is Crow," added Zaq.

Karoly's mouth flattened, but he must have seen I wouldn't budge on this point. "Agreed."

"But instead of us hunkering down here," said Zaq, "I have a better idea. While I was in that cell, I made myself a promise—that when I got out, I'd personally send Moreau to his final grave. So if Ridley agrees, the two of us will go to Paris and stake the bastard ourselves. You can arrange a private jet so no one knows it's us."

I straightened and gave Zaq a delighted smile. "I like how you think. And of course, I'm going. Just try and stop me."

"A wolf-dog indeed," murmured Karoly. He seemed pleased for some reason. "But De Froulay may not agree. He's already punished Philippe."

Zaq's face hardened. "De Froulay can go fuck himself. Moreau's dead, whether or not he put the hit out on us."

His father stroked his lower lip. "All right. If necessary, I'll make it right with de Froulay. Just don't let him catch you."

I stirred. "I can do better than that."

Two pairs of eyes turned in my direction. Despite their difference in appearance, their expressions were so similar—brows tilted up, gaze laser-focused on me—that it hit me anew that Zaq was Karoly Kral's son.

And I was in love with him.

The sense of unreality increased. How had I ended up here?

But I was committed now.

"Better than what?" Karoly prompted.

"I'll contact Primus de Froulay, get his permission. He owes me a favor."

Karoly looked me up and down. His gaze lingered on my hair and eyes. Understanding dawned on his face. "Does he, now?"

"I'll need a phone," I told Zaq. "I don't want to use the same one I've been using."

"In my office," he said, and we trooped down the hall.

Zaq got me a burner phone, and I entered de Froulay's number, the one I hadn't meant to memorize, but had, and sent him a text.

It's R. Can we talk?

Within moments, the phone buzzed with an incoming call. I tapped *Accept*.

"De Froulay? It's me."

His velvety actor's voice sounded in my ear. "How are you, little one?"

"Fine." I hesitated, then reluctantly added, "And you?"

"Very well, thank you."

"Good, good." I glanced at Zaq and Karoly.

Zaq gave me an encouraging smile. His father simply eyed me.

I sipped in a slow breath through my teeth. "I have a favor to ask."

"Go ahead."

"I'm with Zaquiel and Karoly Kral right now. Zaq and I are coming to Paris, and we want your permission to slay Moreau."

He made a low, surprised sound. "You know, then?"

"That he took Zaquiel prisoner? Yeah."

"Yes, Karoly informed me."

"Mm-hum." I knit my brow, feeling like we were talking at cross purposes. "Then what did you mean? What am I supposed to know?"

A short silence. Then he said, "That Moreau is the man who killed Charlotte."

What? My lungs clamped. The room went dark.

For a few seconds, I couldn't breathe or see or hear. It was the opposite of the unreality I'd felt earlier. This was *too* real, like I'd stepped into a bottomless black pool and the waters had closed over my head.

I looked at Zaq, head swimming, mouth moving but no words coming out.

He enfolded me in his arms. "It's okay. I've got you."

I buried my face in the V of his T-shirt.

"Ridley?" asked de Froulay.

"Breathe," Zaq said against the top of my head. His big hand massaged my back. "Take your time."

My shoulders heaved. I managed to unlock my lungs. My breath whooshed in. I kept my nose against his skin, his now-familiar scent a lifeline that pulled me out of the black place until I could think again.

"Ridley?" It was de Froulay again. "Are you still there?"

Zaq took the phone, keeping an arm around my shoulders. "She's here. She's had a shock, is all."

"This is Zaquiel?"

"Yes."

"I can talk." I reached for the phone and Zaq handed it to me. I gripped the phone. "It's me. I'm...okay."

"My apologies," de Froulay said. "From what you said, I thought you'd discovered it yourself."

"You're sure?" I asked. "You have proof?"

"Yes. I have evidence that he and two of his men were in Pennsylvania on that night and a few nights before. I'm following up on the evidence right now, but it was him. I have no doubts about that."

"Okay." I stared unseeingly at the bookcase across from me. "You haven't moved against him yet? You remembered your promise?"

"But of course. I was planning on contacting you tonight, actually. The first man went to his final death five years ago, but the second is in one of my cells. He's admitted traveling to America with Moreau to find you and your mother. He couldn't tell me how Moreau knew about you, though."

The shock had worn off. The anger and hatred I'd carried all these years congealed into something coldly vengeful.

"Moreau is mine," I said between clenched teeth.

Zaq had kept an arm around me. He squeezed my shoulders. "*Ours.*"

We shared a long look that was a mini-conversation. He told me he wanted—no, needed—to be part of this, and I agreed.

I slid my arm around his waist. "Ours."

To de Froulay, I said, "We'll be there ASAP."

"I'll make sure he doesn't go anywhere."

"Good." I took a breath. I'd been undercover for most of my adult life. The habit of keeping secrets was hard to break. But if Karoly Kral was going to use me against the SI Board, then de Froulay should be informed about my previous career. "And that rumor you heard about me being a slayer? It's true."

De Froulay released a pained sigh. "I was afraid of that."

Karoly had rested a lean hip against Zaq's desk, taking in everything, his face expressionless. Now he stirred. "Ask Leo about the money behind the hit on you and Zaquiel."

I nodded and told de Froulay about the attack on me and Zaq. "Zaquiel's man looked into it and found evidence that the order came from the Paris Syndicate."

De Froulay's breath hissed in. "I know nothing about that, I promise you."

I waited a beat.

De Froulay didn't disappoint me. "You think Moreau's behind this as well."

"I'd say it's a certainty. Whoever succeeded in killing us was to apply to Moreau for payment."

"I see," he said grimly. "As soon as we're done here, I'll issue an order revoking the hit. I assure you, I knew nothing about this. Any of it. My apologies to both you and Zaquiel. And to you, Karoly. My only excuse is he was an old friend, and I trusted him."

"About Moreau?" I added. "If you need a cover story for your people, tell them he's been imprisoning members of other syndicates and treating them as blood slaves. It's the truth. I saw it myself."

Karoly's gaze shot to Zaq, and his lips pressed into a hard line.

"Prince Zaquiel?" De Froulay sounded shocked and angry. "He actually drank his blood?"

Zaquiel stiffened, and I squeezed his waist. "Yeah, but keep his name out of it. It wasn't only Zaq, either. Moreau and the Tremblay prima threatened to sell Prince Rafael to a brothel if Zaq didn't do exactly as he was told. I'm guessing there may be others, too. The thralls in his lair, for instance."

Karoly held out his hand. "Let me speak to Leo."

I gave him the phone, and the two primuses got down to planning our next move.

I tried to pay attention, but I was still reeling from the revelation that Moreau was the vampire who'd murdered my mom. How could I have lived in his lair for close to a month without recognizing him? But then, I hadn't gotten a good look at him or the other vampires.

Zaq kept me close, stroking my back and generally radiating calm. I turned my head and took another deep inhale of his Zaq-scent, and that calmed me further.

Karoly ended the call. "It's all arranged. You leave for Paris tomorrow night. I'll have my PA prepare new identities and passports for you both. I assume whatever aliases you used to enter the country have been compromised."

"Yes. My alpha arranged the passports."

He nodded. "My PA will book a hotel for you in Paris, too. When you arrive in Paris, spend the day there. Leo will text your instructions to this phone."

Karoly turned to Zaq. They eyed each other. Then Zaq released me and took a step toward his father. They gave each other awkward man-hugs and broke apart.

"Take care," Karoly told Zaq. "Your mother will never forgive me if you get yourself staked."

"I will. I have to do this." Something dark moved over Zaq's face. "I have to."

"Understood," his father replied. "I would expect nothing else from one of my sons."

Zaq's dark expression morphed into a crooked grin. "Exactly."

I wasn't real up on the nuances of father-son interactions, but I could tell that Zaq was proud of Karoly's implication that Zaq was like him. I disagreed—Zaq was a way better person in my opinion—but I chalked it up to being a guy-thing.

Karoly turned to me. "Moreau won't be easy to kill. I trust you're as good as they say you are."

My smile was all sharp white teeth. "I'm the best."

۞

We arrived at JFK Airport early Friday evening. Our cover was a Kral enforcer—that would be me, my hair glamoured a golden blond, my face borrowed from a New Orleans enforcer who'd been ordered to stay out of sight for a few days—traveling with her human PA, Zaq.

I'd loaded up on blades, the two I'd already borrowed from Zaq and another two that I had stowed in my overnight bag. I also had a thin silver stiletto concealed in the back of each boot. The boots were the only things I had on that were my own. I was wearing all new clothes, courtesy of Zaq, who'd put in a clothing order with a personal shopper via Xavier.

Within two hours, I'd been completely outfitted: two pairs of black tactical pants, a stack of tees and ribbed tanks, and a fitted jacket in a light green leather so soft I wanted to pet it. Also: A couple of tight dresses (one red, one black), short red boots with heels I could actually walk in, and a half-dozen exercise bras and boyshorts.

There was also a stack of sexy underwear that Zaq had picked out himself. I fingered a sheer red chemise and cut my eyes at him, half-amused, half-turned on.

"For later." He wrapped his arms around me from behind and nuzzled my neck. "When I finally get you alone."

Something sparked in my chest—optimism. Maybe we really would have a 'later.'

I turned in his arms and kissed him, and he moved his hands to my ass, pulling me snugly up against him.

"You're going to model them for me." He said it in his firm, you-will-do-this voice, like I didn't have a choice.

I drew a shallow inhale. God, his sexy commands really did it for me.

"Am I?" I asked, pretending to be cool, when inside, I'd melted into a gooey marshmallow.

He nibbled my earlobe. "Yeah."

My eyes drifted shut with pleasure. "And why would I do that?"

"Because I want you to." He punctuated each statement with a nip to my earlobe. "And you want to please me. Because if you do, I'll make you come so good."

My lower belly flip-flopped and I felt a jolt right to my center. "Promises, promises."

He just chuckled. A low, wicked chuckle.

And when it had come time to pack, I'd tucked the red chemise into the overnight bag along with my other clothes.

Zaq wore dark-wash jeans and a black tee. I'd wanted him to wear tight pants and heeled boots as payback for that "thrall" outfit he'd made me wear, but he'd simply laughed and chosen his own clothes.

With his lower face covered in dark stubble, he was rocking the movie-star-on-vacation look. I honestly didn't understand how his so-called human glamour fooled anyone, but apparently no one could see through it other than me and his family.

When we arrived at the airport, the limo driver took us around the back to where a Kral jet waited. Being able to skip going through security was one of the benefits of flying via private jet, one I had to admit I could get used to.

The sun was setting, the sky over New York a wash of purple and pink. That unfamiliar optimism was still with me, making me buoyant.

I told myself it was too soon for that, that first we had to complete this op against Moreau, but it kept bubbling up.

Maybe I *could* live with Zaq and take online classes. I wouldn't even have to decide on a major right away—Leo de Froulay had transferred an eye-popping amount to my account. I could take my time, figure out what I was interested in.

I'd always wanted to know more about art and literature, for instance. And the history of human-vampire interaction, and what could be done about blood addicts.

The driver pulled up near the jet. We got out and he handed us our overnight bags. The door to the jet stood open and a Kral soldier waited at the top of the steps.

As we crossed the tarmac, I glanced at Zaq, wondering if, like me, he was recalling our first meeting.

I sincerely hoped not.

He took my hand and brought it to his lips. "I love you, Ridley."

I shot him a puzzled look, which he read with ease. Another kiss to my knuckles. "I've decided to tell you that as often as I can until you believe me."

My step faltered. Arrested, I looked at him. "Is that what you think? That I don't believe you love me?"

"Am I wrong?"

I shook my head. "It's not that. I do believe you."

Maybe I hadn't at first, but he'd shown me in so many ways that he meant it, especially yesterday when he'd made it clear to his father that he both wanted and trusted me.

Zaq's mouth bent with frustration. "Then what is it? The monster thing? Because I'm sorry about what happened to your mom—so very sorry—but not all of us are like that. And this is who I am. You want me, you have to take the whole person."

An ache bloomed in my chest. I was so bad at this. Like I'd told him, I didn't do relationships.

"It's not that. I know you're not a monster. Even back in Paris, I knew I was wrong about that."

"But—? And don't tell me there isn't a *but*. You have a problem, and I want to know what it is. You owe me that much, at least."

I swallowed. What *was* my problem?

The reasons we couldn't be together seemed to have fallen away.

I'd survived his father. I was pretty sure that Karoly and I could come to an understanding. I'd guard his son even in those camps that Zaq insisted on traveling to without security, and Karoly would allow me to live.

Zaq was still a syndicate prince, but I was no longer a slayer. That was painful for me to think about—crushingly so—but the upside was that I could be with him.

So what was holding me back?

Zaq heaved a breath and dropped my hand. "Scratch that. You don't owe me a fucking thing. Let's get on the plane."

I grabbed his arm.

Zaq's gaze searched mine. "What are you afraid of?"

That I don't deserve you. That I don't deserve anyone.

The answer came from the deepest part of me, the part that was still curled up with the twelve-year-old Ridley in her hideout, hands clamped over her ears to block out her mom's cries.

The twelve-year-old who felt guilty for surviving when her mom had died.

My mouth worked. "That I don't deserve you," I blurted.

His brows snapped together. "What—?"

A black sports car zoomed up, interrupting us.

Zaq gave a pissed-off growl and whipped his head around. Then his eyes widened. "That's Gabriel's car."

A younger, raven-haired, green-eyed version of Karoly Kral emerged from the driver's side.

My hand had gone to the switchblade in my right pocket. I released it and stepped back as the oldest Dark Angel strode toward us.

A broad smile split Zaq's face. "We'll talk later," he told me.

He waited for my nod, then hurried toward his brother. Their arms came around each other in a hard hug.

Tears stung my eyes. It made me so happy to see Zaq happy.

Zaq pulled back. "What the fuck are you doing here? What about Camila? She made it through the transition?"

"Last night." Gabriel grimaced. "It's been the worst week of my life. You were missing, and she was going through a living hell. But she did it."

"Well, damn." Zaq pounded him on the back. "That's great. Just great."

"Congratulate me." His brother's mouth widened in a proud smile. "I'm a mated man."

"I heard. And yeah, congratulations, man. That's good news. The best. She with you?" Zaq peered into the sports car. The only passenger was a man in dark glasses who was obviously a member of Gabriel's security.

"I left her in Montauk planning a flower farm."

Zaq's brows climbed. "A flower farm?" he repeated in a neutral tone of voice.

Gabriel grinned. "An organic flower farm, yet. It's what she wants.

She's going to start with two acres on my property, then expand from there."

Zaq made an amused sound. "I can just picture Father's reaction to that."

His brother moved a shoulder. "He won't care as long as she gives me an heir or two. But what about you? Where the hell have you been hiding? And what's this I hear about a slayer?"

The brothers turned back to me. "This is Ridley," said Zaq.

Gabriel scraped a cool look over me. It was unnerving how much like his father he was, right down to the peaked black brows. The only difference was that his eyes were green instead of espresso.

Zaq beckoned me closer with an encouraging smile. "Come meet my brother."

I walked forward and shook the hand Gabriel extended to me. "It's good to meet you," he said.

"And you," I returned.

He released my hand and turned back to Zaq. "Why do you think I'm here, asshole? You think you get to have all the fun? I'm going to Paris with you."

Zaq broke into a grin. "Great."

They started talking at once, catching up on everything that had happened in the last month, teasing each other in the way brothers who are also good friends do.

Not that I would know; I had no firsthand knowledge of siblings or how they interacted. But I'd seen movies.

I fell back, a hand on my switchblade, and glanced around the tarmac. Zaq had said that everyone flying with us had been thoroughly vetted, but I couldn't forget that Jessa had gotten on Gabriel's staff—and that Crow was still out there somewhere.

The hit might have been called off, but I was still officially a rogue. She wouldn't allow me to get away so easily. And if she could take out Zaq and his brother, she'd consider it a bonus.

But we boarded the flight without any problems, taking off fifteen minutes later. Zaq and Gabriel spent the first couple of hours talking, and then we bedded down, me and Zaq in the bedroom at the rear of the plane and Gabriel on a couch that had been made into a bed.

Zaq cuddled me close. "I love you. And you do deserve me. Just like I deserve you. But love isn't about deserving, it just...is."

I kissed his jaw. Wanting to say *I love you* back. But somehow, I couldn't push the words out.

He sighed but didn't say anything, just tucked me into his shoulder and closed his eyes.

In Paris, we stayed at a trendy little hotel that catered to vampires. Karoly's PA had booked a suite for the three of us under my alias. Zaq was still pretending to be my thrall, while Gabriel had assumed the identity of a bodyguard. If it hadn't been so serious, I would've enjoyed the fact that I'd acquired an entourage comprised of not one, but two, syndicate princes, even if we were the only ones who knew it.

We rested until mid-afternoon, then Zaq and I did yoga together on mats provided by the hotel. I wanted to be loose and ready for whatever went down. By then, Gabriel was awake. We heard him murmuring on the phone to Camila, telling her that he loved her and he'd be home as soon as possible.

"My big bro's got it bad." Zaq grinned at me from where he sat cross-legged on his yoga mat.

He was doing a lot of that—grinning. I'd known he was under pressure, but it was a revelation to see how different he was now. Sociable, easygoing, the kind of man who gets things done, but in his own time.

"Yeah," I said.

He leaned over and nuzzled my neck. "Like I've got it for you. So bad."

I didn't say anything, but I clamped my arms around him. Tears pricked my eyes.

Emotion churned in me. Love for Zaq. Hatred for Philippe Moreau.

"Hey." He enfolded me in his arms. "What's wrong?"

I shook my head and stuffed my emotions down. I couldn't allow myself to feel. Not yet.

"It's okay to cry," he said against my temple. "You've had a rough few days."

I set my jaw. "Not. Until. He's. Ashes."

❧

We ate an early dinner that I barely tasted, then sat around the living room of our suite, sharpening our blades and talking strategy. Gabriel offered suggestions, but deferred to us, saying he was along as backup.

Zaq and I agreed to attack at the same time from different angles

"Although," Zaq said, "a part of me wants to chain him in one of his fucking cells and leave him until he shrivels into a dehydrated husk."

"No argument from me," said his brother.

Both men looked at me. I contemplated leaving Philippe Moreau to rot in a cell, in agony but unable to die because of his magic. Vampires had survived in similar situations for centuries. It was tempting, but I shook my head. De Froulay probably wouldn't agree to it anyway, but that wasn't my main reason for saying no.

"I just want this to be over. And I want to know he's ashes with no chance of being set free."

"Then that's what we'll do," Zaq said.

The time ticked by. De Froulay texted instructions to meet him at ten p.m. at his mansion. We'd drive together to Moreau's lair, where we'd all enter—Leo and I openly, the Kral brothers in the shadows.

We got dressed. I checked my blades again. Rolled my head from side to side, shook out my arms.

And then it was time to leave.

❦ 36 ❧
ZAQ

We took a silver Rolls Royce to Philippe Moreau's lair. Ridley sat next to me, and Gabriel and Leo de Froulay took the seats opposite us.

Ridley's sire hadn't changed since the last time I'd last seen him ten years ago. Same long blond hair, same stunning face, same lean, sinewy body. Except for the fact that he was grim-faced, quiet. I remembered him as charming, larger-than-life—a silent-film version of a vampire—but tonight he was subdued.

At one point he gave Ridley a look of naked yearning, and I realized he wanted to claim her as his. Very much.

She didn't see it; she was staring the window.

I took her hand and interlaced my fingers in hers. De Froulay glanced from our intertwined hands to my face, and I knew he got the message.

Maybe Ridley would let him acknowledge her as his spawn, and maybe she wouldn't. But she was my mate, first and foremost, and whatever she decided, I was part of the equation.

Gabriel shifted his body so he was looking at de Froulay. "So," he said, "I'm still wondering how Moreau came to be involved in this. Other than the fact that he was Prima Victorine's sire, that is."

De Froulay pursed his lips. "Here's what I've discovered so far. Philippe knew Karoly Kral was pushing SI too hard, and he and Victorine came up with a plan to hire SI to take out the Krals. Meanwhile, Tomas Mraz somehow heard about it and got involved. He was on board with the plot to kill the Kral brothers, but not Karoly."

Gabriel nodded. "Mraz said something like that to my father."

"Whether or not Karoly died," de Froulay added, "wasn't important to Philippe. His ultimate goal was to point the blame at me, not Victorine, thereby forcing Karoly to come after me. And if Karoly *had* died before he had a chance to take revenge on me, Philippe would've made sure whoever succeeded him as primus would know I was responsible."

"His mistake," Ridley muttered.

Froulay glanced at her. "What do you mean?"

"You're stronger and smarter than him. He couldn't have won a fight against you."

A pleased smile curved De Froulay's mouth. "Thank you, my dear."

She shrugged a shoulder. "It's the truth. Honestly, I think he might be in the first stages of blood madness. The man's not thinking clearly."

"Then it's time we put him out of his misery," said de Froulay.

"And what about Ridley?" I asked. "He put the hit out on her because she's your spawn?"

"Yes." De Froulay's eyes narrowed. "He'd been trying to kill her for years, but then he lost her when she went into the SI training program. He didn't want to take a chance that she'd succeed me as my heir. He believed she was dead until she resurfaced as Reaper. He couldn't risk staking her once she'd been embedded in his lair, but after she left with you..."

I ground my back teeth. "The man needs to die."

"In that," said de Froulay, "we are in complete agreement."

We turned onto Moreau's street. The limo stopped in front of his lair, and the driver got out and opened the door for us. De Froulay got out first.

I stared past him at Moreau's mansion, feeling a heavy dose of anger along with a rush of adrenaline. The building was very upper-class French, a classic limestone-block building with a wrought-iron fence and bushes that had been clipped within an inch of their life. From the outside, you'd never guess the depravity that occurred within its walls.

Ridley squeezed my hand, wordlessly reminding me to stay focused. I nodded and gave her a small smile, and she followed her father out of the limo.

On the seat opposite, Gabriel caught my eye and gave me a thumbs-up. A rush of love filled me. Gods, I'd missed him and Rafe.

I gave him a thumbs-up back. "Time to get even."

His cheek creased. "You know it."

I faded into the shadows and exited the limo. Gabriel followed a few seconds later, and we trailed Ridley and her father up the brick path to the tall blue door guarded by twin bronze griffins. I couldn't see Gabriel, but I sensed him at my side.

The long-faced butler opened the door. "M'sieur Primus. Mademoiselle."

"Aubin." De Froulay acknowledged the butler with a small nod.

"We're here to see Moreau," Ridley said.

"Of course. Come in." He bowed the two of them inside.

Gabriel and I slipped past the three of them and waited in the foyer for Aubin to unlock the door to Moreau's underground lair.

My mouth was dry, but I wasn't afraid. I just wanted to get to Moreau.

I glanced at the wall where Étan and Blaise had worked me over and smiled grimly. Apparently both vampires had been staked that night they'd captured Rafe. Too bad. I'd like to see them try messing with me now the odds were more even.

Aubin opened the door and we trooped down the stairs. "Is he alone?" de Froulay asked Aubin.

"A thrall is with him, m'sieur."

"*Bien*. Wait at the door. No one is to enter."

Moreau was seated on the same couch he'd been on the night we'd struck our bargain. This time, instead of regarding us from the couch in that lordly vampire way, he rose immediately. The thrall he was with scrambled to her feet and backed up a few steps, her gaze bouncing between the five of us.

"Leo," Moreau said in French. "You honor me with your presence." His eyes gave a telltale flick to Ridley.

With his broad shoulders and long blond hair, De Froulay loomed above the small, darker Moreau like a Viking. He jerked his chin at the thrall. "Leave."

"Yes, m'sieur." She hurried from the room, eyes down, shoulders hunched.

De Froulay waited until Aubin had closed the door behind her before turning back to Moreau. "I believe you know my daughter."

"Yes." Moreau gave Ridley a stiff nod.

Ridley stared back, unmoving. It wasn't a comfortable stillness. It was the stillness of a predator preparing to attack.

Moreau licked his lips and glanced at his primus. "What is this about?"

De Froulay switched to English. "Charlotte Crawford."

"My mother," Ridley added.

"Charlotte Crawford?" Moreau's gaze bounced from his primus to

Ridley to me. If a vampire could sweat, his face would've been dripping. "A thrall?"

The mention of Charlotte was my and Gabriel's cue. We stepped out of the shadows.

Moreau's mouth dropped open. "You," he hissed at me.

"Enough," said de Froulay softly. "I know everything, Philippe. That 'thrall' was carrying my spawn, as you knew damn well."

Moreau's spine stiffened. "What have they told you?"

Ridley and I glanced at each other and moved forward, blades out.

I circled to his right. "That you had me kidnapped and kept me locked up in a cell with no food or water. That you drank my blood while I was fastened to a fucking concrete wall."

"Fuck." Gabriel sucked in a breath and turned an angry glare on Moreau. He had his blade out, but as agreed, he hung back, allowing me and Ridley to make the kill.

Ridley circled to Moreau's left. "That you hunted me and my mom for years. When you found us, you tortured my mom so she'd tell you where I was. And when she refused, you murdered her."

Her accusations fell into the quiet room like hard white pebbles dropping into a still pond.

Moreau blinked several times, then rallied. "It's a lie," he spat at his primus. "You're going to believe these dhampirs over me?"

"Hugo says different," de Froulay replied. "He told me that when Charlotte left, you had her followed, that you knew from the beginning she'd given birth to my daughter. That you didn't tell me because you've been maneuvering to take my place after I'm gone."

Moreau's expression changed, became dangerous. Blue encircled his eyes and his fangs slid out. He broke into fast, furious French. I only caught a few phrases here and there, but it was clear he was denying everything.

De Froulay looked bored. "According to Hugo," he said in English, "you've grown tired of waiting for me to go to my final grave. You egged Victorine on, hoping that Karoly would blame me when his sons died. Because after all, my top enforcer had Zaquiel in his dungeon. How could I not part of this? And now you took out a hit on my daughter and Zaquiel, paid for with Paris Syndicate money. *My* money." His voice had turned so cold, my forearms prickled.

Moreau slipped a hand beneath his suit jacket. He was breathing hard, his gaze darting from his primus to us.

My toothed beast simmered beneath the surface, eager to show itself.

Yes, I told it—and opened myself to the vampire's dark power. My vision sharpened, and I felt energy surge through me.

I bared my fangs at Moreau. "Go ahead," I invited in a guttural voice. "Draw your weapon. We are your executioners, but we agreed this will be a fight with odds like you gave me and Rafe. Three against one seems about right. Or maybe we should drag you downstairs to one of those goddamned cells and fasten your wrists to a wall first?"

Moreau's own fangs slid out. "She's a slayer, Leo," he said without taking his gaze from me and Ridley. "Did you know that? SI is in this up to their necks."

"And you're a traitor." De Froulay's mouth thinned. "Stake him," he told us. "I grow tired of his babbling."

Moreau went for me first. Apparently he'd decided I was the greater threat.

His mistake.

I parried his thrust and shoved him at Ridley.

She chose that moment to release her own vampire. We all felt the whoosh of power. The woman had some serious magic to call on. It glowed in her eyes, made her skin shimmer.

And yeah, she was beautiful. Inhumanly, supernaturally so.

But then, to me, she was always beautiful.

Moreau blanched. His Adam's apple worked. He raised his arm.

"Bastard dhampir," he hissed at her.

I darted behind him, and as he slashed his dagger down, Ridley and I skewered him with our blades at the same time.

He grunted and listed to the side. The rotten stench was almost overwhelming. A second later, it mixed with the acrid scent of his flesh turning to ashes.

I released my handle and so did Ridley. He crumpled to the ground.

He stared up at us with eyes that were already clouding over. "You... were both supposed to be dead by now. I figured you'd fail, and she'd have to kill you. Then Karoly would kill...her."

I grinned darkly. "Guess you blew it."

Moreau's mouth opened again, but all that came out of it was a puff of smoke.

Gabriel came to my side and clapped my back. "Nice job." He curled his lip at Moreau's disintegrating body. "May he burn in a light-filled hell."

"Amen to that," I muttered.

Ridley stared down at Moreau. She'd shut down. Her affect was flat, her emotions a flat line.

My triumph at sending Moreau to his final grave curdled. I reached for her. "What is it, sweetheart?"

She turned empty gray eyes to mine. "I thought I'd feel something. Happiness. Relief. Satisfaction. *Something*. But all I feel is cold."

I enfolded her in my arms. "Let me warm you, then."

✻ 37 ✻

RIDLEY

I shivered. I was so chilled. Encased in ice like I'd been buried in a glacier for hundreds of years.

Or maybe just buried with my mom.

This wasn't how it was supposed to be. Over the years, I'd played little movies in my head of what would happen when I finally caught up with my mom's killers. In those movies, I'd laughed in the monsters' faces. Taunted them with the fact that I was the strong one now, the one with the power. And after I'd staked them, I was elated, triumphant.

Never had I imagined feeling nothing but a weary satisfaction.

It was over. I'd avenged my mother.

But staking Moreau hadn't miraculously brought her back to life, and it wouldn't take away the hole her death had left in my heart.

Zaq wrapped me in his arms. "I love you," he said against my hair.

I made a small, hurting sound and burrowed into his heat.

Gradually sensation returned. Zaq's smell and the strong, steady sound of his heartbeat. His arms holding me and his soft T-shirt against my cheek. Beyond us came the murmur of voices—Gabriel and Leo de Froulay discussing the next step.

A phone buzzed and de Froulay answered, carrying on a short conversation with the person on the other end. Something about Slayers, Inc. and Operation Angel.

"It's over," he told Zaq and Gabriel after he'd ended the call. "The Board has officially pulled the plug on the operation to kill you and Rafael."

"What about Ridley?" Zaq asked over my head. "She's been declared a rogue. SI won't stop coming after her."

"They want Reaper dead," said de Froulay. "So she'll die."

Zaq's body hardened. "What the fuck's that supposed to mean?"

I pulled back so I could see his face. His brows formed an inverted V and his green eyes glittered with challenge.

"There was a fight," de Froulay explained with a sly smile. "Philippe Moreau staked the Reaper. She's ashes now. If we all tell the same story, it will be believed."

I heaved a breath and turned in Zaq's arms so I faced de Froulay and Gabriel. "It won't work. They'll investigate. My alpha will tell them I'm with Zaq. She knows I chose him over my mission."

De Froulay crossed his arms over his chest. "And I'll rebuff them," he returned with regal disdain. "You are my spawn, after all—Princess Renata."

My jaw slackened. I blinked several times.

Princess Renata?

"You'll have to change your name, of course," de Froulay continued. "They might suspect, but they won't be able to prove anything. After all, the idea of a syndicate princess joining Slayers, Inc. is bizarre. SI will look like fools if they insist it's true."

"It could work," mused Gabriel. "SI is on the defensive now. We can make it clear it's in their best interest to accept the story that Reaper died tonight."

De Froulay considered me. "The American accent could be a problem. We'll say you went to boarding school in America, that it was your mother's wish."

Zaq's arms were still around me. He stroked the side of my hip. "Gabriel's right. It could work. And it means we could be together," he added in an undertone. "If that's what you want."

I blinked rapidly. Of course I wanted to be with Zaq. Didn't he know that?

Then I realized that he *didn't* know. I hadn't agreed to mate with him. I hadn't even told him I loved him.

My chest squeezed. What was wrong with me?

I could've died here tonight. *Zaq* could've died.

How sad and terrible would it have been if he'd died without my ever having told him?

I moistened my lips. Gods, I'd been such a coward. Sure, I was brave when it came to physical things, but I was a freaking coward when it came to my emotions.

"What about my colleagues?" I asked. "There are people—slayers—who know what I look like."

"Who?" asked de Froulay.

I chewed my upper lip. Actually, there weren't that many. I'd been undercover for close to a decade, with so many aliases that even my lieutenant didn't know what I really looked like.

That left Crow, and probably Twilight, although I trusted Twilight not to rat me out.

"Two or three," I said.

"We can take care of them," said de Froulay.

I narrowed my eyes. I knew what "take care" of them meant. "No. Absolutely not. If I do this—and I haven't said I will yet—no one dies because of me. And I'll choose my own name."

And why was I objecting to such an insignificant detail when the real issue was Leo de Froulay claiming me as his spawn?

De Froulay stunned me by saying, "It was your original name. The one Charlotte gave you. My people tracked down the record of your birth. You were born in Montreal, actually. I believe Philippe may have arranged for Charlotte to shelter there. Maybe he had a plan for you, a plan she found out, because she left Canada a few weeks after your birth."

"Renata?" I tried it out, but it sounded foreign to me. I was *Ridley*. "I didn't know. She changed my name when I was too young to remember."

De Froulay's expression softened. "Still, it is your name."

Zaq rubbed a soothing circle on my stomach. "You don't have to decide anything right now."

"No, it's okay." I drew in a breath and stepped away from Zaq. It was important to me that Leo de Froulay knew I could stand on my own. "A syndicate princess—me? I don't know."

De Froulay raised one of the dark brows that were so like mine. "You have a better idea?"

My mind raced. But I had nothing. Hell, if it weren't me they were talking about, I might even have agreed it was the best solution.

But it *was* me, and I couldn't wrap my mind around the idea of Ridley Crawford as Princess Renata.

Gabriel spoke again. "Think of it as another alias. You're used to taking on new personas. This will simply be another one."

My gaze flashed to him.

"And you could be with Zaq—"

Zaq interrupted. "Let her think, would you?" He pulled me to the side. "What do you want to do?"

My throat hurt with unshed tears. I looked from Zaq to Leo de Froulay and back to Zaq.

I could have Zaq. An ache blossomed in my heart. My throat felt sore.

"No pressure," he said in a voice for my own ears only. "I love you, Ridley Crawford. I could give a fuck if you're a syndicate princess. I'm not part of that world anyway."

And that's when I knew what to do.

My heart ached and my throat was sore because my love needed to be expressed.

I wasn't sure I knew how to be Zaq's lover, let alone his mate.

But he wanted me, and I was going to do my damnedest to deserve him.

So I just said it. Not giving myself time to overthink it.

I put my hands on either side of his face. "I love you. And I want more than anything in the world to be your mate."

He blinked, and I realized I was scowling. I shook my head at myself, relaxed my frown.

"I love you," I repeated, and added, "That's a promise. And you know I keep my promises."

A smile germinated in his eyes, spread to his face. A slow, heart-rending smile like an angel might give you if he was in love with you.

And yeah, I knew I was the luckiest woman on the planet.

He slipped his hands under my forearms and past my wrists so his arms twined through mine and held my face, too. "Love you, too, beautiful. So fucking much."

I gave him a wobbly smile, and in that instant, the bond between us came fully to life. I felt Zaq's love, intense, true. It didn't erase the pain of my mom's death, but his love did ease the hurt, like the bright colors of spring after a long winter.

De Froulay cleared his throat, and we released each other and faced him.

Gabriel smirked at his brother and Zaquiel grinned back.

"You'll do it, then," de Froulay said.

I gave a small nod. "I'll play Princess Renata, but only if you keep it on a need-to-know basis. Renata's going to be a princess like Zaq's a prince. You can tell your allies and your top people about me—enough to make it convincing to SI—but don't expect me to live in Paris or attend Paris Syndicate events."

"You can say you did it to protect her," Gabriel inserted. To me, he said, "And maybe you could attend a Paris party now and then. To make it convincing."

De Froulay looked like he wanted to argue further but he looked from Zaq to me and nodded. "Very well. A few parties a year."

I nodded. "Fair enough." Gabriel was right; if I wanted people to believe I was a Leo's daughter and a syndicate princess, I'd have to show up in Paris, at least occasionally. Even if I'd rather stab a fork into my thigh than make nice with a roomful of syndicate vampires.

"Let's go home," Zaq said.

I gave him an uncomprehending look. Home? I hadn't called any place home for so long.

"My place in New York," he corrected. To de Froulay, he said, "We'll be in touch, but for now, Ridley needs to rest and recover."

De Froulay nodded, and Zaq took my hand. "Ready?"

Gabriel was already at the door, holding it open for us.

Aubin hovered beyond him. His gaze swept the room, taking in Moreau's ashes. His Vincent-Price sangfroid didn't waver. "I'll get someone to clean that up."

I slanted a look at Zaq. "Home." I tested the word out, absorbed in the wonder of what he was offering me.

I liked saying it.

No, I fucking *loved* it.

But first, I turned to Leo de Froulay. "We'd be honored if you came to our mate ritual." I halted, then added, "Father."

Because I was pretty sure that's what my mom would've wanted, for me to give de Froulay a chance.

"And I'd be honored to attend, Renata," my father returned gravely.

I gave a small nod. "Good."

"We'll be in touch," Zaq added.

"I'll clear my schedule as soon as I receive the invitation."

I twined my fingers through Zaq's and bumped my shoulder against his. "Okay," I said. "I'm ready. Let's go home."

EPILOGUE 1

RIDLEY

TWO MONTHS LATER

We held our mating ceremony under a fat October moon in Zaq's mom's lush garden. It was a small, intimate gathering of family and a few friends.

Behind us was Zaq's family home, a Victorian Gothic dream of turrets and wraparound porches and intricate woodwork that overlooked the Chesapeake Bay. Silver fairy lights were strung above the garden walkways.

In the two months since Zaq and I had returned to New York, everything had worked out pretty much as Leo and Gabriel had intended. Reaper was dead and Ridley Crawford along with her, and I'd become Renata de Froulay—Ren for short.

Me, a syndicate princess.

Sometimes I wondered if I'd taken a wrong turn and landed in Bizarro World, where everything was backward and upside down.

But it was worth it, because it had brought me to this moment, facing Zaq in a candlelit gazebo, a bouquet of fragrant white roses and lavender in my hands. He gazed down at me unsmiling, the candlelight reflected in his green eyes so the gold flecks glinted like tiny stars. Even if I couldn't sense his emotions through our link, I would've known how much this meant to him from his serious expression.

He'd regained the weight he'd lost but kept the sexy scruff because he knew how much I liked it. The silky gray shirt he wore with black pants shimmered in the dusky light, clinging a little to his chest and making his lean, powerful body look good enough to eat...and lick...and suck...

But that would have to wait until later.

Zaq held out his hands. "Ready?"

All the spit left my mouth. But I wanted this, more than anything.

I handed the bouquet to Camila Vittore. Mila, as she'd asked me to call her, had turned into a friend. A newly-made dhampir, she'd asked me to teach her some of my fighting moves. She was so cute, but determined.

"Ready," I told Zaq, and took his hands, my heart so full I wouldn't have been surprised if it had burst right out of my chest and flown to him like one of those winged-heart cartoons.

My one regret was that Twilight couldn't have attended. I'd have liked to have at least one friend at my side. But she'd dropped off the grid. I hoped that meant she was on another assignment, and not that she'd gotten in trouble for helping Rafe.

Crow seemed to have backed off. The Board of Directors had assured Karoly that she was on a new assignment. I wasn't convinced we'd seen the last of her, but I refused to dampen my newfound happiness by worrying about her. Not tonight, anyway.

Zaq and I had elected to say our own vows. He went first, and had me tearing up before he was finished, saying how I was his heart and he hadn't realized what his life was missing until he'd met me.

Then I said mine. "You're my heart, too. I never even let myself hope that there was someone like you out there. Not for me. And that you love me, that you feel the same way, is the greatest gift I can imagine, and I promise to treasure and nurture that gift for as long as we both shall live."

We finished with the ancient words, first him, then me. Words I'd never thought I'd speak, but that seemed right when spoken to Zaq.

"My heart is yours. My body is yours. And my throat is yours."

I'd already accepted the mate bond back in Paris, but as I spoke the ancient vow to Zaq, I felt a jolt clear from my head to my toes, like the connection had been cemented into place, never to be broken.

Zaq's eyes widened and glowed blue at the rims, like he'd felt it too. His gaze flicked to my throat, where I wore the simple white-gold necklace he'd gifted me with just that morning.

I swallowed, a shiver of arousal racing up my spine to join the tingles left behind by the mate-bond jolt. I hadn't told him yet, but I'd decided that tonight I'd take that final step and let him drink from me. My mating gift to him.

Zaq took my hand and slid a worked-gold band onto my ring finger, then I slid one on his. That was for me; I'd wanted us to wear wedding rings, even if they weren't traditional for vampire matings.

We descended the steps of the gazebo and were immediately

surrounded by Zaq's family—his mom and father, his brothers and their mates. My father was there too, and a few of Zaq's friends, including Xavier.

Zaq's mom engulfed me in a tight hug. Rosemarie Kral was wonderful, a combination of warmth and practicality. I'd expected our first meeting to be awkward, even though Zaq assured me she didn't know I'd kidnapped him—or that he'd even been kidnapped. The cool way she assessed me made me wonder if he was right.

Now she said, "Welcome to the family, Renata."

I hugged her back. "Thank you."

"And I want you to call me *Mom*. If you want to, of course."

Something prickly pressed against the back of my throat. "I'd like that," I rasped. I cleared my throat and finished, "Mom."

The jazz quartet we'd hired for the occasion launched into a song. Zaq took my hand and we danced, and then Leo de Froulay asked for a dance.

We'd asked people to dress for a garden party—no suits or formal dresses—and Leo looked gorgeous as ever in a black button-up shirt dotted with tiny crescent moons. But over the past couple of months, I'd spent enough time with him to learn to see past his inhumanly beautiful exterior to the man beneath.

A man who wanted to claim me as his daughter, and not because I was the only offspring he'd sired. No, he wanted to claim me because he'd loved my mother.

It was Karoly Kral of all people who'd helped me see that.

"Leo let your mother go," he'd said one night a few weeks ago when we'd somehow ended up alone after a late dinner in New York with him and Rosemarie. "He'll never tell you this, but Charlotte didn't want to be changed into a vampire or a dhampir, and she didn't want to live as his thrall. So he let her go. For a vampire, especially a primus, there's no greater way to show love. We're damn possessive."

"Congratulations," Leo said now. "It was a lovely ceremony."

"Thank you." I waited until he'd steered me through a turn with an easy grace. When we faced each other again, I smiled up at him. "I'm so glad you came."

A muscle worked in his cheek. His grip on me tightened ever so slightly. "So am I."

We danced in silence for a minute. Then he said, "You'll call me if you ever need anything."

I nodded. "But I won't need anything."

I glanced over his shoulder at where Zaq stood with his brothers, the three men sipping whiskey and harassing each other in a joking way.

Leo's gaze followed mine. "Still, the offer will always be open. Anything I can do for you, anything I can give you—it's yours."

"I won't need anything," I said again, "except a father."

His gaze snapped to mine. "A father?"

"Yeah." I gave him a crooked smile. "Someone to stay with when we're in Paris. Someone to talk with about books, and help me with my French. Someone I can go to for advice. Not that I'll always take it, but I promise I'll at least listen."

His cheek creased. "I'd like that. Very much."

The song ended and he took me back to Zaq. We stayed another couple of hours, and then Zaq took my hand and drew me deeper into the garden. Before I knew it, we walking on a path through the woods.

"Where are we going?"

His mouth tugged up at the corner. "Quiet, woman. This is me kidnapping you."

I blinked, then shot him a grin. "Shouldn't we say goodbye?"

"No way. I don't trust my brothers not to play a prank on us."

"So where are we going?"

"Gabriel has a little house in the woods about a quarter-mile away, and I asked to borrow it. Mom had her people clean it and leave us snacks—wine, chocolate, etcetera. There's even a hot tub."

I turned and walked backward on the narrow path. Fortunately I was wearing Doc Martens, so this wasn't difficult.

"You had me at hot tub. Well, the wine and chocolate are an excellent selling point, too."

He took my hands and put them on his shoulders and kept walking me backward like we were dancing.

His grin was wolfish. "Actually, *mate*, I can have you any way I want now."

I gave a little hop and flex of my body, looping my arms around his neck and wrapping my legs around his hips. He caught me and held me against him.

"Maybe," I said against his whiskey-flavored lips, "I'm going to *have* you."

He gave a muffled groan.

The cabin was an A-frame nestled among the trees. Light streamed from its plate-glass windows. Zaq carried me up the stairs and opened the door.

I barely had time to take in the beautiful glass-and-wood interior because he kept walking through the large, open space to the bedroom at the back. I unwrapped my legs from his hips and slid down his body.

He kept me close with his hands on my ass. His gaze searched mine. "You felt it, didn't you? When we said the words."

"Yeah. It was—"

"Like taking a punch to the heart."

"In a good way," I agreed. The already strong bond linking us had intensified when we'd said the ancient words binding us permanently together.

Zaq backed me to the wall and kissed me, his body pressing me to the wall, his tongue sliding over mine.

My dress was a sleeveless black knit that I'd bought in New York, very simple and very expensive, with a scoop neck and a short skirt that showed off my legs. The tiny skirt also made it easy for Zaq to reach under my dress and palm my bottom.

He kissed me long and slow and sweet. When he lifted his head, he said, "What are you wearing under here? It feels like you're naked."

"A thong. I kissed my way along his jaw. "Mila helped me pick it out so I wouldn't have panty lines."

"Fuck me," he said reverently.

"It's red," I added helpfully. "To match my bra."

He swore under his breath. "Let's see."

He pulled the dress up and over my head. Tossing it on a chair, he swept his gaze over me. "You are so damn beautiful." He thumbed my nipple beneath the sheer red bra. "You don't even know it. When you go out without your glamour, men stare at you like you've put a compulsion on them."

I laughed and shrugged. I started unbuttoning his shirt. "You're exaggerating. You're the one people stare at."

"Nah. But I like that you don't notice."

"Mm." I opened his shirt, helping him shrug out of it, and dropped it on top of my dress.

Talk about beautiful. Zaq's chest belonged in a museum along with other pieces of art, except then I wouldn't be able to pet his sculpted muscles and play with the curly dark hair scattered over his pecs.

Next came his pants. I unzipped them and he took them off along with his boxers and shoes and socks. Meanwhile, I removed my own shoes and socks.

He moved back to where I waited against the wall wearing only his necklace and the barely-there red underwear. Framing my face in his hands, he gave me another kiss, then unclasped my bra and tossed it in the direction of our other clothes.

He slid a hand down my stomach and fingered me through the thong. I was so wet, I knew he could feel and smell it.

"Gods, I want you. I thought this night would never end. It's been three days since I had you and it feels like a month. Sleeping without you was the worse idea I ever had."

"I missed you," I admitted. It had been his idea to sleep in separate rooms once we'd arrived at his parents' mansion, to make this night extra-special.

"Never again," he said, a growl. "From now on, you're in my bed. No excuses."

His hands moved over me, massaging and stroking my ass, then he jerked the thong down. I stepped out of it, and he threw it in the direction of my bra.

Standing up, he scooped me into his arms and sat on the king-sized bed. I turned so I straddled him.

He made another rough, growly sound, one that vibrated in my chest and stomach. He pinched my nipples, caressed my waist and hips.

I, in turn, wrapped my fingers around his length, squeezing and releasing, rubbing the tip against my opening.

He pulled my hand away and turned us, laying me down on the soft sea-green coverlet. He kissed his way down my body, nuzzling my inner thighs.

My breath jerked in and out. I wanted him inside me, but first, I wanted to tell him about his gift. I propped myself on my forearms, trying to order my spinning thoughts.

"I have something for you."

"I don't need anything but this." He licked up my sex, swirling his tongue around my clit.

I took another deep, jagged breath. "This, you want."

I came up a little higher so I could set my hand against his cheek. My hair was held back by tiny clips, but I used my free hand to pull it away from the right side of my neck, offering him my throat.

His eyes cut to mine. "You want me to drink from you?"

I nodded. Excitement shivered over my skin.

He crawled up my body. "You're sure?"

"Absolutely."

His eyes darkened. "You are. I can feel it. Oh, sweetheart. This is going to be so good."

He gave me a hard, hungry kiss, then grabbed a condom from a drawer and rolled it on. "Scoot up higher on the bed."

I pushed the coverlet down and positioned myself further up the sheets. He took himself in hand and came on the bed, moving between my bent legs and stroking me with his erection. The walls of my sex constricted, like it was trying to pull him inside. Then he was there, filling and stretching me and sending pleasure pulsing through me.

His eyes were rimmed blue, his face hard, a little dangerous. But I *felt* his strength, his control, and I wasn't at all afraid, just turned on.

He kissed my neck, thrusting in and out. I twined my arms and legs around him, taking him as deeply as I could, showing him how much I wanted this.

He interlaced his fingers through mine and pressed them onto the bed on either side of my head. Holding me down so he could move in and out at the pace he set. Dominating me with his body while his fangs teased my throat.

I sucked in a breath as heat swirled in my belly. I felt a tiny quake of fear then, but it just sharpened the pleasure. Because this was Zaq, and I loved and trusted him.

He sank his fangs into my carotid and my body arched off the bed. He withdrew and thrust back in, deeper, rougher.

I felt like I was being possessed. Taken. Devoured.

He was right, it was the best fucking I'd ever had. Like fireworks were going off in my head and around the bed.

"Yesyesyes," I cried out and "Please, please, please."

I was shattering, breaking apart. And then he did something with his pelvis that pressed against the perfect spot and sent me flying, the pinwheels and bottle rockets and Roman candles exploding around and in me.

He released my throat, licking the marks, and pounded into me, not so controlled now.

Some instinct made me rear up and sink my teeth into his throat. I wasn't even aware I was doing it until I tasted him in my mouth.

I drank deep and he gave a raw groan. "Gods, that feels so good."

Energy filled me.

Zaq's energy.

An amazing, ecstatic energy.

It felt like life. It felt like love. I'm pretty sure my heart did sprout wings and fly to his, and his heart was right there to meet mine.

I withdrew my fangs, licking the marks I'd made, and chanted, "I love you, I love you, I love you."

He tensed and broke his rhythm, thrusting in and out, his lean angel-face contorted like he was in the best kind of pain.

He came with a low growl and hung over me, sucking in breaths like he'd run a hard race. He was hot and a little sweaty, which amped up his Zaq-scent to a level that should've been illegal, it smelled so good.

Touching his forehead to mine, he gave back my words to me, "I love you. I love you. I love you."

We shared a lingering kiss, then he eased out of me and flopped next to me. He turned his head and smirked. "I think I'm going to like having a mate."

I grinned back. "Me, too."

I kissed his chest, then headed to the bathroom to clean up. He was next, then he rejoined me in the big bed.

He tucked me into his shoulder—the spot I'd claimed as mine—and murmured sleepily, "Wanna get in the hot tub?"

"Later." I pulled the top sheet over us and snuggled closer.

"Mm." He shut his eyes and then he was asleep.

But I remained awake. Still kind of astounded at how my life had changed since that morning at Charles de Gaulle.

I was learning how to be part of a couple. After being alone, just having a person who was mine was a luxury, like a fluffy, silk-covered down comforter when you're used to thin wool blankets.

I was learning to prioritize my emotions, whatever they were. Joy. Sadness. Fear. Anger. Love.

And I was working on believing I deserved all of this, especially Zaq.

Because I did deserve him, just as *he* deserved *me*.

Staking Moreau hadn't fixed the hole my mother's death had left. Only living my best life would do that.

I liked to think that Mom would've approved, that somewhere out there, she was cheering me on.

I released a contented sigh and burrowed deeper into Zaq's shoulder.

Zaq stirred and kissed the top of my head. "Love you, Ren."

"Love you, too," I said, and closed my eyes.

EPILOGUE 2
TWILIGHT

FOUR HOURS EARLIER
Reaper looked like a fairy princess, blond and deceptively delicate, standing with Zaq in the candlelit gazebo.

As they spoke their vows, I swept my gaze over the guests.

Gabriel and Camilla. Rafe and Zoe. Both couples looking crazy in love. Hell, I hadn't known Princess Zoe could smile like that, and I'd been her stylist—and shadow—for two memorable weeks this summer.

Karoly and Rosemarie Kral were present, of course, and so was Leo de Froulay and a sprinkling of Zaq's friends, including Prince Brien of the Maritime Vampire Syndicate.

Karoly Kral had gotten his wish. Reaper was officially dead, but her intel, given under an alias that had been ascribed to another slayer, had been enough to pressure SI to grant him a seat on the Board of Directors.

And the woman I knew as Reaper had been reborn as Princess Renata of the Paris Syndicate.

My gaze returned to Prince Brien. His blond hair shone in the moonlight, his square-jawed face solemn. He stood like he was at parade rest, his feet apart, his hands clasped behind his back. Somehow he made it look like the perfect pose—not too casual, not too formal.

Everything about the man was perfect from his symmetrical face with a hint of stubble to his broad shoulders to his long legs. The kind of perfection that made me itch to muss him up.

Like I had that last night in Montreal...

I resolutely focused my attention on Renata, or Ren Kral, as she was known now. Trust Reaper not to appear at her mate ritual in anything resembling a wedding dress. Instead, she wore silver Doc Martens and a short black dress. Her platinum hair was brushed into a simple, shoulder-length style and held back with small, diamond-encrusted clips on each side. A plain white-gold chain encircled her neck.

Zaq gazed at Reaper like he was torn between wanting to worship her and eat her up. And she was literally glowing, she was so in love with him.

They were too adorable; if I were still Lainey Q, I'd sneak a photo of them and post it on Insta.

But I wasn't Lainey Q anymore. That alias had been buried two months ago. I was here as a server for the company catering the party. The Kral Syndicate had vetted me, of course, but Crow had made sure I passed their background check.

I'd dyed my hair black and added a white Cruella de Vil streak. Under my black pants and white shirt I wore a false belly to make me look thick around the middle, and I'd made up my face to look like a woman in her forties. Heavy perfume disguised my scent.

Brien rubbed his nape and glanced around, and I realized I was staring at him again—and that the ceremony had ended.

Zaq and Reaper descended the gazebo steps, holding hands. They were surrounded by people congratulating them.

I filled a tray with blood-wine and carried it around.

Reaper was doing better than okay. Leo de Froulay had claimed her and she'd been welcomed into the Kral family as well. Rosemarie Kral seemed prepared to mother her, and Karoly Kral was smart enough to see she was a two-fer—a built-in bodyguard for Zaq, who was known for traveling without security; and a link to the Paris Syndicate.

Acid filled my throat.

Because I was here to take that away from her. The dagger tucked into a cavity of my false belly was a cold, heavy weight against my stomach.

Crow had recruited me herself to take out Reaper. "She'll let you get close to her," she'd said. "You can tell her you have intel about me."

Crow was furious at how Reaper had betrayed her and SI. Crow didn't seem to comprehend that she was at fault, that Reaper had been pushed into it by Crow's fanaticism.

Problem was, I agreed with Reaper, not my alpha. We'd been wrong to go after the Krals, and Reaper deserved a chance at happiness.

Reaper probably didn't even remember this, but once, long ago, she'd taken a new—and homesick—slayer trainee under her wing, showing me around, practicing marital arts with me during her (rare) free time. She'd even reminded me to stay hydrated so I didn't pass out from the constant, extreme exertion. And when I mastered something, she was always there with a fist-bump or an approving nod.

The hairs on the backs of my arms raised; Crow was watching from the shadows. She'd said she was there as backup, but I suspected she'd swoop in during the confusion following Reaper's death and slay as many Krals as she could.

I made up my mind. I put my tray down and returned to the white caterer's van. The keys had been left in the ignition so it could be moved if necessary.

I climbed into the driver's seat. Tucking the dagger into a pocket of the door, I started the van and turned it around.

Crow appeared at the passenger-side door, blue eyes glowing in the dark. I unlocked it and she got inside.

Her lips were pulled into an angry line. "What the hell, Twilight?"

"I had to abort the op."

She gaped at me. "Why? What happened?"

"Not here." I pulled out of the driveway, drove a few hundred yards down the road. The Krals' property backed up to a park. We were surrounded by woods. Autumn leaves skittered before the headlights.

I pulled onto the berm and put the van into park.

"Well?" Crow demanded.

My fingers clenched on the steering wheel. I was a human. A highly trained human, yes, but at a disadvantage when fighting supernaturals like Crow. I'd have just one chance to do this.

I reached into the door pocket, palmed the dagger and drove it into Crow's heart in a single fast move. I didn't even draw a breath so as not to tip her off.

I hit my target dead-on. Crow's mouth formed a shocked 'O.'

I heaved a breath. "I'm sorry. I really am."

Her hand went to the blade's handle, trying but failing to remove it. "Why?" she croaked.

I looked at her. There were so many things I could say. That Crow had become a zealot who'd lost her moral compass. That I was almost certain she was working on her own, that the BOD hadn't approved Reaper's death sentence. That I was sick of the lies and the killing and wanted out.

In the end, all I said was, "Reaper looked so happy."

Crow's eyes glazed over. Smoke from her burning body filled the van.

I climbed out of the van and went to her side. Opening the door, I gathered her into my arms and carried her into the woods, where I laid her on the newly-fallen leaves. She'd be ashes within minutes.

I pulled off the false belly and threw it deeper into the woods. The van

I left where it was and hiked up the hill to where I'd hidden my motor-
cycle in the trees.

The last thing I saw were the lights of the Kral mansion in the
rearview mirror.

"You're welcome," I told Reaper, and aimed my bike for I-95.

Hello, you lovely reader—
I hope you enjoyed reading my Vampire Syndicate Dark Angel Trilogy as
much as I enjoyed writing it!

And yeah, Twilight and Brien have a story, ***Fallen***. I fell in love with
Twilight and had to see more of her!!

FALLEN (Vampire Syndicate, Book 4)

The slayer and the vampire prince...
He's the enemy, a Vampire Syndicate prince who bought me at a blood-slave auction.
Trusting him is dangerous, but loving him could be fatal.

TWILIGHT
To save a friend, I stake my alpha in Slayers, Inc. and disappear, hoping my superiors will believe I died along with my alpha.
But you don't quit Slayers, Inc. until you're too old to fight...or dead.

A member of SI's shadowy Board of Directors tracks me down. One last job, he tells me, and he'll make things right with the organization.
The catch? I have to go undercover as a blood thrall in the dangerous world of vampire syndicates.

BRIEN
Twilight shouldn't be up for sale. She made it clear she'd never be anyone's thrall.
But there she is, the main attraction at a private auction.
The woman I'd do anything, pay any amount to have.
So I buy her.
But is she who she's pretending to be—or have I brought the means of my own destruction directly into my bedroom?

A white-hot vampire mafia paranormal romance!

ALSO BY REBECCA RIVARD

THE VAMPIRE SYNDICATE

Tempted

Pursued

Craved

Taken

Fallen

VAMPIRE BLOOD COURTESANS

Ensnared: Star

Compelled: Cerise

THE FADA SHAPESHIFTERS

Stealing Ula: A Fada Shapeshifter Prequel

Seducing the Sun Fae

Claiming Valeria

Tempting the Dryad

Lir's Lady

Shifter's Valentine

Sea Dragon's Hunger

Saving Jace

Charming Marjani

Adric's Heart

Thanks so much for reading!

Want to be the first to hear about my vampire romances and other steamy paranormal romance books?

Sign up for my newsletter: www. rebeccarivard.com/newsletter

ABOUT REBECCA RIVARD

USA Today bestselling author Rebecca Rivard read way too many romances as a teenager, little realizing she was actually preparing for a career. She now spends her days with vampires, shifters and fae—which has to be the best job ever. When she's not writing, she walks, bikes and kayaks in the Chesapeake Bay area with her guitar-playing, storytelling husband.

Rivard's novels have received numerous awards, including the RONE for Best Long Paranormal (*Craved*); the PRISM (*Charming Marjani*); and the Paranormal Romance Guild Reviewer's Choice Award (*Saving Jace*).

In addition, seven of her books have been awarded the coveted Crowned Heart Review from *InD'Tale Magazine*.

www.ingramcontent.com/pod-product-compliance
Lightning Source LLC
Chambersburg PA
CBHW031335020726
47499CB00005B/1271